LOVE STORIES

A Novella Collection

SAMANTHA YOUNG

Love Stories

A Novella Collection

by Samantha Young
Copyright © 2021 Samantha Young

Edited by Jennifer Sommersby Young
Cover Design by Hang Le
Photography by Regina Wamba

ALSO BY SAMANTHA YOUNG

On Hart's Boardwalk (a novella)

The Hart's Boardwalk Series:

The One Real Thing

Every Little Thing

Things We Never Said

The Truest Thing

The Adair Family Series:

Here With Me

There With You

Young Adult contemporary titles by Samantha Young

The Impossible Vastness of Us

The Fragile Ordinary

Writing as S. Young

War of the Covens Trilogy:

Hunted

Destined

Ascended

Warriors of Ankh Trilogy:

Blood Will Tell

Blood Past

Shades of Blood

The Seven Kings of Jinn Series:

The Seven Kings of Jinn

Of Wish and Fury

Queen of Shadow and Ash

The Law of Stars and Sultans

The True Immortality Series:

War of Hearts

Kiss of Vengeance

Kiss of Eternity: A True Immortality Short Story

Bound by Forever

Fear of Fire and Shadow: a standalone adult fantasy romance

THE FORBIDDEN CHRISTMAS GIFT

CHAPTER ONE

EVAN
Mid-December

Edinburgh, Scotland

B ing Crosby crooned, "It's Beginning to Look a Lot Like Christmas," and he wasn't wrong. Standing in the atrium of Shaw's Department Store on Princes Street, it definitely couldn't get any more Christmassy for me. Strands of gorgeous fairy lights cascaded over the balconies of the gallery floors above us. I stood at Santa's Grotto, surrounded by fake snow and glitter, while a twinkling forty-foot Christmas tree towered above.

Oh, and I was dressed as one of Santa's Little Helpers.

With glitter shimmering on my cheeks and my petite

figure wrapped in a green velvet elf dress, I looked all of sixteen, I was sure of it.

For months now, I, Evan Munro, had been trying my hardest to make my brother's best friend—my boss—see me as something other than his best friend's wee sister who was not only twelve years his junior but the woman he offered a pity job to.

Okay, so it was a little harsh to call it a pity job. The situation demanded more respect than that. After all, when I graduated from university, I'd struggled to get *any* work, never mind the PA position at Shaw's. However, it was safe to say I only got the job because my big brother Patrick asked his successful best friend, Reid Shaw, to give me the position on a trial period.

One would think, in this difficult economy, that I'd do anything to keep the job.

For instance, I wouldn't be *mooning* over my boss with an infatuation the size of said planetary satellite. But I couldn't help it.

Until recently, I'd become obsessed with showing Reid that the twelve-year age gap between us didn't matter because I was a mature, wise-beyond-my-years woman who would rock his freaking world in and out of the bedroom.

After the events of the last few months, I thought I'd made progress.

And I had.

But it still didn't matter.

Because to Reid, I would always be his best friend's untouchable little sister.

Weeks ago, wearing this costume in front of Reid would have mortified me. Now I couldn't care less.

In fact, it was pretty damn funny.

I was sure Reid would never see me as a woman he could

take seriously again, but as I smiled at the excited faces of the kids lining up to see Santa Claus, I no longer cared.

Fine.

That wasn't *entirely* true.

It hurt like hell.

But I had a little something called self-respect, and if Reid was too afraid to take a chance on me because of Patrick, then he wasn't the right man for me.

Bing's voice trailed off and Mariah Carey flooded the department store's sound system.

Santa, some guy called Gary I only met an hour ago, gestured to me and then to the pile of presents under the Christmas tree. I stifled my chuckle as the bells attached to my pointy-toed elf shoes jingled as I walked. A little girl with laughing brown eyes caught my attention, and we shared a giggle together just before I bent down to collect the next gift from under the spectacular tree.

A whoosh of cool air hit my backside, and I straightened, blushing. The elf costume was not only roasting hot, but it came with a stiff petticoat that prevented the mid-thigh-length skirt from covering my bum when I bent over. Everyone was probably getting an eyeful of my red-and-green-striped bottom.

I was wearing elf stockings.

And my dress was high-necked, the sleeves long, with the collar and wrists trimmed in white fur.

Seriously, I needed to learn how to say the word *no*.

Feet jingling and bell tinkling on my matching festive green hat, I strolled over to Santa and gave him the present. He winked flirtatiously at me.

Charming.

I tried not to wrinkle my nose at his impropriety.

The young boy at Santa's side took hold of the brightly

wrapped gift, all distress at talking to a strange man disappearing as his mum came to take him away. That was my cue.

I shuffled over to the front of the line and smiled at the waiting father and his little girl. I bent toward her, knowing I was probably giving Santa a clear view of my stockinged arse. Everything about the costume was silly and childish, except for the arse-revealing part. It was supposed to be worn by the sixteen-year-old high school girl who couldn't show up to be Santa's elf because she had the flu.

Margaret, the manager of the women's department, had volunteered me since I was the only one who could fit into the costume. While I should've asked for Reid's permission first, seeing the panic on Kerry, our event coordinator's face, I knew I had to help her.

We'd advertised Santa's Grotto everywhere, and parents had purchased tickets for their kids to visit Santa and take home a quality gift for Christmas. Determining Reid would be more annoyed if we let down customers, I reluctantly donned the elf getup.

And now, the object of my affection would probably never look at me the same way again if he caught me in it. Not that it would make a difference.

Pushing through my disappointment, I smiled at Santa's next customers as the father handed over their ticket.

"What's your name?" I asked the little girl with the blond pigtails. She was adorable in a red velvet dress and matching shoes.

"Belle," she murmured shyly.

"It suits you perfectly." I beamed, drawing a smile from her. "Would you like to meet Santa?"

After glancing up at her dad for reassurance, Belle took my hand, and I led her over to Santa and then stood off to the side. While Gary kept throwing me looks that would definitely put him on the Naughty List, he was great with the kids. He had a joyful, booming voice and pulled off "Ho, ho, ho!" with grand aplomb.

My favorite Christmas song came over the sound system. Wizzard's "I Wish It Could Be Christmas Everyday." While the department store employees had to listen to the same Christmas album all day every day in December, I spent most of my time at my desk outside Reid's top-floor office—where he'd banned all Christmas music.

Scrooge.

God, I wished I didn't adore the brooding bastard.

Anyhoo, it was nice to listen to Christmas music all morning, and I relaxed, feeling less ridiculous (sort of) and falling more comfortably into my role.

Swaying my hips to the music and singing under my breath, I forgot to feel moody and lovesick for the first time in months.

My toe bells jingled as I skipped toward the Christmas tree to collect Belle's present. I bent over without thinking, singing to myself.

It was a wonder I didn't feel his glare singeing my arse.

Because I certainly felt it when I stood up, turned with a flourish of my petticoats, and smiled just as my gaze collided with Reid's.

He stood to the side of Santa's Grotto, a fierce glower furrowing his brows, arms crossed over his chest as he glared.

"What the hell are you doing?" he mouthed slowly before pressing his lips into a hard line. His eyes lowered down my body and back up again. Somehow, his expression grew even darker.

Damn it.

I guessed it didn't look all that professional for his personal assistant to dress in a teenager's elf costume.

My lips widened into a sheepish grin, followed by an equally sheepish shrug, as if to say, "What can you do?"

In answer, he crooked his finger at me to come to him.

It was appalling the way my body reacted to the commanding gesture, as if I'd just been summoned to the bedroom.

Mortified, frustrated, and irritated that he had such power over me, I gave him a slight shake of my head. Reid's eyebrow raised at my defiance, but I ignored him. We'd decided that I needed to find a new job, and that was exactly what I'd done. My time at Shaw's was up after Christmas, and Reid would no longer be my boss. So defying him wasn't really an issue.

Instead, I moved toward Santa, who took the present with another lascivious wink in my direction.

The whole time, I could feel my boss's stare burning into me.

I knew he was beyond annoyed at this point.

A niggle of concern filtered through my newfound "could give zero fucks" attitude.

Maybe Reid would ask me to leave sooner.

And even though I kept telling myself I didn't care what he thought of me, I knew it would sting horribly if he made me pack my things and leave him.

I wasn't prepared for it.

Not yet.

I still had two weeks of secretly pining for him and hating him in equal measure.

I wanted those two weeks!

They were mine.

I flicked him a look beneath my lashes.

He was still there.

Glowering at me.

Oh, dear.

I was definitely on someone's Naughty List.

CHAPTER TWO

EVAN
Early October

Three months ago

The thing is ... I'm actually a really professional person. Normally. Ask anyone.

The current situation didn't highlight that virtue, but I promise it was true.

It was just very hard for me not to press my ear to Reid's office door so I could listen in on his conversation with Emmy.

I wouldn't usually.

I might be infatuated with my boss, but his relationship with Emmy was none of my business.

However, yesterday, I had the unfortunate task of relaying

to Reid that his girlfriend had rung up a whopping five grand bill under his personal account for the store. Reid had gone quiet at the news, giving nothing away regarding his feelings on the matter.

Then, today, I'd been in the staff room trying to defuse a quarrel between Ailsa, the salon manager, and Louis, the beauty department manager. Apparently, Ailsa had recommended a product to a customer that we didn't stock, and this ruffled Louis's feathers. While he was sort of right that she should only recommend store products, I couldn't help but understand why Ailsa was pissed off at him for his condescending attitude.

Handling staff disputes was not part of my job description. It should fall to George, the general manager, to Human Resources, or to Reid himself. Reid, however, had no patience for tattletales, as he called them, and George was in a meeting with our events coordinator for the upcoming Halloween sale. Human Resources were surprisingly good at avoiding human contact outside of their own department. Reid had thus asked that I "see to the problem regarding the staff." This had been happening more and more lately, since I had a knack for conflict resolution.

"So," I was saying to Ailsa and Louis, "if Ailsa thinks this product is a better one than the products in Shaw's, I'll talk to Reid about stocking it. That way, we all win. Yes?"

Louis gave a little huff, but nodded.

Ailsa beamed.

That was when I saw Emmy floating by the staff room wearing four-inch heels, her diaphanous trench coat billowing behind her as she strutted down the hallway toward Reid's office.

"Uh ... I have to go. We're all good?" I gave Louis and Ailsa a thumbs-up before scurrying out of the staff room before they could stop me. "Back to work," I threw over my shoulder.

Emmy was already in Reid's office by the time I caught up. The woman had outrageously long legs.

That was when I abandoned all common decency and pressed my ear to the door.

I was shamefaced, but not nearly enough to stop myself.

"Three months is nothing," Reid said calmly.

While my boss could glower for Scotland and brood and cut a person with a look so dirty I'd seen grown men crumble under it, he rarely raised his voice. He was always so in control. It made me want to ruffle his feathers.

And by ruffle his feathers, I mean drive him so wild with passion he falls on me like a wild thing.

Flushing hot at the imagery, I squeezed my thighs tight and tried to concentrate on the somewhat muffled conversation beyond the door.

"Do you know how many men would die to have me in their bed?" Emmy countered.

At her arrogance, I stifled a snort.

So she was tall, voluptuous, and gorgeous.

Big deal.

If she had a beautiful heart to go with her pretty facade, then she would have been right. Reid would be lucky to have her.

Unfortunately, Emmy was kind of a snooty cow. She looked down her nose at Reid's staff and expected them to snap to her every demand, and was what she referred to as a socialite. A socialite? Did those even exist in Edinburgh? Apparently so, because Emmy didn't work for a living. She had a degree from St. Andrews University, so she wasn't stupid, but she was from a wealthy family. Between their money and Reid's, Emmy didn't seem to think working was a productive use of her time.

9

Did I sound judgmental?

I wasn't usually judgy.

But I was judging her. I admit it.

The thing of it was, I couldn't understand how this lack of work ethic could appeal to Reid. My brother's best friend hadn't gotten to where he was in life without serious hard work. He'd grown up around the corner from us in Dalkeith, a town about thirty minutes southeast of Edinburgh city center. A town I still lived in, occupying a tiny one-bedroom apartment a few streets over from my parents' house.

Reid had grown up with a single mum, Annie. She'd worked her arse off to keep a roof over Reid's head and food in his stomach. Like us, they didn't have much, but they had each other, and Annie had my parents while Reid had Patrick. I hadn't come along until my brother and Reid were twelve years old, so by the time I was old enough to really get to know Pat and Reid, they'd left home. Despite how easy it might have been for them to fall in with the wrong crowd of boys in our estate, they'd both stuck in at school and gotten into the University of Edinburgh. While Patrick then studied for his medical degree in Manchester, Reid got his MBA at a top business school in London. We'd see them over the holidays, as Annie and Reid always spent Christmas with us. I wasn't aware of Reid back then. I was only a kid, after all, and just excited to have my big brother home.

Reid returned to Edinburgh before Patrick, and we didn't see much of him at all.

My brother returned home two years later to complete his foundation program as a doctor at a general practice in the city. It was then we saw more of Reid. Not loads, but more.

And I developed my first real crush.

I remember it clearly.

I was fourteen years old. It was Christmas, and Patrick

was spending the night with us, rather than staying at his flat. Like always, Annie and Reid came over for Christmas Day.

I'd noted that Reid didn't smile much.

But he smiled at me as he strolled into my parents' sitting room and wished me a happy Christmas. His smile set off a riot of flutters in my belly, and I found myself tongue-tied and flustered around him.

The feeling never really went away, although it lost its intensity as I got older and saw him less and went off to the University of Edinburgh to pursue my own degree in business management. An MA that proved useless when I left school and competed with a ton of other young people with similar degrees and very little experience.

After six months of job searching with no luck, Patrick said Reid was looking for a new personal assistant at his department store, and he was willing to give me a shot.

I hadn't even thought about my old crush.

All I'd thought about was the great pay and the fact that my first job would be working with one of the most successful entrepreneurs in Scotland.

After working for several companies over the years, networking and accruing stock and investments, Reid purchased an aging department store in the heart of Edinburgh. Situated on the main thoroughfare of the city center, Princes Street, the department store had lost its luster years ago, as many had because of online shopping. Reid bought the store and the three shops that shared the same turn-of-the-century building. Knocking through into those meant he could create a much bigger department store.

While he maintained its nineteenth-century charm, he created a mini empire with everything from clothing to home furnishings to electronics to beauty to a salon and spa and topped it off with a fine-dining restaurant on the level below the office floors. He created an atmosphere where people wanted to shop, and he catered to those in the city who had money to do so.

Everyone thought he would fail.

In the last three years, the store had gone from strength to strength, proving all the naysayers wrong.

Unfortunately, success meant Reid was a busy man. Too busy to think about women beyond the convenience of having a partner with him at a business dinner and someone to satisfy his sexual appetite. While not necessarily a womanizer, Reid was definitely a serial monogamist. He had a few rules when it came to women.

They had to be accepting of his long working hours.

Everything was on his schedule.

And he didn't do immaturity. Which meant he never dated a woman younger than twenty-eight. Patrick told me that. It didn't make sense to me at all. I knew women twice my age way more immature than me. That ridiculous rule stung.

Did I mention my youthful crush returned when I started working for Reid and was now growing into full-blown infatuation? It wasn't just because Reid was tall with the athletic physique of a swimmer, or that he had the most beautiful glimmering dark eyes and wickedly boyish grin. I suspected Reid had much passion and feeling buried beneath his cool, overly controlled facade. For instance, he was loyal and generous to a fault. I wasn't supposed to know, but my parents were in financial difficulty because of a second mortgage they'd taken on the house and were in danger of losing it. Reid paid off their debt. No questions asked.

I could only imagine how much of a hit that was to Dad's pride. Reid would have handled it delicately, though. I'd seen him handle businessmen with a deft touch, and he loved my dad, so I couldn't imagine him not handling him with care.

Then there were the many charities I knew he donated

to. Anytime I tried to ask him about them, he just blew me off. But I worked for him. I saw the good he did without wanting accolades.

And all his staff were competitively paid. If one among them had a personal problem that interfered with their duties, Reid had instructed Nicola, our Human Resource manager, to create a supportive environment for them and to put measures in place to help.

His staff were a priority.

When I mentioned this, he replied, "Happy staff are productive staff. Productive staff bring in more sales."

All that was true, but I still thought he was a big softie, really.

For the last six months, I'd seen Reid with two women up close and personal. The first was Anushka. She and Reid had been dating for three months before I appeared. His PA before me was a lovely older lady called Janet. She'd retired.

Anushka was unhappy that Reid's new PA was a twenty-three-year-old, not entirely unattractive (I hoped) woman. Again, Patrick filled me in on that. After about two months of me working for Reid, Anushka grew increasingly paranoid. At her jealous insistence that Reid fire me, he fired Anushka instead.

Emmy appeared on the scene about a month later.

And she was the worst.

While I truly got the sense Anushka had genuine feelings for Reid, all Emmy saw was Reid's success and what his money could do for her. Patrick told me (if you hadn't already guessed, my big brother was a bloody gossip) that Reid had to stop at his mum's house in Dalkeith one night while Emmy was with him. Despite Reid wanting to buy his mum a nice house somewhere else, she didn't want to leave. Instead, he paid off her mortgage, the darling man.

Anyway, back to the story. So Reid goes to Annie's to drop

off the new phone he'd insisted on buying her when her old one broke, and Emmy had stayed in his car, dramatically terrified to get out, as if Dalkeith were the ghetto. While the estate we grew up in was a little run-down and very working class, the insinuation that it was dangerous was insulting.

Patrick had been pissed when Reid told him Emmy had said "he was never to bring her back to that dump again." Reid had shrugged it off. When I asked Patrick why, he said Reid wasn't serious about her. He was only interested in their sexual relationship, so there was no point getting upset about her attitude.

I got upset.

Mostly at the reminder that the snooty cow got to have sex with Reid.

Reid who looked after his body with the same careful discipline he brought to all areas of his life. There was a staff gym on the top floor that Reid used first thing in the morning, every morning.

I'd once found him in there, shirtless.

The image was BURNED on my brain.

"I don't care how many men would die to have you in their bed," Reid said to Emmy. "Go find one of them."

"What?" Emmy screeched.

I winced.

There was a moment of silence and then, "I called you in here to discuss the charges on my store tab. I'm not a man you can use like this, Emmy."

"Use you? I'm using you," she said indignantly. "As if you aren't using me. Reid, I'm at your bloody beck and call. You do realize that's not how normal relationships work? They're about give and take. Outside of the bedroom, you're all about take. Surely, a little compensation for being one step up from an escort isn't a lot to ask."

"An escort?" he replied coolly.

I knew that tone. If Reid hadn't been happy before, he really wasn't happy now.

"Yes, an escort. And I'm worth more than that. You think you can break up with me? I'm breaking up with you." Footsteps moved toward the door, and I skittered quickly back to my desk, staring at my computer like I hadn't been eavesdropping.

The door to Reid's office opened, and I heard Emmy say, "You're an unfeeling bastard, Reid, and you're going to die alone for it."

I tried not to let my jaw drop in shock at her awful snipe.

She stepped out into the hall, closing the door behind her with a little slam. She cut me a dirty look and strolled away.

"Good riddance," I called out to her as if I were calling a cheery "good day."

Emmy glanced over her shoulder, pausing. "Excuse me?"

"Go-od. Rid-dance," I drawled.

"Screw you," she huffed and marched away.

"No thanks," I muttered to the screen. "Can't afford you, babe."

A snort sounded from the doorway, and I looked up to find Reid leaning on the door frame of his office.

I grimaced. "Sorry. Not professional, I know."

"No. But funny."

I smiled sympathetically. "She's wrong, you know."

He raised an eyebrow. "About?"

"You're not an unfeeling bastard who is going to die alone."

Reid's expression closed down. "Has Butler called?"

I knew by the very fact that he didn't want to talk about what Emmy had said meant she'd drawn blood. Hating that she'd wounded him, I suggested, "Why don't you finish up early? I can handle everything here."

"I'm fine. Let me know when Butler calls. If he doesn't

call by three o'clock, you call his assistant." He disappeared back into his office before I could reply.

Hours later, once the store was closed at seven and the staff had all gone home, except for the night maintenance crew and security, I knocked on Reid's office door.

In my hand was the bottle of eighteen-year-old Macallan I'd bought from our small whisky department with my staff discount. Grabbing two glasses from the staff room, I approached Reid.

The man didn't seem to have anyone to talk to except Patrick, and sometimes guys couldn't say the things they wanted to say to each other. Especially two proud Scots who thought it only appropriate to cry at football, funerals, or at the death of a beloved family pet.

"Come in."

I stepped into the office, using my arse to close the door behind me. Reid raised an eyebrow at my entrance as I held up the items in my hands. "Thought you might need this."

I expected him to reject the idea and tell me to go home. Instead, he exhaled heavily and pushed away from his desk. He gestured to the sofa and coffee table at the back of the small room, and I made my way over to it. Ignoring the flutter in my belly and the slight increase of my pulse, I placed the glasses on the coffee table and opened the whisky as Reid approached.

The rich, spicy scent of his cologne caused a flush across my skin as he settled onto one end of the sofa and relaxed back into it. I handed him a tumbler of whisky, and he muttered his thanks before taking a sip. I tried to ignore the movement of his strong throat as he swallowed. And the way his fingers clasped the glass. He had gorgeous hands. Masculine but graceful. Big knuckles. And his forearms. Gosh, he had lovely forearms with thick veins and sun-kissed skin and only a dusting of hair across the top. I'd never noticed so much about a man before, but Reid's hands and forearms totally turned me on.

Okay, everything about him turned me on.

He had cut cheekbones, a square jaw, and a wicked grin. Reid would almost be too perfect, but thankfully, he wasn't. He'd broken his nose playing rugby when he was fourteen, and it had healed slightly crooked. Somehow, this just made him rugged and sexier.

Damn him.

Taking hold of my glass, I sat at the other end of the sofa. It was a small two-seater, so we weren't exactly miles apart. Studying him as I sipped my drink, I enjoyed the smooth warmth of the alcohol as it slid down my throat. Reid possessed a strained weariness to his features that made me want to touch him. Comfort him.

His eyes slid toward me, and I held my breath at his study. "I didn't know you drank whisky."

I nodded. "Got a taste for the stuff when I was at uni."

Reid smirked. "Most students have less expensive tastes."

"I'm not most people."

He didn't respond, just leaned forward, elbows to his knees, glass cradled between his palms. His expression turned contemplative as he stared into the golden-amber liquid.

Though it was unpleasant to think about him brooding over another woman, as his wannabe friend, I had to ask, "Did you have strong feelings for her?"

Reid raised his eyebrows as he looked at me. "Emmy?"

I nodded.

He shook his head. "Less than I should have."

"What does that mean?"

Instead of answering, he threw back the entire glass and reached for the bottle to refill it.

"You can talk to me, you know. If you need to."

"You're my employee," he reminded me. "I shouldn't even be having a casual whisky with you."

I scoffed. "Reid, you've known me forever."

"Another reason not to talk about this with you. Your brother is my best friend. And he's a fucking gossip." He threw me a quick grin.

Chuckling, I nodded. "Too true. But unlike Patrick, I am a vault."

Settling back against the sofa, Reid took another sip and murmured, "There's nothing to say."

"I don't think that's true." I'd grown to know Reid very well over the last six months, and he always seemed to have this never-ending source of energy. But lately, he'd seemed ... restless.

And today he just seemed exhausted.

"Do you miss Anushka?" I prodded.

Reid shook his head, his dark eyes troubled. "Not as much as I should. It never seems to be as much as I should. That's the problem." He smirked unhappily. "You promise our conversation does not leave this office?"

"Of course."

"I always ..." he sighed as if frustrated with himself as he scrubbed a hand over the dark hair he styled short. "It was just Mum and me growing up, you know. I always thought that once the success came, everything else would fall into place. Wife, kids."

Surprise and longing burned through me.

Reid always came across as the perennial bachelor. I'd never have guessed he had plans to be a family man.

Apparently, I didn't know him as well as I'd thought.

"I wanted what me and Mum never had. I wanted to give her a family. A daughter-in-law. Grandchildren. But I keep fucking up."

"How do you keep fucking up?"

"I never make time to do it right with a woman. The store always comes first. What kind of family man would I make? A pretty shitty one. I'd end up turning my wife into my mum, essentially leaving her to raise our children on her own."

I considered this a moment, sorry for the bitter self-recrimination I heard in Reid's tone. I understood then that he felt he'd failed. In all his success, in this one aspect of life, he felt he was failing. "Reid, have you ever considered that you just haven't met the right woman?"

"Emmy doesn't count, but I've been with a lot of good women over the years."

"A good woman doesn't equal the right woman."

"You mean like a soul mate?" He scoffed. "I don't believe in that, Evan."

I made a noise of irritation. "I'm not talking about soul mates. I'm talking about the person who feels like they … fit. The person who drives you wild." Considering how controlled Reid was in everything he did, I asked (and hoped for a negatory answer), "Haven't you ever been infatuated with a woman?"

"I've dated plenty of attractive women."

"That's not what I asked." I chugged my whisky and leaned over to refill it, trying not to roll my eyes at his clue-lessness. "Haven't you ever met a woman who made you lose your common sense? Who made your skin hot and your blood pump and everything else but kissing her, touching her, ceased to matter?" I blushed a little, imagining being said woman.

Reid tensed, gazing at me speculatively. "Have you ever met a guy who did that for you?"

I thought about Luca and lowered my gaze, feeling the old hurt still after all this time. "Once."

"Who?" he demanded.

Wondering at his sudden glower and the reason behind it,

I took a slow sip, knowing my lack of rush to respond would irritate him. Reid liked everyone to give him the answers to his questions with speed and efficiency.

"Evan?" He leaned toward me. "Who? Does Pat know about this guy?"

"I asked first."

"What?"

"I asked you first if you'd ever met a woman who made you feel that way."

"No," he bit out. "Your turn."

I shouldn't have felt pleased by his response, but I really did. In fact, it elated me. So much so, I had to hide my smile in another sip of my drink.

"Are you deliberately being irritating?" Reid asked.

I smirked sadly at him. "No. I just ... haven't spoken about it. To anyone." Not even to my best friend, Cass. She'd asked. But I'd been too raw about the whole thing for a long time. My infatuation with Reid, however, had eased the hurt Luca left behind.

Concern flashed across Reid's expression. "Did someone hurt you?"

"Emotionally, yes. His name was Luca. He was an Italian studying at Edinburgh. I met him in second year. I'd never met anyone like him. Italians are so affectionate and open and charming and passionate. At least he was. We dated for just over a year. I'm pretty sure you knew that."

Reid frowned. "I knew you had a boyfriend at uni, but no one said anything about him hurting you."

"I told everyone that we broke up because he was going back to Rome."

"What really happened?"

"I let myself get wrapped up in him. He's one of those guys who makes you feel beautiful because he genuinely finds women in all their forms gorgeous. Too much. But the sex was amazing," I admitted, unable to look at Reid when I said it. "I think I let my hormones ignore all the warning signs. One day I was in the library and this girl came over, sat down beside me, and told me Luca had been cheating on me with her and had gotten her pregnant. She thought I should know. And when I confronted him, he didn't deny it. Told me people weren't meant to be monogamists." I finally met Reid's angry gaze. "I argued that if that was how he felt, then he shouldn't have misled me into believing he loved me and that we were each other's only one."

"I'm sorry. He sounds like a fuckwad."

"Oh, it got worse. I shared a flat with four other girls. My best friends. One of them confessed to me after the fact that she and Luca fucked a couple of times behind my back."

"Jesus Christ."

"Yeah." I took a long swallow of whisky, remembering the betrayal. I coughed a little and wiped at my lips, placing the glass on the table. "Part of me was terrified I'd never be able to trust people again."

"And can you?"

"Yes," I answered firmly. "Two people who don't understand what loyalty entails will not make me bitter or distrustful. Luca wasn't the right guy for me. I confused lust for love. I never felt truly comfortable around him. Looking back on it, we never talked about anything serious. Anything real. I think the right person is someone who makes you vibrate with awareness." I grinned, thinking of how much Reid did that to me. "And distracted as hell. But also be the one person you can trust to talk to about anything. To be comfortable enough with to be who you really are, to say how you really feel. You haven't met her yet, Reid. It doesn't mean she's not out there."

"Says the twenty-three-year-old who has all the time in the world. I'm not getting any younger, Evan."

I snorted. "You're talking as if you're ancient. You're only thirty-five, Reid."

"Men have ticking biological clocks, too, you know," he teased, surprising me.

"No, they don't," I disagreed, laughing. "You have nothing to worry about in that regard. But maybe if you had fewer rules, you'd meet the right woman."

His brow furrowed in confusion. "What rules?"

"Patrick said you have rules," I explained. "No dating women who'll nag about your schedule, no dating women who don't understand the store comes first, and no dating women younger than twenty-eight." I tried not to emphasize the last.

"Your brother needs to keep his mouth shut," Reid muttered.

"Are they true?"

He shrugged uncomfortably. "Aye. And clearly, the reason I'm still alone. I need to let them go. Except for the last." He refused to meet my gaze. "The last is a firm rule."

Disappointment burned in my gut along with the whisky. "Why?"

Still not meeting my gaze, he shrugged again. "I've dated younger women. They're too immature." He cut me a look. "I was born older than my years, Evan. I don't want to be with a woman who is disappointed I'm not interested in clubbing or going to music festivals or taking selfies together for social media."

Feeling irritated by his assumptions, I griped, "Not all twenty-somethings are into clubbing and music festivals and social media."

He raised a querulous eyebrow.

"They're not. Some of us have other interests."

"Maybe you do," he conceded. "But I haven't met many others who do. Plus, I'm not screwing around. Contrary to what people think, I'm looking for someone to start a family with. Women my age are ready for that," he sighed, closing his eyes as he pinched the bridge of his nose. "Not that I can seem to slow down enough for it to matter."

"You'll find her," I promised him. *It's me, you fool!* "One day, you'll find her, Reid."

He opened his eyes, looking at me through a low-lidded gaze. "You think so?"

His secret longing for a wife and family made my infatuation increase to ovary-exploding levels. I shifted uncomfortably, feeling the blush stain my cheeks.

All I had to do was slowly but surely prove to my brother's best friend that I was Mrs. Right. That I was a mature twenty-three-year-old who wanted the same things as him.

"I know so." The words came out hoarse with emotion.

Something in my voice caused Reid to stiffen, and as our eyes held, I felt a thick tension fall between us. I wanted to dive on him. Crush my mouth against his and show him that there was a woman out there who wanted him for his loyalty, his determination, his secret sweetness, and his understanding of what was truly important in life. I wanted to show him that for the right woman, he would loosen the reins on the store to be with her.

To be with me.

Something flared in his eyes before his expression shut down. Then he leaned forward and patted my knee. "You're a sweet kid, Evan. Thanks." He stood abruptly and strolled across the office to the coat stand in the corner where his suit jacket hung. Shrugging into it, he said, "You get home okay?"

Deflated, and a little embarrassed, I stood up, too, at the subtle rejection and hint for me to leave. "Oh, of course. I'll see you next week."

"Have a good weekend." He held the door open but wouldn't meet my gaze.

"Yeah, you too," I muttered, hurrying to collect my things so I could get the hell out of there.

"You're a sweet kid, Evan."

Ugh.

Shot to the damn heart.

However, hours later, after the mortification left me, determination returned.

I didn't imagine that moment on the couch between us.

And Reid's response felt a little contrived. Like he was trying to put distance between us.

Maybe I was a nutter and completely wrong.

But I had hope that I wasn't.

And I had time to prove to Reid that I was a woman. A mature woman.

The right woman.

CHAPTER THREE

REID

Mid-November

I was distracted.

Evan was distracting me.

And the level of distraction was irritating.

We crowded around the small conference room table. Kerry, my events coordinator, my sales and marketing team, and George, my general manager.

At my side, of course, was Evan, my personal assistant.

That alone made Evan off-limits.

The fact that she was my best friend's wee sister and twelve years my junior made her forbidden.

I shifted uncomfortably in my seat.

It was the forbidden thing, I told myself.

That was what was making me hot.

Not the way her skirt molded to an arse that was surprisingly round and luscious. Or the way her curvy hips accentuated how tiny her waist was. I could probably span it with my hands. I'd watched her sashay ahead of me into the conference room, mesmerized by the exaggerated feminine shape of her. I'd heard Evan complain to her mum about her hips and thighs as if they were a bad thing.

"If God was going to give me curves, why couldn't he give me boobs?" I'd overheard her moan to Jen, Pat and Evan's mother.

The memory had me flicking a surreptitious look at my PA's chest before glancing quickly away. Small but perfectly formed breasts strained against the tight fit of her black shirt.

Why had I never noticed how fucking gorgeously made Evan Munro was until last month?

Okay, not gonna lie, I'm a man—I noticed her arse around the year she turned eighteen.

But only in passing, as a man is wont to notice an exceptional arse.

Now her arse was an obsession.

Ever since we had that drink in my office, something had changed between us. This tension needed to evaporate because it was playing havoc with me.

"Haven't you ever met a woman who made you lose your common sense? Who made your skin hot and your blood pump and everything else but kissing her, touching her, ceased to matter?"

Not until now.

It was like her question had created a monster between us.

Evan took a sip of coffee from the mug she'd brought from home. It had arrows pointing upward and beneath it the words, "This is what an Awesome Employee looks like."

Fuck, she was adorable.

My eyes drifted to her mouth as she licked the coffee off her lips.

Everything about Evan, other than her hips and spectacular arse, was delicate and stunning. She had Jen's doll-like features, large, beautiful, thickly lashed dark eyes, a button nose, and a small but very kissable mouth. Evan's chin was a little pointed, giving her a mischievous quality that only made me think very bad thoughts.

"... Mr. Shaw?"

Realizing my name had been said, I looked blankly over at Kerry. "Sorry?"

She flicked Evan a strange look before turning back to me.

I tried not to squirm over my event coordinator's suspicious gaze.

"I asked if you were happy for us to post a competition on Instagram for locals to enter to win a chance to watch the Christmas tree being piped in?"

The Christmas tree at Shaw's was an event in itself. We had to remove the side door to the building, and a crew of men carried the forty-foot tree into the store's atrium. It was then erected by the use of pulleys while people rappelled from the ceiling to decorate it in fairy lights. We had a bagpiper pipe in the tree, and I invited staff to watch.

"Aye, that's fine," I replied. "Only two winners and their plus-ones."

Kerry opened her mouth to protest. I cut her off. "Part of the magic is customers asking how we get the tree into the store. They prefer the staff's tall tales to reality."

"Reality is pretty impressive, too, Mr. Shaw," she argued.

"I said no."

"Okay. Two winners and their plus-ones."

"Now the sale," I said, determined to focus on anything but the petite woman at my side who smelled bloody amazing. Three weeks ago, I'd caught Evan in the perfume department mooning over a perfume called Black Opium by YSL. It was one of the more expensive ones, and she bemoaned its price. It irritated me that Evan wouldn't buy herself the perfume, even with her discount. I'd picked up a box and told Greta, one of the staff in the perfume department, to add it to my tab.

Evan had looked dumbfounded by the gift.

Not wanting her to read too much into it, I casually called it a bonus and walked away before she could question me.

Now she wore the perfume every day. It had a heady, musky scent that made a man want to chase it with his tongue.

Fuck.

Patrick would kill me if he ever guessed what ran through my mind when I thought about his wee sister.

And I'd deserve to die.

Slowly. Painfully.

Suddenly, the door to the conference room flew open and a red-faced boy in the store's uniform stood panting in the doorway. I tried to remember his name and failed.

"Mr. Shaw." His eyes were round with panic. "We've had to call for an ambulance. Customer down in the men's department."

Shit.

I stood up, pushing my chair away with force. "George, Evan, with me," I demanded, hurrying out of the room with my manager and Evan at my back.

The whole time we stood in the elevator waiting for it to reach the men's department floor, I wondered what the hell I was going to do. We'd had fainting spells in the store before, but never someone who required an ambulance.

As it turned out, I didn't need to do anything.

Evan pushed past us, striding after the junior staff member who'd alerted us to the situation.

By the time George and I caught up, Evan was kneeling beside a man perhaps in his late fifties who was sitting on the floor, gray-faced and clammy. A woman of similar age stood to the side with Alan, the men's department manager, looking ready to pass out with worry.

Evan placed a reassuring hand on the man's chest. "What's your name, sir?" she asked softly.

"Gerald," he wheezed out.

"Hi, Gerald, I'm Evan. Are you experiencing chest pain?"

He nodded.

"And breathlessness?"

He nodded again, wincing.

"Are you allergic to aspirin?"

Gerald shook his head.

"Good." Evan turned toward George. "Run to the pharmacy as quickly as you can and grab a packet of aspirin and some water. And make sure the side entrance isn't blocked for the ambulance."

My general manager didn't question her authoritative tone.

"Are you a medic?" asked the worried woman I suspected was Gerald's wife.

"I'm a qualified first aider," Evan replied.

How did I not know this? Surely that was something I should know about her, especially as her employer. My entire staff should know who the first aiders in the building were.

The wife looked near tears. "Will my husband be okay?"

"He's doing fine," Evan evaded, patting Gerald's arm. "The ambulance will be here soon."

"Is he having a heart attack?" The wife began to cry.

Gerald shot her a concerned, pained look.

Evan rubbed her hand down Gerald's arm to soothe him. "I don't know for sure. But some aspirin should help until the paramedics get here."

For a few more minutes, Evan spoke quietly and calmly to the man, and he stared into her eyes, seeming to relax. Not long later, George appeared, breathless and sweating with the goods in hand.

I watched on from the side as Evan helped Gerald take the aspirin with some water. She did it with that same mature calm and the small, reassuring smile she'd worn since we'd arrived on the scene.

Minutes later, the paramedics made their way through the department to Gerald. I was completely focused on Evan, who quickly and efficiently relayed the man's symptoms to the paramedics and told them she'd given him aspirin.

"Are you a doctor?" one paramedic asked in a tone I didn't like.

I stepped forward. "She's one of my first aiders."

The paramedic nodded. "Fine, fine, good. Can you make sure everyone's out of the way, sir?"

Evan and I did just that, cutting a path through the store for the paramedics to maneuver with no fuss. Customers watched as we passed, the store brought to a standstill in some departments because of it. It barely registered with me.

I was completely and fully aware of the small, incredibly capable woman at my side.

Once the ambulance departed, I turned to Evan, staring into her gorgeous dark eyes and said gruffly, "You were wonderful."

She beamed, her smile causing this ache in my chest I didn't understand. "Thanks. Happy to help him. He should be okay."

"You were so calm and in control."

It was bloody impressive.

George appeared, and then Alan and the young boy who'd come running to alert us to the situation. They surrounded Evan, marveling at her handling of the situation and congratulating her.

The overwhelming urge to snatch her up from the lot came over me.

"Haven't you ever been infatuated with a woman?" Her question from weeks ago came back to me.

My answer then was no.

But it had changed.

Evan with her sunny disposition, her kindness, her surprising maturity, the ease with which I could talk to her, had become an obsession. I wanted to possess every inch of her, like a fucking territorial caveman, and I'd never felt that way about a woman.

It had taken me twenty years to find a woman who filled my thoughts and drove me to distraction.

And it would have to be my best friend's little sister.

It wasn't the forbidden thing that got me hot.

She did.

It was the forbidden thing that made it hurt.

Because I couldn't have her.

CHAPTER FOUR

REID
Early December

It was very difficult to avoid a personal assistant.

Something about their entire job revolving around *personally* assisting, I suppose.

There was no getting away from Evan at work, as much as I tried.

The woman was driving me to madness.

Was this love? This insanity?

Searching for the sound of her voice, the tinkle of her laughter, the smell of her perfume.

This knot in my gut and the absentmindedness that seemed more appropriate for a teenager than a full-grown man.

I'd taken to sending Evan home earlier than usual. It had been a bad habit of mine to let her work almost as late as I did, but I'd insisted she leave at the end of her workday. She'd tried to resist, but my snapped demand that she do as she was told halted any further arguing. In fact, she'd started to treat me with a cool distance that was driving me up the wall.

I should be grateful for it.

Yet every time she smiled at another staff member or laughed on the phone with someone, it made me miss the ease between us all the more.

It was for the best, I kept telling myself.

My eyes flicked to the wall clock, and I wasn't surprised to discover it was past eleven o'clock. I'd been working later once Evan left the office because it was the only time I could fully concentrate.

Damn the woman.

My phone buzzed on my desk, Patrick's name on the screen.

Guilt suffused me.

I'd been avoiding Pat, too, ever since I realized how I felt about Evan.

However, knowing he wouldn't be calling at this late hour without a reason, I answered, hitting the speaker button.

"Reid, can you do me a favor, mate?" Pat asked without preamble.

"Of course."

"Evan is on a Christmas night out with the girls. Her friend Cass got blootered. Bad breakup or something. The rest of the girls have buggered off and left Evan to deal with it alone. She phoned me just before her phone died. The taxi drivers won't take Cass while she's that smashed. I'm in Aberdeen for work, so I can't get to her. She's on George IV Bridge near Frankenstein's. Will you go get them, mate, and take them back to Evan's?"

Shit.

"Of course," I repeated as I stood. "I'm still at the office so I won't be long."

"Great, thanks. Also, get a fucking life and stop burning the midnight oil." Pat hung up.

Worry quickly propelled me out of Shaw's. I hated the thought of Evan stranded on a busy thoroughfare where drunk bastards might try to take advantage of her while she was looking after a friend. But there was a part of me dreading seeing her again.

I'd parked two streets back from the store on George Street. The icy December wind bit at my nose and cheeks as I hurried toward the vehicle past crowds of revelers enjoying Friday-night barhopping. Some, like Evan, might even be on their Christmas night out with friends or work colleagues. Every weekend running up to Christmas would see the city filled with women wearing short dresses and high heels, some carrying their coats because alcohol made them feel impervious to the winter chill.

Right now, Evan was one of those women out in the windy city, probably inappropriately dressed for the weather. It surprised me for more than one reason to get the call from Pat. Evan didn't seem like much of a party animal. She preferred quiet nights out in cocktail bars or at the theatre or restaurants.

My kind of woman.

I'd never been the clubbing type.

Mum said I was born eighty years old.

Too old for Evan.

But are you really? She's mature for her age, that devil on my shoulder insisted.

"Fuck," I muttered, growing impatient as I sat at traffic lights on Princes Street. Princes Street Gardens were brightly lit, most of the trees covered in fairy lights, the Ferris wheel colorful in the night sky.

Finally, the traffic lights changed, but there were more to contend with on my way to Evan, and it seemed to take an eternity to get to George IV Bridge. Eventually, I drove forward, my eyes searching the pavement filled with men and women dressed to the nines.

Then, there, not far from Frankenstein's, I saw Evan crouched near a barely conscious blond propped against the building behind them. I hit my indicator and swung the car beside them, even though it was illegal to park there. I couldn't give a fuck.

Hurrying out of the car, I approached Evan, who wore a long wool coat and scarf.

"Evan."

Her head whipped in my direction, and I blinked rapidly at the vision before me.

She usually wore her dark hair in a no-nonsense ponytail at work. Now it fell in long, silky waves around her face, and she had done something with her makeup that made her look older and more mysterious. Her eyes, which were naturally beautiful, were fucking stunning. Striking.

"Reid?" Her lips parted in surprise. "What are you doing here?"

"Pat called. He's in Aberdeen."

"I know. I thought he'd call Dad."

"I'm closer." I lowered to my haunches beside her, my attention moving to the blond woman. Her eyelids sat heavy and low as she peered up at me, expression slack and pale. "How is she?"

"Cass has thrown up twice. I've given her as much water as she'll take." Evan shook a half-filled bottle, her expression strained with worry. "None of the damn taxi drivers would take her in this mess. They said I needed to phone an ambulance. But she's just wasted."

I nodded and stood, only to bend down and haul her friend up into my arms. She was dressed in an oversized faux fur jacket that shifted with the movement, blinding me. Evan yanked the jacket down into place so I could see where I was going. Cass drunkenly looped her arms around my neck while I gazed down at Evan.

"Get the back-passenger door of the car," I directed.

She threw me a look of pure hero worship before rushing across the pavement to my vehicle.

Lowering Cass into the back seat took a little more finesse than one might think. We ignored drunken shouts from young men walking past and eventually slid Cass along the back bench.

"What if she throws up in your car?" Evan asked, worrying her bottom lip with her teeth.

"It'll clean."

"It's a Jaguar."

"It'll clean," I repeated. "Get in before you freeze."

"I'm wearing a coat," she muttered, but hurried to jump into the passenger seat.

It was only when we drove away that I relaxed.

"It was great of you to pick us up. I never let my phone die when I'm going anywhere, but some stupid app must have been running on it, eating up my battery."

I shot her a quick look. "What happened tonight?"

"Cass broke up with her boyfriend. They've been together three years. He took a job in London, and Cass didn't want to move there, so she ended things. Some girls we went to uni with decided she needed a Christmas night out. They bought her shots and she kept flinging them back. Within an hour, she was blootered." Evan's tone was angry. "Then the lot of them left me. Said they were going clubbing and I could either put Cass in a cab home and come with them, or deal with her."

"Very nice."

"Aye, bloody charming." Evan glanced over her shoulder at

Cass. "She'll be okay. Though it'll be one helluva hangover in the morning."

"Why didn't you just go with them?" I asked, though I already knew the answer.

"One: She's my best friend and I'm worried about her. I want to stay with her to make sure she doesn't choke on her own vomit. And two: The thought of being squished onto a crowded dance floor while strange men try to press up against me isn't my idea of a good time, believe it or not. I've been told on more than one occasion that I'm, and I quote, 'a boring old fart.'" Her tone was only slightly amused. There was a hint of hurt there.

"Who said that?"

"Friends. A guy I started dating not long after Luca. It didn't last long. He just wanted to go out on the lash every weekend, preferably without me."

"You're not boring just because getting pissed isn't your idea of fun," I replied dryly.

Who were these fuckers she was friends with?

"You're just saying that because you're thirty-five and past all that."

I frowned at the reminder of our age difference. "I was never really about that, even at your age. Pat, the lads and I, did our fair share of drinking when we were students, but clubbing was not my thing. We'd go to a pub or hang out at the dorms."

"How did you pick up girls, then?" she asked cheekily.

I threw her a cocky grin. "Before, sometimes during, and after classes. At the student union bar. The library—"

"Okay, okay, okay." She held up a hand. "You got laid a lot at uni. Very good."

It was on the tip of my tongue to tease her and ask her if she was jealous. I quelled the instinct.

There was a frown in Evan's voice when she asked, "Why are we going the wrong way?"

"My place is closer. We can take care of Cass. There's room for you both to crash there."

"Won't we be intruding?"

"Why would you be intruding?"

"Well, I've never been to your place before. I assumed it was because you're so private."

I was a private man, but not so much I didn't want Evan to see my space.

Whatever thoughts I had about putting distance between us had flown out the window as soon as I had her in proximity. I wanted to talk with her. Be near her.

It didn't take long to pull up to my apartment building in Newhaven. I lived in one of the penthouse apartments and had a fantastic view over the Firth of Forth estuary.

Parked in my private spot, I got out and rounded the car to get Cass. She mumbled in my arms as Evan took my keys and led the way. The reception was closed at this time of night, so all was quiet as we made our way through the lobby and onto the elevator.

"Thanks again for this," Evan said as the lift climbed upward. She stared up at me with adoring, big dark eyes. I wanted to ask her how she planned on repaying me, making it clear by my tone that I'd prefer sexual favors.

I stifled that urge too.

We got Cass into my flat. The main living space was large and open plan with a bank of windows that overlooked the water. Together we got Cass onto one end of the oversized sectional in the middle of the sitting area.

"I'll get water." I turned, shrugging out of my jacket and placing it over a bar stool at my island. I collected water for Evan and Cass from my fridge.

When I returned to the ladies, Cass was out cold, her face

pressed to the back of the sectional. Evan had removed her own coat and scarf and stood from sitting at Cass's hip.

My eyes lowered, and I felt my hot blood travel south.

I'd never seen Evan wear anything so daring.

But then I guessed I didn't know everything about her.

The red velvet dress was perfect to celebrate Christmas. But it wasn't the kind of dress she could wear at her family Christmas get-together, that was for damn sure. The dress had long sleeves, but that was where any demureness ended. It had an exaggerated V-neck that Evan might have assumed wasn't overtly sexy because she was so small breasted. She'd be wrong. The hemline hit her mid-thigh, and the velvet clasped tightly to the curves of her hips. For such a small woman, she had great fucking legs. Strong thighs, shapely calves, slim ankles.

All lengthened by sexy, gold strappy heels.

"You look amazing," I blurted out without thought, dazedly handing her a bottle of water.

Evan's eyes widened a little at the compliment. "Uh, thanks."

I had to drag my fucking eyes off her hips. Trying to focus on Cass, I said, "She seems okay." I placed the bottle of water on the coffee table near her.

"Aye, she'll be fine," Evan muttered. "Thanks again." She looked around the room, her gaze stopping on the bank of windows. "Your place is fantastic."

I was pretty pleased with my flat. I was glad she liked it. "Thanks."

She turned to me and teased, "Pity you don't spend more time here."

If I had you in my bed, I might.

Thankfully, I didn't say that out loud, but I might as well have for the thick sexual tension that sprung between us as we gazed into each other's eyes.

"Tea," I blurted.

Evan blinked in confusion. "Huh?"

"Do you want a cup of tea?"

"Oh. Yeah, sure."

Grateful to have something to do, I busied myself in the kitchen.

Unfortunately, when I returned, Evan was sitting on the opposite arm of the sectional to Cass, the coffee table between her and her unconscious friend whose soft snores now filled the room. That wasn't the unfortunate part.

The unfortunate part was that sitting down caused the velvet dress to strain across her thighs and shift upward, revealing more of her olive-skinned legs.

She wasn't wearing any tights.

Fuck.

Even though it was toying with disaster, I sat down close beside her, inhaling the perfume I'd bought her. Feeling territorial, I couldn't meet her eyes as I handed her a hot mug.

"Were you at work when Patrick called?" she asked.

I nodded.

Silence fell between us. Usually our silence was comfortable.

Not now. The air crackled.

I wasn't even shocked when Evan said bluntly, "Did I do something?"

I forced myself to meet her gaze. "What?"

She wrinkled her nose in consternation. I wanted to press a kiss to the tip. "You've been aloof with me lately. Even a little irritable."

Hearing the sadness in her tone, I cursed myself for being such a bastard. "It's not anything you've done. It's me. I'm sorry."

"Has something happened? Can I help?"

For a moment, I couldn't speak. The overwhelming need

to pull her into my arms and tell her just holding her would do the trick was intense. And hard to fight. I felt huge next to her on that couch. She'd be light and fragile in my arms. Except for those luscious thighs. I could almost imagine them gripping my hips as I thrust up into her as she straddled me.

God, she'd be small and tight.

Would she even be able to take me?

Feeling myself grow hard and almost dizzy at the thought, I stood abruptly and wandered over to the window. Willing the heat out of my body before I lost control, I sipped at my tea and tried to think of things that disturbed me. Like the time Pat and I walked in on Pat and Evan's parents fucking in the kitchen when we were twelve.

We were supposed to be staying at my house that night and had surprised them.

Scarred for life.

All four of us.

"Reid." Evan sidled up next to me, her perfume driving me nuts.

She was driving me nuts.

This was ridiculous.

I was seconds from grabbing her up in my arms and taking her into the bedroom.

"How's Pat doing?" I asked, trying to distract myself.

If the subject change confused her, she didn't say anything. "Haven't you two spoken recently?"

"I've been busy. I keep meaning to call ..."

"He's fine. In Aberdeen for a medical conference. And trying to decide whether he should give in to his attraction for a receptionist at his practice. He thinks it might be unprofessional to start something with her."

Way too close to the bone. I turned away, heading into the kitchen to put my mug in the sink. Taking a few deep breaths, I moved back into the sitting room to find her still standing at the window.

Her back was to me as she stared out at the dark water. Light from across the firth spilled over its inky ripples.

Evan turned her head ever so slightly, as if she sensed me staring.

And something about the loneliness I saw within her broke me.

I crossed the distance between us, drawing to a halt as the back of her head touched my upper chest.

I heard her quick inhale, and my dick hardened.

"Evan," I exhaled, shaky with need as I touched her arms, my hands coasting up the soft velvet of her dress.

I could see over the top of her head, see her chest rising and falling with shallow breaths.

Her cheeks flushed, her lids lowered, her lips parted on little pants of excitement.

My fingers slipped under the fabric at her left shoulder, and I pushed it down her arm until the neckline gave way and one small, beautiful breast popped free.

Her large, rosy nipple tightened in the cool air of the apartment.

"Jesus Christ," I murmured, in awe, desperate to taste her.

Instead, I cupped her breast in my large hand, engulfing it, kneading it, my thumb plucking at her nipple. My other hand settled on her hip, squeezing it, caressing it, learning the shape of her. I buried my head in her neck, kissing her soft skin, my tongue tracing the scent of her perfume as I rolled my hips against the top of her arse. I wanted her to feel how hard she made me.

A moan drifted out of her. "Reid." Her hands settled on my outer thighs, and she undulated her arse against my dick.

It was like a switch going off.

Lust covered my mind in a haze.

Whirling her around in my arms, I hoisted her into them, bringing her mouth to mine. She wrapped her legs around my waist as my lips and tongue devoured her. Feeling my way there, I carried her to the opposite end of the sofa. Laying her down, I covered her with my body, my kiss hungry and punishing.

She tasted like everything I'd ever wanted.

I needed inside her.

"Fuck, Evan." I broke the kiss to pull at her dress, freeing her other breast. "I need to see every inch of you." I pushed up the hem of her skirt to find her underwear. "You're the sexiest woman I've ever met. I've never wanted to be inside a woman more."

"Oh my God," she panted, her eyes gleaming with desire and something far more dangerous to my heart. "You keep talking like that, and I'm going to come."

"*You* keep talking like that and *I'm* going to come." My fingers brushed her sex, feeling how wet she was. "Oh, fuck, Ev. I can't wait. I've waited too long." I fumbled for the buttons and zipper on my suit trousers, desperate to drive my dick deep inside her.

"Urggh, urggh." The loud, pained moans were like a bucket of ice water over me.

My eyes flew to the other side of the room.

Cass.

Fuck.

I'd forgotten she was even in the room.

Looking back at Evan, I saw her shock, too, and she quickly fumbled to cover herself.

Evan Munro was hurrying to cover herself because I had just mauled her.

Pushing off her, reality crashed back down.

I had nearly fucked my PA.

My best friend's wee sister.

Patrick would kill me if he found out about this.

Shaking from my complete loss of control, I climbed off her and marched across the room to get away from her. Running my hand through my hair, I tried to get a handle on my emotions.

Everything I prided myself on—self-control, honor, loyalty—was being compromised because of my feelings for this woman.

It couldn't go on. I'd end up losing who I was to her.

"Reid?"

I squeezed my eyes closed at the uncertainty in Evan's voice.

Then I turned to her, my chest aching, my gut in a knot as I realized what I had to do. "This shouldn't have happened."

She looked crestfallen.

Rejected.

And I fucking hated myself for it.

"You're Pat's little sister," I reminded her.

"It's none of his business."

I scoffed. "Evan, come on. I can't jeopardize my friendship with him and your parents."

Her expression darkened. "That would be true if this was only about sex."

Tell her it's not.

Tell her the truth.

But I knew if I did, it would only make it worse for both of us. "You're too young for me," I lied.

"I see." Her voice was brittle.

"We just need to pretend like it didn't happen."

"I can't pretend. I'm going to make some calls over the weekend. I'll find somewhere else to work."

The air in my apartment turned icy with my displeasure. "Very well."

Evan crossed her arms over her chest, hugging herself.

It took what little self-control I had left not to cross the room and embrace her.

"There's a guest room, if you'd like to sleep in there." I was coolly polite.

"No, thank you. I'll stay out here and keep an eye on Cass."

So I hid away like a coward in my bedroom.

When I woke up early the next morning, Evan and her friend were gone.

And I felt truly alone for the first time in thirty-five years.

⚜

One week later

IF THE DISTANCE between Evan and me had bothered me before I'd pawed her in my apartment like an adolescent boy incapable of controlling himself, it was much worse now.

Evan had taken to looking right through me, even when we were discussing work.

I hated it.

It chafed badly.

I wanted to grab her by the shoulders and tell her to stop.

But that would be unfair.

After all, I was the one who said nothing could happen between us.

All week, I'd waited anxiously for her to tell me she'd gotten a job elsewhere. As the days went on with no word from her, however, a part of me hoped she'd been bluffing. The masochist in me just wanted Evan near, no matter if she was giving me the cold shoulder.

A knock sounded at the door, drawing me out of my distracted thoughts and back into my office.

"Come in."

Evan strode in. Her pretty features were smoothed into a perfectly blank expression.

I tried not to look anywhere else.

Those pencil skirts she wore drove me mad.

"Yes?" I sat back in my chair, pretending indifference toward her.

Evan drew in a breath and then exhaled, betraying her cool countenance. Then she stepped up to my desk and laid down an envelope. "You'll find a month's notice in there."

My stomach dropped. It took me a moment to speak. Finally, I replied, "You found a job, then?"

She nodded, staring directly into my eyes. "You must have mentioned how good I was at my job to Josh Baxter. When he heard I was looking for a position, he hired me as his PA."

Josh Baxter?

Josh fucking Baxter.

I was going to kill him.

Swallowing my anger, I had to clench my jaw to stop furious denial from roaring out.

Josh was two years younger than me. We'd been friends for a few years, meeting as equals in the Scottish business world. He'd opened a gym at the tender age of twenty-six and now had a chain all over the central belt of Scotland. Evan had accompanied me to a charity benefit five months ago when Emmy hadn't been able to attend. He'd asked after Evan with a look I knew well. He wanted her. I'd explained she was a brilliant PA, Patrick's wee sister, and completely off-limits to him.

That absolute fucker.

Visions of him touching Evan exploded through my brain, and I reeled back from my chair. "No." I stood up.

Her lips parted in shock. "Excuse me?"

I knew I was being a controlling dick, but I couldn't stop

myself. "I said no. Find another job. One not with a known womanizer."

She crossed her arms over her chest and raised an eyebrow. "I think not."

"Evan ..." I practically growled her name in warning.

"I'll finish up to Christmas and start with Baxter in the new year. End of discussion." Evan turned and marched with that alluring swing of her hips toward the door.

Heat pumped through me as I imagined chasing her across the room, pressing her against my door, my straining dick thrusting against that impressive arse of hers.

And I knew Josh Baxter would inevitably want her too.

The thought filled me with a horrific feeling. My throat was closing with it, my heart racing too hard. A knot tightened in my gut.

It was jealousy, I realized.

An emotion I was not familiar with.

But Evan slammed out of my office before I could protest any further.

A huge part of me wanted to follow her out and demand that she find another position elsewhere. Or better fucking yet, stay!

I didn't want to become someone I wasn't just because I was jealous. That thought stayed me.

Not wanting Evan to hate me any more than I feared she already did, I slumped in my chair.

Missing her already.

CHAPTER FIVE

EVAN
Mid-December

As soon as Belle and her father walked away with gift in hand, Reid was there. He strode up onto the platform where Santa sat and bent down to whisper something in Santa Gary's ear.

Whatever it was, it had Gary blanching beneath his fake white beard.

"Hey, mate." Gary pulled away from Reid, his words just loud enough for me to hear. "No harm meant, aye."

Reid cut him a dark look before turning it on me.

I bristled at his displeasure as his gaze raked down my body and back up again. "They needed an elf," I whispered.

Suddenly he was before me, his chest almost touching me. "And you thought it would be a good idea for my PA to dress up in a ridiculous costume? Why couldn't someone else do it?"

"You're making a scene," I said through gritted teeth as I beamed up at him. "The kids are waiting to meet Santa."

He flicked a look over my shoulder, and his scowl eased. When his gaze returned to mine, he said, "As soon as you're on break, I want you in my office."

Irritated that he was being so uptight about the whole thing, I gave him a brief nod and then whirled to face the line of kids again. As I talked with a shy little boy, I eventually felt the heat of Reid's stare disappear. When I turned around toward Santa, my boss was, thankfully, gone.

❧

"Is it true Mr. Shaw is unhappy about this?" Kerry hurried toward me as I walked through the atrium in my costume, drawing stares from customers.

As promised, I was on my way to deal with Reid during my break. I waved Kerry off as she walked along with me. "It's fine. I should have asked him before I agreed to do it. He obviously needed me for something and is annoyed I wasn't there for him. Which is fair enough."

"Oh, God, I feel awful for getting you in trouble."

I shrugged. "How much trouble can I really get into? I'm leaving, remember?"

"Right." Kerry frowned. The announcement I was leaving had confused most of the staff. When asked why I was moving on, I lied and said I needed a new challenge. I knew they weren't buying it. Who needed a new challenge after only working in a job for nine months?

Oh, well.

Let them gossip.

I left Kerry standing in the beauty department and made my way to the elevators. Swiping my ID card across the screen below the buttons for the customer areas, I unlocked the staff floor buttons. With a shaking hand, I pressed for the top.

Why I was so nervous, I had no idea.

I couldn't possibly still care what Reid thought of me.

Yes, I could.

Ugh!

By the time I reached his office, my heart hammered against my rib cage. I knocked softly.

"Come in."

My belly fluttered at the sound of his voice.

Damn him.

I stepped inside and found him walking around his desk to lean against it. He crossed his arms over his chest and his right ankle over his left.

His dark eyes gleamed with something that could have been anger or lust. Maybe even both.

That look made my palms sweat.

Reid's gaze lowered down my body and back up again.

I shifted uncomfortably, feeling a deep, low, needful tug in my belly.

While earlier he'd called the costume ridiculous, I got the distinct feeling he was imagining ripping it off me.

Oh, boy.

"You wanted to see me?"

His eyes returned to mine. "Didn't you think it appropriate to ask first before you played Santa's Little Helper for the day?"

"Probably. But we had paying customers waiting to meet Santa. They needed me."

"I needed you. We were supposed to go over the applications for your replacement today."

My replacement.

I hated how much that word stung.

"I assumed you could do that on your own."

"You assume too much." Reid abruptly pushed up off the desk and strode toward me.

I braced myself, my breathing shallow.

The air between us crackled. Reid's eyes held a dark intent.

To my confusion, he brushed past me. I glanced over my shoulder, wondering where he was going.

He looked back at me as he stopped at the door and then very deliberately locked it.

Oh. My. God.

"Reid?" I could barely hear over the rushing of blood in my ears. The damn elf costume was suddenly way too hot. The stockings chafed.

"It doesn't matter," Reid said.

"What doesn't?"

"The applications. I've already chosen your replacement."

That damn hurt shoved its way through, confusing me all the more. Why was he saying that when he looked like he was ready to devour me?

"Oh?" I frowned.

He nodded and prowled across the room. I sucked in a breath as he cupped my hips in his hands and pushed me backward. I stumbled a little at first but then dazedly allowed him to move me across the room, my silly elf shoes jingling all the way.

Until my arse hit his desk.

I was panting now at the unadulterated desire in his eyes.

"I've decided to replace Evan Munro with Santa's Little Helper." He smirked, bending his head toward mine.

Wait!

What was happening here?

Yanking myself out of the sexual fog he so easily cast over me, I pushed against his chest, stopping his descent. His brow furrowed, his eyes questioning.

"Don't," I said, almost pleading and hating myself for it. "I can't be just a casual fuck to you."

Reid's expression hardened with anger. He wrapped his hand around my nape, a possessive, territorial, claiming gesture that secretly thrilled me. "Is that what you think of me?"

Trying, and failing, to control my breathing, I whispered, "You said I was too young. That we couldn't because of Patrick."

"I was a damn fool," he said hoarsely, his lips almost brushing mine. "I can't let you go. I can't stop thinking about you." His gaze moved from my mouth to meet my eyes, and his grip on my nape tightened. "You're all I think about, Evan. You've driven me to goddamn distraction. If I don't get inside you soon, I'm going to lose my mind."

"But—"

"It's not just sex," he cut me off. "You're in my blood. I've never felt this way about anyone."

Just like that, all my defenses crumbled.

Exultation gleamed in Reid's eyes as he read my expression. He massaged my nape, sending shivers down my spine. His lips brushed mine, and he commanded, "Spread your legs, Ev."

I made a sound from the back of my throat as arousal flushed through me, and I slowly spread my legs.

Just like that, whatever control Reid had snapped. He crushed his mouth down on mine, his kiss voracious, his tongue exploring, chasing mine. It was the deepest, dirtiest fucking kiss of my life, and I loved it.

I clung to his waist, trying to draw him closer, to feel him between my legs.

As we kissed, he reached beneath my petticoat and tore at the stockings. I broke away, panting, "My costume!"

"The costume is indecent," he replied, nipping at my lips,

trying to pull me back into the kiss as he yanked the tights down my thighs.

"It's the demurest elf costume ever!"

Reid pulled back, scowling. "Every time you bend over that fucking Christmas tree, your skirt flies up. Every father in that line got a view of your spectacular arse, and Santa wasn't doing a very good job of hiding how much he was enjoying himself."

"This costume is ridiculous," I argued.

"Yes, and yet somehow I've been fighting a hard-on since I first saw you in it." Reid reached down and pulled off my elf shoes. My tights followed.

"Reid!" I braced my hands on his shoulders for balance.

"Please tell me you're wet," he practically begged as he coasted his hands along my thighs and curled his finger beneath my underwear.

"I'm always wet for you," I whispered, almost mournfully.

Whatever he heard in my tone stopped him. He cupped my face with his other hand, his thumb brushing my mouth. "How long?"

I knew what he was asking.

"Since I was fourteen," I admitted, knowing there was no point hiding it now. I'd loved him in some way or another since I was a kid.

His expression was so tender, if I could have melted any more, I would have been a puddle of feels at his feet. "Patrick is going to kill me," he replied hoarsely.

I stiffened.

Reid shook his head. "But you're worth it, Ev."

Just like that, I couldn't wait. I needed him. Now.

I told him as much, fumbling at the slim leather belt looped through his black suit pants.

We were frantic, hot skin and searching hands. Reid took

over releasing himself, while I shimmied out of my underwear and kicked them across the room.

Then he was there, revealed to me.

Hot, hard, and thick.

Watching him roll a condom over his length was the sexiest show on earth.

"Oh my God." My inner muscles squeezed as if they could already feel him.

"I wanted you naked and bare to me the first time we did this ... but I just can't fucking wait to be inside you." Reid pulled me across the desk to meet him, one hand clasping my nape again, the other gripping my hip beneath my skirts.

I gasped against his mouth as he prodded between my legs.

He thrust at the same time he kissed me.

Pleasure-pain exploded in a cascade of shivers down my spine and the back of my legs, tingling all the way to my toes. I was small; he was thick.

It was a tight fit.

Slipping my hands over his rock-hard arse, I wrapped my legs around his hips. He glided out of me and pumped back in. The slight burn eased, and all I felt was the overwhelming, amazing fullness of him moving inside me. I reveled at the feel of his muscles shifting beneath my hands, and I dug my fingers into his cheeks, begging for more.

"Harder!" I broke our kiss to pant.

Reid lifted his head. Our eyes locked as he moved his hand from my nape to my other hip so he could steady me.

Then he fucked me in earnest.

I had to let go of him to hold on to the desk.

Biting back my cries of pleasure, I held Reid's eyes the whole time he drove into me. His expression was fierce with need, his eyes glittering under the light, teeth slightly bared as he took his pleasure from me.

Surprise flickered over his face. "I'm ... I'm going to come. Fuck." He slipped a hand between my legs and rolled his thumb over my clit.

"Oh God, oh fuck, oh God." My head fell back on my shoulders as that tight, winding tension building inside reached the heavens.

And shattered with the bliss of it all.

I cried out, forgetting where we were as my inner muscles rippled around Reid in voluptuous tugs.

His eyes widened with the sensation. "Evan!"

My body was still pulsing with release as he throbbed inside me, his hips shuddering against mine as he climaxed.

I reached for him, kissing him through the last of it, desperate kisses that turned languid and luxurious as our orgasms eased.

Finally, Reid lifted his head to cup my face in his hands. "Jesus fucking Christ."

I grinned and agreed, "Yeah."

"It's not enough," he groaned, peppering sweet kisses down my chin and throat. "I need you again."

As much as I didn't want to remind him, I whispered, "I have to get back to the grotto."

With a heavy sigh, Reid nodded and reluctantly eased out of me.

I winced a little.

"You okay?" He frowned.

"More than," I promised him.

His eyes roamed my face. "No regrets?"

"No regrets."

"You're not leaving me."

I grinned. "Was that a question or a demand?"

He scowled, but his tone didn't match his expression. "Evan ... please don't leave me."

Tenderness flooded me. "What about Patrick?"

Reid sighed again. "If he cares about us, he won't stand in our way."

"I don't want to cause problems. I know how much his friendship means to you, and vice versa."

"It does." He slid his hands beneath my skirt again, causing goose bumps to chase his touch. "But I told you, I've never felt this way about anyone before. If I let you walk away, I'll regret it for the rest of my life."

His words caused me to smile so big, I probably looked like a moron.

Reid didn't seem to think so, though. He smiled, squeezing my thighs. "Happy?"

I nodded. "Extremely."

"Good." He leaned his forehead against mine. "Because it's my new mission in life to make you happy. So happy you'll never want to leave me."

"I approve of this mission," I teased, pressing kisses to his bristly cheek until I reached his ear. And then I took a plunge of faith and confessed, "I love you, Reid."

He jerked back, making my heart sputter with fear.

But then he demanded, "Don't say it if you don't mean it."

Trying to quell my smile, I replied, "I mean it. No way has anyone ever made me feel the way you do."

Confusion flooded me as he reached past me for his wallet. At the same time, he kicked off his shoes and the trousers that had fallen to his ankles.

"What ..."

He was pulling out another condom. "Take off the dress. You're going to be late."

"Reid?"

"You just told me you love me. I want to say it to you while you're naked and on your back and I'm buried deep inside you."

I'd never taken off a dress so fast in my life.

Minutes later, I was sprawled across the couch in Reid's office. We were both gloriously naked.

And he made love to me as he murmured how much he loved me over and over again.

Neither of us cared how loud we were or if anyone heard us.

All we saw was each other, all we felt was each other, and all we heard were those three little words whispered between us as we connected in every way two people could.

CHAPTER SIX

EVAN
Christmas morning

My heart lurched when the doorbell rang. My palms sweated when Mum called out as she passed the living room from the kitchen, "That will be Annie and Reid. I'll get it."

I heard their loud greetings of "Happy Christmas" to one another, Reid's voice more of a rumbling murmur in amongst our mums' higher-pitched tones. The feeling in my stomach was familiar. I'd felt that deep, nauseating sensation that time my high school bestie convinced me to jump from the top diving board at the swim center.

Suffice it to say, my anxiety was through the roof.

After two weeks of keeping our relationship secret, Reid and I had decided to tell our families on Christmas morning. It was a gamble and possibly selfish if we ended up spoiling everyone's day. However, it was the one time our families would be together and in a guaranteed good mood. And we lived on the hope that this news would be a gift to our parents.

Reid had wanted to tell Patrick on his own, but I didn't think that was fair. It wasn't all on Reid.

Mum ushered Annie into the sitting room first, and Reid's mum came straight to me. I stood on trembling knees to embrace her and accept her soft kiss on my cheek.

"Happy Christmas, Annie."

"You too, sweetheart." She clasped my face in her hands, her dark eyes filled with tenderness. "You look beautiful. And happy. My son's treating you right at that office, then?"

As hard as I tried, I couldn't fight the blush that heated my cheeks. "Of course."

The corner of her lips turned up in a knowing smirk and suspicion rippled through me.

Did she already know?

My eyes flew past her to Reid.

Happiness engulfed me at the mere sight of him. The man made me giddy. Every morning I went to work, excited to be there, to see him, to steal secret kisses in his office. To leave before him, but then meet him by his car and drive to his apartment for dinner. Afterward, we made love. And then we'd lie in bed, talking about everything and nothing. Laughing. Cuddling.

Until he had to take me home.

Not this last week. He'd insisted I leave clothes at his apartment so I could sleep over.

Waking up in his arms, safe and content, was the best feeling in the world. And while it had been amusing for Reid to drop me off a block from the department store so it didn't appear as if we'd arrived together, I looked forward to the day we could walk through it hand in hand.

There would be gossip.

But I didn't care what people thought.

Correction: I only cared what our families thought.

Reid held my gaze for a second or two, hiding nothing of his feelings for me. Then Dad embraced him, breaking the moment.

I felt a little discombobulated as we got the Christmas greetings over and Annie laid the Christmas gifts she'd brought under the tree. Patrick and Reid were the last to embrace.

"Happy Christmas, mate." Pat clapped Reid on the back.

"Happy Christmas. You doing all right?"

"Well, you'd know if you ever picked up the bloody phone," Pat teased, but there was an edge to his voice as he sat down on the sofa. His posture was relaxed, but his questioning gaze never left Reid.

Reid swallowed. Since the man was excellent at hiding his feelings, including nervousness, I felt more than a surge of discomfort for him. I wanted to cuddle into him. Instead, I could only sit down on the edge of the sofa and stare.

"Been busy," Reid eventually said. "No excuse, though, sorry."

In truth, he'd been avoiding my brother because he hated lying to him.

Studying Patrick's face, I knew he knew Reid was lying or being evasive at least. His eyes narrowed.

"Well." Mum clapped her hands together. "Why don't we open presents first before we have breakfast?"

My stomach lurched again as Reid and I looked at each other.

It was time.

"Actually." Reid stepped toward me, and I drew slowly up from the sofa to meet him. He slid his arm around my waist and cuddled me into his side. I could hear his heart thudding fast and loud at my ear. It was just as fast and loud as my own.

"Evan and I have something to tell you. I hope it's good news." Despite the dramatic gasp from my mum, our eyes were on Patrick. Reid repeated, "I really hope so, Pat."

Patrick was expressionless.

"You're together?" Dad asked, pushing up out of his armchair.

"Yes, sir," Reid replied. "I love your daughter very much."

I would never grow bored hearing that.

"Oh my God," Mum cried out, hurrying over to hug us. "This is wonderful news!"

I laughed at her exuberance, relieved as Dad drew Reid into another hug, this one including a hard clap on the back and the murmured words, "You take care of her, or else."

"I promise," Reid replied solemnly.

"Come here," Annie said as Mum stepped aside. She was sniffling now, like we'd just announced we were having a baby or something. I stepped into Annie's welcoming hug, and she whispered in my ear, "I'm so happy it's you."

"I love him," I promised her, tears thick in my throat.

"I've known that awhile, sweetheart." She cupped my face again and beamed. "I was just waiting for my son to notice. Thankfully, he's a smart one."

I laughed at that as Reid overheard, huffing good-naturedly before hugging his mum.

All of that was lovely.

More than lovely.

It was a better reaction than either of us could have hoped for.

Yet there was an ominous silence from Patrick's spot on the sofa.

Reid took my hand in his, squeezing it tight. "Well, Pat?"

My big brother leaned his elbows on his knees and stared up at us. "She's my wee sister."

I blanched.

Uh-oh.

"I know," Reid replied. "But I can't help how I feel about her."

His gaze came to me now. "He's twelve years older than you."

"That means nothing to me. It's just a number."

"He's your boss."

"We'll make it work."

"People will talk."

"We don't care."

Patrick looked at Reid. "You never stick a relationship out."

Reid's hand tensed in mine. "Evan is different."

Patrick stood up. He was shorter than Reid by two inches, but somehow he seemed bigger than all of us at that moment. "If you hurt her, I will kill you."

It wasn't an empty threat.

"Patrick," Mum admonished. "You're ruining a happy moment."

"No, it's fine," Reid assured her. He released me to walk over to his best friend. He held out his hand to Patrick. "This is my promise to take care of her. You've trusted me in the past. Trust me now."

Patrick eyed the offering, then returned his gaze to Reid's. "I've never had to trust you with anything as valuable as Evan before."

Okay, so my heart melted at that.

Tears pricked my eyes as I felt Mum squeeze my shoulder. Flicking a look at Dad, I saw nothing but pride for Patrick on his face.

"I know." Reid's voice was hoarse. "I'll earn that trust, Pat. I promise you."

We all held our breath as silence stretched between them … and then, finally, my big brother shook Reid's hand.

Mum blew a loud puff of air between her lips. "Oh, thank God for that."

THE ATMOSPHERE WAS strange after our announcement. While Annie and Mum brimmed over with joy, Dad was chilled as ever, but Patrick's uncharacteristic brooding caused tension. Reid and I sat together, casting each other concerned looks. The last thing I wanted was to cause a breakdown in their lifelong friendship.

Mum refused to acknowledge the tension, continuing on as if Patrick was fine.

We'd just finished exchanging gifts when Mum told Dad to come and help her put together the breakfast in the kitchen.

"Can you wait?" Reid asked.

Mum paused from standing up to sitting on the arm of Dad's chair. "Why?"

"There's one last gift." There was a surprising nervous tremor to Reid's voice.

"Oh?" Annie asked.

Reid nodded, his expression serious, almost strained, as he stood and retrieved his jacket from over the back of a dining chair. Confused, I watched him remove something small and dark out of the pocket.

I was less confused when he returned and went down on one knee in front of me.

Blood whooshed in my ears. I was immobilized with shock.

Was this happening?

Was this a joke?

WHAT?

I gaped at Reid in question, seeing a jumble of emotions

fight for supremacy in his gaze. Then his hands moved in front of him and a million of my own emotions flooded me.

He held up a black velvet ring box.

He opened it.

Nestled inside, sparkling in the winter sunlight flooding my parents' front room, was the most beautiful diamond ring I'd ever seen. It was a platinum band with delicate filigree work that encased smaller diamonds along the top half of the very slender band. Clasped in the middle was an oval diamond. It was perfect. Not too over-the-top for my small hand.

And exactly my taste.

But it was an engagement ring!

We'd only been dating two weeks!

I didn't have to say that. He read it in my expression. Reid reached for my hand, his fingers curling around it. "I know it's soon."

"Uh-huh." I nodded. It was very soon.

What scared me the most, however, was how much I still wanted to yell "YES!" at the top of my lungs.

"You know me, Ev." He tugged on my hand. "You know I'm a man who goes after what I want. It's why I'm successful. Business is one thing ... finding the woman I want to spend the rest of my life with is the most important thing that will ever happen to me. I never thought I'd find you. I didn't even know feeling so much for someone was possible. And it hasn't been easy. It's been complicated. But all the best things are. And you, my love, are not just what I want. You're everything I need to be happy. And I don't see any reason to mess about for the sake of what we're *supposed* to do. I love you. I want to spend the rest of my life with you. And I want it to start right now."

"Oh my goodness," I whispered, feeling raw and terrified

and thrilled and excited ... because I wanted and needed him too. So much. It was overwhelming.

"Will you do me the absolute honor of marrying me, Evan Munro?"

Some people would call us crazy.

Impulsive.

I didn't care.

I grinned, nodding, as I threw myself at him, almost taking him to his arse. Reid gave a bark of surprised laughter and caught me, his arms bound tightly around me.

"Is that a yes?"

"Yes!" I reared back my head to yell, "Yes, yes, yes!"

He kissed me, hard, possessive, and it was inappropriate in front of our families, but I didn't care. And as he did this, he fumbled for my hand, blindly sliding the engagement ring on my finger. I broke the kiss to stare down at it, disbelieving this was real.

"Happy Christmas, Ev," he murmured huskily in my ear.

My gaze moved from the ring to his face. "Best one ever."

He grinned and opened his mouth to reply, but the words were cut off as our mothers fell upon us in joy.

"It's finally happening!"

"Let me see the ring."

"Oh my God, it's beautiful!"

"You should get married next Christmas."

"A Christmas wedding would be stunning."

"A sleigh! She could arrive in a sleigh!"

"Oh, heaven! And we could have a Christmas choir singing her up the aisle."

"And we—"

"Enough!" Patrick yelled.

A deafening silence fell over the room, and my heart sank.

Patrick glared at Reid.

Oh, boy.

But then a smirk curled the corners of his mouth. "You didn't have to propose to convince me. Marriage is life, mate. She's cute, but have you really thought this through?"

I reached past Dad for the large cushion on his armchair and chucked it at my brother.

He laughed, blocking it with his hands.

Relaxing, Reid stood and looked between Dad and Patrick. "I have your blessing, then?"

Dad mock scowled. "Think you're supposed to ask that before you ask the bride."

"Och, Harold, that's not how it's done now," Mum said. "Stop teasing the poor boy."

I snorted at Mum calling Reid a boy.

Patrick grinned. "Aw, are we teasing you, wee man?"

Reid rolled his eyes. "I take it that means I have your blessing?"

My big brother looked at me, his gaze softening. "If you make Evan happy, that's all I care about."

"You'll be my best man, then?"

"Who the fuck else would be?"

Assured all was well with the guys, Mum and Annie crowded in, bombarding me with wedding plans already. My ears were ringing. I felt a little faint.

"Enough!" Reid repeated Patrick's command from earlier, pushing through the mums to get to me. I grabbed onto him like a lifeline. "Let Ev breathe, for Christ's sake."

"We're just excited," Annie replied.

"And I'm glad. But let Ev get used to the idea of being engaged before you shove Christmas wedding plans down her throat. There will be no Christmas wedding."

"There won't?" I asked.

Reid stared down at me. "I don't want to wait a year. Do you?"

My heart. Honestly, I couldn't withstand another

romantic word out of his mouth or I'd expire on the spot. "No. I don't want to wait."

"Oh, but—"

"You heard them," Dad interrupted Mum, taking her by the shoulders and physically steering her toward the door. "Now let's go make breakfast. I'm sure everybody needs sustenance after all the excitement."

Annie trailed at the back of Mum, still discussing wedding plans.

Reid pulled me in tight to his side and kissed my temple. "Have I mentioned lately how much I appreciate your dad?"

"He is wonderful." I covered Reid's chest, his heart, with my hand. The engagement ring sparkled in the light. "And so are you."

"Best Christmas ever," Reid murmured, his eyes hot with love and desire.

"Best Christmas ever," I agreed. "Can't wait to celebrate on our own tonight."

"Oh, dear God," Patrick groaned, reminding us he was still there. "I'm in pain. Physical pain. New rule." He wagged his finger at us. "When I'm in the room, we will all pretend that yours is a spiritual union in name only."

Reid shook with laughter at my side. "Really?"

"I will end you," Patrick warned. "If you break this rule, I will end you."

Chuckling, I teased, "What if I break the rule? I mean, technically, I was the one who just reminded you that your best friend is bonking your wee sister."

Patrick cut me a wounded look. "Too soon, Ev. Too. Damn. Soon."

"Aw, fine, fine." I hurried toward my brother to give him a reassuring cuddle. "I'm a nun, and Reid is happy to spend a long, sexless life with me. Okay, sweetie, that better?" I patted his back.

"Yes," he grumbled like a little boy. "Much."

"Good news, though." I pulled back and gave him a tender smile. "You can rest easy knowing your best friend found a woman who loves him for who he is. And your wee sister found a man who treats her like a queen. That's a nice Christmas present for a big brother."

"Aye." He nodded, a little gruff now. "Aye, it's a pretty good Christmas present."

"You should have invited your receptionist for Christmas breakfast, and then we'd all be in on the joy." I winked.

"Oh, that's right, Ev, tell the whole world."

"That Dr. Munro is hot for his younger receptionist? Yes, yes, I will tell the whole world."

Reid laughed at our backs, and Patrick cut him a filthy look. "Remember, the best man does a speech at the wedding," he warned.

"I have no secrets from Ev."

"But you do from Annie."

That wiped the smirk off my fiancé's face. Reid reached for me, pulling me toward him. "Okay, stop baiting your brother, Ev."

It was my turn to laugh. "Oh, this is going to be so much fun."

Really.

Best. Christmas. Ever.

NEW YEAR'S EVE

CHAPTER ONE

RYAN

"Will Joe be there?" I asked my sister as I watched Gil work at adding the new lock and second dead bolt to my apartment door.

Shaw sighed heavily, causing the phone line to crackle. "No. He said he's got a meeting during the holidays that he can't miss. Who arranges a business meeting over the New Year?"

Apparently Joe.

Somehow, I didn't think he was telling the truth.

My little sister, Shaw, had called to ask me if I wanted to spend New Year's Eve with her and her husband, Dex, at a cabin in Lake Tahoe. Dex's dad Joe knew the guy who owned the place, and he'd offered Joe the cabin over the holidays for free. He'd decided not to use it but had said Dex and Shaw should and invite a friend or two to go with them.

"Dex is pissed. He wants to spend New Year's Eve with his dad, you know. It's his dad's year."

Dex had alternated the holidays with his parents since their separation when he was only four years old.

"Well, I'm in." Hell yeah, I was in. The only reason not to go would've been Joe, and he wouldn't be there.

"Great!" My sister sounded relieved. "I did not want to leave you alone."

She'd said the same about Christmas, and because I didn't want her worrying about me, I'd spent an awkward few hours with her, Dex, and Joe until I feigned feeling ill and left early.

I regretted leaving. But not just because I'd left my sister early on Christmas.

No, I regretted it for an entirely different reason.

But alone on New Year's Eve? "I would have been fine," I lied. Maybe four days ago, I would have been fine. Not now. Not after what happened.

Gil packed up his tools, shooting me a look that said "I'm done."

"Sweetie, I've got a call coming in I need to take. Call me later to discuss the details, yeah?"

"Yes!" Shaw yelled excitedly. "Wait until you see this place."

We hung up, and the absence of her voice made me feel lonely and exhausted.

Gil gave me a disapproving look. "You didn't tell her?"

I shook my head. No way. It was my job to look after Shaw, not the other way around. She might have gotten married at the crazy age of nineteen, but she was still my baby sister and still mine to protect. Even from worrying about me.

"Sounds like you're planning a trip together. How are you going to explain the shiner?"

I tentatively touched my bruised cheek. "Walked into

something."

My building manager rolled his eyes. "That's original."

"Is it done?" I asked, not wanting to talk about it. I'd done all the talking I needed to do with the cops. And it was technically still the holidays. I would not let this ruin my favorite time of year.

"All done." Gil handed over a new set of keys. "Like I said, the co-op board is going to move their asses on the new security system at the front entrance."

I nodded, even though I was thinking *too little too late*.

Gil had been riding the co-op board's ass for years about the cheap entrance system that continually broke. Most of the board didn't live in the building but rented out the apartments, so they weren't invested in the daily maintenance of things. It was my luck that the entrance system had broken this past week and Gil hadn't gotten around to fixing it. That was the last time I'd ever choose a first-floor apartment just because I wanted to live in a certain area.

Seeing the guilt flicker across Gil's eyes, I shook my head. "No. Don't do that. Not your fault."

"Yeah." He exhaled heavily and pulled open my apartment door. "You call me if you need anything."

"I will. Thank you."

As soon as he left, I locked the door and slid the dead bolts home.

Leaning against it, I stared into my small apartment and wished like hell it was New Year's Eve already and I was at Lake Tahoe. My little sanctuary had become a place I feared.

And I hated that.

I hated that someone could do that to me.

A four-foot Christmas tree sat in the corner of my open-plan living area. I'd twined fairy lights over the too many bookcases that filled the small room. A wreath hung on the wall above my largest radiator. I'd replaced my oven mitt with a Christmas one and hung it over the oven door handle. My Christmas tea towels were folded on my small kitchen counter. A Santa Claus sat propped on the breakfast bar near the wall in case he toppled.

My place looked cozy and warm.

But if you knew better, you would see the tree was a little squished because I'd knocked it over a few nights ago. My glass coffee table with the bowl of glitter-speckled acorns and furry snowballs was missing after we annihilated it in the struggle.

I took a deep breath, trying to alleviate the tightness in my chest.

Maybe I'd take the tree down early this year. Get rid of the reminder.

In two days, I'd have some distance from the place, and when I returned, it would feel like home again. It had to. There was no other option. No one was going to make me feel afraid in my own home.

As brave as the self-administered pep talk was, hours later, I was still awake. I'd curled up on my sofa with my blanket and pillow, my ears pricked for the slightest sound. I'd barely slept since it happened.

Giving up on sleep entirely, I made some hot cocoa and grabbed my e-reader. Needing something light, easy, and romantic, I downloaded a rom-com. Unfortunately, it was about a woman who was crushing on her father's best friend.

It hit a little too close to home.

I shut off the e-reader and tried (and failed) to forget the last time I'd been alone with Joe.

It had been two months ago at Dex's twenty-first birthday party.

I groaned as I sipped my cocoa, almost choking on it. I deserved to choke on it! What an idiot. What a *selfish* idiot. As someone who had always prided herself on being thoughtful and responsible, what I'd done at Dex's party was the complete opposite. Why Joe Colchester could make my brain fritz and my hormones take over, I'd never know.

The problem was that I was deeply, *deeply* attracted to my little sister's father-in-law.

Memories assailed me, taking me back to Dex's party.

Since arriving at Joe's, I'd had insistent flutters in my belly waiting for him to show. Shaw had opened the door, and Dex led me out to the pool where most of the guests were hanging out. Joe's house had an enormous yard and a swimming pool, perfect for hosting parties. All of Dex's family, as well as his college friends, were in attendance. His mom, Renee, was too—she and Joe were friends and the best example of co-parenting I'd ever seen. Renee had brought her husband, Alan, and Dex's two half-siblings, twins Austin and Hopper. I was standing around, beer in hand, talking to Shaw and Renee while Dex hung out with some guys from school when I felt him.

The hair on the back of my neck rose, and I turned to look toward the house.

There he was.

Joe Colchester.

Bifold doors separated his kitchen from his patio, and they were pushed all the way open so the inside flowed to the outside. Joe surveyed the party in his yard, a slight smile curling his mouth. I felt a deep tug low in my belly at the mere sight of him.

I had never been this viscerally attracted to a man in my life.

He was rough, rugged, masculine, and charismatic. With a prominent, bold, aquiline nose that crooked slightly to the right from a break years ago, and his deep-set, dark eyes, there was nothing pretty about Joe Colchester. Joe was a sexy, successful forty-year-old who owned his own business. Started off as a mechanic and opened up his own garage. Then another and another ... until he had garages all over the state of California. He was a smart guy who rolled with the times, so a few of those garages specialized in converting gas engines to electric.

At six four, Joe had that loose-limbed swagger cowboys were famous for, and the upper body of a man who kept himself in great shape. I hadn't seen him with his shirt off, of course, but I had a good imagination, and his T-shirts had a tendency to strain against the most amazing biceps. Like right then. His navy plain tee stretched across his broad, muscular chest in the most delicious way.

Yum.

He kept his dark hair longish, and lately he'd been sporting salt-and-pepper scruff that only drew attention to his mouth. A mouth with a full lower lip that made a woman want to nibble on it. I'd had many a fantasy about that mouth.

It was wrong.

I knew it was wrong.

But from the moment I met Joe two years ago, I was instantly attracted to him. He was the kind of guy I didn't even know still existed. Gruff with a rumbly, deep voice and a quiet, sly sense of humor. A great dad who would do anything for Dex and now Shaw.

And a serial monogamist.

Shaw liked to gossip wildly about Joe's love life, and I liked to listen intently.

According to Dex and Shaw, Joe was the most loyal guy on the planet. He'd never dream of cheating on a woman. Unfortunately, he also didn't seem to know how to settle down. He dated a woman for a few months and then moved on. And he had a type. Usually dark-haired beauties who were looking for a guy to take care of them in every way—emotionally and financially.

In other words, my complete opposite.

Joe was a protector and a provider. He enjoyed taking care of people. He enjoyed taking care of his women, knowing that they needed him. And nine months ago, to my overinflated devastation, he'd started dating Nicole. Nicole was thirty-six, divorced, and *adorable. Petite, dark-haired, gorgeous face, and she had this tinkly, feminine laugh that was infectious. She was also a sweetheart. I wanted to hate her and couldn't. She'd been in a terrible marriage, had a nasty divorce, and openly admitted she was looking for a man who would take care of her since she'd never had that. There was something about Nicole that made you want to scoop her up and protect her. And that seemed to work for Joe in a big way.*

When they got past the four-month mark, it surprised Dex.

The sixth-month mark and Shaw speculated there might be a proposal brewing.

The very idea crushed me.

Joe and I got along. We shared a similar sense of humor and an ability to be together without having to fill the silence with conversation. Our time together would almost be wonderfully comfortable if it weren't for my feelings. I was so aware of every aspect of his being that I think he must sense something because a tension always crackled between us.

I'd like to imagine it was sexual tension, but no—he was with Nicole.

Plus, I was not a petite brunette with a need to be taken care of.

I was a tall redhead. And I was staunchly independent.

Suddenly, Joe looked in my direction, and our eyes locked. My breath caught in my throat as my pulse picked up speed. Trying to be casual, I raised my beer bottle in greeting, and he flashed me that gorgeous, boyish, wicked smile of his.

I felt that right between my legs.

Dirty girl.

He glanced behind him, looking for Nicole, and thus the reminder that Joe was off-limits in more ways than one. Except I noted she was nowhere in sight.

As if reading my mind, my little sister's voice drew my attention. "They broke up," Shaw whispered.

I turned to look at her, my heart skipping an actual beat. "What?"

Shaw's expression was impassive. "Yup. Two weeks ago."

"Who broke it off?"

"Who do you think? Joe did. It devastated Nicole because for her, it came out of nowhere. Dex tried to ask his dad why, but he said it was his business. Oh, shoot, he's coming over. Pretend we're talking about something else."

How could I? My mind was racing. So was my adrenaline. And it shouldn't be!

Just because Joe was single again didn't mean I could do anything about it.

I was still sixteen years his junior. And I was still his son's wife's big sister.

This selfish feeling of elation was awful and needed to stop.

"Hey, Ryan." Joe's rumbly voice was like a caress of his fingers across my nape.

I turned toward him with a genuine smile. "Hey. How are you?"

"Good." His dark eyes studied mine before dropping to my beer bottle. "Want a whiskey?"

Knowing my preference for whiskey—a taste we shared—it was so sweet and considerate that he'd asked. But I was afraid if I started too early on whiskey, I'd get drunk and do something regrettable. "I'll take one later."

"I'm gonna go say hello to Dex's friends," Shaw said, reminding me she was there.

Joe blinked as if he hadn't even seen her and gave her a nod as she beamed at him and hurried around the pool. His eyes caught on Renee, who sat on a lounger with her husband while the twins played in the water. Joe and his ex-wife nodded in greeting, and Renee's gaze flickered to me for a moment. She frowned and then turned back to her husband to whisper something.

My skin flushed, like she'd caught me doing something wrong.

Sometimes I wondered if my crush on Joe was obvious to everyone or if I was just being paranoid.

Laughter caught my attention across the other side of the pool where Dex's friends and Shaw chanted, "Chug, chug, chug!" to Dex as *he drank beer straight from the keg. I shook my head in dismay. "I think he's taking this turning-twenty-one thing a little too seriously."*

Joe grunted. "Why is it that smart kids are also the stupidest?"

I laughed, meeting his half-amused, half-annoyed gaze. "I honestly don't remember being that stupid."

"It was only three years ago," Joe teased. "If you were that stupid" —*he gestured to his son whose face was turning a worrying red*— *"you'd remember it."*

"I don't remember ever being that young."

His expression softened. "Yeah, I guess not."

I'd been raising Shaw practically on my own since our parents died when I was fourteen years old. We'd gone to live with my mom's nice enough but completely self-absorbed and uninvolved aunt Rachel.

She had left it to me to raise Shaw, who was only ten at the time.

I'd been concerned when Shaw told me she wanted to become an environmental lawyer. Not the environmental part. As a freelance sustainability expert, I was proud of that. It was the law part. Shaw was an idealist, an optimist, and I didn't want a life in law to beat that out of her.

Then, I was as horrified as any parent might be when she told me a year ago that she and Dex had eloped. I knew he loved her, and I adored Dex, but they were young, and I was even more afraid my little sister's optimistic and idealistic nature would be crushed by a short, failed marriage.

Our concern for Shaw and Dex was one of the reasons Joe and I had bonded. However, we'd conceded that for two college kids, Shaw and Dex were handling marriage and school fairly well. They had help from Joe. He let them move into the apartment above his garage so they didn't have rent or utility bills. The strain of financial worry was not a factor in their marriage, which surely helped a lot.

I would have helped, too, if I could, but I was still paying off my student debt.

And Aunt Rachel had moved to Italy as soon as I left for college.

She'd left us the house, but it meant I was raising a sixteen-year-old all alone while attending classes and working part time. Once Shaw started college, Rachel had put the house on the market, and I'd had to find an apartment.

I was not a typical twenty-four-year-old.

I was all grown up.

Something passed between Joe and me as we stared into each other's eyes. Something that made my belly flutter wildly and my skin flush hot. Thankfully, I wasn't a redhead with pale skin that flared pink at any sign of embarrassment. Both Shaw and I got our unusual coloring from my mother, who had red-gold hair, olive skin, and green eyes. We were her copies, except for our eyes. I had our mother's eyes while Shaw had the same blue as our father's. We'd both gotten Mom's height too. I was five ten, and Shaw was five eight.

Joe suddenly cleared his throat and wrenched his gaze from mine to his son's. "It's hard to believe when they're acting like that, that they're married."

I nodded in agreement. Even if I weren't a forty-year-old woman trapped in a twenty-four-year-old's body, I wasn't the type to have fun over a kegger. Give me an excellent book or a movie or a quiet bar somewhere over a college party any day of the week.

"I heard you broke up with Nicole." Ugh. Why? Why was that the first thing out of my mouth?

Joe flicked me an indecipherable look before taking a sip of his beer. "Yeah. It didn't work out."

I wanted to ask why, but he was giving off very definite "I don't want to talk about this" vibes.

"How are the contracts going for the place in Las Vegas?" I asked instead, referring to the building he wanted to buy to convert into a new garage. It would be his first garage outside of California.

His broad shoulders instantly relaxed at the subject change, and he gestured to his patio lounge chairs near the house where we could chat away from the noise of the music and revelers. When we sat down on the outdoor sofa, I did my best to keep some distance between us. Joe talked about the business for a bit and then reciprocated with, "How's it going with that idiot at the smoothie company?"

I was stupidly pleased that he remembered my latest job and the VP who had driven me nuts. As a freelance sustainability expert, companies who couldn't afford to have a full-time employee responsible for sustainability research hired me to develop new workflows to increase productivity while lowering their carbon footprint. I went in, assessed how their company currently ran, supplied a sustainability evaluation, and then advised them about recycling and waste reductions, that sort of thing. I loved my job.

But sometimes, certain employees within a company wanted me to offer miracle suggestions that allowed them to make as few changes as possible. It just didn't work that way. The vice president of a California smoothie company I'd recently worked for didn't understand the need for me to be there. Despite my credentials, including a degree in environmental science and business, he'd treated me as if I were an airhead doing a useless, flaky job.

"Oh, I finished up with them two weeks ago. I'm on a new account, working for a national footwear company. The excitement of landing that makes up for the asshole VP who treated me like dirt the entire three months I was there and then added insult to injury by having the audacity to ask me out when I was leaving."

Joe raised an eyebrow. "This guy sounds clueless."

"Oh, and does not like rejection," I replied. "Bitter little man. When I turned him down, he called me a frigid bitch."

To my surprise, Joe's face darkened with anger, and his voice was rough as he bit out, "He what?"

I blinked at the dangerous bite to his tone. "It's cool, Joe. I don't have to see him again."

He took a deep pull of his beer, but I could see his grip on the bottle was tight with annoyance.

"It was just a name. I've been treated worse. Sexual harassment isn't a new thing."

Wrong thing to say.

He cut me a dark look. "You think it's okay to put up with that shit?"

I reached out to squeeze his arm in reassurance, pretending not to delight in how hard the muscle was beneath my fingers. "No, of course not. And I don't. Joe, I'm good." I retreated after his gaze flickered down to where I was touching him. "You know I can handle myself."

"Doesn't mean you should have to. This is the problem with being freelance." He turned toward me, and I could feel a familiar lecture coming on. "You don't have the protection of a company behind you when you have to deal with these kinds of guys."

I sighed. "A company might not do anything about it. In fact, they might tell me to suck it up and deal with it. Whereas, I can say, 'Hey, I don't put up with bullshit misogyny or sexual harassment. Find another sustainability advisor.'" I grinned, tossing my hair playfully.

His eyes flickered to the movement and then back to me. His tension eased a little. "Anyone does anything to you that crosses the line, I want to know."

A part of me thrilled at his protectiveness.

The other part of me feared it.

It wasn't wise to rely on someone to feel safe, loved, and protected. If they went away, by choice or not by choice, they suddenly left you without that sense of home.

And Joe was off-limits.

There was no way I could let myself rely on him. I'd only end up hurt.

"I can take care of myself," I reiterated, but gave him a small smile so I didn't sound harsh.

"And what I'm saying is that you don't need to take care of yourself all the time. You have a family."

Ugh. That was a bucket of cold water if ever I needed one.

Joe was family.

Looking away, I sipped my beer and decided it wasn't strong enough after all. "You know, I think I'll take that whiskey now."

. . .

AND THAT WAS my last vivid memory from the party.

I got drunk.

I got drunk, and I remembered moving closer to Joe on that couch as we chatted the evening away. But the memories after were vague. Blurry.

Except for the memory of me kissing him.

Joe had gone into the house for something.

I followed.

I kissed him.

I couldn't remember much about the kiss at all, only that it was probably short because I remembered Joe gently removing me from his person and handing me off to Shaw to sober me up. Thankfully, she didn't know about the kiss.

That kiss. Selfish. Irresponsible. And stupid.

Joe was my brother-in-law's father.

He was sixteen years older than me.

And I was not his type.

I was independent; I was strong; I was focused.

I didn't need anyone to look after or protect me, and everyone who knew Joe knew that was what he got off on.

I also wasn't a petite, dark-haired beauty.

That was fine.

I liked who I was, even if I wasn't for Joe.

Rejection stung, though.

And I didn't want to face Joe for the first time since the party after the week I'd had.

I was not in the headspace for that.

So it was good he wouldn't be at Lake Tahoe.

I could lick my literal and metaphorical wounds while I spent my favorite time of year with my favorite person in a beautiful place far, far away from the scene of the crime.

And maybe I'd even get some sleep.

Bliss!

CHAPTER TWO

JOE

I knew that stubborn glint in my son's eyes.

I was pretty sure he'd gotten that from me.

Wiping the sweat off my face with a nearby towel, I stepped back from the punching bag that hung from the ceiling in my office and waited for Dex to say whatever it was he'd come here to say.

The whir of engines and buzzing of tools could be heard in the distance, muffled after Dex closed my door.

I kept my primary office in the first garage I'd opened, near the college. It was five minutes from the house where I'd raised Dex near the McKinley Park area, five minutes from California State, and five minutes from an apartment that belonged to the greatest temptation that had ever been put in front of me.

Hell.

I knew why Dex was here.

"You're spending New Year's Eve with us at Lake Tahoe," my son said.

Yeah.

Knew that was why he was here.

After taking a swig of water to collect myself, I sat on the edge of my desk and lied, "I can't. Got that meeting."

I hated lying to my kid.

It was Ryan Baillie's fault.

She'd put me in this shitty position.

Well ... it wasn't all her fault.

My dick wasn't entirely blameless.

"Dad, I know you're lying."

I narrowed my eyes at my kid. He might be right, but I didn't like being questioned by him. Or anyone. Especially when I felt guilty as hell.

Dex raised an eyebrow and crossed his arms over his chest.

While my son had gotten his coloring from his mother, all blond-haired and blue-eyed, resisting the dominance of my darker gene coloring, he had my build and features. He looked like a young, blond version of me. Except my kid also got his mom's open, optimistic nature. It didn't bother me he lacked my aggressive drive. He had his own ambitions. Wanted to be an environmental lawyer, and I was proud of how hard he was working to do that.

Even if he scared the shit out of me by getting married to Ryan's little sister Shaw.

I still wasn't one hundred percent sure a college romance could survive, but a year in and those two were still as annoyingly loved up as ever.

My kid was happy with Shaw.

That was what mattered.

Currently, he was not happy with me.

Dex enjoyed having his family around him. And he'd been

stubborn about us sticking to his alternating holiday routine for as long as I could remember. His mom got him for Christmas and New Year holidays and Easter one year while I got him for Thanksgiving and Halloween. Then we alternated the following year. He'd never grown out of it. If it was my year with him, nothing was to get in the way.

This year was my year with him.

But something—no, some*one*—had most definitely gotten in the way.

Christmas dinner at my place had been awkward as fuck, and Ryan leaving early had only made it worse.

"I know about Ryan," Dex blurted out.

I tensed, feeling a knot form in my gut.

My son took a step toward me, his expression somewhat sympathetic. "Dad, you may be my father, but you're a guy. I'm a guy. I get it. A hot, drunk twenty-four-year-old throws herself at you, and you forget yourself. You forget who she is."

I frowned. "You saw the kiss?"

Dex snorted. "I saw the make-out session."

"I—"

"It's cool, Dad. I saw you push her off and take her to the kitchen for a glass of water. Then you handed her off to Shaw to sober up," Dex huffed. "It's not ideal that you've had your tongue in my wife's sister's mouth, but it happened. It's over. And we all have to get along for the rest of our lives. You and Ryan need to get over the awkwardness, because we can't have another Christmas like that again. It really upset Shaw that Ryan took off."

Get over the awkwardness?

It was hard to do that when I couldn't stop thinking about Ry.

Dex had no idea the incredible willpower it took to remove Ryan Baillie from my mouth.

"You've been avoiding her. Shaw is getting suspicious, but

she thinks it's something to do with us. That you're fed up with us living rent-free. That you really don't approve of our marriage."

Shit. "You know that's not true."

"I know. But I can't tell her what *is* true. Ryan raised Shaw. Shaw worships the ground her big sister walks on. As for you, Shaw thinks the world of you. She thinks you're the absolute shit. And guess what? She wants the absolute shit for her sister. I tell her you two kissed, and she'll start planning the wedding."

Shock moved through me alongside something ridiculous that felt a bit like hope. "Shaw would want that?"

Dex scowled. "Yeah, because she's a dreamer and a romantic and thinks her sister can move heaven and earth. I know better. Dad, I've watched you go through woman after woman, and I know you're not the settling-down type. You would not only screw up Ryan, who doesn't deserve it, but you could screw up my marriage to Shaw if you fuck over Ryan. Never mind the sixteen-year age gap and how that might not look so hot in twenty years' time."

Indignation ripped through me, but only because he was saying the things I'd had to remind myself of over and over for the past two years. "I'm not screwing around with Ryan."

"I know, I know. You just need to ignore whatever stupid crush she's got on you. Okay? Off-limits," he reiterated, making me feel like a rebellious teenager. "The point is New Year's. Shaw sees right through this bullshit about a business meeting over the holidays. I don't want to spend New Year's Eve with a bunch of people I don't really care about. I want to see in the new year with my dad, and I want my wife to stop worrying that my dad disapproves of us."

The old guilt manipulation. I scowled at him. "Fine. I'll be there."

"It's your friend's cabin, so I'm sorry if Ryan being there is uncomfortable for you," Dex added regretfully. "But she's got nowhere else to go."

An ache, sharp and tender, flared across my chest. The thought of Ryan not having somewhere to go disturbed and upset me more than I liked. Ryan had walls up a mile high. She didn't want to rely on anyone. She wanted to take care of Shaw and not the other way around. It was like she was afraid to let anyone take care of her. For some fucked-up reason, it just made me want to be there for her more. "She should be with her family. Shaw is her family. I wouldn't want anything else for her."

Dex narrowed his eyes with uncharacteristic suspicion, looking so much like me.

"What?" I shifted uncomfortably.

"Nothing." Dex shrugged. "So, we're confirmed? You're coming?"

"Tell Shaw I got out of the meeting," I replied.

My son snorted. "Right. Shaw, Ryan, and I are driving up together. We'd offer to drive you, but I don't think we'll all fit into one truck with all of our shit ..."

Like I wanted to be trapped in a confined space with Ryan for two hours. "I'm taking my truck. In fact"—I thought about how I hadn't had a moment's peace in months—"I might head up there a day early."

"You should. You work too much." Dex clapped me on the shoulder and grinned. "See you there."

"Yeah, see you in—there." I'd almost said, "See you in hell."

Because that was what it would be.

Trapped in a cabin on Lake Tahoe with a woman I wanted but couldn't have.

Yeah, New Year's Eve in hell.

CHAPTER THREE

RYAN

Driving in snow was not one of my favorite things. Thankfully, I'd been lucky to get a rental last minute. The SUV handled the snow-dusted roads, leading me to the lake much better than my small Honda could. Still, I was tense as I sat forward in my seat, my eyes glued to the dark road, peering through the falling snow, as I drove up through the hills on the winding road of the El Dorado Freeway. The snow was thicker here than it had been on the highway, and I slowed to begin my descent as I hit Emerald Bay Road.

Sweat gathered under my arms with the tension.

But I was almost there. According to my GPS, this road would take me down to Lake Tahoe where Joe's friend had a large cabin right on the water.

When I'd agreed to spend New Year's Eve as a third wheel with my sister and her husband, I thought we'd all be driving up together. But Shaw had called yesterday morning to tell me she and Dex wanted to have a night alone, so they were driving up early. I'd told her I would be happy to leave them to their romantic cabin and spend New Year's at home, but Shaw got really upset at the idea, so I gave in.

And now I was driving at a crawl as I made my way through the snow. Exhaustion pulled at me. I was actually grateful for the tension that kept me awake.

The things we do for family.

To my great relief, I finally reached the lake. I only knew this because of GPS—I couldn't see anything beyond my headlights. The lights caught on the signs outside each entrance to the cabins at the end of a woodland-surrounded road.

My headlights hit a snow-dusted sign that declared it was No. 6, and I slowed, turning down onto its private road. As I approached, the driveway opened to reveal a medium-size cabin with a truck sitting outside. I narrowed my eyes as my headlights lit up the vehicle.

That was Joe's truck.

My heart rate kicked up for a few seconds as I pulled beside it.

Then I remembered that Dex had the same truck as his father.

Calming down, I turned the rearview mirror toward me and double-checked my cheek and eye. Thankfully, the swelling had gone down completely, but there was still bruising. Hopefully, my makeup covered it because no amount of makeup seemed to conceal the dark circles under my eyes.

I hadn't slept since Christmas Eve.

I didn't even know how I was functioning.

Just like that, now that I'd reached my destination, an overwhelming wave of weariness crashed over me.

As much as I'd come here for Shaw, I'd also come hoping

that being away from my apartment and being with my people would allow my body to relax.

That I'd sleep.

A sudden knock on the driver's side window scared the crap out of me.

"Shit!" I yelled, turning to glare at the knocker as my heart pounded.

Light spilled down from the cabin, casting shadows over the face peering in at me.

Oh, hell no.

Joe.

I stared, shocked and confused.

Then he opened my door, resting his arm along it and his other on top of the car. His expression was grim as his deep voice rumbled through me. "Looks like there's been a communication problem."

⚜

I WAS GOING to kill Shaw.

Following Joe up the porch stairs and into the cabin, I vowed to kill my sister. Yet I couldn't even find the energy to be all that angry with her. My ankles felt like they had twenty pounds of stone tied around them, and I was grateful Joe had taken my luggage. I didn't think my fingers could grip onto anything.

In fact, as soon as the heat from the log-burning fire hit me, something happened.

I stopped inside the open-plan living area. Joe's body wavered as he continued walking ahead of me. His voice sounded distorted, like I was underwater.

The room tilted and little black dots scattered across my vision.

I thought I heard Joe shout my name.

That was the last thing I heard before the dots joined together and all I saw was black.

⊗

THE FIRST THING I was aware of was the throbbing in my cheek, near my eye.

Confused, it took me a second to remember the assault, and then my eyes flew open in panic.

Daylight streaming into an unfamiliar room greeted me, and the tightness in my chest worsened as I tried to remember where the hell I was and what was happening.

"You're awake."

The familiar voice drew my attention. Turning my head on a soft pillow, I found Joe sitting in an armchair by the side of the bed. His clothes and hair were rumpled and his eyes a little bleary, like he hadn't slept.

Despite my confusion, I relaxed.

"Where am I?" The words croaked out of me. My mouth was so dry.

"Lake Tahoe." Joe leaned forward, his eyes narrowed. "You don't remember last night?"

Slowly his voice brought back the memories.

I'd passed out upon arrival.

When I woke up, Joe was trying not to freak out. I promised him I just needed to sleep, that I hadn't slept in days. He tried to ask questions, but I'd fallen asleep on him.

"What time is it?" I pushed into a sitting position, glad to feel the strength back in my arms. While there was a heaviness in my head, my eyelids felt lighter for having slept.

"It's midday, New Year's Eve. You've slept around fifteen hours."

Holy crap.

Guessed I needed it, though.

Joe's expression darkened as he stared at my face. "When you fainted, you hit the floor on your cheek pretty hard. I put some ice on it. Funny thing, though ... the ice took off your makeup and beneath the fresh swelling were bruises."

Shit.

I looked away. "Joe ..."

"What happened?"

Protecting my sister from what had happened was one thing. Protecting myself from Joe's need to protect was another. While I wanted many things from him I couldn't have ... I didn't want his protection. I didn't need it. I was alone. And I didn't need the illusion of not being alone.

"You know, I'm starving. While my sister was setting us up, did she happen to stock the cabin with food?"

I whipped off the covers and stopped when I realized I was in my sleep shorts. I glared at Joe.

He shrugged nonchalantly. "I couldn't let you sleep in your jeans."

I glanced down at my top, grateful to see it was the thermal Henley I'd been wearing upon my arrival. Still, Joe had taken off my jeans.

I experienced a tingle between my legs at the thought.

Okay, I was definitely better.

"Oh." I slipped out of bed, skirting him and feeling his heat without even touching him. "Food?"

The creak of the wooden floorboards told me Joe was following me out of the room. The floors were toasty beneath my feet, suggesting underfloor heating. In fact, the entire cabin was comfortably warm, even though the fire from the log burner had died during the night.

I came to a stop in the middle of the open-plan room.

Because ... the view.

Beyond the sitting room were sliding doors that led out onto the deck. And beyond the deck was Lake Tahoe.

Crossing the room, I peered out through the doors at the majestic view of tranquil water surrounded by snow-dusted trees on the hills that sloped down toward it.

"Wow."

"Pretty spectacular, huh?" Joe came to a stop beside me. So close, his shoulder brushed mine. I glanced at him to find him watching me. His eyes narrowed on my upper cheek. "Why do you have a shiner, and why did you pass out from exhaustion?"

Sighing, I turned back to the view.

I could feel Joe's aggravation growing.

Part of me was thrilled that he gave a shit.

The other part was terrified of it.

"I'm not letting you leave here until you tell me."

I scowled. "You're not the boss of me, Joe."

He was silent so long, I finally looked at him.

And wished I hadn't.

Excitement scored through me at the heat in his eyes and the obvious way he was fighting it. The muscle in his jaw ticked before he yanked his gaze away. His voice was gruff, almost hoarse. "You're not leaving here until I get answers."

Indignation killed the excitement. "Didn't you hear what I just said?"

"Cut the crap, Ryan." He glared at me before crossing the room toward the kitchen. "A woman I care about fainted, and she has a fucking black eye. Of course, I want to know what happened."

I followed him into the kitchen. I tried not to react to him saying he cared about me and failed. My tone was softer now. "Joe, it was nothing. And I don't want you making a big deal out of it because I don't want Shaw to know."

He contemplated me, then surprised me. "Coffee? Bacon sandwich?"

Both sounded great. I slid onto a stool at the island. "Yes, please."

"Good. And you can tell me what happened while I make breakfast."

"Technically, it's lunch."

He cut me another look.

"Or brunch," I muttered with a shrug, staring out the side door of the kitchen. Beyond were snow-covered trees, providing privacy between us and the neighbors. "My sister isn't here, is she?" I asked, even though I knew the answer.

"Nope. They changed their minds a few days ago. Said Shaw wasn't feeling too great."

My sister had lied to me and Joe to get us at this cabin alone. Together. "You know this wasn't an accident, right? My sister did this to us deliberately. What was she thinking?"

"Shaw later. You first."

I watched Joe move around the kitchen as he made coffee, unable to ignore the way his long-sleeved tee molded to every inch of his perfect body. I thought about him unzipping my jeans last night when I was out for the count. Of him tugging them off and then rummaging through my luggage for my pajama shorts. Of him pulling the shorts up my legs. He must have seen my underwear. I tried to remember what pair I was wearing.

Oh, well.

I shifted as renewed heat flooded between my legs.

I so wished I'd been awake for that moment so I could've studied Joe's face.

Had he liked what he'd seen?

"Well?" he asked impatiently as he slid a steaming mug across the island toward me.

I took a bolstering sip and then stopped at the realization he knew exactly how I took my coffee. This was Joe. So I was inappropriately attracted to the man, and I'd thrown myself at him when I was drunk. But he was still Joe.

As much as it scared me to rely on anyone, he was my friend.

I met his dark gaze. He was worried about me. It was plain to see. "Promise not to tell Shaw."

He frowned. "I don't like keeping secrets."

"Considering the high possibility that the little busybody is trying to play matchmaker with us, I wouldn't be too concerned about keeping secrets from her."

Joe gave a huff of unamused laughter. "Right."

I took another sip. Remembering Christmas Day set off a spark of unwanted adrenaline. My hand shook around the mug, and I lowered it quickly.

Joe caught the movement anyway. "Hey ..." His voice was soothing as he reached out to cover my hand with his. "It's okay. I'm here." He held my gaze. "Gotta admit you're scaring me a little, baby."

I shivered at the pet name he'd never used with me before. It was so intimate. Something a lover might call me. And I stupidly wanted to launch myself across the island and into his brawny arms. Instead, I slipped my hand out from beneath his and dropped it in my lap. Staring at the counter, unable to look at him now, I shrugged. "I'm making a bigger deal out of it than it was."

"Ry, I'm losing patience here. I got a million ugly things going through my head right now, and I need to know that I'm wrong about all of them."

"Sorry." I forced myself to look at him. "I'm not used to anyone but Shaw caring."

That seemed to piss him off even more. "Well, I care. I care a fucking lot."

"Joe ..." I shrugged, helpless against his concern. "Christmas Day. After I left early ... when I got home, my door was ajar and the lock broken. And I was stupid. I was so stupid." I shook my head at myself. Everything they tell you not to do, I did. "I went into the apartment, and there was a guy in my bedroom. He was high, had a garbage bag filled with my stuff ... but he had"—my eyes filled with tears—"he was going through my jewelry box, and he had my mom's locket in his hand. I didn't think. I just went for him. We grappled and found ourselves in the living room. I pushed him into the tree, and when he got back up, he charged me, and we fell into the glass coffee table."

Joe sucked in a breath.

"I was so lucky—it was only a couple of minor cuts on my back. But he punched me hard, and he was out of it ... if my neighbor hadn't heard the commotion and come running, it could've been so much worse. The guy took off. He didn't get any of my stuff. But ..." I ran a hand through my hair, embarrassed at what I was about to admit. "He scared me. I'm scared. I ... until last night, I hadn't slept since it happened."

Movement drew my eyes up, and I watched as Joe marched around the island. "What ..."

Suddenly he hauled me off the stool, his arms bound tight around me, crushing me to him. Joe buried his face in my neck, breathing hard.

Realizing he wasn't just comforting me but himself, I closed my arms around him, too, my fingers curling tight into his shirt.

For the first time in days—no, years—I felt something I hadn't since I was fourteen.

Safe.

And the fact that I felt that, and that Joe needed to be comforted after hearing about my ordeal, made me realize this wasn't just a one-sided attraction.

What was between us wasn't simple attraction.

And that made it infinitely more dangerous for both of us.

CHAPTER FOUR

JOE

I wanted to find the bastard who had attacked Ryan. Who had shaken her up so badly, she hadn't slept in days. The thought of what might have happened to her if her neighbor hadn't shown up made me sick to my stomach.

My arms tightened around her and I breathed her in, reassuring myself she was here and safe in my arms. Her perfume and the feel of her soft curves against my body were sinking in. Causing a blood-flow problem.

I gently released my hold and guided her to her stool. I then took a few steps back while she stared up at me with those big green eyes, looking confused.

"You okay?" My words were hoarse. I cleared my throat and rounded the island to put some distance between us.

"I'm fine."

A bite of defensiveness flavored her words. It irritated me.

"You know it's okay not to be fine, Ry. It's okay to need someone. And believe it or not, Shaw is not a kid anymore, and she doesn't need you protecting her from shit. What she needs is for her sister to be okay."

Her chin lifted stubbornly. "I *am* okay."

She made me want to round the island and kiss the stubbornness right out of her. Somehow I stopped myself. "You think not sleeping for five days is okay?"

"I didn't have to tell you, and now you're throwing it back in my face?"

Hurt glimmered in her gaze. My gut twisted, and I softened my tone. "No. But it doesn't make a person weak to ask for help. It doesn't make you weak to need someone."

"Yes, it does."

"Jesus, Ryan, you can't go through life thinking that."

"I'm wrong?" She pushed off her stool, her chest heaving.

I tried not to notice anything about her other than the hard edge in her voice, but it wasn't easy. It was difficult not to remember sliding the jeans off her long legs last night. I'd tried to avert my gaze as much as possible, but those legs of hers were branded on my brain. Feeling a fresh surge of hot blood heading southward, I cleared my throat. "Yeah, you're wrong."

"How can I be wrong?" Ry crossed her arms over her chest.

"Because we're built to need each other."

"And leave each other," she whispered hoarsely, and the devastation in her eyes killed me.

"Ry ..."

"Needing people only hurts in the end. I'd rather go it alone."

"So you're telling me you don't need Shaw?" I pushed.

"It's different. *She* needs *me*."

God, her heart was all fucked up from losing her parents.

"No, baby. You need her to need you. But more than that, you love her. So in the end, you just need her. And you should tell her when shit like this happens." I gestured to the fading bruises on her cheek.

Ry's expression turned mulish. "I don't think I should tell my baby sister anything. She clearly can't be trusted."

Knowing she referred to our current predicament, I sighed, running a frustrated hand through my hair. "I came up here a day early. Then Dex called to say Shaw wasn't feeling so great, so they were going to stay home."

"Shaw told me she and Dex were coming here early, and that's why I had to drive myself. And I hate driving in the snow."

"You shouldn't have been driving anywhere on no sleep." Jesus, anything could have happened.

"I don't need a lecture, Joe. You're not *my* father-in-law."

"Oh, I'm well aware of that."

Whatever she heard in my voice made her eyes turn hot. Ry didn't blush like most redheads, but her eyes gave her away.

Shit.

Why would Shaw do this to me?

"Shaw thinks the world of you. She thinks you're the absolute shit. And guess what? She wants the absolute shit for her sister. I tell her you two kissed, and she'll start planning the wedding."

"Christ." I leaned back against the counter and squeezed my eyes shut.

Shaw saw more than anyone suspected. She knew there was something between me and Ryan.

"She did this because of me."

I looked at Ry.

She turned, giving me her profile as she stared out the side door to the woods surrounding the cabin. "I think she might have seen me kiss you at Dex's party." She flicked me a quick look but couldn't meet my gaze. "I'm sorry about that. I don't remember much, but I remember you having to push me off, which is beyond mortifying. I was drunk. I'm sorry."

That was how she remembered it?

A part of me wanted to let her continue believing it. It would be easier. But it would also make me a dick. "That's not how it happened."

Ryan turned to me, her eyes round. "It wasn't?"

I shook my head. "You kissed me, yeah. But ... I kissed you back."

Her lush lips parted, drawing my attention. I could still feel them against mine. Still taste her.

"What ... what happened?"

"I remembered you were drunk and that I'm not an asshole, and that's when I stopped the kiss. Not really a kiss." I smirked. "We were most definitely making out."

Ry looked confused now, and she was breathing heavier.

It was making me think ungentlemanly things.

"And Shaw saw this?"

"Not that I'm aware of. Dex did. But he warned me off you, so this wasn't his idea."

"He warned you off me?" She looked hurt.

Clearly, she was missing the big picture here. "Ry, I'm your sister's father-in-law. And I'm sixteen years older than you. Dex knows ... you and I shouldn't go there."

"But you want to?"

I stared into those gorgeous fucking eyes and imagined sinking myself deep inside her. Oh, yeah. I wanted Ryan Baillie more than I could remember wanting any woman. Even as a horny goddamn teenager, I couldn't remember wanting a girl the way I wanted Ry. Because it wasn't just sex with her. For the first time in my life, I wanted a woman to belong to me and to belong to that woman in return.

She was just the goddamn wrong woman.

Off-limits.

"Dex is too important to me." I reminded myself, and her. "I won't do anything to screw up my relationship with him. Shaw must have kept him in the dark about this."

Ry lowered her gaze, shielding her thoughts from me. "Yeah, Shaw's too much of a romantic. She doesn't live in the real world sometimes."

Hearing the hint of bitterness in her words was like taking a knife to the gut. I'd hurt her. "Ry—"

"Don't." She waved off my words, not meeting my gaze again. "I get it. I'm not really your type, anyway. And we're totally different people. I don't want a guy who needs to take care of me, and you love women who want to be taken care of. A little attraction between us isn't worth the cost to our family. I don't need anyone. I'm fine alone. And this ... is just a disaster waiting to happen, so I'm going to head out." She strode out of the living room, leaving me seething.

Not my type?

Was she fucking kidding me with that?

I loved women who want to be taken care of?

What was that shit?

A little attraction?

I moved to go after her and set her straight, but stopped myself.

Dex was right. I was sixteen years older than Ryan, and she deserved better than to be tied to someone that much older. If we had kids, I would be in my sixties when they were still only in their twenties.

I don't need anyone. I'm fine alone.

My gut twisted at the thought of Ryan spending her entire life keeping people at a distance. Of that gorgeous, funny, sweet woman being lonely. And the thought of her returning to that apartment where she'd been attacked made me break out in a cold sweat.

Dex was wrong.

Yes, in the past, I'd dated women until I got bored.

But I had never felt about any of them the way I felt about Ryan Baillie.

Before I could stop myself, my feet were taking me to her.

CHAPTER FIVE

RYAN

I was shaking as I hurried into the bedroom where I'd slept last night. If I was so cool about being alone, about not needing anyone, then why did it feel as if Joe had just ripped out my guts?

It was stupid of me to feel this way.

Of course I was not as important to him as his son.

Dex should come first.

His devotion to his son was one of the reasons I loved Joe so much.

My breath caught.

Loved?

No.

I didn't love Joe.

I shook my head, searching the room for my jeans.

I couldn't love Joe.

No way.

Trembling even harder, I spotted my jeans in the corner, folded on top of a chest of drawers. Hurrying over to them, I pushed down my pajama shorts and was just reaching for the jeans when Joe suddenly marched into the room.

My heart lurched in my throat as he drew to an abrupt halt.

His cheeks flushed at the sight of me standing in nothing but my Henley and plain cotton underwear.

Joe's gaze dipped to between my legs, and the area throbbed in response.

"Joe?" I whispered hoarsely.

His hot, dark gaze drifted down my legs and back up my body, drinking every inch of me in. "One," he rasped, his voice hoarse, "not my type?"

I shivered. "Small, petite brunettes ring a bell?"

"Apparently, they don't make my dick as hard as a tall redhead with legs that go on forever and the most beautiful fucking green eyes I've ever seen in my life."

I gasped, my gaze falling to see his jeans straining with his erection. Oh my God. My skin flushed from head to toe, and my breasts suddenly felt heavy with need.

"Two," Joe continued in that thick voice, "I don't have a thing for women who need to be taken care of. Do I like to take care of my woman? Yes. But the woman I care about has an independent streak a mile wide, and I like it a fuck of a lot. Three: This isn't just a 'little attraction.'" He took a step toward me, determination and need dark on his face. "This is a code-red situation."

"Code red?" I could barely breathe.

"Code red. I can't live my fucking life because all I can think about is you."

Oh my God.

"Joe—"

His eyes flashed. "I want to hear you say my name just like that as I move inside you."

Oh. My. God.

"Joe—"

Then he rushed me. Our bodies collided seconds before our mouths did.

Joe's kiss was ravaging. It was a man's kiss. Dark, deep, and sexual. His stubble rasped against my skin.

His hand fisted in my hair as he held me to him, and I grasped onto him as he plundered my mouth. It was as if Joe couldn't kiss me deep or hard enough.

I whimpered against his tongue as his other hand gripped my ass to pull me into the hard-on straining the zipper of his jeans. The whimper turned to a moan, reverberating into his mouth. Joe ground his hips harder into me, squeezing my ass. I slid my hands under his tee in answer, shivering at the delicious feel of his smooth, hot skin beneath my fingertips.

He groaned as I touched his nipples. The sound rumbled in my mouth as we kissed harder, bruising each other's lips.

I needed him inside me. I wanted to be overwhelmed by Joe. To have all my senses captured by him. To feel and taste and smell and hear nothing but him, all around me, over me.

Inside me.

Fumbling for the button on his jeans, I made that very clear.

Then suddenly, I was in his arms for a few seconds before finding myself on the bed, Joe covering my body as we pawed at each other's clothing. Or what little I wore. Joe broke our kiss to whip off my Henley, and I reached around my back to unhook my bra. He took hold of it and ripped it away from me, throwing it over his shoulder. His fiery eyes devoured my naked breasts.

"You were over one Saturday," he said, even as his hips undulated against me with a mind of their own. "Nicole was there too. You were both in your bikinis. But I couldn't stop looking at you. Every time you laughed, I wanted to kiss the sound into my mouth. I wanted to press you up against the pool, rip off your bikini, and suck on your nipples."

Wet slickened between my legs. "Joe."

"I broke up with Nicole after that." He reached for my breasts, caressing them, plucking at my nipples as they tightened into hard points. "I couldn't be with one woman when all I could think about was another. And all the nasty, dirty, grown-up things I wanted to do to her."

"Do them," I begged, my mind a haze of lust. "Joe, please. I want you so much."

"God, baby, you have no idea how much I want you back." He kissed me again.

I frantically pulled off his shirt, breaking the kiss to do it, wanting to explore his beautiful body ... but then he bent his head to my breasts, sucking a nipple deep into his mouth, and I forgot about everything but what he was doing to me.

I cried out, arching against him.

His long fingers curled around my underwear, and he tugged so wildly, I heard them tear.

Neither of us cared as he yanked my underwear down my thighs. They got caught around my ankles, and I kicked to get them off. My patience was obliterated. "Come inside me. Please, Joe, now."

"Fuck," he murmured, his eyes wild with need. "You kill me." He kissed me again. Prolonging my need. Toying with me.

In answer, I fumbled for his zipper. As I slid my hand inside his boxers to feel his throbbing, hard heat, he slipped his hand between my legs, sliding his fingers into me. The wet he found there made him grunt into my mouth. He tore his lips from mine, and my chest rose and fell in frenzied breaths as he stared into my eyes with a passion that blew my mind.

"You're soaked." His face hardened with need, and he gently captured the hand I had wrapped around him and removed it. He pinned my hand to the bed.

Anticipation made me squirm beneath him. Joe never broke eye contact as he shoved down his jeans and boxers just far enough to release himself.

The fingers of my free hand curled into the bedcovers until Joe captured it, too, and held me down. My panting filled the room, and I let my legs fall open wide as he nudged against me. I moaned into his mouth.

He pushed into me. Hard.

My desire eased his way considerably, but he was big, thick, and that overwhelming fullness I'd been desperate for caused a pleasure pain to zing down my spine.

"More, Joe," I begged.

"Fuck, Ryan," he growled, his head bowing into my neck as he pumped into me.

If everything was out of control before, it turned wilder than I could have imagined. I'd never been so consumed. Everything was about the hot drive of him inside me. My hips rose to meet his hard thrusts, my cries and his groans filling the entire cabin.

I couldn't touch him, could only take what he had to give, and it was so goddamn exciting, I knew I was going to come quickly. The tension inside me tightened, tightened, tightened every time he pulled out and slammed back in.

"I'm close," I gasped.

He released one of my hands to grab my thigh and pulled it up against his hip, changing the angle of his thrust. I reached for him blindly as the tension inside of me shattered. I think I even screamed.

My orgasm rolled through me, my inner muscles rippling and squeezing around Joe. His hips pounded faster and then momentarily stilled before he cried out my name, his grip on my thigh bruising as his hips jerked with the swell and throb of his release.

As his climax shuddered through him, he let go of my thigh and slumped over me. Joe's warm, heavy weight surrounded me, and I slid my hands across his back. He was solid and real.

Our labored breathing rasped in my ears.

My heart pounded.

Finally, reality intruded.

I was sprawled on a bed with Joe between my legs, inside me. He was still wearing his jeans because we'd been so frantic to have each other, he didn't even undress fully.

It was the best sex I'd ever had.

But we hadn't used a condom.

Joe had come inside me.

CHAPTER SIX

JOE

"You didn't use a condom," Ryan whispered, sounding panicked.

The words cut through my post-sex bliss haze.

Shit.

I raised my head from her neck to stare into Ry's wide eyes. "You on the Pill?"

"Yeah, but that's not the point."

Realizing what she meant, I cursed under my breath. "I'm clean. I have never forgotten to use a condom before. Not since I got a girl pregnant at eighteen."

She raised an eyebrow like she didn't know whether to believe me.

"Ry ..." I cupped her face in my hand, my fingers brushing the slight swelling around her eye where the fading bruises were. It killed me I hadn't been there to protect her. "Do you still not get it? When it comes to relationships, I have been in control my whole life. I've never been so fucking desperate to have someone that I forgot to put on a condom. Not after I acted like a stupid kid with Renee and knocked her up. Not ... until now. I have no control over how I feel about you. If I did, this wouldn't have happened at all."

To my shock, hurt saturated her features. "I know that probably sounds romantic to you ... but to me, there is nothing romantic about not being someone's *choice*." She tried to push me off her, and I took hold of her wrists to pin her back in place. Ry growled up at me in frustration, and fuck if I didn't get hard inside her again. That *definitely* hadn't happened to me since I was a teenager.

She sucked in a breath, feeling me.

"This is a choice. I made a choice as soon as I followed you into this room. I love my son," I said, my voice gruff with emotion, "but I can't bear the idea of you thinking I don't want you or need you enough to fight for this. Because I do. I have tried not to for nearly two years because I didn't want to complicate everything for everyone. Dex thinks I'll just get what I want from you and move on ... But he doesn't know I'm in love with you. It took me years to find you, and I'm a selfish bastard for wanting to keep you, but if you feel even half of what I feel, I'm willing to fight for this."

I felt her relax beneath me, her features softening with wonder. "You love me?"

"Don't you love me?" My heart pounded now, waiting for her to crush it—or not.

"I ... I ..." Tears filled her eyes, and she strained against my hold. "Get off me, Joe. Please, get off me!"

I instantly let go, gently pulling out and rolling off. An ache I'd never felt before gripped tight to my chest as Ryan scrambled from the bed to get away from me. Jesus, was I a foolish asshole thinking a young, vibrant woman like her would want something serious with me, a man sixteen years her senior? Had I read the situation so wrong?

As she hurried to dress, I felt paralyzed.

Until her soft sobs cut through my hurt. "Ry ..." I pushed off the bed, but she turned her head toward me as she pulled up her jeans. Tears streamed down her face.

"Don't," she choked out. "Please. Don't. I'm going to get in my car and leave, and we're not going to speak of this again."

Fuck me. I looked away because looking at her hurt too much. "We can never talk about this if that's what you want. But I'm not letting you drive back to Sacramento alone. You've barely slept all week, and you haven't eaten in God knows how long."

"You think I can stay here? After that?"

I glared at her as I got off the bed. She averted her gaze as I pulled my boxers and jeans up. "Yeah, but don't worry. I'll stay out of your way." I stormed out of the room, shaking. Jesus Christ. I'd been crushed by a fucking twenty-four-year-old woman.

I should never have followed her into that room.

RYAN

It was hunger pangs that forced me out of the bedroom a few hours later. Joe, thankfully, was nowhere in sight. His truck was still here, so I guessed he'd gone for a walk.

Guilt suffused me.

And cowardice.

While I'd felt euphoric at Joe's confession of love, I'd also felt absolutely terrified by it.

I'd never expected to feel for any man the way I felt about Joe.

But the truth was, he was older than I was... and one day he wouldn't be here anymore, and I was so scared of that. Wasn't it easier to walk away now than to fall deeper and deeper in love with him, only to inevitably lose him?

I could kill my sister.

After shoveling down some cereal I found in the pantry, I grabbed my phone out of my purse. It needed to be charged, but there was just enough battery to call Shaw.

She answered on the third ring. "If you're calling to berate me, please don't."

I slumped on the corner sofa near the crackling fire. Joe had obviously gotten it started before he escaped the cabin. My heart ached with renewed guilt. "Why did you do this?"

"Because she's nuts!" Dex yelled in the background.

It made me smile sadly. "I take it Dex found out."

"Yeah, and he's not happy with me, but I told him if my little plan works, he can't give you or his dad a hard time."

"Shaw ..." Tears filled my voice.

"Oh, Ry, shit ... I'm sorry. Did I read it wrong? You don't love Joe back?"

There was that word again.

"What made you think Joe and I are in love?"

"Because her head is in the clouds!" Dex called out. Shaw obviously had me on speakerphone.

"No, it isn't. Anyone with eyes can see it. Even Renee can see it. You just don't want to because Joe's your dad," Shaw replied to Dex. "Please tell me I'm right, Ry?"

"I can't talk about this in front of Dex."

"Oh, for God's sake," Dex grumbled, much louder in my ear this time, suggesting he'd taken the phone from Shaw.

"Dad isn't answering his phone, so I texted him. I told him that if this is what you really want, then I won't stand in your way. I just hope you've thought it through. There's an age difference here, Ry. And I don't want my dad to fuck you around. I told him I will kill him if he does."

I closed my eyes, my self-recrimination at its boiling point. "Dex ... it's your dad you need to worry about. Not me."

"What does that mean?"

"I ... know that he would never hurt me or mess me around. What's happening or not happening, however, is between me and him. I appreciate you're okay about everything, but I can't discuss this with you."

There was silence on the other end of the line.

Then, "Ry ... okay. Fine. But try not to hurt my old man. He's the best fucking guy there is, and if Shaw's right about how he feels about you ... yeah ... shit, just let him down easy."

Tears slipped down my cheeks as a reply stuck in my throat.

Shaw's voice was gentle in my ear now. "I love you, Ry. Whatever you do, I'm here. I know whatever is holding you back isn't about what other people think because you've never cared what other people think. It's one of my favorite things about you."

"Shaw," I whispered brokenly. "I'm scared."

"Of what?"

"Of losing him."

"Oh, Ry." Understanding filled her voice. "It is scary to love someone that much. We know that better than anyone. But you know what's scarier? Regret. Looking back on your life, safe but lonely, and wishing you hadn't let fear win."

CHAPTER SEVEN

RYAN

After returning to my bedroom in the cabin, I'd heard Joe's arrival. I'd heard him puttering about in the kitchen and at one point heard him murmuring, so I knew he had to be talking to someone on the phone.

I wondered if it was Dex.

The hours passed like days as I watched the clock on my phone tick toward midnight.

Toward the new year.

Every time I looked at the bed, images of Joe straining above me filled my head.

I kept hearing him telling me he loved me.

It seemed like a miracle that Joe Colchester was in love with me.

It was my wildest fantasy come true, and I'd spit all over it.

Shaw's wise words haunted me throughout the day.

The fact that my sister had guessed I was in love with Joe before I even realized I was would've been funny if the whole situation didn't feel so tragic.

"But it doesn't have to be tragic," I whispered to myself.

If I let go of my fear, or at least tried to overcome it, I could make me and Joe so happy.

And Shaw was right. I didn't care what people would say or think about us. Not as long as we loved each other.

But what about when you lose him?

The thought filled me with agony.

Yet ... wasn't I already in pain? Was losing him any worse than pushing him away?

No.

The thought of never touching Joe again or tasting his kiss or feeling him move inside me made me feel like the world was ending.

"You have to try," I whispered.

I had to try.

And I couldn't let Joe go on thinking I didn't love him just to protect myself.

Decision made, I pushed up out of the chair just as the clock neared twenty minutes to midnight. My belly grumbled with hunger as my heart pounded in my chest.

Joe sat on the sofa, a glass filled with beer in one hand, while he stared in a trance at the flickering fire.

I could feel myself losing my nerve at the mere sight of him, even as I wanted to lie my body atop his. A foil-covered plate on the island caught my attention, and I moved toward it. Stalling.

Beneath it was a roast beef dinner. Joe had cooked. The smell from earlier had given me hunger pains.

"That's yours."

I started at his voice. He stared blankly at me.

"Thank you."

He lifted his chin and turned back to the fire.

Hungry and nervous, I sat down at the island to eat. But after a few forkfuls, my nerves got the better of me. Pushing the plate away, I was readying myself to talk when he spoke first.

"Is it Dex? Because I spoke to him today, and he's okay with the idea of us."

I spun around to face Joe.

His expression was still hard and defiant. His walls were still halfway up, even though he was trying to understand me.

"It's not Dex."

"The age gap? You worried about what people will think? That I'm a dirty fucker going after a woman almost half my age?"

"I don't care what people will think. And you're not a dirty fucker, so don't call yourself that. You're forty, Joe, not eighty. And I'm twenty-four, not some innocent eighteen-year-old."

His lips twitched at that but then pinched into a straight line before he muttered, "So, you just don't feel about me the way I feel about you?"

"You scare me," I blurted out.

Joe's eyes flashed dangerously. "What?"

At his biting tone, I shook my head. "Not like that. God, never like that. In fact, I've never felt safer with someone in my life. You're what home should feel like."

Joe sat up, looking baffled. "Then I don't understand."

Drawing up my courage, I exhaled slowly. "I'm sorry I hurt you or made you feel like your feelings aren't reciprocated. Of course, they're reciprocated, Joe." I hurried on before he could interrupt. "But I'm scared. Scared of needing you as much as I do. Scared of losing you."

His expression hardened. "You don't trust me."

"No!" I pushed off the stool, crossing the room only to stop midway as Joe stood up, too, dumping his beer on the side table as he did. "I ... everyone *goes away*. That's just the natural course of life. I knew I had to suck up the fear of losing Shaw because I loved her and there was no changing that ... but I wanted to go through life protecting my heart as much as possible. Trying to love as few people as possible."

"Baby ..." His voice was thick with understanding.

"But whether or not I push you away, there's no getting around it. I love you. And I can throw off my fears and enjoy a life with you ... or I can let fear win."

"What have you decided to do?"

I smiled tremulously. "I won't regret you. I won't look back on my life and remember this moment and wish I'd done something different. I love you, and I can't believe you love me back. I will never throw your love back in your face again. I promise, Joe, I pr—" The words were cut off by his kiss as he hauled me into his arms.

Between hungry kisses, we divested each other of our clothes, and I found myself sprawled across the rug in front of the fire. Joe towered above me, all muscle and solid, masculine beauty. His erection strained toward his taut stomach as he dragged his gaze slowly down my body.

"Open your legs, baby," he murmured.

I did as commanded and grew wet at the hitch in his breathing. "Come inside me, Joe."

"First, I'm gonna kiss you." He lowered to his knees, pushing mine apart, and then he buried his head between my legs.

My gasps of pleasure filled the cabin as he licked and sucked until the tension was too much and I shattered into a million blissful pieces. I was tight and swollen from my climax as he pushed inside me, but I didn't care. All I cared about was being connected to this man in every way possible. I wrapped my arms around him as he moved over me, in me, our eyes locked in passion.

"I love you so fucking much," he groaned.

"I love you too."

"I'm never letting you go." His thrusts grew harder, his words catching on his pleasure, "You're not going back to that apartment."

I moaned, gripping my thighs to his hips, rocking into his throbbing drives. "You're not the boss of me."

"Ryan," he warned, grabbing my hands to pin them to the floor.

I couldn't think past the heat building deep inside me. "Joe—"

"You're moving in with me."

"Ask nicely!" I managed to bite out.

He slowed his thrusts, laughing softly. "Okay, baby, move in with me. Please?"

"Yes, yes, yes ..." I pushed my hips against him. "Just make me come, Joe. Don't stop."

"Ask nicely," he murmured against my mouth.

I grinned, pushing against his hold. He released me and I wrapped my arms around him, pulling him closer. "Please fuck me to orgasm, my darling Joe."

Dark desire saturated his expression. "Say it again."

Knowing exactly what he wanted, I brushed my lips against his and whispered hoarsely, "Fuck me, Joe. Fuck me, hard."

My words shattered his control and soon I was coming around his powerful thrusts.

"Ryan!" Joe roared as he flooded inside me.

His chest heaved against mine as he tried not to crush me with his weight. I held him to me, loving the feel of him over me, inside me. Face suffused with wonder and satisfaction, he shook his head. "It's never been like this. Never."

"For me either," I promised.

Joe grinned, his obvious happiness filling me with joy too. Then his eyes flickered up to above the fireplace where a clock was mounted on the wall. "It's past midnight. We missed bringing in the new year."

I laughed, caressing his face, drawing his gaze back to mine. "I think we brought in the new year perfectly. After all, we should always start the new year the way we mean to go on."

His deep chuckles filled my ears as he rolled to his side, pulling me with him. I rested my cheek on his chest, my leg curled over his, keeping him inside me.

"I meant what I said." He broke our pleasurable silence a few minutes later. "I don't want you going back to that apartment. It doesn't make you weak to lean on me a little. And I want you with me. I want to wake up every morning to see you sleeping beside me."

I smiled against his chest, dizzy at the thought. "Isn't it too soon?"

He tipped my head back. "I don't care. All I care about is you."

"Okay," I agreed, excited and nervous at the prospect. "I want that too."

"You want babies?" he asked abruptly.

More people to love and worry over? The fear almost caused me to lie, but I stopped myself. "I do."

"Do you care I'll be an older dad?"

"Not if you don't care. Joe, you know our age difference doesn't matter to me. I don't see your age. I just see you. I just ... I just love you."

"Then that's all I care about." His expression was serious.

"I'm going to make you so fucking happy, you won't be able to stand it."

I grinned, already so happy I couldn't stand it. "I believe you."

"Happy New Year, baby."

"Happy New Year, Joe."

LOVING VALENTINE

CHAPTER ONE

MICAH
AGE 16

I was heating soup on the electric hob when the electricity went out.

Dread filled me because I knew it wasn't a power cut.

My mom hadn't paid the bill.

Cursing under my breath, I waited for my eyes to adjust to the dark before moving through the room toward the window. Upon peeking out, sure enough, I saw lights on in the apartments on the opposite side of the building.

Resentment and aggravation built inside me, but I forced it down and found the camping lantern I had buried in the back of my closet. Once it was on, I poured my lukewarm soup into a bowl and tried not to hate my mom.

Two weeks ago, she took off with some guy she'd met online. Some shithead who didn't care that my mom was an alcoholic addicted to painkillers so long as she gave him what he wanted. Mom said he was taking her to Florida to the beach, and they'd be back in three days.

She hadn't returned.

And she wasn't picking up her phone.

My job at Billy's Burgers would barely pay even half the bills now, never mind when school started in two weeks and I returned to part time. I was determined not to quit school.

But if Mom didn't come back soon, I might not have a choice.

A knock at the door made my stomach lurch. If it was our landlord, I was screwed. Another knock followed it. Harder this time.

Then, "Molly? Micah?" a familiar voice called.

It was Mrs. Fairchild. Relief and embarrassment filled me in equal measure. Getting up off the couch, I wavered over answering the door.

"Micah?" She sounded really worried.

Mrs. Fairchild was Mom's childhood best friend. They grew up together in South Glastonbury. Both girls' parents were moneyed, so Mom and Mrs. Fairchild attended a private school. But when my grandfather died, it turned out he'd hidden that he was in debt up to his eyeballs. They took everything. My grandmother couldn't handle it. Turned to drink.

While Mrs. Fairchild went off to college, Mom moved into her own place and worked in a fast-food joint, just like I was now. I never met my grandmother, and I didn't even know if she was still alive. All I knew was that not long after the sperm donor responsible for impregnating my mother took off, I was born. Mom's dependency on alcohol was a gradual thing. I'd been dealing with the worst of it since I was ten.

Last year, Mom hurt her back on a cleaning job and got addicted to the painkillers her doc gave her.

Things had gone downhill between us.

Then, three months ago, Mrs. Fairchild, now a lawyer, moved back to South Glastonbury with her lawyer husband and their daughter. She wanted to check on Mom. Our situation shocked her. She'd been coming around a lot and even gave Mom money.

Little did she know Mom would use it to take off on me.

I was humiliated that Mom didn't love me enough to stick around. It took Mrs. Fairchild calling my name in rising concern for me to open the door.

Relief flooded her pretty face. "Micah. Thank God. Are you okay? I've been calling your mom ..." Her voice trailed off as she looked beyond me into the dark apartment, lit only by my camping lantern. She pushed inside—she was nosy like that. "What is going on here?" she asked, her voice tight. Concerned. Annoyed.

I shrugged.

Mrs. Fairchild's eyes narrowed. "Micah, where is your mother?"

Unable to meet her gaze, I shrugged. "I don't know."

"How long has she been gone?"

"A few weeks, I guess. She said her and some guy were going to Florida for the weekend but ... she never came back."

Mrs. Fairchild let out a stream of curses that surprised me. She was always so proper and ladylike.

"I'm sorry. Forgive me, but this is unacceptable." She gestured around the apartment. "You have no electricity." She marched across the kitchen and pulled open the refrigerator. It was empty. "Oh, for goodness' sake, Molly, what are you thinking?" Mrs. Fairchild slammed the fridge shut and strode toward the apartment door. When she turned to me, the light from the hallway shone in her blue eyes. They were bright with unshed tears. "She has a good kid ... and she leaves him all alone." She shook her head, and I flinched in embarrassment. "Oh no, no ... don't you take this on yourself. This is on Molly. Not you. Now." She crossed her arms over her chest. "Go grab your things. Pack everything that matters to you."

"Why?"

"I'm not leaving you here, Micah. You're coming home with me. You can stay with us until we can reach your mother."

My voice was hoarse with emotion. It pissed me off. "What if you can't reach her?"

"We'll figure that out later. For now, let's just go home."

⚜

IT WAS about a twenty-minute drive in Mrs. Fairchild's gold Lexus SUV from South Green to her house in South Glastonbury. The Lexus had white leather seats. I'd never been in a vehicle so fancy in my life. It still had that new-car smell.

A twenty-minute drive, and it was like driving into a different world. It was greener around here, for a start. The houses were nicer, with more land around each of them, the buildings and gardens well maintained.

I couldn't believe my mom grew up in this neighborhood.

We'd passed a lot of houses that were of average size. But the street we'd turned onto stood out from the rest. It was a quiet court, surrounded on three sides with large, New England-style houses and lots of trees. The driveway we pulled into belonged to the biggest house of them all. While the other homes were clad in painted wood siding, this house was red brick with varying triangular rooflines, a circular drive, and a three-car garage.

"Holy shit," I muttered under my breath, looking up at it.

Mrs. Fairchild's lips twitched. "Micah."

"Sorry. I just ..."

"I know it feels worlds away from what you're used to. But I promise, we're just like any other family."

I raised an eyebrow.

Mrs. Fairchild chuckled. "Okay, as a family, we're like any other family. As people ... we're financially blessed compared to many others. But we don't take it for granted."

"You don't have to apologize or explain it to me. You work hard for what you have." Even if they only had it in the first place because they had a step up in life to begin with. But I didn't say that out loud. My mom was proof that a step up in life at the beginning didn't mean a damn thing if you didn't take hold of the opportunities offered to you.

"We do. Come on in. Jim was ordering takeout when I left, and he always orders way too much, so there will be plenty of food."

My stomach grumbled.

Striding through the double-door entrance after her, I drew to a stop, taking in the spacious hallway, the wide staircase that led upstairs, and the warmly furnished rooms on either side of me.

"We're home!" Mrs. Fairchild called as I followed her through a family room, a library room, and a dining room to get to the kitchen. The kitchen stretched along the entire back of the house. Sliding doors led out into a backyard with a pool, currently covered for winter.

"We're?" A tall man stood at an island opening takeout cartons. His eyes widened at the sight of me and then drifted to my duffel bag.

I braced myself, feeling like an intruder.

"Jim, this is Micah, Molly's son. Micah, my husband Jim."

"Nice to meet you, Mr. Fairchild," I said.

Jim chuckled as he rounded the island. His dark eyes glittered warmly as he reached for my hand. "Please, Mr. Fairchild's my father. Call me Jim."

I nodded, but I wasn't sure I'd be able to do that. It would be like calling Mrs. Fairchild Caroline. Too weird.

"We'll be back in a minute." Mrs. Fairchild took her husband's hand and led him out of the room, presumably to fill him in on my situation.

My pride stung.

It was fucking humiliating taking her charity, but I didn't know what else I could do. I didn't want my future to fall to shit because my mom took off, and I didn't want her life for myself. With a 3.9 GPA and as captain of the swim team, I was on course to receive a scholarship, preferably to Boston University. All this with a part-time job. I couldn't screw it up.

If that meant accepting Mrs. Fairchild's help, then I guessed that was what it meant.

"And who are you?"

A girl's voice made me whip around.

I'd remember the sight of her always because it was like someone had punched me in the gut. All the air went out of the room.

The girl was about my age, I'd guess. She had long, thick, pale-blond hair that spilled around her shoulders in shiny waves, and the prettiest dark-brown eyes I'd ever seen, filled with humor and curiosity. Her lush lips quirked upward at the corners. She grinned and killed me with her dimples.

Dressed like one of those hippie-girl images from the seventies, she wore a thin gold circlet around her head like a crown. Her dress was long, fitted at her tiny waist, then flowed to her feet. It was a light pink with oversized sleeves that narrowed at her wrists.

I'd never seen anything like her.

It wasn't just her sense of style ... it was the way happiness and warmth radiated from her.

I didn't even know her, and yet I sensed she was *good*.

Beautiful all the way through.

"Do you talk?" she teased.

I cleared my throat, my heart hammering. "Uh. Yeah. I'm, uh—"

"Oh, good." Mrs. Fairchild strode back into the kitchen with her husband at her side. "You've already met Valentine, our daughter."

Even though it should have occurred to me that was who she was, I was disappointed as hell.

Valentine Fairchild was most definitely off-limits.

CHAPTER TWO

VALENTINE
AGE 15

F ive months.

That was how long Micah Green and I had been dancing around our chemistry. And we definitely had it. According to my friend, Kim, who had been dating older guys since she was thirteen, when two people were truly attracted to each other, there was this electric tension between them. The plethora of romance novels I devoured every month (that my mother didn't know about) verified Kim's claim.

For five months, Micah had been living with my family. His mom Molly took off, left him, and when my mother finally tracked her down, Molly refused to come home. So Mom and Dad, being lawyers and all, sorted things so that Micah could stay with us for the rest of his high school career. Then they went further by pulling strings at the private academy I attend so he could start his junior year there. My parents even gave him his own car because he also made the swim team and so he finished his school day later than I did.

You would think Micah would have problems fitting in at my school, coming from such a different background.

But no! He fit in better than I did.

Whereas most kids there were ambitious and academic, I much preferred being in my room sewing myself a wardrobe no one else had. That was if we were allowed to wear our own clothes and not the mandatory black-and-red plaid uniform.

Although I *did* cover the left lapel of my blazer in cute, custom-made brooches, and the teachers finally gave up telling me to remove them.

But I digress.

My palms were sweaty.

I'd just lied to my English teacher that I needed the restroom. The truth was, I knew this was the period Micah used the darkroom for his photography class. Although he was super smart and academic, he was also artsy. Like me. Micah wanted to be an architect, which I thought was impressive.

He thought my clothing designs were amazing.

"You're so talented, Val," Micah had said when I showed him my clothes and the Singer sewing machine I'd begged my parents to buy when I was twelve.

Sometimes Dad would tell me I was clever and talented when I walked downstairs in one of my new creations. But Mom would just give me that look, because she knew I'd spent all my time sewing instead of studying.

It was appalling to my parents that their child was a B student instead of the A student she could be if she only applied herself.

I shook off those thoughts as I tried to act casual, walking through the school halls. Sometimes I let myself get too worked up about Mom and Dad. Today wasn't about my parents. It was about Micah. The one person who made me feel good about myself. Who told me it was okay that I couldn't envision myself at college. That it didn't make me a bum because I wanted to get out in the world and get a job and start living my own life, rather than spend another four to seven years in the land of academia.

There were moments when I caught Micah looking at me in a way that made me sure he got butterflies in his stomach like I did whenever he was near me. I still remember the first day we met when I found him in the kitchen. He'd looked so sad and hurt. Those gorgeous gray eyes full of pride and anger and gratitude all at once. Then he'd seen me, and he looked at me like no one ever had before.

He stared at me like he thought I was beautiful.

I grinned, my heart racing just thinking about it.

So okay, it was weird that we lived together, but maybe we didn't have to tell Mom and Dad right away. In fact, that was why I'd put off approaching Micah about our feelings. I thought it would go down better with my parents if I was sixteen. And I was sixteen in January. Next month.

Yet, I found I couldn't wait past Christmas.

I wanted to go to bed on Christmas Eve knowing that Micah was mine. Best Christmas present ever!

Holy crap, it felt like my heart was going to explode out of my chest as I approached the darkroom. The light was on outside—he was in there processing. Which also meant I had to slip in really fast and close the door so I didn't mess up Micah's photos. His photos were pretty good. Mostly of buildings and architecture. I didn't personally get his fascination with them, but I loved his passion. So few boys our age had genuine passion beyond the instant gratification of gaming, sports, and sex.

"Here we go," I whispered before taking a deep breath.

I gently pushed open the door.

I'd barely gotten it wide enough to slip through when my heart plummeted into my stomach.

A guy who looked awfully like Micah from behind had a girl pressed up against the counter at the back of the room, kissing her hungrily as his hand worked beneath her skirt.

"Micah, oh my God, don't stop." A familiar breathy female voice filled the darkroom.

I knew the perfect profile of the girl who threw her head back in pleasure.

Christy McAlister. Senior. Brunette. Five foot ten.

Student body president.

Cheerleader.

My exact opposite.

I quickly pulled the door closed before either of them saw me.

Tears burned in my throat and eyes.

This whole time Micah was screwing around with Christy?

Christy only dated older guys. Not younger ones!

Of course, she'd break her rules for Micah.

And he'd been in there ... touching her!

Oh my God, I was such an idiot.

I'd look back on this moment as an adult and cringe, but when you're fifteen, in love with a boy, and you find out you're the exact opposite of the kind of girl he likes to be with ... let's just say it feels like the world is ending.

Tears streaming down my face, I hurried back to my class. I explained to my teacher I wasn't feeling well, and she took me to the office. They said I had to wait while they called my mom.

I tried not to let the tears flood out.

Mom calling my cell only made me it harder not to cry.

"Mom." My voice broke on the word.

I wanted to tell her the truth. That I loved Micah, and he liked someone else.

But I could never tell her that stuff. She always made everything I felt seem small and childish.

"Valentine, are you okay?" She sounded concerned, making me feel terrible for thinking badly of her. "The school just called."

I sucked back more tears as I lied. "I threw up. I really don't feel well."

"Okay. I'll come get you."

"No. I'm okay. I just need to go to bed. Can you just ask the school office to call me a cab?"

"I hope it's only something you've eaten and not a bug. You've got end-of-semester exams to concentrate on."

Gee. Thanks for the sympathy, Mom.

"Right."

"Oh, sweetheart, I didn't mean it like that. You know how I get. I just want you to do well. I'll tell them to call that cab. Feel better."

Not long later, I texted her when I got to the house, but I didn't feel better.

First, I stopped in the doorway of Micah's room, just down the hall from mine. It had once been a guest room.

Now it smelled like Micah, and he had posters and drawings on the wall. Mostly posters of his favorite bands, books, and artists, as well as sketches of building designs he'd imagined. He was so talented. So smart. Smarter than me.

Smart like Christy.

Of course, he was into intelligent, stupidly gorgeous cheerleaders with legs up to their ears.

I promptly returned to my room, curled up on my bed, and sobbed until my entire body ached.

IT COULDN'T HAVE BEEN that much longer when my eyes cracked open at the feel of a hand on my arm.

I knew who it was without turning my head.

The last person I wanted to see.

"Hey." His deep voice made my chest hurt. His palm brushed down my arm in comfort. "Kim said you had to come home early."

My swollen eyes moved to the vintage alarm clock on my bedside table. School had only just let out. "Shouldn't you be at practice?" I sounded rough, croaky.

"Cupid, you don't sound so good."

I squeezed my eyes closed at his nickname for me. He thought it was interesting that my parents, who didn't seem all that romantic, would give me such a romantic name. But they met on Valentine's Day. Hence, my name. And Micah's pet name for me.

A pet name I moronically thought meant something.

Turned out it was because he saw me like a little sister.

"I'm fine. Practice?"

"Four guys on the team got detention today. Coach was so mad, he canceled practice. And then Kim told me you left school 'cause you were sick. I got worried." He pulled on my arm, so I turned to look at him.

His handsome face clouded over, those amazing gray eyes filling with suspicion and concern. "You've been crying. You're not sick, something happened." Micah seemed suddenly fierce. Like he'd fight off an army for me.

The vision of him and Christy in the darkroom flashed in my mind, and I turned away from him. "Nothing. I'm okay."

Hurt silence filled the air between us.

I never shut out Micah.

But that was the problem.

"Valentine." He leaned over me, brushing my hair off my face. I suppressed a shiver. "You're really worrying me."

"There's nothing to worry about," I whispered, my voice cracking as I fought back more tears. "It's just stupid girl stuff."

"Oh. Is it ... is it your period?"

I looked at him in surprise. Most boys (even my dad!) couldn't even say the word, let alone think it.

Micah grinned. It was crooked and boyish. And I was so in love with his smile. "I grew up with just my mom. I'm not squeamish. Girls get periods, it sounds like they suck, and I don't envy you. Unfortunately, they're kind of a big deal in the perpetuation of humanity, and you ladies have to bear it for us men because we have a zero-pain threshold. And the baby thing. No way we could do that. So ... thanks. For all of that."

I couldn't help it. I laughed at his rambling.

His eyes brightened. "That's better." He shook me gently. "Come on, Cupid. Tell me what's wrong."

A tear escaped before I could stop it. "It's not my period ... I found out today that the boy I like likes someone else."

He seemed shocked. Uncomfortable. His hand withdrew from my arm.

I turned away. "Told you it was stupid."

"Hey, hey." Micah leaned over me again, and I couldn't help but meet his gaze. He studied my face like I was precious. I wished he wouldn't. It confused me. "Any guy who doesn't see how unbelievably special you are isn't worth all these tears."

Right.

Except he was.

I lowered my gaze so he wouldn't see the truth.

"Come here." He hauled me into his arms. A big part of me wanted to shove him away. But I loved the feel of Micah's strong arms around me. I pressed my cheek to his shoulder and held on as he whispered against my hair, his voice gruff, "There is no one like you, Val. No one. Don't waste your time on any guy who doesn't realize how fucking lucky he is that you want to be with him."

I smiled sadly and held on a little tighter as my dreams of us each being part of one whole disappeared.

I decided then and there that I would take Micah Green's advice to heart.

CHAPTER THREE

MICAH
AGE 18

"Are you in a mood? Is it because I danced with Steve? You know we're just friends."

I looked down at my prom date, trying to figure out what she was saying.

Me in a mood. Dancing with Steve. Right. I shook my head at Alison. "No. I'm not in a mood. You know prom's not really my thing."

Alison chuckled and then grabbed me by the lapels. "It's your senior prom. I'm going to make it your thing." She dragged me onto the dance floor and I did my best, pretending like I wasn't searching the room as we swayed to a cheesy song.

The truth was, I was in a mood.

I'd been in a mood my entire junior and senior years.

That was what happened when you were deeply, miserably fucking in love with a girl you couldn't have.

And to top off this shitty year, she was my friend's prom date.

I couldn't believe Graham had asked Valentine to our senior prom.

I couldn't believe Valentine said yes.

She'd dated quite a few losers over the past eighteen months. My little pep talk when I found her crying over some guy I didn't even know but wanted to kill had worked a little too well.

But Graham was the worst of the lot.

There had been times when I first moved in with the Fairchilds that I thought my feelings for Valentine might be reciprocated. I wouldn't do anything about it because I couldn't reward their kindness by going after Val, but there was a part of me that felt elated she might feel the same way. Instead, I screwed around with a couple of cheerleaders and hoped they'd take my mind off my whopping crush on the daughter of the people who had turned my life around.

It didn't work.

Little Cupid was in my blood.

As it turned out, I wasn't in hers. She'd made that clear by dating half the guys in my class.

"You *are* in a mood. I can feel the tension in your body," Alison huffed.

Alison had been elected student body president and head cheerleader after Christy went off to college. It wasn't that I had a thing for cheerleaders. I had a thing for smart girls who were as ambitious as I was and didn't want to get weighed down by a high school romance.

"I need to use the bathroom. I'll be back in a sec."

I'd seen Valentine dancing with Graham a little while ago, his hand on her ass.

He hadn't said it to me, because he knew I'd fuck him up, but he had to be thinking he was getting laid tonight. It was prom night.

Over my dead body.

Cursing under my breath, I escaped the ballroom of the fancy-ass club the school had rented and found the men's room. I tried to shake off the black cloud hovering above my head before going back out there.

As I was leaving the restroom, however, something caught my attention in my peripheral. I turned toward the hallway that led to a closed-off part of the members-only club.

Cupid. Sitting on the floor, knees to her chest, her arm around some crying girl I didn't recognize. As the girl wiped tears from her cheeks, something inside me eased upon seeing Valentine.

I leaned against the wall and watched Cupid as she comforted the girl at her side.

Eventually, she pulled the girl to her feet, hugged her, and then led her toward me. Val's eyes brightened when she saw me. Her companion blushed and hurried away from us, joining the line into the women's restroom.

Val and I met each other in the middle. I tried not to check her out. It was really goddamn difficult. She'd designed and made her own dress, and she was a knockout in it. Lately, she'd become obsessed with this '50s vibe. It suited her. Over the past eighteen months, her body had changed. I'd heard her complaining about it to her mom, and it took everything within me to tell her she had nothing to worry about.

She was all tits and ass.

And the '50s vibe worked for her big-time. It showed off her curves.

Like now, in her strapless, cherry-red dress that fit like a second skin. The hem stopped just below the knee, and the heart-shaped neckline showed off Valentine's cleavage a little more than I'd like. I wasn't too happy about that. Neither was her dad.

But the whole Marilyn Monroe thing worked.

My gaze dropped to the floor because I couldn't look at Val without wanting to kiss the hell out of her. Instead, my eyes caught on her high heels. Tall, with an ankle strap. Her legs looked fucking amazing.

Shit.

"Cupid." I cleared my throat, swinging my gaze back up to her gorgeous face.

Her dimples creased, her dark eyes glittering. "Hey. You okay?"

"I'm fine. What about you?" I gestured to the girl she'd been comforting.

"Oh, her name is Heather. We're just newly acquainted."

I raised an eyebrow. "You just met, but she was sobbing on your shoulder?"

"Yeah. Come on." She tucked herself into my side, her arm around my back. I automatically curled my arm around her. Her head just came to my chest. To me, she was the perfect fit.

She smelled good too. Always did.

As we walked toward the ballroom, Valentine continued, "Heather's a sophomore. Invited by that jackass junior, Steve Johnson. He's danced with every hot girl since he got here and then started making out with another girl fifteen minutes ago."

"Asshole."

"Yup."

"Where are her friends?"

Val shrugged. "I don't know."

This was why I loved her. When Valentine saw anyone in pain, stranger or otherwise, she had to stop to help. Even if it interrupted her good time. "You're amazing, you know that?"

She grinned up at me, those dimples I'd wanted to kiss a million times popping again. "*You* always make me feel that way."

"It's because it's true."

Something flickered in her eyes, and I felt her tense against me.

Could she see it? Sometimes I wondered how she could *not* see it?

How much I adored her.

"Dance with me." It was out of my mouth before I could stop it. But I didn't want to stop it. I couldn't make Valentine Fairchild mine. The Fairchilds were already constantly fighting their daughter about her future. They'd told her no serious boyfriends until college. She'd told them she wasn't going to college. It was causing major tension. They saw me as a brother figure to her, the buffer that kept their relationship from growing too hostile.

If I suddenly announced I was in love with her, our entire family dynamic would implode. And I couldn't risk hurting the Fairchilds like that. Not when I owed them everything.

But I could have this one dance with her.

Valentine smiled and took hold of my hand, leading me to the dance floor even though *I* asked *her*. I tried not to notice the guys staring at her. The guys who wanted her. Or to think about the guy who would be lucky enough to have her.

To really have her.

All of her.

Instead, I pushed that agonizing thought aside and pulled her into my arms. Her sweet curves pressed into my body. Her fingers tickled the strands of hair at my nape. Her perfume drifted over me, dragging me deeper under her spell ... until everything around us disappeared.

It was just me and Valentine. Swaying to music I couldn't even hear.

I couldn't hear anything but her voice as she murmured against my chest, "This is nice."

It was more than nice.

It was right.

Perfect.

I tightened my arms around her waist and fantasized we were here together. That we'd just met at school like two normal kids would.

"Are you excited about college?" Val suddenly asked.

Part of me was. Instead of BU, I'd gotten into MIT. Going to a private academy had its advantages. MIT had one of the best architecture programs in the world. Sometimes I couldn't believe it. It was a partial scholarship, and the Fairchilds were paying the rest. I'd promised I'd pay it back as soon as I could after graduating.

Another reason their daughter was off-limits.

"Well?"

While yeah, it blew me away to be attending MIT, I was going to miss Cupid like fucking crazy. Not being able to walk down the hall, knock on her door, and just sit and talk shit for hours about everything and nothing. To make her laugh whenever her parents were coming down hard on her. To make her whole face light up when I praised her newest creation.

To feel her with me when my mom screwed up and had to go back to rehab for the hundredth time. To have her lie beside me and not say a word because she knew all I needed was her next to me.

"Let's not talk about it. I'm all talked out."

Her fingers stroked down my nape, and I shivered as she whispered, "Okay."

It was tempting to take hold of her hands and put them somewhere else, but that was useless. Wherever she touched me would go straight to my dick. I was eighteen, for fuck's sake, and in love with her.

Thinking about how things could be between us if life had turned out differently, I asked, "What would your dream date be?"

Valentine met my gaze. She seemed surprised by the question. "My dream date?"

"Yeah. Not who or anything like that." I didn't want to know that shit. "Where would you go? What would you do?"

She bit her plump bottom lip. I glared at it. Wanting it.

Finally, she released it and melted into me with a laugh. "You'll think it's cheesy."

"No, I won't."

Her dark eyes warmed. "No, you won't, will you?"

"Cupid?"

Her eyes drifted past me as she smiled and confessed, "My dream date would be ... okay, so I saw it in a movie and I thought it was so simple but really romantic. And perfect. This guy turned the rooftop of his city apartment into a wonderland. There were fairy lights strung everywhere, vases of flowers, flower petals, candles flickering in the dark. And in the middle of it all was a picnic. Music playing in the background." She shrugged. "How romantic to be up there in a city of millions but feel as if you're the only two people in the world. Hanging out under the stars with the one person you most want to be with." Her eyes returned to meet mine when she said the last.

And I swear my heart stopped.

"Yeah," she whispered, "the one person you want most to be with."

Valentine was looking at me like she wanted me to kiss her.

Shock, thrill, anticipation all blasted through me at the thought of her reciprocating my feelings.

Mostly, I couldn't stop staring at her mouth and thinking how I could almost taste her.

My need for her short-circuited my common sense.

I bowed my head toward her, and I felt her body press deeper into mine as she rose to meet me. Her mouth was almost on mine. Just one more breath—

"There you are!" Alison's voice was like an explosion.

Valentine and I practically jumped out of our skins. Dazed, I dragged my gaze to find my date at our side with Graham, Val's date.

"Can I cut in?" Graham glared at me before turning to Val with a smile. He pulled her across the dance floor before I could stop him.

Then Alison wrapped her arms around my neck like Valentine just had.

It didn't feel the same. Her touch didn't zing through my blood like bliss.

My attention returned to Cupid.

Our eyes met as she looked past Graham's shoulder.

"So that's why you don't date anyone seriously," Alison said.

Reluctantly, I turned my attention to her. I was being a dick, wasn't I? "Sorry?" I vowed to focus on her for the rest of the night.

She grinned, but there was a tinge of sadness to it. "You love Valentine. I always kind of suspected it, but that moment between you was so hot, there's no denying it now."

Her words were like ice through my veins. "I don't know what you're talking about."

"Don't, Micah. Only Graham and I noticed. And I won't say anything. You can't be with her. I get it. The Fairchilds have done a lot for you."

I frowned, extremely uncomfortable to have something so private known by anyone.

Alison leaned into me. "You know my mom remarried last year, right?"

Confused by the random change of subject, I nodded.

"Well, the guy she married has a son. He's a freshman in college. And I have an insanely large crush on him. Crushing on your stepbrother? Not cool. And never gonna happen. So I get it." She gave me a commiserating look.

"I'm sorry." I didn't know what else to say.

"Me too." Her arms tightened around my neck. "But that's why we have each other. To distract us from who we really want and can't have."

Sadness overwhelmed me, and I buried my head in her neck, holding her closer.

Maybe I should be more excited about college. It would get me the hell away from the torment, and maybe I could finally get over Valentine.

CHAPTER FOUR

MICAH
AGE 19

My palms were sweating.

I clenched them into fists and told myself to toughen up. Ye of so little faith. I wasn't going into battle. I was finally letting myself lose a battle I should never have been waging.

And I couldn't believe it was Mom of all people who made me see things clearly.

But last year, my mom had worked really hard to stay clean after rehab. Caroline practically forced her to stick with it, and that woman could be the most stubborn person on the planet. Sometimes that was an outstanding quality, say, for helping someone like my mom deal with addiction. Not so great for supporting (or not, in this case) her daughter.

Valentine.

The person I was on my way to see now.

As soon as she hit eighteen, Valentine moved to the city, got three jobs, and rented an apartment with a friend she'd met at a flea market two summers ago. Summer. Summer was flaky and smoked a lot of jay. I worried Val couldn't depend on her. But Valentine was a little defensive about her, so I kept my mouth shut. She was getting enough crap from her parents about her life choices on a daily basis. She didn't need me doing it too.

Part of me was a little concerned that Valentine was drifting through life, but I continually reminded myself that she wasn't me. She didn't need to know what her future might look like. There was still time for her to find the thing that made her happy. I thought she'd do something with her clothes designing, but so far she was bartending, working in a chocolate shop, and answering customer service calls for a small internet start-up.

Val seemed content.

Mostly. She got hassled a lot by her parents, which I know wasn't fun. We'd both stayed at the Fairchilds' place for Christmas, and my mom joined us. Mom and I were more than a little uncomfortable when Caroline chose Christmas Eve as the "perfect time" to give Valentine shit about her future. I thought Val's head was going to explode with rage.

Thankfully, Jim stepped in before I did and asked Caroline to promise not to say another word the entire holiday. However, it hung in the air between mother and daughter, the awful tension.

That wasn't why my palms were sweating as I made my way across town to Valentine's crappy apartment. The apartment I wanted to get her out of but knew I never could because one of the many reasons I loved her was her thousand-mile-long independent streak.

Nah, my palms were sweating because Mom had given me a big kick up the ass on Christmas Day.

. . .

HANDING Mom the rinsed plate to put in the dishwasher, I tried to think of something to say. We'd offered to clean up since Caroline and Jim had cooked. Valentine looked ready to offer to help, too, but her mom had shaken her head. It was a not-so-obvious attempt to give me and Mom alone time.

It wasn't like we hadn't been alone over the last two years. But every time I tried to speak, the well of shit that bubbled up inside just kind of choked me.

"Caroline's too hard on that girl," Mom whispered.

I gave her a sharp look.

She smirked. "Yeah, I know. Those in glass houses, right? I know I'm not in the position to judge, but ..." She glanced over her shoulder to make sure we were still alone. The Fairchilds had retreated to the family den to watch Christmas movies. "I once was Valentine. The kid among the overachievers who just wanted to experience life first. She's got more grit than me, though. I can see it in her eyes. She'll be okay. But Caroline needs to ease up, or she'll lose her like my mom lost me."

Unease niggled at me because I knew Mom wasn't wrong. "Hopefully, it won't come to that."

"Hopefully."

I moved to hand her another dish.

"She's in love with you, you know."

The dish slipped between my fingers, but Mom's reflexes were fast, and she caught it before it crashed to the floor.

She gave me a reassuring smile. "You really didn't know?"

"Valentine?" I leaned heavily against the counter.

I didn't want her opinion to give me hope, but ... I couldn't help it.

"You should tell her how you feel."

She knew I loved her back? "What?"

Mom covered my hand with hers. "Sweetheart, you two couldn't be more obvious if you tried. And yet, neither of you seems to recognize how the other feels."

"Obvious?" Did the Fairchilds suspect?

It was as if she was a mind reader. "Caroline sees only what she wants to see, but I can tell Jim knows. He just doesn't know how to feel about it."

"How can you tell Valentine feels the same?" I could barely hear anything over the pounding of my heart. I'd spent a year and a half at college trying to distract myself from the girl I'd left behind. Sometimes it felt like it was working, that the distance was helping. But I couldn't let her go. When I had time, I'd check in on her in the city, and we'd spend all day together. Then I'd find myself back at square one, fucking pining for her.

"The way she looks at you. The way she lights up from the inside out when you walk into the room. You make her feel good about herself, and I don't think many people in her life make her feel that way." Mom squeezed my hand. "I'm so proud of the person you are."

Emotion thickened my throat. "Thanks."

"Don't waste a moment of your life. Not like I did. You need to tell her, kid."

Guilt pierced me. "They've helped us. Both of us."

She knew I referred to the Fairchilds. Mom frowned. "Yeah, they have. And I'll be forever grateful for what they've done for you in particular. But that doesn't mean you owe them your happiness. So what if you and Val dating makes them a little uncomfortable at first? They should feel lucky as hell to have you being the guy sharing their girl's life. And they'll eventually come around when they recognize what a good thing it is."

So there I was. On my way to tell the girl I loved, I loved her.

It had taken me more than a few weeks to work everything out in my head. Until I realized I was wasting time overthinking everything. Mom was right. I owed the Fairchilds. But not my happiness. And not Valentine's either.

Today was Valentine's Day.

It was a little cheesy, but I thought how one day, looking back, it would make my Valentine smile.

As scared as I was, excitement and anticipation moved through me. We'd take it slow. It would be really fucking difficult not to throw her on the nearest bed after wanting her for so long, but we had to do this right. Dates and getting comfortable in a new reality together first. Sex later.

Scowling at the broken building entrance, I made a mental note to talk to her landlord and then hurried up the three flights to Valentine's apartment. Taking a deep breath and releasing it slowly, I hammered my fist on the door before I could talk myself out of this.

Hearing nothing, I deflated.

I should've called first.

But I could've sworn that this was the day she worked customer service for the internet start-up, which she did from home.

Maybe she was on a call.

Shit.

Deciding this was too important not to interrupt, I knocked again.

Finally, I heard movement beyond the door. A few seconds later, the door whipped open and a guy stood there, scowling, wearing nothing but a pair of jeans.

He looked like he was in his mid- to late-thirties.

He also definitely looked like a guy who'd just been interrupted having sex.

Summer's boyfriend?

"Can I help you?"

I bristled at his tone, wondering where the hell Val was. "Yeah, I was looking for Valentine, but I guess—"

"I'm here, I'm here!" I heard her call from the back of the apartment.

My heart plummeted as she suddenly appeared beside the older guy. She'd thrown on a dress, but there was no disguising her flushed cheeks or messy hair.

Fuck me.

It was like someone had stuck a knife in my gut.

At my silence, Valentine flushed. "Sorry. Introductions. Micah, this is Dillan. Dillan, this is Micah. Micah is a family friend. Dillan is ..." She looked up at him, her lips twitching with amusement.

The bastard smirked down at her. "Dillan is late for work." He gave her a quick kiss and disappeared down the hall, out of sight.

I stared at Valentine, trying to mute the betrayal I felt.

Because she technically hadn't betrayed me, and I would be a hypocritical bastard if I tried to say she had. In my efforts to get over her, I hadn't exactly been a monk.

We stared at each other, the silence awkward and awful.

Then the bastard returned, fully dressed. He kissed Valentine, longer, with tongue, until I wanted to rip off his fucking head. "Later, baby." He scooted past me with a knowingly smug expression, and I tightened my hands into fists at my sides to stop from lunging at him.

"Come in." Valentine broke the silence, stepping back from the doorway.

What I really wanted to do was leave.

And roar my frustration and rage out into a dark sky somewhere.

Instead, like I was on autopilot, I followed her into the run-down space that acted as both kitchen and living room.

"What brings you to my part of town?" she asked, running her fingers nervously through her hair.

I tried not to notice how kiss-stung her mouth was and

failed. Clenching my jaw, I looked away. "Just in the neighborhood. Thought I'd stop by. Didn't mean to ... interrupt."

"Oh, it's fine."

"Who is he?" I picked up a book from the side table. A romance novel. I assumed it was Val's. Pretending to read the blurb, I waited for her to speak.

"He's my boss. He owns the bar I bartend at."

Disbelief scored through me.

Was she fucking kidding?

I turned to face her. "Are you insane?"

She flinched like I'd slapped her. "What?"

"Cupid, how could you be so stupid? You don't fuck your boss." My anger took over. "Jesus, he looks twice your age. Too old for you. And is he too married for you too? Is that the reason for the clandestine fuck in the middle of the day? Are you really that much of a screwup?"

The color drained from Valentine's cheeks.

The hurt and betrayal in her gaze was worse than anything I was feeling.

I wanted to take back what I'd said. It was ugly. It was so fucking ugly. Assumptions based on nothing but jealousy and rage.

Tears filled her eyes, and I hated myself.

"Val—"

She raised a palm. "Don't. Now I know ... now I know what you really think of me. I ..." She brushed away her tears angrily and huffed, "I always thought you were the one person who really saw me. But you're just like them. And I've decided I don't need people in my life who make me feel like a failure." She stormed toward the door and threw it open, gesturing for me to leave. "You can go."

"Valentine, I didn't—"

"You can't take it back." She shrugged miserably. "It's out there now. Always between us."

"That's not ... I was just surprised ... I didn't expect—"

"Just stop, Micah."

Everything I wanted to say wouldn't come out.

I left.

And I would curse myself for years to come for not telling her right at that moment that I was in love with her, I was a jealous bastard, and it had made me say things I didn't mean.

CHAPTER FIVE

MICAH
AGE 22

The table, as always, was covered in delicious goodness. Turkey, ham, chicken. Stuffing, mashed potatoes, candied yams, sweet potato casserole, green bean casserole, corn bread. Not to mention the three kinds of pie for dessert: pecan, pumpkin, and chocolate.

The Fairchilds always went all out on Thanksgiving.

But that wasn't the reason I always came back.

I was a graduate student and had my own place in Boston with a few of the guys I'd met in college. All of them but Wells went home for Thanksgiving. I could've stayed with him.

However, I had hope.

That she would be there.

She never was.

Caroline had inadvertently pushed Valentine away as much as I had.

Not that she didn't stay in contact. We emailed. We texted. It wasn't the same. But it was something.

She talked with Jim too.

And for some reason, I really thought she'd be here this year. She was turning twenty-one in January ... time was slipping away.

Mom was the only one who noticed my disappointment when I realized Valentine wasn't coming. She didn't say anything. The one good thing that had come out of the last few years, other than me getting closer to becoming a qualified architect, was my mom. We were closer. We were building trust again.

"Didn't Valentine say she'd call?" her grandmother asked for the ninetieth time. "A child who feels loved and wanted would have called by now."

If Caroline came down hard on Val, her mother came down hard on her. She'd been making these little digs at Caroline for the past three Thanksgivings.

"My daughter knows I love her." Caroline glared at her mom.

Caroline's dad tsked. "Your mother means nothing by it. Lose the tone, Caro."

Shit.

"I don't have a tone." She sniffed and stuffed more food into her mouth.

Jim stared forlornly at his dinner plate.

They missed their kid.

I missed her too.

Mom and I shifted uncomfortably.

"I'm not saying you weren't right to guide her on her future, but you have to know when to let go and just let your child make her own mistakes."

"I know that, Mother."

"And Valentine seems perfectly happy. That's all anyone can ask for."

"Really? Because when I was growing up, you made it clear that my happiness depended upon how successful I was in life and thus how proud I made *you*."

"Jesus," Mom murmured under her breath.

Things were about to go south.

A sharp ringing from the TV on the wall behind Jim jolted us.

"Oh, thank God," Jim muttered. "That'll be Val." He tapped his phone as he turned toward the TV, and suddenly Valentine's beautiful, beaming face filled the screen.

"Happy Thanksgiving!" she cried, waving at us.

"Happy Thanksgiving!" we called back.

I was so busy staring at her face, it took me a minute to register the background.

"Where are you?" Jim asked.

Although it was dark out, palm trees blew in the breeze behind her.

And she was wearing a white dress.

Valentine giggled. "I have a surprise. I'm in Cancun."

"Mexico?" Caroline asked, leaning toward the screen. Her face paled. "Valentine ... what is that on your left hand?"

Her dimples popped as dread filled me.

She raised her left hand, showing off the gold wedding band, and then a guy stepped into the shot. A guy in a tuxedo. Holding her close. Like she was his. "Louis and I got married!"

The room erupted.

Dazed, I barely registered what was being shouted at the television by both parents and grandparents.

Valentine had only been seeing this guy for three months.

He owned a comic book store. That was all I'd known about him.

Her parents thought he was a loser.

Her grandparents changed their tune, said Valentine was wasting her life.

I could hear her arguing with them, but I couldn't look at her.

I got up from my seat and was leaving the room when I heard her shout at them she didn't need their approval. From the way the four of them turned on each other, I assumed Valentine had cut off the video.

Feeling sick to my stomach, I grabbed my coat with my car keys and rushed outside for a deep gulp of crisp, cold, fresh air.

I stopped for a minute on the front lawn, trying to catch my breath.

Instead, my mom caught up with me.

"Micah."

I turned to her.

I guessed everything I was feeling must've shown because her face crumpled. "I'm so sorry, baby."

Mom embraced me, and I held on as tight as I could. Tears burned in my eyes and throat until I knew I had to leave, or I was going to lose it.

As I drove back to Boston that night, I vowed I would stop loving Valentine and finally, finally, move the fuck on.

CHAPTER SIX

VALENTINE
AGE 26

Over the years, I'd told myself I'd give up my addiction.
It was always a lie.

And for the millionth time, I found myself internet stalking Micah Green.

Scrolling through his Instagram, I think a masochistic part of me got off on the unbearable sense of longing and regret I felt every time I saw his smile. Like I deserved to feel that way for having screwed up my early twenties. Not that removing people who make you feel bad about yourself is screwing up. Like my parents, Micah wrote me off as a failure, something my brief marriage and subsequent divorce only seemed to prove.

My grandparents were a little more forgiving, so I still had contact with them. Dad tried. He never stopped trying. And honestly, I think it would break my heart all over again if he did. Yet, I still didn't totally trust him not to hurt me.

I snorted bitterly. I still didn't completely trust anyone not to hurt me.

Sometimes I didn't even trust myself.

It was hard to after I'd thrown myself into one romantic relationship after the other, hoping to forget the object of my unrequited love. I guessed I thought if I was enthusiastic enough that I would really fall in love with one of them. I talked myself into being in love with my ex-husband, Louis. But Louis turned out to be a giant man-child. And he cheated on me. The only good thing to come from that relationship was Mindy.

I'd met my best friend Mindy at one of Louis's theme nights at the comic store. We both loved retro clothing, and we both designed and created our own. It took us a few years to save and get our finances in place, but we finally opened our dream boutique clothing store.

And it was an enormous hit in the neighborhood. Plus, we made a killing because of our large Instagram following. We'd had to employ a small team of seamstresses and admin staff just to help us fulfill our online orders.

I'd proven my parents and Micah wrong. While I'd cut my parents out of my life after my marriage (and subsequent divorce), Micah had cut me out of his. For a while, I wondered (hoped?) that maybe my feelings weren't unrequited, and he was angry and hurt. Like the way he'd look at me sometimes ... or the night at prom when I could've sworn he was going to kiss me. And the way he reacted to Dillan, the idiot boss I had a short fling with.

After Micah had left that day and I'd calmed down, I wondered if it was jealousy that made him lash out. I went back and forth, arguing with myself that what I'd felt from him in those moments was real versus me just projecting my unrequited feelings onto him.

Mom finally solved my inner turmoil by giving me the cold, hard truth about Micah.

During one of my many arguments with her, she'd yelled at me that even Micah didn't want me in his life because I was too similar to how his mom used to be. Unpredictable, unreliable, and a screwup.

A screwup.

That was what he had called me.

And it hurt.

I couldn't even tell you how much that hurt to hear my mother repeat it all over again.

Mom tried to apologize. To say she didn't mean it.

People who loved each other said hurtful things in the heat of the moment. But my problem with my mom was that it happened too damn much to be healthy.

Fuck, it killed, but I had to cut those ties.

Just like Micah cut his ties with me.

So why couldn't I let him go?

My life was good! I had my own business at twenty-six, a successful one.

Why did I care if Micah was sexier than ever or laughing in the Commons with his model-like girlfriend of the hour? Though, to be fair, this one had been around longer than the others. According to his Instagram, the elegant "E" had been in his life for six months.

E was exactly Micah's type. Tall, stunning, brunette, and according to his comments about her, very smart.

What he considered my opposite.

He was right about everything but the smarts. I was way over letting people make me think I wasn't intelligent just because I wasn't academic. And I might not be stunning, but

I wasn't exactly hard to look at. Some guys liked the whole adorable, curvy, quirky thing I had going on.

"Ugh." I glowered at a candid photograph he'd posted of himself hugging a mind-bending building in Peru. He faced the camera, grinning that boyish smile. He looked happy.

That summer, he and his girlfriend along with another couple had taken a trip to Peru to tour the amazing architecture. Micah looked like he was having the time of his life.

He was a stranger now.

Sadness enveloped me.

"Dear God, you're stalking him again." Mindy's voice right at my ear made me jump a mile.

"Fuck!" I glared at her. "You're a sneaky ninja."

She grinned, showing off the cute gap between her two front teeth. "No ... you were just lost in your mooning again over he who shall not be named."

I turned my phone over on the boutique checkout counter. "No, I'm not."

My best friend gave me a knowing look. "Uh, yeah, you are. But I have just the thing to distract you."

"Oh?"

She whipped out her phone, tapped the screen a few times, and then shoved it in my face. I stared into the smoldering, dark gaze of a very cute indie band front man-looking dude.

"His name is Ville, and he saw you on our Instagram page and is obsessed with you. He asked for your number."

"Ville and Val. Really?"

"What? His parents are Finnish."

"Mindy—"

"Don't Mindy me. He's a recent friend of Xander's." Xander was Mindy's longtime boyfriend. "Xander approves of him. Says he's a nice guy. An up-and-coming artist. They've shown his work in galleries. He's not some bum, I promise."

"Let me see his photo again."

She grinned and practically squealed as she handed over her phone. I scrolled through his Instagram. He didn't seem to be a poser, which was good. A lot of the photos were of his art, which was also quite good. "He's talented."

"Is that a 'yes, I'll go on a double date with you and Xander and in five years' time thank you for setting me up with the man who gave me my babies Vilandra and Veronica'?"

I shook my head, laughing at her nonsense. "Let's just try the double date first."

"Whoop!" She did a little happy dance. "I'll let Xander know. I'm in such a good mood now, I'm even going to do a stock check."

"Wins all around." I hated stock checking.

"I THINK the size 10 is a perfect fit."

"I don't need the 12? You're sure?"

"You go with the size 12, you lose the shape. You have such a cute waist. Why not show it off?"

My customer smiled, uncertain. "Really?"

"That's just my opinion. You're the one wearing the dress, and you have to be comfortable in it."

She sighed and turned to the mirror, studying her lush figure in the tight-fitting '50s pencil dress. "Maybe I should try the flare dress again."

I nodded patiently. We'd been in the changing rooms for thirty minutes trying to decide on an outfit, but it was for her ex's wedding, so I understood—this dress needed to be perfect.

After handing her a couple of dresses that required a petticoat underneath to give that awesome '50s prom-dress vibe, I heard the antique bell over the shop door tinkle loudly.

"I might have to disappear for a second to deal with another customer," I told her.

"Oh, of course. You've been amazing."

I walked toward the front from the changing rooms and heard a loud, female voice say, "Oh, this place is perfect. Jenny was right."

The compliment made me smile, proud.

"We'll definitely find something for the '50s costume–theme dinner. I wonder if they only do women's costumes."

Costumes?

My smile abruptly disappeared as I strode out to see who this person was that thought my store could only possibly be a costume store.

A tall, heterosexual couple stood holding hands with their backs to me while the woman studied a silk prom dress.

"This isn't a costume shop," I announced to the back of their heads.

Then they turned to me.

And it felt like the shop floor disappeared out from beneath my feet.

Micah.

Standing in my store.

Holding the hand of the stunning E from his Instagram.

"You're, like ... kidding, right?" E dragged her gaze down my body and back up again. I wore a purple pencil dress with a stiff white bow attached to the low neckline. "People actually dress like this? Like, every day?"

"Elizabeth," Micah warned.

What was he doing here? "Micah."

"Valentine."

"Oh, you two know each other?" Elizabeth narrowed her eyes.

Micah gave her a quick look before returning his stony stare to me. "Valentine is the Fairchilds' daughter."

"Oh. I almost forgot they had one."

She knew my parents?

Anger bristled across my shoulders, but I didn't let her see. I didn't let him see. "How can I help you?"

Elizabeth stepped forward, her condescending gaze darting from one item to the next. "Well, we've been invited to a '50s theme dinner. I'm looking for something ... chic. Maybe I'm in the wrong place, though."

"Funny, a second ago, I thought I heard you say this place was perfect."

She gave me a shark's grin. "Sometimes something that looks pretty at first looks a little cheap on closer inspection."

God, he really knew how to pick 'em. "Yeah ... I often think people's souls are a lot like that. You know, beauty on the outside, a whole bunch of ugly on the inside."

Her eyes flashed, but she shrugged. "Whatever." A black dress I'd designed myself drew her attention. It was reminiscent of Audrey Hepburn's famous black dress in *Breakfast at Tiffany's*. "Ooh, this might be perfect." She released Micah's hand to hurry over to it. "Do you have this in a size 2?"

Minutes later, she'd wandered off to the changing room, dress in hand, and I was alone with Micah.

The air crackled with animosity as we glowered at each other. He was dressed stylishly in a fitted coat, dark jeans, and black ankle boots. His hair was different, shaved close at the sides, a little longer on top. He even had some fashionable stubble that I really wanted to mock but couldn't. I didn't mock, no matter how angry I was. Mocking was petty. When I insulted a person, the insult was direct, true, and based on my grievance with them.

I hated how good he looked.

Finally, I blurted, "Did you know this place was mine?"

He shrugged. "I'd heard something."

The old hurt and defensiveness rose at his casual dismissal of my business. "Clearly it doesn't meet your standards of success, but we're doing really great, actually."

Anger clouded his handsome face. "What the hell does 'it doesn't meet my standards of success' mean?"

Oh, don't play the innocent. "You and your catty girlfriend, coming in here and mocking it as a costume store."

Micah looked away, guilt flickering across his expression. "She meant nothing by it."

"Oh, please. Your girlfriend was being condescending. But then it doesn't surprise me. She's absolutely your type."

If he could have fried my ass with the heat of his glare, he would have. "What the hell does that mean? I don't see you in years, and I get this shit? What the fuck is that?"

Don't ask me where my bravery came from or why I decided to put it out there ... all I knew was that I'd had enough of Micah pretending to be someone he wasn't. A perpetually good guy! He wasn't. I'd had enough pretending that he hadn't hurt me. "It means that the whole time I've known you, you've always been attracted to style over substance."

"That's not true." He took a step toward me. If the air crackled before, it was snapping and angry and electric now.

"Yeah?" I stepped toward him too. "I like to think I'm a pretty great person no matter what you or my parents think. I'm good, I'm kind, I'm hardworking, and I don't shit on people to get ahead in life. But that still wasn't good enough for Micah Green. All of it didn't come with long legs, a shitty attitude, and lethal ambition."

Just like that, he froze. The color bled from his cheeks. His voice sounded hoarse when he said, "What are you talking about?"

I was on a roll. The word vomit kept pouring. "Oh, come

on. You knew. Everyone knew. Even my parents knew I was in love with you. But you made it clear which side of the fence you were on in that situation, didn't you? It was perfect for all of you. My parents got the kid they always wanted, and you got rid of the pathetic girl who made you uncomfortable mooning over you all the time. Because that's what I was to you—a chubby failure. God forbid Micah Green think with anything other than his dick when it comes to women."

I gestured to the changing room to emphasize my point. "The girlfriend—I barely even know her, and I can already tell you that her beauty is only skin-deep, baby. Have a nice life with that." I marched into the stock room, leaving him gaping at me in disbelief. I trembled from head to foot, but I felt triumphant.

I felt like a weight had been lifted off me.

I'd finally said, in less than two minutes, everything I'd ever wanted to say to him.

Everything he never thought I'd have the guts to say to his face.

After explaining to Mindy I needed her to cover the store because Micah was out there, I headed up to our apartment above it.

No more internet stalking. No more pining for a guy who was never really the right guy.

It was time to date again, this time with conviction.

I wasn't sure Ville would be Mr. Right, but at least this time I'd give a guy a real shot.

CHAPTER SEVEN

MICAH
AGE 27

"*Oh, come on. You knew. Everyone knew. Even my parents knew I was in love with you.*"

I shook my head, trying to get Valentine's voice out of it.

I couldn't.

It had been three days since our altercation in her store.

Three days since my whole fucking life got turned upside down.

"*Because that's what I was to you—a chubby failure. God forbid Micah Green think with anything other than his dick when it comes to women.*"

Squeezing my eyes closed, I tried to shove her words away.

Tried not to care.

But this ache in my chest, deep and gnawing, wouldn't shift.

"You look like you're in physical pain."

Opening my eyes, I found my best friend and roommate, Wells, standing at my side. It amazed us both the same firm offered us jobs after we graduated. We'd interned at Watkins & Holtz but never expected we'd both get something permanent there. Their firm specialized in making eco-living beautiful and interesting, an aesthetic Wells and I sought to achieve in our designs.

"I think I am."

He sipped his champagne, following my gaze to Elizabeth. She was across the room, elegant in the chic black dress she bought from Valentine. When Valentine's business partner, Mindy, took over for Val in the shop, she'd told Elizabeth the dress was Valentine's design. I swear Elizabeth wasn't going to buy it when she heard that, but her better side won out.

And whatever Valentine had said about Elizabeth, she did have a better side.

Problem was, that side of her was never fully engaged.

I hadn't just come to this conclusion because of Val's split-second judgment of my girlfriend. Elizabeth's attitude had been bothering me for months. Yet I felt caught. I'd made the stupid mistake of saying yes to a date with the daughter of Richard Meyer, a partner at the firm. He set us up. I thought it was a great idea. Elizabeth was sexy as hell, smart, and independent. However, for the last few months, I'd pushed her snide comments about almost everyone to the side.

She had her moments of kindness too.

Elizabeth did a lot of work for charity organizations.

"You can break it off with her, you know." Wells turned to me, a knowing look on his face. "Richard won't fire you. Look, I saw it in Peru, man. The woman is gorgeous, but she can be downright nasty. And controlling. Every time she swapped out the food you ordered for a salad, I thought my head was going to explode. Cherry can't stand her. She almost left Peru because of her."

Cherry was Wells's girlfriend, a sustainability expert we'd met through our work.

We'd spent three weeks in Peru touring the country to study the architecture. Our firm had actually let us do it as research. It was supposed to be the time of our lives, but tension had seethed among the four of us toward the end of the trip. I hadn't realized it was all down to Elizabeth. "You should've said something."

"I didn't think I needed to."

"I saw Valentine," I blurted out.

Wells knew all about Valentine Fairchild. And how I'd felt about her. His eyes widened. "When?"

"E saw her store online and wanted to visit. I didn't know how to say no."

"More like you didn't want to say no."

I shrugged. "Okay, I admit I wanted to see her."

"And?"

I felt like I was going to throw up. "While E was in the changing room ... Val let me have it. Basically implied I'm a shallow piece of shit because I'd rather have someone like E than someone like her."

"What the hell?"

I looked him straight in the eye. "She outright said she used to be in love with me ... and she said I knew it. That everyone knew it. But I didn't want her because she didn't meet my shallow standards."

Wells looked like he'd been punched in the gut for me. "Fuck, man. What did you say?"

"I didn't say a thing. I was in shock. And then she walked out."

We were quiet a moment as we watched Elizabeth move

through the crowd of employees and their other halves, a born hostess.

Then Wells said, "It's not on you. She obviously doesn't know you that well, after all."

"I pushed her away because of her parents. I called her a screwup. I cut her out of my life when she married that prick." My heart hammered. "I could have prevented all of it if I'd just grown a pair and told her how I felt. So it is on me."

"How do you feel about her now?"

Remembering how every part of me came alive as soon as I saw Valentine the other day, I knew the answer. Not only that but I'd been internet stalking her for years. Scrolled through her Instagram and Facebook photos until my eyes blurred. After her divorce, I wanted to go to her, but I'd been afraid it would send me back to that place where I constantly pined for her. With distance, the pining was kept at a minimum.

Yet in doing that, I'd broken her heart as much as she'd broken mine.

"I need to end things with Elizabeth."

Wells clapped me on the shoulder. "About damn time."

THE RIGHT THING TO do after breaking up with your girlfriend was to wait at least a month before moving on, right?

I could barely wait a week. I guessed that made me a prick.

But the heart wants what it wants.

I'd promised I'd give it some time before I went to Valentine to clear the air between us. But I'd been home on a Friday night, working on some plans for a couple who were building an eco-home on a tiny plot of land in Beacon Hill at the end of one of the historical row houses. It was a miracle we'd even gotten planning permission.

Wells and Cherry were out on a date.

Fingers itching, I reached for my phone and opened Instagram. The first photo on my feed was from Elizabeth's account. She hadn't blocked me.

Now I knew why.

The photo was of her kissing a guy in what looked like a nightclub. The caption stated, "He's a better kisser than the last guy I dumped."

Nice.

Elizabeth wasn't exactly devastated when we broke up. She was more pissed off that *I'd* ended things.

"You do not get to break up with me. No one breaks up with me. I'm ending this. And don't think for one second you can come crawling back when you realize what an epic mistake you just made."

She'd swaggered out of the café as if she'd been told her favorite store didn't carry her shoe size anymore, not like she'd just ended a six-month relationship.

Not gonna lie, her reaction made me feel like less of a prick.

And if she wanted to tell the world she dumped me, have at it.

I shook my head, disbelieving I'd wasted Peru on her, and typed Valentine's name into the search. Finding her account, I tapped on her latest photo and felt that goddamn ache grip me tight.

She was out with Mindy tonight. She'd posted a selfie of them in a bar and tagged the location.

Jesus, she was so beautiful, it killed me.

Those dimples.

Those sultry eyes.

My attention moved to the location tag. They were in a bar near here.

Screw it.

Not fifteen minutes later, I pushed through the door of the crowded bar, searching the patrons' faces.

I found Valentine sitting in a booth across from Mindy. There was a guy next to Val's friend but Valentine sat alone. I worked through the crowd and didn't even say hi before I slid onto the bench next to her.

She looked up at me in shock. She'd pulled her hair into a high ponytail, elongating her eyes, which already looked huge and "come fuck me" because of her eyeliner. I loved Val's style. It was feminine and sexy, and she did not know just how much of both.

"Hey, Cupid." I gave her a coaxing smile.

A bunch of emotions flashed across her face, none of them positive. Fuck. "What are you doing here?"

"Saw you here, thought I'd say hi." I looked at her friend Mindy and the guy I recognized from their shop's Instagram account. It was Mindy's boyfriend, Xander. Christ, I sounded like a stalker. I shouldn't know these things. "Hey, Mindy." I held out my hand to Xander. "Nice to meet you. I'm Micah."

Xander peered at me warily through his thick, black-framed glasses but shook my hand. "Hey. Xander."

"Uh ... dude, you're in my seat."

Glancing up, my stomach dropped. A tall, wiry, good-looking guy was frowning down at me, a tray of drinks in his hands.

This was a double date.

Valentine was on a date.

And this guy was exactly her type.

No, I reminded myself. You *are her type.*

I would not repeatedly make the same mistake.

Feigning ignorance, I grinned and shimmied closer to Valentine, forcing her along the bench toward the wall.

"Plenty of room for three." There was no way I was letting him sit beside her.

I was pretty sure I heard Mindy cover a snort of laughter with her hand.

"I'm Micah," I said as the indie guy reluctantly slid in beside me and passed out the drinks.

"Uh ... Ville."

I grinned at the thought. "Ville and Val? Really?"

"What are you doing?" Valentine hissed under her breath.

I ignored her. "How long have you two known each other?"

"First date." Ville flicked a wary look at me and then Val.

Excellent. Definitely wasn't going to feel bad about messing this up for him, then.

I turned to Valentine, looked into her huge, dark eyes, and I realized at that moment that I couldn't waste another eleven years of my life. If I didn't say something now, even if it was humiliating and she rejected me, I would end up without her. And if I said what needed to be said and I still ended up without her, then at least I could say I actually goddamn tried.

"I broke up with Elizabeth."

Valentine gaped at me. "What?"

"You were right. Not about why I was with her or that a woman needs to look or be a certain way before she interests me," I said, glaring at her for those unfair comments. "But that sometimes she could be a not-nice person. And I didn't want to be with someone like that."

Valentine stiffened. "Good for you."

"You were wrong about everything else."

Her eyes flashed angrily. "I don't think so."

"Then you don't know me as well as you think you do."

"Did you or did you not call me a screwup and then cut me out of your life when I married Louis?"

"Wait, you were married?" Ville peered around me to ask.

Mindy put her palm up to his face, her gaze fixed on us. "Shush it, Valo."

"What? It's Ville."

"Ssshh." She cut him a pleading look and turned back to me, leaning in. "Continue."

I tried not to laugh as I turned to Valentine. She'd transferred her glower to her best friend. "*I* was the screwup. I was jealous and pissed, and rather than manning up and admitting how I really felt, I let you go. But you should know, I have never regretted anything more in my life. And God, Cupid, I have missed the hell out of you."

Angry tears filled her eyes. "You can't do this to me."

"Hey, look, I'm clearly in the middle of something here," Ville said loudly, pushing away from the table. "I'm just gonna go."

"No!" Valentine turned to me, her expression furious. "You go."

"I can't do that."

Her eyes widened in shock.

"Yeah, okay, see you." Ville stalked off, pushing through the crowded bar.

That was fine with me.

Triumphant, I turned to Val.

She looked ready to kill me.

I could deal with that.

"Don't look so smug. And let me out of here." She pushed at my chest. "Seriously ... I'm feeling claustrophobic."

Sensing her genuine panic, I winced and slid from the booth to let her out. "Cupid—"

"Don't call me that!" She shoved past me, her face crumpling just before she rushed away.

I moved to follow her, but suddenly, Mindy was in my face, holding me off. Xander turned out to be at least two inches taller than me, and he stood at Mindy's back like her bodyguard.

I wasn't getting past them without going through him first.

Great. I didn't think beating up Val's friend would endear her to me.

"I didn't mean to ..." I ran a hand through my hair in exasperation. "I didn't come here to upset her."

"Why did you come here?" Mindy didn't look accusatory. In fact, her entire attitude tonight made me think I could have an ally in her.

"Because our wires have been crossed for more than a goddamn decade. And I came here to clear the air. To be honest. Didn't quite work out."

"Val is just pissed because you have the power to hurt her," Mindy admitted. "But don't stop trying. As long as you don't plan to hurt her, don't stop trying."

"I don't plan to hurt her. I plan to love her."

She grinned, her blue eyes brightening. "Then don't give up. We'll be at a vintage market in Somerville on Saturday. I'll DM you the address on Instagram."

Feeling a lot more hopeful than I was minutes ago, I raised an eyebrow and teased, "You know my Instagram account?"

"Oh, please ... you clearly stalked Val's Instagram to find us here. The fact that she stalks you should come as no surprise."

"She stalks me?" I grinned.

She rolled her eyes. "You two are hopeless. You better be there on Saturday, Green."

"Oh, I'll be there."

CHAPTER EIGHT

VALENTINE

"What do you think of this one?" I held up a '50s raffia handbag. "It needs a little TLC, but I think we could make this beautiful *and* make a killing on it." At the answering silence, I turned to Mindy to find her scanning the outdoor market. Was she looking for someone or something? "What's with you? You've been distracted all morning."

Mindy whirled, her short, dark curls flying around her face. "I'm not distracted. You said something about a bag?"

I held it up. "You are definitely distracted."

"How much?" She turned the tag and frowned. "Let me try to whittle the price down first."

I let her take the bag to the seller because she was better at haggling than I was, and turned to see if the woman was selling other accessories with potential.

"Do you think this is too yellow for me?"

The familiar voice caught me off guard.

My eyes flew up from the bin I was raking through to find Micah on the opposite side of it, holding a yellow bikini top to his chest. What the hell was he doing here?

I straightened, my hands flying to my hips. "I think it's too 'in Somerville' for you. What are you doing here?"

First, he hunted me down using Instagram (according to Mindy) and ruined my date, and now he was here? I hadn't posted I was at this market.

How did he—

Mindy!

Whipping my head in her direction, I found her watching us with avid interest. At my glare, she gave me a half grimace, half smile, waved the bag at me as if in triumph, and then darted off.

That little interfering ... "I'm going to kill her."

"Don't." Micah dumped the bikini back in the bin and stepped into my space. I wanted to retreat, but that would only prove he affected me. "She's just trying to help."

"Help with what? Mess with my head again?"

He frowned down at me. His gray eyes were too easy to drown in. I wanted to look away. I didn't want to be sucked back in. "Why did you say what you said in your store if you didn't want to clear the air between us?"

"I said what I said because it was true, and I wanted you to know I know what kind of person you really are."

Hurt flashed in his eyes and guilt crushed me. "You don't really mean that."

"Micah, why are you here?"

"You know why." He took hold of my upper arms and bent his head toward mine. His expression was everything I'd ever wanted from him when he looked at me. Yet now that I had it, I was terrified. "You have to know that I have always felt the same way. From the moment I first saw you."

I shook my head.

"I just ... for so long, I felt like I owed your parents. I didn't want to upset them."

"So you wanted me. Just not enough?"

His grip on me tightened. "You remember the day I came to see you? It was Valentine's Day, and when I got to your apartment, you had that guy there. Your boss."

"Hard to forget. You assumed some pretty not-nice things."

"What I should have said"—Micah pulled me closer, his breathing uneven—"was that I was sorry. I was saying all those shitty things because I had come over to tell you I loved you and I wanted to be with you. And I was angry and jealous as hell."

Oh my God. I'd been right all along, and I'd let my mother make me think differently.

"Micah." All that time wasted. "You should have said something. He was just a fling! If you had just *said* something—"

"I know. I know." He wrapped me in his arms, burying his face in my neck with a groan. Was this happening? It felt so surreal. "Christ, I know. You have no idea how much I wished I'd said something."

"I should have said something too," I whispered, softening beneath his touch. I couldn't let him take all the blame. "It's on me too."

"Go on a date with me."

I stepped out of his embrace at the abrupt demand. My heart raced. Excited butterflies sprung to life in my stomach. But fear had a tight grip on me.

Micah had the power to devastate me.

And too many people I'd loved had hurt me already.

I didn't know if I could trust that he wouldn't do it again. "We're too different."

He scowled. "That's bullshit."

I let out a huff of laughter. "It would never work. It's been years, Micah. We're strangers now."

"No. We're two sides of the same coin. We got split in half for a while, but we'll fit good as new again if you'll let it happen."

Why did he have to be so romantic? "You have to mean this, Micah. This can't just be because you miss me and are confusing our old friendship for something else."

"We were never friends."

I flinched like he'd hit me.

"I mean," he hurried to explain, "I never just thought of you as a friend. I don't go around fantasizing about making love to my friends."

Heat stained my cheeks. "Oh."

He studied my reaction and his grin turned wicked. "If we're putting the truth out there, I have been thinking about doing very dirty things to you since the moment I moved down the hall from your bedroom."

I burst into laughter, covering my hot face with my hands.

Was this really happening?

Gentle but strong fingers curled around my wrists and gave them a little tug. I let Micah lower them.

"Go on a date with me. Just one date."

"I need to think about it."

Micah winced. "Cupid, we have been overthinking this since the moment we met. Please. Just one date."

His eyes were big and pleading.

Jesus, he was too handsome for his own good. I groaned, feeling my defenses crumble. "Okay. One date. Just one."

WEDNESDAY, September 22

. . .

MICAH: Three days until I see you again.

Val: U're really committed to this daily countdown thing, huh?

Micah: I'm ignoring your lack of enthusiasm.

Val: That bodes well.

Micah: Trust me, when I'm inside you, you'll be voraciously enthused.

Val: Cocky much? Just try to make it thru the 1st (only?) date, Green.

Micah: I can't fucking wait. And 1st of many. Definitely not only.

THURSDAY, September 23

MICAH: Are your favorite chocolates still Ferrero Rocher?

Val: Yes. Y?

Micah: Are your favorite flowers still peonies?

Val: What r u up 2?

Micah: Peonies?

Val: Yes.

Micah: Send me a pic. I miss your face.

Val: Sent. Send me one too. I may or may not miss urs back.

Micah: You look beautiful. You always look beautiful.

Val: Thank u. U look srsly hot. Damn u.

Micah: 🍫 You're so romantic, Cupid.

Val: I thought that was romantic!

FRIDAY, September 24

. . .

VAL: So can u at least tell me how I should dress for this supersecret date?

Micah: Dress like you.

Val: Helpful.

Micah: I thought so.

Val: I might dress like Catwoman.

Micah: Yes! Do that!

Val: I'm not dressing like Catwoman.

Micah: Yeah, maybe keep that one for the bedroom.

Val: Aw, in ur dreams, Green.

Micah: Since I was 16.

Val: 😼

SATURDAY, *September 25*

Micah: I can't believe I get to go on a date with you tonight.

I STARED down at the text I hadn't answered since this morning. I hadn't known what to say. What I really wanted to say was, "Me too! I'm a ball of nerves and excitement and feel like all my romantic dreams are coming true."

But if I said that, then I was opening myself up to being hurt before we even went on the date.

A knock sounded on my apartment door, and I almost jumped out of my skin. Mindy had taken off with Xander after we closed up shop for the day. She said my nervous energy was making her restless.

I understood. I was "vibing big-time," as Mindy would say.

Taking a deep breath, I shook out my hands and cast one last look at my reflection in the long mirror that hung on the wall near our front door. Instead of my every day '50s look,

I'd bought a dress for the occasion. It was not my usual style but when I tried it on, it made me feel beautiful. Mindy convinced me to buy it. It was a deep red that contrasted well with my blond hair and it was long and flowy. The sleeves were full but tight at the wrist and it had a flattering neckline that showed more than a hint of cleavage.

I'd left my hair down, curled into soft waves with my flat iron, and had spent almost an hour on my makeup.

The truth was, I'd never gone to this much effort for a guy before. And I didn't mean the time I'd invested in my appearance. There was a hell of a lot of emotional investment here.

Please be worth it, Micah.

Micah stood on the other side of the door when I opened it, his hands in the pockets of his coat. He was wearing a dark-gray waistcoat that matched his suit pants.

Minus the newsboy cap, he looked straight out of the TV show, *Peaky Blinders.*

It was hot.

He was HOT.

Reaching for my coat, I returned his soft smile. His eyes filled with as much anticipation as I felt.

"Let me." He stepped into the apartment and took my coat.

With my back to him, I bit my lip, admitting only to myself how much I enjoyed his gentlemanly manners. I'd never had a date hold a door open for me before, never mind help me into my coat. Once I had my arms in the sleeves, Micah settled his hands on my shoulders and gave me a little squeeze. "You ready?"

I turned to him, inhaling his spicy, delicious cologne. He was close enough to kiss. "I'm ready."

Those gorgeous gray eyes of his dropped to my mouth.

The air crackled between us.

"Should we go?" I whispered, just as he seemed to lean in for a kiss.

Micah blinked rapidly, as if coming out of a daze. He stepped back. "Yeah. Uh, yeah, let's go."

Outside, he hailed a cab and when we got inside, he gave the driver an address I didn't recognize. "Where are we going?"

Micah smiled and reached for my hand. "You'll see."

I stared at our entwined hands as we sat in tense silence while the cabbie made his way through the city. It wasn't tense as in *bad*; it was tense as in *electric*. Micah casually brushed his thumb over the top of my hand, back and forth, back and forth. Shivers sprinkled down my spine at the caress.

He was turning me on with a mere touch.

I didn't know if I let out a disgruntled sigh or what, but Micah smiled at me, somewhat smugly. He raised our hands to his lips and kissed the back of mine.

I melted.

Oh, yeah ... minutes into the date and already he was getting behind my defenses.

Dangerous, dangerous man.

Thankfully, fifteen minutes later, the car stopped in front of a block of red-brick apartments in Allston. After Micah paid the cabbie, I stood on the sidewalk, staring up at the building. "Where are we?"

Micah took hold of my hand and repeated, "You'll see."

As he led me into the building and up the stairs, I worried that he'd brought me to his apartment for our first date. It was not only presumptuous; it was way too fast. Heart racing, I bit my tongue, hoping I was wrong.

We reached the top floor and then passed through a door at the end of the hall; it led to a dark flight of stairs.

Confused, I stayed quiet and followed him up. He pushed open the door at the top, leading us out onto the roof.

Shock. Amazement. Wonder flooded me.

The roof had been transformed into a fairy-tale wonderland.

Garden trellises covered with flowers and strung with ropes upon ropes of fairy lights created a cocoon around a picnic area. There were candles placed here and there, too, their flames dancing in the soft breeze.

Pots and vases of peonies covered the space, and in the middle of the trellis arrangement was a fur blanket with a picnic basket. Beside it were several bowls of golden-wrapped Ferrero Rocher, as well as an ice bucket complete with champagne and two champagne flutes beside it.

And soft indie rock music played from a dock beside the picnic basket.

My dream date.

He remembered.

I didn't expect to react like I did.

The sob burst out of me.

Suddenly, I was in Micah's arms as I cried against his chest. "Cupid, tell me these are good tears?"

I nodded, unable to speak through the intense emotion clogging my throat.

Micah's voice was gruff. "I have loved you for a very long time."

Finally, I raised my head, my fear still prodding me even as I felt myself letting go. "You don't know me anymore."

"I do," he replied fiercely, his grip on me tightening. "I know you. And I miss you like crazy. I've been walking around for years missing a piece of me, an immense piece of me. And that emptiness won't go away unless I have you. I know I promised not to push, not to move too fast, but I needed you to know—"

I pulled his head down to mine and cut off his desperate words with a kiss.

He groaned, lifting me into it, turning it wild and voracious. I clung to his neck, my feet now inches off the ground.

When he finally lowered me to the rooftop and we parted to breathe, I confessed, "I still love you too. And that you did all this for me ..." I gestured around us. Somehow, it had changed everything. It was a reminder of who he really was to me. The person who made me feel special and *seen*. "Micah, I don't want to go slow with you. I want to stop wasting time and start making up for the time we lost."

It was difficult to keep our hands off each other as we settled to have the picnic of sandwiches and snacks Micah had put together. We laughed and reminisced about the past, caught up on each other's lives, the things we'd missed. Touching and kissing in between, a slow foreplay that was driving me crazy. Hours passed up there in the sky, the city lights in the distance, surrounded by people but all alone. Together.

When Micah took me downstairs, I should have let him call me a cab like we'd planned.

Instead, I whispered, "I want to see your apartment."

We both knew what I meant.

"Are you sure?" he whispered back, his eyes shadowed with desire.

I nodded.

I barely saw his apartment when he let me into it. We were too busy hurrying toward his bedroom. As soon as the door slammed behind us, we became frantic arms and hands trying to undress each other. It was like being stuck in a scorching desert with too many clothes, desperate to feel nothing but air on our bare bodies.

Except we were desperate to feel nothing but skin against skin.

Laughing and stroking and kissing, we eventually ended up on Micah's bed naked, his body braced above mine. When he slid a hand between my legs, my breath caught.

Micah was touching me.

It was like a beautiful dream.

I lifted my hips, widening my legs, inviting him as he slipped two fingers inside me. My need for him eased his way, and Micah's face was suddenly harsh with lust.

He kissed me, lowering his hips so I could feel his hot erection throbbing against me. Then his lips left my mouth to discover my body. He kissed every inch of me, sucking on my nipples until they were distended and tender, kissing between my legs, his tongue laving at my clit until I came. And then he started all over again.

"Micah, I can't," I moaned, my nails biting into his back. "I need you. I need you."

"It should have been me," he whispered, suddenly sounding pained.

He raised his head from my breasts, and I saw regret mingling with his passion.

I stroked his face. "Micah?"

He leaned into my touch. "I should have been your first, Cupid."

Yes, that would have been perfect. Instead of with Graham in the back of his parents' Range Rover. But I wouldn't go back. Not if it led to this moment. "What does any of it matter as long as you're my last?"

My words, the promise in them, shattered whatever control Micah had. He leaned over the bed and opened the drawer of his bedside table to remove a foil. His eyes were dark with need as he ripped open the packet with his teeth. The taut desperation low, deep in my womb coiled tighter as I watched him roll the condom up his thick hardness.

Micah's hands depressed the mattress on either side of my

head, his chest lifting off my body. He nudged my knee with his, and I opened my legs wider at his silent request.

I gazed into those beautiful gray eyes, letting him see everything I felt.

He stared back at me, his cheeks flushed, nothing but love and tenderness in his gaze. "This is a dream come true, Cupid." Then he pushed into me, and I grabbed onto his waist, holding tight at the pinch of pain. Micah was bigger than I'd expected.

I felt full. Overwhelmingly full and surrounded by him.

He withdrew a little and then pushed back in, the slight pain eclipsed by pleasure.

"Yes," I gasped, tilting my hips up to pull him deeper.

He let out an animalistic growl that made me unbelievably hot.

I cried out as he thrust, pushing deep, hitting that perfect place inside me, and gliding slowly out again. I arched my hips, trying to pull him back in.

"Cupid," Micah grunted, and his thrusts picked up speed. Then his features hardened and he froze over me. "Fuck, fuck, fuck."

"What is it?" I breathed hard. "Don't stop. God, don't stop, Micah. Please."

"I'm sorry." He stared down at me, something like awe in his eyes, his muscles straining in his arms. "I'm just ... I've fantasized about being inside you a million times, and now that I am ... fuck, I'm so turned on, I'm gonna come too soon, like I'm a fucking kid again."

He looked boyishly frustrated by this while I gloried in the feel of my feminine power. It made that low, savage, needful part of me pulse with want. "Come, then." I arched into him again. "Just come. I'm not getting out of this bed anytime soon, so we have all night to come as many times as we can."

Micah groaned with need. Then his thumb was on my clit, the delicious pressure leading me toward climax. My hips lifted against his as I came around him, and his suddenly jerked as he shuddered and throbbed through his own release.

I wrapped my arms and legs around him, loving the heavy weight of him.

Not long later, I reluctantly released him so he could take care of the condom. When he returned, he stood over my body, his hot gaze taking in every inch of me. I'd never been that confident about my body. I was soft around the tummy and thighs. While I had a small waist, I wasn't trim. Curvy hips, lots of tits and ass.

I'd held sheets to hide myself anytime I was in bed with a guy ... but something about Micah's expression made me feel like the sexiest woman on the planet. I sank into his mattress, bit my lip to stop the moan that wanted to escape from his mere perusal, and I widened my legs in invitation.

Then he was on me again, his enthusiasm making me laugh.

My laughter turned to giggles, then to gasps, followed by sighs and moans.

Then screams of pleasure as he took his time wringing bliss out of my body.

And when we were finally partially sated by the wee hours of the morning, Micah curled me in his arms and whispered, "I love you, Valentine. Always have. Always will."

For the first time since I was a kid, I felt safe.

I let myself trust him, trust that *his* love was unconditional. "I love you, too, Micah Green."

EPILOGUE

MICAH
AGE 28

Valentine Fairchild walked toward me in a white dress Mindy had designed for her.

It was just Valentine's style.

She was an absolute angel to behold.

But she could've been wearing a plastic trash bag and I wouldn't have cared, as long as she was walking down that candlelit aisle toward me.

My mom sat in the first pew on my side of the church, watching Val make her way to me with a bouquet of peonies clasped in her hands. Mom dabbed at her eyes, her joy for us genuine. Her boyfriend, a widower named Rick, who actually seemed like a decent guy, sat at her side as her date.

Wells stood at my side as my best man. Cherry sat next to Rick, a big smile on her face. She and Val got along great. But I knew they would.

And on Val's side was Mindy in her maid of honor dress, her boy Xander in the second pew from the front on the bride's side.

In the front pew sat Caroline, Jim, and Val's grandparents.

The relationship between the Fairchilds and their daughter might never be easy, but I was trying to help repair old wounds, and it meant something that they were here and that they were happy for us.

I felt them all cheering us on. But I only had eyes for her.

This nervous energy had been rushing through me for days. Probably months.

Valentine had talked me into waiting almost a year before we married.

A fucking year.

It was like a lifetime.

Now it was finally here.

And that nervous energy finally relaxed as I held Val's hands and the reverend announced, "I now pronounce you husband and wife."

I gazed into the warm, kind, beautiful dark eyes of Valentine Fairchild Green and whispered, "You happy, Cupid?"

She grinned, her dimples popping with joy she couldn't contain. Val threw her arms around me, pulling me into a hug that made me stumble, and we laughed as we held each other tight.

It was the only answer I needed.

EMBER IN THE HEART

CHAPTER ONE

EMBER

"This cannot be happening." I glowered out of our living room window at the moving van sitting in our neighbor's driveway. More specifically, I glowered at the man standing in front of the moving van. To my sister, Jade, I demanded, "Did you know about this?"

Jade raised her hands defensively. "I swear Colt never said a word."

Colt was my elder sister's fiancé and the business partner of the man currently moving into the house next door.

A man I couldn't stand.

"I think we're all being very rude and should probably go out and welcome him to the neighborhood," Celeste, our second-youngest sister, remarked as she peered curiously at him. "His kid is cute."

"Kid," I huffed, rolling my eyes. "He's a man-child. No *man-child* should be raising a child."

"That can't be helped," Jade admonished. "His ex took a job in Paris so Foster is now a full-time dad. Colt said they're both having a hard time adjusting."

Foster. Foster Darwin. Quite possibly the rudest man I'd ever met. My attention strayed to the little girl standing in the driveway, her hand held tight in Foster's as they watched the moving team unload. She wore a somber expression on her sweet little face. "How could a mother abandon her child for a job?"

"We don't know the circumstances," Celeste reminded us.

"True," I murmured.

"I'm done peeping out the window." Jade started for the front door. "Foster is Colt's best man. It would be weird if I didn't say hello."

Celeste hurried to follow Jade.

Lifting the hem of my full-skirted maxi dress, I marched out of the house, bounced down the porch steps after my sisters, onto the lawn *I* cared for, and hopped over my flower beds and onto Foster's driveway.

Foster was my new neighbor.

The universe had a sick sense of humor.

"Foster!" Jade called, and the man in question turned, adorable daughter in hand.

"Jade?" He frowned, coming toward us.

His little girl's face brightened with curiosity.

"Colt didn't tell me you bought this house," Jade said after kissing his cheek. "Why wouldn't he tell me?"

"You live here?" He nodded at our house.

"For now. Once Colt and I are married, I'll move in with him, but this is our family home. Our parents left it to us. Ember and Celeste live here too."

At the mention of my name, Foster's lips pressed together into a tight line.

Yeah, the feeling's mutual, buddy.

"Hey, Georgie, do you remember me?" Jade crouched to eye level with Foster's daughter, who nodded shyly. Jade held out her hand. "It's nice to see you again."

Georgie eyed my sister's hand, then her face, considered her, and then tentatively placed her hand in Jade's. My big sister beamed that stunning smile of hers. "Are you excited about your new house?"

Georgie's answer was to step behind her father's leg and bury her face in the back of it. Foster settled a hand on her head, stroking her hair in comfort. I refused to let the sign of familial love melt my anger toward him. "She's a little shy."

Jade stood. "Of course, I remember. And it's a big day."

"Yeah." Foster stared expressionless at our house for a second. "It is weird Colt didn't mention you were my new neighbor."

"Did I hear my name?"

We turned to see Colt Baron striding up Foster's driveway, a twinkle in his blue eyes, a mischievous smile curling his lips. "Hey, angel." He stopped to press a kiss to my sister's mouth, winked at her, smiled at me and Celeste, and then turned his charm on Georgie. "How's my princess doing?"

Georgie stepped out from behind her father and went to Colt with animation. She held out her arms, and he swept her into them with ease. Catching the look of longing on my sister's face, I wished we were standing next to one another so I could squeeze her hand. Colt was four years younger than my thirty-eight-year-old sister, and he wanted kids. So did Jade, but I knew she worried they'd have a hard time getting pregnant because she was a little older. I wanted to reassure her because I couldn't imagine a universe in which my kind, beautiful, patient sister wouldn't be a mom.

Both of us had been in prior relationships, but being the romantics we were, we didn't want to settle down for less than utter certainty that we'd found *the one*.

It was quite by chance she met Colt. Jade was an English teacher at a local high school, and one of her student's moms was going through a bad divorce. Parent-teacher conference night came around, and that mom's younger brother decided to accompany her so she wouldn't be alone for her first post-divorce conference. That brother was Colt.

At his and Jade's engagement party, Colt told all his guests how he walked into Jade's classroom and felt like he'd been hit by a thunderbolt. He'd never seen a more beautiful woman in his life. And to his amazement, she turned out to have an even more beautiful soul.

I'm glad he saw that in Jade. It was the truth. She had patience and an endless well of forgiveness and compassion. I continually told myself to be more like my big sister. Unfortunately, I didn't always succeed.

I glowered at Foster as he chatted with Jade.

Feeling eyes on me, I yanked my focus from the rude man and found Colt smirking at me. Georgie was now at his side, holding his hand, quietly watching the moving team in the background.

My suspicious gaze on my soon-to-be brother-in-law, I questioned his motives, not telling us about Foster buying the neighboring house. He'd been witness to the engagement party incident, so it would be common courtesy to give me a heads-up!

Bristling, I crossed my arms over my chest and intensified my displeased glower. Colt grinned, flashing that boyish smile Jade had fallen for. To be fair, I couldn't imagine Colt's intention was to be cruel or devious. He'd proven himself to be kind and generous. In fact, he was the perfect match for my sister.

I wondered how he and Foster became business partners and best friends.

Never mind the age difference—Foster was only twenty-five—they seemed to have completely different personalities. Where Colt was inclined to smile and laugh, Foster grunted and glared.

My cheeks flushed as I remembered the engagement party and our first meeting.

"ARE YOU NERVOUS?" I asked Jade.

"A little. Colt invited business people I haven't met before."

"Well, at least you don't have to worry about impressing the in-laws," I cracked, taking a sip of champagne.

Jade's lips parted in shock. "Not funny."

I winced. Colt's parents died in a car crash when he was nineteen. It was one of the things he and Jade bonded over, considering our parents had died on a hiking trip when Jade was twenty-three and I was twenty-one. "I'm sorry. I know better. Maybe I'm nervous. I'm sorry."

My sister patted my arm. "It's fine. And why are you nervous?"

I gestured to the decorated suite Colt had rented at this five-star hotel. The guests were scheduled to arrive within minutes. "Look how fancy."

"You don't like it?"

"It's beautiful," I assured her.

While our parents left us a big old house, our inheritance was really just enough to pay the cost of keeping it. My dad inherited the house from his father, and folks thought we had more money than we did. Our parents were never the fancy types. Five-star hotels and material "stuff" weren't their thing.

Colt, however, was determined to give Jade the best of every-thing, and he could afford to. He ran an extremely lucrative real estate company with Foster, called Baron & Darwin.

The engagement party, much like the upcoming rehearsal dinner and wedding, had been organized by a professional planner. She'd taken Jade's favorite colors (pale metallics like champagne, silver, and rose gold) and incorporated those into her design. The overall effect was understated elegance. It suited Jade, and I told her so.

My sister relaxed. A little. I wrapped my arm around her slender waist. "Hey, you have nothing to be nervous about. You are sweet, smart, and beautiful inside and out. Pure class from head to toe." It was true. Her blond hair was styled up off her neck, diamond earrings Colt bought her for her thirty-eighth birthday sparkled in her ears, and her pleated silver evening dress contoured her slim figure. It was sleeveless, with a fairly modest V-neck and a slightly less modest slit in the skirt. The dress shimmered under the chandeliers, making my sister look like a human star.

"Thank you." She studied my face with her earnest blue eyes. Honestly, it wasn't any wonder folks asked if we were really sisters. Except for the shape of our noses and mouths, we didn't look a thing alike. "Why are you so nervous?"

"I was kidding. I'm not nervous," I assured her. I was comfortable enough in my own skin to not care what people thought of me, but I wasn't sure what kind of crowd Colt's social circle was. Serious business types didn't really have a lot in common with a thirty-six-year-old, single massage therapist who ran a spa and New Age store out of the same building.

Watching Colt chat with our younger sisters, Moon (a thirty-three-year-old lawyer who lived with her wife, Linzi, and their adopted daughter, Jilly, in the city), Celeste (thirty years old, twice divorced, lived at home with me and Jade, a nail technician at my spa), and Luna (twenty-eight, divorced, remarried and now a stay-at-home mom) across the room, part of me hoped they behaved themselves. Moon would behave herself because secretly, she and Linzi would be dying for the party to end so they could go home to Jilly. But Celeste and Luna were wild cards. Get enough champagne in them, and there was no telling what they'd get up to.

"Colt won't mind," Jade said, and I realized she'd read my thoughts when she continued, "If Celeste and Luna get a little wild later."

"Let's just hope there's no stripping involved," I muttered, taking another sip of my drink.

Jade winced at the reminder—Luna stripped at my thirtieth birthday party, an event that sparked one of the darker periods in our relationship.

"Sorry, shouldn't have mentioned it. Did I tell you how gorgeous you look?" Jade smiled, changing the subject.

"Thank you." While I was sure all the ladies would wear dresses of a similar ilk to my sister, I couldn't help but be myself, though I did pay careful attention to Jade's wedding colors when I chose it. I was her maid of honor, after all. My dress was a blush/rose gold-colored, silk-georgette gown, fitted at the waist with a full skirt. The sleeves were sheer and billowy but tight at the wrists. All of that was pretty demure, except for the plunging neckline and tie-opening back. And I had boobs, so it was daring. There was a lot of tape holding me into it. "Not too much?"

My sister grinned. "Just enough. You look hot. Who knows, maybe you'll meet someone."

I tried not to roll my eyes. Ever since Jade had fallen in love, she'd become determined that there was still hope for me too. I wasn't sure about it anymore, and honestly, I was okay with that. My life was great. I no longer needed romance to feel fulfilled.

Guests began streaming into the suite, and Colt turned toward us, gesturing to Jade.

"I better go."

"Have fun," I reminded her.

AROUND TWENTY MINUTES LATER, I stood chatting with Celeste, Moon, Linzi, and Luna. It was rare for us all to be in the same room at the same time these days, so I enjoyed our random chatter about everything and nothing while Jade made the rounds with her fiancé.

"Oh my God, you can't let me drink too much of this," Luna said, grabbing another glass of champagne as a waiter passed by. Her eyes *popped wide, expression sheepish. "I'm not used to alcohol anymore. It'll go straight to my head."*

"Loosen up." Celeste clinked her glass against Luna's. "Girl, you spend twenty-four seven looking after three kids. I think you can let loose for a night."

"So true."

"Hey, sisters." Jade bumped my elbow and I turned to greet her. She wasn't alone. "Colt and I wanted to introduce you to Colt's business partner and best man. Guys, this is Foster. Foster, these are my sisters."

Colt stood next to an extremely tall, handsome young man who nodded at each of my sisters, his lips pressed tightly together. When he got to me, our dark eyes connected, and the breath whooshed out of me. His lips parted as if I'd surprised him, and he searched my face, perusing my body, slowly, hotly, before returning to meet my gaze.

I shivered.

He had an angular jaw, just a hint of scruff on his cheeks, full lips, and beautiful brown eyes as dark as my own. Foster's brown hair was almost black, and he wore it short but a little longer on top, swept back off his forehead. He was the kind of good-looking that was so perfect I usually found it a turn-off ... but something about those glittering, brooding eyes held me utterly captive.

Which was ridiculous because I knew from what Jade had told me, the guy was eleven years my junior. I was absolutely not into younger men. They weren't done maturing yet, and even the "yet" in that sentence was often optimistic.

Tell that to your body.

"Hi." I held out my hand to break our tension-filled staring contest.

To my shock, the heat I thought I'd seen in his eyes turned ice cold. He looked at my hand as if I'd just offered him a glass of pee. Politeness dictated he take my hand, but it was like shaking a limp noodle. He let go so fast, my arm dropped like a dead weight at my side.

Foster avoided my gaze and said to Colt, "I need to find my date."

Jade caught my eye, her brows pulled together in confusion. I shrugged, because I didn't know what had happened either.

Still, for some bizarre reason, I found myself looking for the weirdo as the night progressed. At dinner, I spotted him at a table three over from us Bonet sisters, seated next to a stunning, age-appropriate redhead dressed in a conservative pencil dress.

Throughout the evening, I wasn't short of dance partners, which was great because I loved to dance. To my pleasant surprise, Colt's friends and business associates weren't the stuffy, pretentious types I'd prejudged them to be. A lot of those folks were fun and hilarious, and I had a good time.

During a slow dance with a man old enough to be my father, but also a perfect gentleman who kept his attention on my face (couldn't say the same for some of my other partners), I looked over his shoulder and my eyes got tangled in Foster Darwin's.

He stood on the edge of the dance floor. A quick glance told me his date was dancing with another man. But his eyes were on me. Another shiver prickled my nape.

"I'm sorry, sweet lady, but I'm going to have to cut this short for a restroom break." My partner grinned sheepishly.

I laughed and patted his shoulder. "No problem."

Seconds later, I was alone on the dance floor, but I could still feel Foster's eyes on me. I should ignore him. I knew I should. But curiosity compelled me across the room. He visibly tensed as I drew toward him. His shoulders (fitted perfectly inside a tailored, dark-gray three-piece suit) pulled back and his eyes narrowed. That was probably my cue to veer off course, but I reminded myself that this guy was Colt's best man, and we were going to be in each other's lives.

I also remembered Jade telling me Foster had a five-year-old daughter with his ex, and while that was young to have a kid, I knew from personal experience that kind of responsibility made you grow up fast. Maybe Foster was a mature twenty-five.

I stopped before him, tilting my head to meet his eyes.

God, he was tall.

"Hey."

He nodded warily at me.

My brows drew together. Why was he acting so strange? Determined to break the awkwardness between us, I gestured behind me. "Would you like to dance?"

Foster looked out at the dance floor, then back at me, his expression unreadable. He opened his mouth and replied, "Not really."

For a moment, I was shocked and was pretty sure I stood there gaping at him like I'd never seen another human.

Then he added insult to injury by marching away without another word.

What. An. Asshole.

A HALF HOUR LATER, a very drunken Luna was pulled off a dining table by the party planner; Moon and Linzi, horrified by the scene, left early; and now Celeste and Luna were leading many of the guests in the conga and flirting outrageously with all the other drunks, no matter the gender.

The intoxicated revelers were really getting into it, but as my eyes wandered over the remaining guests seated at tables, I saw the exchange of mocking looks and caught a few people talking about what an embarrassment my sisters were for Jade. It made me angry, on top of the indignation Foster had incited. What was wrong with having some drinks and a good time? They weren't doing any harm.

Needing a breather, I escaped from the ballroom, hurried down the corridor, and turned the corner to brace myself against the wall, out of sight. Fanning my hot cheeks, I tried to get a hold of myself. The last thing Jade needed was me adding fuel to the fire by losing my shit in front of some of her stuck-up friends. Plus, I reminded myself, it wasn't all of them—just a few.

I wasn't there long when the murmur of deep voices grew louder —and then I recognized to whom they belonged, and they were walking toward me.

"Why did you bring her if she's pissing you off?" Colt asked.

"Because my father asked me to," Foster replied. "It's just easier to agree to the date and then tell him we aren't compatible."

"Or you could tell your dad to go fuck himself."

"Oh, yeah, I'll get right on that."

"A parent should want nothing but happiness for his kid. You shouldn't be at an engagement party with a woman who sets your teeth on edge. There are gorgeous, single women here, and you can't approach any of them because you agreed to take Janet as your date."

"Who are these gorgeous, single women?" Foster scoffed, and I stiffened at the insult, whether intended or not.

"Hey, watch the tone," Colt admonished. "Two of them are my soon-to-be sisters-in-law."

"Good luck with that. They're a handful."

"They're a little drunk. And it's just Luna and Celeste. Celeste is single. She's cute."

"Isn't she twice divorced?"

"So?"

"Not exactly marriage material for a Darwin."

"You sound like your father, i.e., a total prick."

"You know what I mean."

Colt went silent, suggesting he might know what Foster meant. I didn't. To me, he sounded like a judgmental asshole. He'd be lucky to have Celeste. She was adorable, fun, and a total sweetheart.

"There's Ember. I know you noticed Ember. She's smart as a whip. Damn funny too."

I smiled at that, feeling warm and fuzzy toward my soon-to-be brother-in-law.

"Isn't she like a thirty-eight-year-old spinster living at home with her sister and running some fucking woo-woo occult store?"

Excuse me?

"What has gotten into you tonight?" Colt snapped. "Ember is thirty-six, she co-owns a house she inherited from her dead parents, she's a massage therapist, and she owns a spa and store."

"Well, all that's fine and good, but while you might be into older women, I'm twenty-five, Colt, and not interested in taking on a woman who I assume has a shit ton of baggage. I mean, why is someone like her single at her age?"

That cheeky son of a bitch.

Before I could think it through, I stepped out from behind the wall, and both Colt and Foster looked over sharply. Colt looked horrified. Foster hid his surprise behind a cold mask.

I stared at him like he was a bug and detected the slightest flinch in his expression.

"I'm single because, unfortunately, there are far too many Foster Darwins to Colt Barons. I'd rather be alone than settle for immature man-children who can't even stand up to Daddy."

Taking too much satisfaction from the thundercloud that hung over his expression, I sashayed away, waving off Colt's apology and enjoying the feel of my dress fluttering around my legs as I departed on the last word.

COLT TRIED to apologize again after what happened. Jade was so angry at Foster at first, but then after she spoke with Colt, her attitude annoyingly changed to understanding and forgiveness. Shouldn't your big sister be on your side no matter what?

It didn't matter what age you were. A person needed family to take their side when someone insulted them.

I crossed my arms over my chest, silently listening to them all talk on Foster's driveway, but not participating. In fact, my mind wandered, and I stared over my shoulder at our front porch, thinking how it needed sprucing up for summer. Maybe we could swap out the swing seat for one of those oversized ones that looked like a bed. How comfy would that be, sitting out on the porch with a glass of iced tea on a warm summer's day?

And if spring was anything to go by, we were in for a hot summer.

A tug on the skirt of my dress brought my attention back around.

To my shock, I found Georgie standing in front of me, her head tilted, dark hair spilling down her tiny shoulders, big, dark eyes staring into mine. She gave me a shy smile.

My heart melted. "Hey."

"I like your dress," she said quietly.

I crouched beside her and watched her face light up as the full skirt spread out on the ground around us. "You like dresses?"

She nodded. "My mommy said she's going to send me dresses from Parees." She mispronounced the city.

"Dresses from Paris? Well, you know, they'll be the prettiest dresses in the world."

"As pretty as yours?"

"Prettier."

"Come on, Georgie." Foster was suddenly there and lifted his daughter into his arms. He avoided my gaze as he rubbed his nose against hers and said softly, "Time to see your room."

And with nothing more than a wave to Colt, Foster carried his kid into his house without saying another word to us.

So. Freaking. Rude.

CHAPTER TWO

FOSTER

Holding Georgie's hand, he stood at his daughter's side as the moving team organized her room. He'd paid for two services—moving their belongings and also unpacking and dressing the house. Moving from his apartment, he'd promised Georgie a whole new suite of furniture for her large bedroom, and this was the first time she'd gotten to see it in place.

"The ladies will hang the princess drapes you chose on the bed canopy," Foster pointed out as the two women working on Georgie's room unpacked soft furnishings. He'd asked for G's room to be completed first. They'd get around to painting it whatever color she liked later, but for now, at least he could make sure her first night in her new home was as comfortable as possible. The furniture she'd picked out was white, and the small bed was fit for a princess with four posts. G loved every shade of purple, so the drapes, her bedding, cushions, rug, everything was in a variety of her favorite color. "Do you like it so far?"

Georgie stared around the room, looking bemused. An ache flared in his chest. Weeks ago, G would have been curious about everything in her room. But since Carolyn left for Paris, his daughter had been subdued. No wonder. What child wouldn't be upset that their mother decided to accept a job offer on another continent?

Foster and Carolyn had argued, but there was no arguing with a woman who felt she was owed her chance at the life and career she wanted and would only resent G if she didn't go for it. In the end, Foster decided he didn't want Georgie around a mother who felt that way about her, anyway. But Georgie was five, old enough to realize her mother had left her, and too young to understand it wasn't her fault. He could kill his ex for doing this to their sweet little girl.

Swallowing back his anger, he lifted G into his arms and turned to look out the window. Her bedroom had a large window with white shutters that looked down over their quiet neighborhood. The house was one of the largest on the street, really too big for just the two of them, but it was in a great area, and like the Bonets', their house came with a pool. Georgie loved a pool.

"You can watch the world go by from up here," he said. "I could put a window seat in so we can sit and read together. That sound good?"

G nodded, but her attention was focused elsewhere. Following her gaze, he tried not to tense because his daughter was sensitive and she'd feel the change in him.

But she watched the Bonet sisters. Colt and his fiancée and her younger sisters were still chatting in his driveway. Foster couldn't help himself. His eyes automatically found Ember Bonet.

Now that he was gone, she'd come alive, gesturing with

her elegant hands as the others listened to whatever story she told them. Colt and her sisters burst into laughter, and Foster wished the window was open so he could hear what she was saying.

He couldn't believe his best friend, his business partner, omitted that the house he'd bought was next door to the Bonets. When he'd viewed the place the first time, there were no signs of the three of five sisters who lived there. The second time he viewed it, with Colt, again no sign of them, and the bastard hadn't said a word.

What was he up to?

Was it because he knew Foster wouldn't buy the house if he'd known Ember lived next door?

And not because he'd insulted her behind her back and she'd overheard and slighted him in return ... but because he was pretty sure Colt could tell how attracted he was to the second-eldest Bonet.

From the moment they'd locked eyes at Colt and Jade's engagement party, Foster felt drawn to her. It wasn't like the normal attraction he felt toward a beautiful woman either. It was ... it was like she had some magnetism about her. He'd found himself searching the party the entire night for glimpses of her, feeling something alarmingly like jealousy as he watched man after man invite her onto the dance floor.

He could tell she loved to dance.

And laugh.

She laughed a lot.

Full of joy.

And self-confidence.

It was an alluring combination.

And at eleven years his senior, single, never been married, a "lowly" Bonet who worked at a profession his father did not respect, Ember was as far removed from the kind of woman

Foster was expected to date, and eventually marry, as anyone could be.

Foster couldn't disappoint his family again.

Georgie depended on her grandparents more than ever, and a rift between them and Foster might mean she'd lose them. Moreover, while his business had taken off, there were no guarantees in life … except for the huge inheritance that would guarantee his daughter's future. An inheritance his father would have no problem cutting him out of if he didn't fall in line.

Reluctantly looking away from Ember, trying to ignore thoughts of her flashing, warm eyes and lush mouth, he said to G, "Why don't we leave everyone to get on with the house and you and I go out for ice cream?"

G looked up at him with big, sad, dark eyes, the ache in his chest flaring again. "Can I get rainbow sprinkles?"

"Only if I can?" he teased as he nodded at the ladies organizing G's room. They'd stopped dressing the four-poster bed to watch father and daughter walk by.

G snuggled her head against his chest. "Okay, Daddy."

Her forlorn tone broke his fucking heart.

❧

LATER THAT NIGHT, G was conked out on her new bed after a day of Foster, Colt, and Jade trying to cheer her up. The engaged pair had decided to join them on their trek for ice cream, and ice cream had led to dinner and a walk along the pier. It was clear to them all that the new house really brought it home to Georgie that her mom was gone, that she and her dad were starting a whole new life without Carolyn.

It would've been easier for Foster to keep his place in the city, cut the commute to work down, but he wanted to make up for Carolyn's defection. Yanking his kid out of school to move to the city now that her mom didn't live in the coastal town anymore would have been selfish. Plus, Colt was moving here for Jade, so that meant Foster and G would have friends nearby.

Foster stared around the large master bedroom that looked down over the backyard of his place and the Bonets'. The room was huge and not completely unpacked yet. The team would return in the morning to finish up. There were still rooms in the house that required furnishing, but he'd leave that up to his mom. She lived for that stuff.

Striding across the hardwood floors, he decided he'd need rugs in here. It would be cold in the winter, and the room echoed. Opening the French doors, he stepped out onto the small balcony that hung above his back deck. Movement from the neighbor's yard caught his attention.

Someone was having a late-night swim in the Bonets' pool. Lights situated around the pool illuminated it and the surrounding patio. It was hard to tell which sister was swimming ... until she climbed out.

His mouth went dry.

A green bikini displayed luscious curves.

Ember Bonet.

The object of his lust.

Hot blood rushed south.

He knew from being up close and personal with her that she didn't have the tight, slender body of the young society women he'd dated since he was a teen, bodies honed from frequent visits with a personal trainer and fierce control over their diet. Ember was soft where they were toned. And she couldn't give a fuck.

Her hips sashayed as she strolled toward the house, her heavy breasts jiggling with the movement, and Foster swallowed a groan. Could that woman get any more dangerously sexy?

He squeezed his eyes closed once she disappeared.

It was a good thing she hated him ... otherwise, she'd be a temptation and distraction he might not be able to resist.

❧

THIS COULDN'T BE HAPPENING. Foster tried to modulate his tone so as not to upset Georgie as she sat on the back deck with him, eating the pastries from the local bakery. Sunday was supposed to be pancake day, but the kitchen wasn't unpacked and he hadn't bought groceries yet.

Sunday was also supposed to be a chill day, but he and Colt were in the middle of an important business deal (they were buying out an established but failing real estate company and incorporating it into their brand), and the last thing Foster needed was the nanny he'd just hired calling to inform him she'd found another situation that was better for her.

In California.

Shit.

Getting up from the patio furniture, he stalked toward the boundary between his place and the Bonets', partially hidden by the low fence between them. "And you didn't think to tell me you were interviewing for another job? You didn't think that it might be a major inconvenience for me to be without a nanny the day before she was supposed to turn up?"

"I don't like the way you're speaking to me, and I don't have to put up with it. I'm hanging up now."

And she did.

"Fuck!" he bit out, struggling not to throw his phone in the pool.

"Problem?"

He jumped back from the fence. "Jesus Christ."

Celeste Bonet had appeared on the other side like magic.

She blinked owlishly at him. "Nope. Just me. Sorry if I startled you. I couldn't help but overhear." She gestured to his phone. "You're without a nanny?"

He nodded. "She was supposed to start tomorrow but took another job behind my back on the other side of the country. I leave early for my commute, so I need someone here to get G ready for school, take her, collect her afterward, and be here until I get home," Foster sighed, running a hand through his hair. "How am I supposed to find someone in less than twenty-four hours?" God, he'd have to ask his mother, and he hated asking his mother. She loved her granddaughter, but she always made such a big deal out of it if he asked her to watch G at the last minute.

"I'm sure Colt will understand if you can't go into work tomorrow."

He shook his head. "We're in the middle of a huge deal. I need to be there."

Celeste twisted her pretty face in thought. She looked a lot like Ember, but for some reason, *she* didn't make his heart pound. "I have just the solution. Ember!" She turned to yell across the yard toward the house. "EMBER!"

He winced, glancing over his shoulder to check on Georgie.

She picked at a muffin, watching him somberly.

He gave her a tender smile.

She smiled back.

His heart melted.

God, he never knew it was possible to love another being as much as he loved his daughter.

"What is it?"

Her mellifluous voice drew his attention back over the fence.

There she was, walking toward them in another one of those long, floaty dresses that clung to her curves but hid legs he'd discovered last night were long and fan-fucking-tastic.

"I'm running late for work," she said, staring pointedly *not* at him.

"You're going to work?"

"Michelle called in. Sasha has a fever, so I told her to go home. I'll cover her."

"Michelle is Ember's number three at the spa," Celeste explained. "I'm her number two, but Sundays are strictly my days off." She narrowed her eyes at her sister. "Right?"

Ember made a face. "Don't panic. You are not required today. Now, what is it? I need to go."

She still wouldn't look at him.

It was beginning to piss him off. Even though he knew he deserved it.

"Foster is in a bit of a jam. His new nanny quit before she started, and he needs someone to be here in the morning to get Georgie ready for school and pick her up afterward. You could organize your appointments so they're all in the morning, and I thought you could collect Georgie from school and keep her at the shop with you." Celeste gestured to Foster who was pissed off he hadn't seen where the conversation was going. "Foster can collect her from the store."

"That's not necessary," he said tonelessly.

Ember's eyes flew to him. He couldn't read her expression as she studied his face. "I can do it," she finally said.

"I'm sure you wouldn't know what to do with a five-year-old."

"Why? Because I'm a single, childless, thirty-six-year-old woman and therefore I must not have a maternal bone in my body?"

He bristled at her defensiveness. "Don't put words in my mouth."

"Hey." Celeste held up her hands between them—even

though there was a fence to do that—her expression curious and questioning. "Cool it. Georgie needs someone to look after her. Someone responsible. There's no one more responsible than Ember. She dropped out of college to look after me and Luna when our parents died, and before that, she always helped our parents with us."

Guilt prodded him. He'd forgotten they'd lost their parents young. And he hadn't known Ember dropped out of school to take care of her sisters.

It was more than he'd done for G.

"I really wouldn't mind." Ember's eyes moved beyond his shoulder and softened. "She's a sweet kid."

Colt vouched for Ember. He thought she was the shit.

Still ... "I'd prefer her not to hang out in your store."

Ember crossed her arms. "Why? What do you think is in there?"

He shrugged. "Nonsense occult, paranormal crap that might make my kid uneasy."

She grimaced. "I sell candles, jewelry, crystals, yoga mats, cute yoga gear, and books on meditation."

Oh.

"You should check it out. Meditation has a way of removing large sticks from small assholes."

Celeste choked on a bark of laughter, her round eyes swinging to Foster's in apology.

He glowered at her and then at Ember. "Don't really want my kid around someone with that mouth."

Though he'd like to taste it.

A lot.

A deep, wet taste.

Fuck.

He glanced over his shoulder to check on G again but also so they couldn't see the heat in his expression. How could he be attracted to a woman who continually insulted him? There must be something wrong with him.

"Oh, get over yourself, Darwin." Ember's voice brought his head back around. "I can look out for Georgie until you find someone permanent. Think about it. You know where to find me. Now, I really do need to go."

Foster watched her sashay away, annoyed but hungry.

A throat cleared, drawing his attention back to Celeste.

Her head tilted to the side, and she studied him with a knowing glitter in her dark eyes. "Oh. Okay." She smirked.

What did that mean?

"So ... are you going to take Ember up on her offer?"

"I'll think about it." He spun around and returned to G, willing his pulse to slow.

CHAPTER THREE

EMBER

I loved night swimming. It was a good thing, too, because I also loved food. Swimming and yoga were wonderful exercise, but I'd never be one of those slender, athletic women who looked great no matter what they wore. And I was okay with that. It took me until my thirties to be okay with that, but when I finally let myself be happy with my body and own my curves, it was amazing the kind of peace it brought.

Women spend far too much emotional energy worried about weight. If I could bottle my "could give zero fucks" formula, I wouldn't charge for it. I'd dole that stuff out for free so every woman in the world would be happy and see the beauty in themselves that the people who loved them could already see.

My feet hit the pool wall and I pushed off, propelling myself back toward the opposite end. I saw movement on the patio, realizing a large figure stood there. I startled in the water and stopped moving, floating in the middle. I watched as the tall man strode into the light.

Foster.

"Sorry if I scared you." He crouched, those intense, dark eyes focused on me.

Despite my distaste for him, I was curious about his appearance. Swimming toward him, I came to a stop at the pool's edge. "What are you doing here?"

"I saw you swimming." He thumbed over his shoulder toward his house.

I looked up and saw the light on in the master bedroom that overlooked the backyard. My whole life we'd lived next door to the Cowies. They were around twenty years older than my parents, and their kids were off to college by the time Mom and Dad started popping us out. Deciding to move to a smaller house in Florida, they'd put the house up for sale, much to our sadness. It was weird not having them next door.

Even weirder Darwin had moved in.

"I wondered if your offer was still good?"

Remembering my impulsive offer to look after Georgie, part of me wanted to say no. But I remembered Georgie sitting on the patio furniture, watching her dad with big, melancholy eyes. Her mom had *abandoned* her. In that moment, I'd forgotten about Foster's repellent personality and just saw a father who needed help with his little girl. Until he'd opened his mouth again. His disdain for me couldn't be clearer, so it was more than a shock that he'd come over to accept my proposal.

Swimming to the ladder, I pulled myself out of the water. I hadn't thought anything about my state of undress until I walked toward Foster. He slowly stood from his haunches, his eyes traveling up my body.

And I swear to God, I felt his perusal like strong fingers

caressing my skin.

His Adam's apple moved with a hard swallow as his attention lingered on my breasts.

Surprise halted me a few feet from him.

His focus moved to my face, and although he was quick to bank it, there was no mistaking the heat in his eyes.

Holy shit.

Foster was attracted to me.

I crossed my arms over my chest and then realized the action pushed my boobs out and drew even more attention to them, so I dropped my arms, feeling awkward.

And very, very almost naked in my blue bikini.

"Well?" he snapped.

I raised an eyebrow at his tone and bristled.

Was he mad that he was attracted to me?

Why? Because I was a thirty-six-year-old massage therapist and being sexually interested in me was mortifying to him?

Man-child.

I bet he wouldn't even know what to do with a woman like me.

Screw him.

If he was uncomfortable because he found me attractive, that was his problem. I cocked a hip. "You're asking me for a favor ... don't you think you should at least pretend to be polite?"

Foster narrowed his beautiful eyes. "You do make it difficult."

"I didn't even say a word," I argued.

"It's your attitude." He took a step toward me. "I need help with my kid, and you're deliberately ..." He gestured vaguely to me.

"I'm what?" I moved into him. "Breathing?"

"I don't even know why I bothered." His angry eyes

dipped to my mouth and back up again. "You're clearly not the best person to watch Georgie, anyway."

That pretentious prick. I stiffened. "Why?"

"Excuse me?"

"That's the second time you've questioned my ability to be a responsible adult around a five-year-old. I want to know why, with so little effort to get to know me, you think you do. Know me, that is."

He shrugged. "Just a hunch."

A hunch?

"Well, you're best friends with Colt, so I'm sure he could vouch for me. And probably already has. So why have you made this snap judgment about my capabilities? Is it perhaps because you're a country-club snob who thinks anyone without a college degree, or any woman who hasn't been married by the time she's thirty, is deficient in some way?"

"Now who's jumping to conclusions?"

"Jumping to conclusions? You more than insinuated that a woman who looks like me who's still single at my age—ouch, by the way—must have something wrong with her. Then you've twice implied that I am incapable of looking after a child. Why, when you know so little about me, would you draw that conclusion? Of course, I'd assume it was out of pure elitism and sexism."

"So I'm an elitist and sexist now?" He stepped into me, our chests brushing, and I gasped at the sparks that electrified my skin and set my pulse racing. Foster tensed, his gaze dropping to my mouth again.

Attraction crackled between us, hot and charged.

My fingers curled into fists at my sides as Foster's head dipped toward mine, his breath whispering across my lips. I could feel my mouth plumping at the mere thought of his kiss.

He stumbled back, his eyes wide as if he was shocked by

his own behavior.

I sucked in a breath.

We stared at each other, confused.

Not just confused. My body was taut, completely unsatisfied with his sudden distance.

"This was a bad idea," he said, voice hoarse, before he turned to leave.

Gathering myself, I called after him, "I can look after Georgie until you find someone."

Foster glanced back at me. "Like I said, I think that would be a terrible idea."

It was clear, despite our personality clash and age difference, that there was a physical attraction between us. One I was quite willing to ignore now that my mind wasn't lust-fogged by his proximity. Yet, Foster was so horrified by the idea of being attracted to me, he didn't even want to be near me?

Well, that just pissed me off.

"Scared?" I taunted.

He turned. "Excuse me?"

Ignoring his dangerous tone, I continued, "You have no logical reason for turning down my very kind offer. Unless you're such a snob that you can't associate with a massage therapist with no known blue blood in her family history?"

"You're determined to think the worst of me."

I shrugged. "Change my mind."

"Fine," he bit out. "I'll leave for work a little later tomorrow so I can be there to explain to Georgie you'll be watching her this week. But I usually leave at six thirty. Is that too early?"

"Not at all."

"Fine."

"What time shall I come over?"

"Seven fifteen."

"I'll see you then."

His eyes flicked down my body one last time, and I saw a muscle tick in his jaw before he marched out of sight down the side of the house. Without saying good night.

"We really need to work on his manners."

⊗⊗⊗

THE JEWELRY in my store held Georgie transfixed. I watched her look over the stands and towers and glass cabinets filled with jewelry, some costume, some handmade in precious metals. After I'd dropped her off at school yesterday morning, I'd switched around some of my clients so that all my appointments ended before the school day did. Those who couldn't accommodate, my three other massage therapists covered.

Raven, a friend from high school whose real name was Mindy Watts, managed my store during the day. Growing up she'd been envious of the unusual names my parents had given me and my sisters, and so she'd adopted the name Raven. To be fair, she looked way more like a Raven than a Mindy.

I'd let Raven go home to her teenage kids early, since Georgie and I could watch the shop until Foster showed. We did her homework in between customers.

The first day with Georgie went well, though slightly awkward. She was a shy kid who didn't talk much. That didn't worry me. I used to be a shy kid. What worried me was the sadness in her eyes. No five-year-old should be that glum or serious.

My phone beeped on the counter, and I saw it was a text from Foster. Swiping my phone screen, I leaned in to read it.

Sorry, meeting ran late, just getting out of the office now. Please, can you provide Georgie with dinner? Foster.

I sighed. So goddamn formal.

I texted him back.

No problem.

I still wasn't loquacious with Georgie's dad, afraid that in being so, we'd end up in another argument. Jumping off my stool, I grabbed my purse and called to Georgie, "Hey, honey, your dad is running a little late, so we're going to do dinner without him."

She walked toward me. "Is he coming home?"

I frowned. "Of course. He just got out of the office, though, and the city is ninety minutes away. So we're going to close up here and grab some dinner. How does Penny's sound?"

It was her turn to frown at me.

"You've never been to Penny's Diner?"

Georgie shook her head.

"You like chicken nuggets? And milkshakes?"

Her eyes lit up, making me smile.

"I'll take that as a yes." I held out my hand. "Penny's is the best place in town for chicken nuggets and milkshakes."

༺༻

As I ate Penny's famous and delicious cheeseburger, Georgie dipped a nugget into ketchup and stared around the diner at the other occupants. We were lucky to get a table since tourists descended upon our town spring through summer. But I knew Geraldine, Penny's head waitress, and she found us a small table in the back.

Noting Georgie's attention was fixated on something, I looked and tensed. A mom and her daughter, around Georgie's age, were settled in a booth, two older boys on the opposite side, and the mom and daughter had their heads together, giggling at something.

My chest ached at the wounded expression on Georgie's face.

She was way too young to feel the horrible emotions she was experiencing right now.

God, I could kill her mom.

"You okay, honey?"

Her little mouth trembled as she replied, "Jenna Green said mommies don't go away like Mommy did. Jenna said Mommy must have really not liked me, and that's why she went to Parees."

Ugh, that was a punch to the gut.

Jenna Green was a brat. I leaned across the table. "That's not true, Georgie."

"But Mommy went away."

"For a job. A very important job." I didn't know if that was true, and truth be told, I didn't think there was any job more important than being a mom. As far as I was concerned, that was the deal you made with the universe once you had a kid.

"Jenna Green said her mommy said being a mommy is an impotnant job and that my mommy didn't love me because she thought Parees was more impotnant than me." Tears shone in Georgie's eyes, and she looked seconds from bawling.

Jenna Green's mother was on my shit list.

I quickly waved down Geraldine. "We're just going to the bathroom. We're not leaving."

"Sure thing, Em. I'll watch your stuff."

"Thanks." I stood and scooped up Georgie before she could protest. She was heavier than she looked, and I had to shift her onto my hip. I was grateful she looped her arms around my neck and let me take her to the restroom.

Locking the door behind us, I gently lowered Georgie to her feet, noted the tears had sprung loose, and got down to her level to hug her tight. She wrapped her little arms around me, and feeling her tremble, hearing her little hiccups, I had to hold back my own tears. This angel had rapidly gotten under my skin.

Eventually, I eased her away and rummaged in my purse for tissues to dab at her cheeks.

"Honey, your mom loves you," I told her, sure it had to be true. "She just needed to do this, and she knows how much you love your dad. She thought it might be great for you to spend more time with him." I shouldn't be lying to a five-year-old. I knew that. But I couldn't have her thinking her mom didn't love her. "And your dad is so happy to have you with him."

To my shock, she didn't look certain of that either.

Despite my conflicted feelings about Foster, there was no doubt in my mind that he loved his kid.

Yet, it seemed her mother's abandonment had filled Georgie with insecurities no kid should feel.

Time to chat with Foster.

᠀᠀

AFTER OUR TALK in the bathroom, we returned to our table, but Georgie had lost her appetite so we went home. Not long later, Foster arrived. Leaving Georgie to watch a cartoon in a living room that had been transformed overnight by a team of stylists, I followed Foster into his office after asking to speak privately.

As I closed the double doors behind us, Foster leaned against his sturdy antique desk and crossed his arms over his chest. He hadn't shaved in the last few days, his hair looked like he'd been running his hands through it, and a weariness in his eyes made him appear older than his twenty-five years.

Twenty-five.

When I was twenty-five, he was only fourteen.

I shuddered.

Don't think about that.

"What's going on? Is G okay?"

I told him about the incident at the diner.

Foster bit out a curse, turning to glare at a bookshelf. He gritted his teeth.

"I'm sorry if I said the wrong thing to her."

"What else could you say?" he asked, his voice hoarse with emotion.

I sighed. "I'm telling you because obviously you need to know, but also because I got the distinct impression that she doesn't feel sure you're happy she's living with you full time."

He glared at me incredulously. "What?"

"She's five and extremely smart and intuitive for her age. No matter what we say, she feels, rightfully, abandoned by her mom. It's made her insecure. You're going to have to work overtime to make her feel wanted."

Foster continued to glower at me.

I forged ahead. "I understand you work in the city, and you're doing your best to get back home after office hours. I understand you probably still have to work through the night. But my advice is that Georgie needs stability. She needs your evenings while she's awake to be all about her, and she'll need your weekends too. No working … and no …" I waved vaguely, remembering the gorgeous redhead at the engagement party. "Women who aren't permanent."

"Are you done?"

My spine stiffened at his tone.

Foster pushed up off his desk and prowled toward me. I forced myself not to retreat.

"Who do you think you are, schooling me on how to father my daughter?"

"I'm not trying to school you. It was advice."

"And the insinuation that I'm the kind of father who not only ignores my daughter but brings strange women around her."

Okay, so perhaps that was a little judgmental. "I only—"

"Maybe you should keep your nose out of it." He stopped so close to me, we were almost touching. "My child, my business."

Scowling, I responded, "You asked me to look after her. This is me looking after her. Holding her in my arms while she cried over her mother's abandonment was heartbreaking." Tears glistened in my eyes at the memory. "I'm just trying to help."

He seemed stunned as he studied my face. Then to my shock, his expression softened and his eyes warmed. Suddenly, he was unbearably good-looking. "Fine," he said, his voice gentle. "Then I'll accept that your judgmental advice came from a good place and forgive you."

I grimaced. "I can die happy."

He leaned into me. "You are such a pain in the ass."

"Back at you. You take everything I say the wrong way and assume the worst."

"*Back* at *you*," he retorted.

Then his dark gaze dropped to my mouth and just like the flick of a switch, electric tension sizzled to life.

Feeling my body react, wanting to melt toward him, I retreated. "Well, then, maybe we should call a truce. From this point onward, we both agree to assume that the other has only good intentions."

Foster considered this and said in a bored monotone, "I suppose we can try that."

It was difficult not to offer a pithy response to his enthusiasm.

"Fine. Good. That's settled, then. I'll see you in the morning."

I'd turned toward his door when he murmured, "Do you swim every night?"

Halting at the strange question, I glanced over my shoulder. His expression was unreadable. "I try to. Why?"

"Why do you do it?"

"Because I ... I like it."

He seemed disappointed by my answer.

I frowned. "I started night swimming after my parents died. Jade and I became guardians to Celeste and Luna. Moon had just left for college. Jade was getting her teaching degree and was almost finished ... so I dropped out of college to look after the girls." An ache flared inside me at the reminder of what might have been. "I wanted to be a teacher too. But the girls were more important. Losing Mom and Dad, bearing the responsibility of parenthood at twenty-one ... suffice it to say, I didn't sleep well for a while."

His expression was filled with understanding, and something even more dangerous.

Tenderness.

"So you swam to exhaust yourself."

I nodded, struggling to regulate my breathing. "Yeah. Then it just became a habit."

"I'm sorry."

"For what?"

"For what I said at the engagement party. For the unfair comments I've made since."

Shocked, in a good way, I smiled at him. Really smiled.

He looked stunned, like I'd kicked him in the gut. He blinked a few times.

"Thank you," I said. "And I'm sorry for insulting you in return. Let's do better."

Foster swallowed hard and nodded.

An awkward, tension-filled silence fell between us, and I took that as my cue to leave.

CHAPTER FOUR

FOSTER

He was obsessed.

There was no other word for it.

Ember Bonet had become an obsession.

At night from his bedroom window, he'd watch her swim, like a stalker, waiting for her to return safely into the house before he'd go to bed. When he got home from work, he wanted her to linger, and not because he didn't love spending time with Georgie but because he liked the changes he saw in G around Ember.

Upon taking her advice that night in the office where she'd smiled at him and he'd felt the beauty of it, he'd talked with Georgie and assured her of his love. And every night since, after he read to her, he'd tuck her into bed and tell her how much he loved her and how glad he was they got to be together now.

Between that and Ember's influence, Georgie was back to her old self again, proving kids really were resilient.

At work, he interviewed nannies, but he had a hard time picking one when the woman next door had captured G's heart. But he knew it wasn't fair to Ember to keep asking her to work her schedule around his daughter, so he'd narrowed the choices down to three women.

And he needed to choose soon.

Not just for Ember but to give Georgie stability, and selfishly, for him.

Because he needed to get over Ember.

He needed to rid himself of this overwhelming desire to be in her company all the time.

"Why?" Colt asked when Foster confided in him about his attraction.

The answer: it all came down to his parents and having Georgie so young.

Carolyn got pregnant when they were in college, which was a mammoth disappointment to his father, Edward Darwin. His father was the president of an insurance corporation, and the Darwins had been leading members of New England society for over a hundred years. His mother was Madeline Bourne—her family really did date back to the *Mayflower*.

As their only child, Foster was required to act, think, and succeed with the family reputation always in mind. Having a kid at twenty was the end of the world for the Darwins. Determined it wouldn't derail them, they insisted Foster remain at college and tried to force him to marry Carolyn. He refused. Another point against him. But he did stay in college and accepted his parents' help with childcare.

For the first couple years, Foster wasn't the best father. He'd worked hard at business school, but he'd also been working his ass off to make connections. Through hard work and a bit of luck, he met Colt, and the rest, as they say, was history.

However, one weekend, it was his turn with Georgie. She was barely two and toddling all over the place ... his parents had fallen in love with their granddaughter, and he was watching his father have a conversation with G.

And he realized ... his father was *having a conversation* with his daughter.

Foster hadn't been there for her first word, and now she was speaking in sentences.

He hadn't been there for her first crawl or her first step.

While he loved his parents and knew they loved him, he'd vowed he'd have a closer, more hands-on relationship with his kids. And he was already failing.

At that moment, everything changed.

Carolyn wanted to finish school, so he asked to take Georgie more. They split their time with her down the middle. He was in a great situation to be able to afford a nanny while he worked.

But he wasn't in a situation where he could disappoint his father again.

Something he had to remind himself constantly as he followed G and Ember down onto the busy beach.

How had he gotten himself into this?

Oh, right, he had a hard time saying no to his daughter at the moment. And this Saturday, as if she knew a new nanny was on the horizon, G had begged him to ask Ember to spend the day at the beach with them. She'd done it in front of Ember so there was no way out of it.

He eyed how Ember's summer dress molded to her ass and had to admit he was looking forward to seeing her in her bikini in bright daylight. Her warm laughter floated back to him on the breeze, followed by his daughter's adorable giggles.

Something overwhelming filled his chest watching them as they found a spot to settle. As G helped Ember stretch out towels on the sand, he stumbled a little at the sight.

G had inherited his dark hair and eyes, and it was the first time he realized that it would be easy for people to confuse G for Ember's kid.

They had the same coloring.

And a bond that was beginning to worry him.

Once the new nanny arrived, Ember would probably disappear from G's life.

Fuck.

"Come on, slowpoke," Ember called out to him, grinning, her eyes hidden behind oversized pink-and-blue sunglasses that G immediately decided she wanted as well. Ember, having already predicted that might happen, had brought a child's pair from her store's stock.

G wore hers, too, making them look even more alike.

Unnerved, Foster attempted to shrug off his strange emotions and helped them set up.

"Water?" Ember asked them, patting the top of their cooler.

"I want to swim!" G announced.

"I'll take her." Foster jumped to his feet, eager for distance from his neighbor. He already wore long swim shorts, but he pulled off his T-shirt for the upcoming foray into the ocean. Glancing down at Ember, Foster caught her ogling his stomach. There was a gym at the office, and he and Colt always had an hour workout slotted into their daily schedule. It showed in his six-pack, and he was suddenly very glad for his hard work because Ember looked close to drooling.

He smirked, and she turned away. "I'll, uh ... I'll watch our stuff."

"Em, my dress." G went to Ember for help. Instead of him. *Hmm.*

But Ember deftly untied the little straps to reveal G's purple swim dress underneath. "I brought a hair tie to keep your hair dry."

He watched as his daughter stood patiently while Ember gathered her thick hair into a cute little bun thing on top of her head.

"All set." Ember blew raspberries on G's neck, making her erupt into giggles again.

His heart fucking melted.

"Come on, angel." His voice sounded gruff to his ears as he took G's hand and led her down to the water.

☙❧

AS IT TURNED OUT, Ember in a bikini in broad daylight was a glorious thing. She was sunbathing, her olive complexion turning a dark gold. Her green bikini looked amazing against her skin tone.

Hell, everything about her looked amazing.

Grinning mischievously at him, G lifted a finger to her lips to silence him, and he smiled. Then she tiptoed over to Ember and shook her swim dress so all the seawater on it sprayed across their neighbor's bare skin.

Squeaking in surprise, Ember shot up, shoving her sunglasses into her hair. "You little—" She launched at G, pulling her into her arms so she could tickle her. Foster laughed as his daughter's infectious cackles filled the beach, drawing amused stares from nearby families.

"Since I'm all wet now, anyway," Ember said and jumped up, ruffling G's messy bun, "I might as well take a dip."

Foster, his eyes hidden behind his sunglasses, took the opportunity to really look at her.

He wanted to feel her soft body against his, to kiss his way up those lethally long legs, to pleasure her and hear her husky moans fill his bedroom, to taste her nipples and squeeze her gorgeous, full tits in his hands as he pumped into—

Fuck!

He looked away as he felt hot blood travel south.

Just looking at her in public was making him hard, like he was a fucking teenager.

"Daddy, I'm going back to the water with Em."

"Okay, angel." Fine with him.

He needed a minute.

Slumping down on the towel, he made the mistake of watching Georgie and Em walk away.

Ember's ass was almost as good as her tits.

Then he became aware of something that really pissed him off.

He wasn't the only one staring at Ember Bonet. His gut twisted in annoyance.

While there were plenty of gorgeous women on the beach, Ember stood out because of her sensual curves. Natural sexiness oozed from her.

To his agitation, Foster realized he didn't want other people to see that in her.

He wanted her all for himself.

And wasn't that a very dangerous thought.

Not long later, G and Ember returned, and he refused to stare at Ember in her wet bikini. It might kill him. Instead, he focused on making sure G was fed. She'd just finished her sandwich when a little girl came over and asked if she wanted to build sandcastles. At his nod of permission, the two girls set up camp between both their parents' spots and played together.

"She's doing awesome. I see such a change in her in just two weeks."

Foster turned to Ember. "Yeah, it's great. You've been a huge help. Thank you."

"It's been my pleasure."

Christ, even hearing her use the word *pleasure* got him hot. This was ridiculous.

And even though he told himself to change the subject to anything that might distract him from his attraction to her, the next thing he blurted out was, "So, I take it you're not seeing anyone?"

Shit.

He couldn't see her eyes behind her glasses, but her lips parted as if he'd surprised her.

"I mean, I haven't seen you with anyone."

Ember leaned back on her hands, stretching her legs. His eyes dropped to her thighs and he swallowed hard. "No, no boyfriend."

He dragged his gaze up to her face again. "Why?"

She gave a huff of laughter. "Because I haven't met anyone lately."

Me. You've met me.

Jesus, Foster, don't be stupid.

Pushing away his inner dialogue, he prodded, "But there have been boyfriends, right?"

"Right." She grinned. "There have been a few."

"None of them felt like marriage material?"

Say no.

Her silence spoke for itself, and his stomach dropped.

"I'm sorry, I shouldn't—"

"No, it's okay. I just ... I don't want you to think badly of my sister if I tell you."

Foster raised an eyebrow. "Okay?"

Ember turned to him. "There was someone. We dated for a few years, and I honestly thought he'd pop the question at my thirtieth birthday. He didn't. Instead, Luna, my youngest sister, got drunk and stripped. Apparently, this got him so hot, he couldn't help himself."

"You're kidding me."

She shook her head, lips pinched. Then, "They started seeing each other behind my back that night. I found out weeks later when I walked in on them having sex in his apartment."

Jesus Christ. The betrayal ... Anger churned in his gut. Ember had given up her education to become Luna's guardian, and she'd thanked her by sleeping with her boyfriend?

"We broke up, but he and Luna ... Luna fell pregnant. They got married, but then he proved he really was the ultimate asshole by taking off. So she moved back in with us, and we helped her out for a while with Casey, her daughter, until she met this older guy, Garret, and married him. Now they live in the city, and they have two of their own kids, Anna and Lucas. Luna's a stay-at-home mom."

"I saw you with her at the engagement party. You two seemed fine."

"We weren't for a while, but we got through it."

"You forgave her?"

She shocked him by replying, "Of course. Luna has always been impulsive, and she was very young when she cheated with Kyle. Not just literally but emotionally and mentally. Besides, she doesn't have the best taste in men. I can say that because once duped, I've never been duped again. But Luna's husband ..." Foster could tell she scowled behind her glasses. "He cheats on her all the time. And she puts up with it. I don't know if she thinks she deserves it, or she just doesn't want to give up the cushy lifestyle he provides. I have no idea. I've tried talking to her about it, and we always end up arguing. My youngest sister is the one I understand the least."

"I'm amazed by your capacity to forgive," he admitted. "I don't think I can forgive Carolyn for taking off on G. I can't help how bitter I feel about it."

Ember reached over and covered his hand with hers. "That's totally different. You're bitter on Georgie's behalf. No mother should choose a job over their five-year-old. It's okay not to forgive her for that. You're hiding the anger from Georgie, which is all that matters."

The urge to close the gap between them, to wrap his hand around her nape and drag her against him so he could kiss the life out of her was so great, he had to lean back.

She removed her hand from his, misinterpreting his withdrawal. Foster wanted to haul her into his arms, uncaring of who could see them. But he stopped himself.

Instead, he confessed, "I worry I'm not doing this right. That I'll fail G."

Ember gave him a tender smile. "Foster, the fact that you worry about it means you're doing it right. And if no one has said it already, I'm sorry, and this is me rectifying that—you are an amazing dad. You're only twenty-five years old, and you've got your shit together. You know what's important. You know it's her."

"Thank you." He could barely get the words out for the emotion choking him. "It means a lot that you think that."

Silence fell between them, allowing the sounds of the water, the seagulls, the chatter of the busy beach to fill the void.

Then Ember murmured, "Don't look now, but you've caught the avid attention of two fangirls."

He looked at her. "I don't care."

She twisted her luscious mouth before replying, "You

sure? They're hot, and unlike the teenage girls who were ogling your six-pack earlier, these two are age appropriate."

It should have alarmed him how uninterested he was in hot women his age checking him out. In fact, it did alarm him a little.

But that didn't stop him from caressing every inch of Ember's body with his hidden gaze instead of looking in their direction.

Ember tensed as if she could feel him staring at her. Then she shoved her sunglasses up into her hair, and he saw the bemusement in her eyes.

"Like I said," he uttered, his voice hoarse with want, "not interested in *them*."

Before she could reply, G threw herself at him, and he caught her just before she face-planted on his chest. "Daddy, come see our castle!"

Nice timing, angel, nice timing.

Because he'd been about to make a huge mistake.

CHAPTER FIVE

EMBER

"Y ou miss them, don't you?"

I looked up from my breakfast to find Jade and Celeste staring at me with big, concerned eyes from across the table. It was the end of my first week without Georgie (and Foster). The new nanny started a week ago, and other than catching glimpses of them in their yard, I hadn't seen much of the Darwins.

"You should go visit. I'm sure Georgie misses you," Jade insisted.

I shook my head. "I haven't been invited."

And stupidly, I'd expected Foster to text at some point and ask me to come over or grab a milkshake with them ... or something.

Stupid, stupid, stupid.

"It's a Sunday. They'll be home, you're home," Celeste said. "Why don't you make your lemonade and take it over?"

I grimaced. "Like a desperate spinster from the fifties?"

"That's severe and unfair," Celeste admonished.

"You know what I mean. I have to be careful with how my behavior appears."

Jade cocked her head. "When have you ever cared what people think?"

"Not people—Georgie. And Foster. I don't want to be that middle-aged woman who can't take a hint." Melancholy was a sharp ache near my heart. "No, I won't go over uninvited."

My sisters exchanged a look as if I were a problem to be solved.

"It's not a big deal."

"Tell that to your mopey face."

I scrunched my nose at Celeste. "Stop being childish."

"Pot, meet Kettle."

Jade pushed away from the table. "I'm meeting Colt in half an hour. We're making final decisions about the venue today."

"Good luck. Have fun."

My sister paused. "I promised I wouldn't say anything, but I feel like if I don't, you and Foster might miss an opportunity here."

Frowning, I turned in my seat to meet her gaze. "What's going on?"

Jade's eyes lit up. "Foster likes you."

My pulse skittered. "What?"

She nodded, barely containing her excitement. "He told Colt he's extremely attracted to you."

Extremely attracted to me.

Yes, I knew that.

The man did not hide that fact.

But there was a difference between like and attraction. "Attracted to me or likes me?"

"Well ... both."

"So why hasn't he done anything about it?" Celeste asked. "He doesn't seem like the kind of guy who doesn't go after what he wants."

I gestured to my younger sister as if to say, "Yes, thank you, I agree."

Jade narrowed her eyes on Celeste before focusing on me. "I don't know why he's holding back. I think Colt knows, but he won't tell me. But maybe he thinks you think he's not mature enough. I mean, you did call him a man-child. Several times."

Hope was a wretched blossom blooming deep within. I tried to shove it down. "It's more than likely I'm the opposite of the kind of woman he usually dates."

"In what way?" Celeste frowned.

"I am neither in my twenties, beautifully athletic, a college graduate, nor am I from a good East Coast society family."

"You don't really think that stuff matters to Foster, do you?" Jade retorted. "He had a child when he was still in college. Not exactly Mr. Perfect Society Guy."

Hmm. That was true. Maybe I was projecting his initial attitude about me onto who I knew him to be now. And hadn't we decided we were going to see the best in each other?

Still ... "Like Celeste said, Foster is a man who goes after what he wants. If he wants me, he knows where to find me."

"Does that mean you would be interested?"

I shrugged. "Certainly in sex. Anything more than that ... I'm not sure."

Jade's face fell. "But you're not the casual-sex type."

"There is a huge age difference between us, and I might not look so hot to Foster when I'm sixty and he's still forty-nine. However, I am attracted to him, so ..." I shrugged, feeling butterflies at the mere thought. "I wouldn't say no to sex with a hot younger man. As long as he knows what he's doing."

The thought of Foster's mouth and hands on my body made me shiver with unfulfilled desire.

❧

FOSTER DARWIN WAS the last man I'd ever let near my body with his hands and mouth!

In fact, he could rot in hell for all I cared!

Instead of my leisurely breaststroke across the pool, I furiously powered through the water in the front crawl. Back and forth, hammering out my hurt and rage.

I tried not to think of the events earlier that day, but I couldn't stop seeing it.

A warm near-summer's day, I decided to spend it outside, pottering in our garden. The pool took up most of the back-yard, but flower beds lined the front lawn and hanging pots decorated the porch. I'd bought some fresh plants and was near the flower beds adjacent to Foster's driveway, digging in the cool soil, when an Escalade swung up onto his drive.

An older woman in gray linen pants, a white, high-neck blouse, and matching gray linen jacket hopped out of the SUV. She wore sunglasses, but I felt her stare and sat back on my heels. A man who looked an awful lot like an older version of Foster rounded the hood.

"Grandpa, Grandma!" Georgie shouted. She dashed down the porch and across the driveway as fast as her little legs could carry her.

My heart pounded at the sight of her, and I felt stupid tears prick my eyes.

Jesus, I missed that kid.

And I was so thankful to see her happy as her grandfather

swung her up into his arms for a hug. I smiled, watching them greet one another, noting Foster had appeared on the driveway too. As Georgie turned her head to look at him, she caught sight of me.

Her pretty little face lit up. "Em!" She took off across the driveway before anyone could stop her, and I dropped my gardening implement just in time to catch her.

The feel of her in my arms made me emotional, and I hugged her tight without touching her with my dirty hands. Then she let me go, and I realized she'd gotten soil on her pretty purple dress, anyway. "Oh, honey, I got you dirty."

"G, you can't just attack Ember like that." Foster came toward us, frowning down at her spoiled dress. "You'll need to get changed now for lunch with Grandma and Grandpa."

Her face fell.

"It was my fault," I said, even though it wasn't.

"I'm Madeline Darwin." Foster's mom hovered on the boundary between our yards. She offered me a smile. "You are?"

"Ember Bonet."

"She's Jade's sister," Foster said without looking at me.

"Oh." Her smile wilted a little, but she gestured to the flower beds. "I love to garden too. Isn't it therapeutic?"

I nodded, though I barely paid attention. I was too busy staring at Foster, wondering why he refused to acknowledge me.

"This is my husband, Edward. Edward, come meet Foster's neighbor. She's Colt's fiancée's sister."

"I heard."

I stiffened at his dismissive tone and scowled as he said, "Georgie needs to change into a clean dress, so we better move if we want to make our reservation."

"Can Em come?" Georgie asked, staring up at her dad with big, pleading eyes.

Just as I was about to open my mouth to protest, Foster replied firmly, "Absolutely not." Then he took her hand and walked away. She stared back at me, her lower lip trembling.

I know the feeling, kid.

I gave her a weak smile and a little wave.

It only made her face fall further.

Remorse filled me.

"Georgie seems close to Jade's sister." I heard Madeline say as she followed Foster up the driveway.

Edward grunted in displeasure.

And that was when Foster replied, "Not really. She watched G for a few days while I searched for a nanny. That's all. We barely know each other."

See?

Rot. In. Hell.

I glared as I hurtled across the pool.

"Ember."

I was so mad at him, I was hallucinating his voice?

"Ember!"

I paused mid stroke.

"Ember!"

Turning my head, I caught sight of a shadowy figure leaning over the fence.

Foster.

"What do you want?" I asked flatly.

"Can you come over here?"

Screw you, asshole. "Not really."

"I can't be long. My parents are still here ... but G was asking for you a lot after we saw you today, and I wondered if maybe she could hang out with you one evening this week?"

"I don't think that's a good idea." Guilt consumed me, but I couldn't be around someone like Foster.

"Why?"

"Because I have very good hearing. You said we barely

knew each other, which is a lie. And I don't associate with people who are too embarrassed to introduce me properly to their parents."

Silence reigned from the other side of the fence.

My hurt and rage built, so I resumed my laps, ignoring his presence.

A few minutes later, water splashing at the other end of the pool startled a cry from me. I whirled to see Foster swimming in my direction.

What the hell?

I backed away from him. "What are you doing?"

His face was grim. "Apologizing."

Scowling, I shook my head, grateful when he stopped before we touched. "You can't apologize for a fundamental personality flaw. You clearly think it matters what family a person is born into, and I don't. And I can't be friends or associate with anyone who would think I'm less worthy because of who my family is or isn't. By the time you get to my age, Foster, you'll realize none of that shit matters."

Frustration flashed in his gorgeous eyes as he floated before me.

In nothing but his boxer briefs, I realized.

Heat flushed through me, and I hated my attraction to him more than ever.

"I already know that shit doesn't matter. I do. But my relationship with my family is complicated. However," he said, moving closer, "that does not give me the right to treat you that way." Contrition softened his gaze. "I hurt you, and I hurt G ... and that's not cool."

Confused, I looked away. "I ... what do you want from me?"

"You don't want the answer to that question."

My breath caught at his hoarse response, and I finally looked at him.

Desire darkened his expression, his features taut with it.

"Foster ..."

Suddenly, he wrapped a hand around my nape and dragged me across the water to collide with his hard body. As his mouth crushed over mine, Foster groaned, and the vibration sparked my desire like hands down my body, fingers teasing my nipples, whispering across my belly and sliding home between my legs. His kiss grew harder, more demanding and desperate. We panted into each other's mouths, refusing to break the kiss.

When I became aware of his erection digging into my stomach, I was lost. Arousal was a luscious flip, deep and low between my thighs. My lust grew as Foster's hand slid up my waist, brushing my heavy breast and coming to a stop at the halter-top string. He broke the kiss, pulling back only an inch to stare into my eyes. His lips were swollen, his expression wicked.

He tugged on the bikini strings, and I gasped as the wet material fell into the water, revealing me to him.

"Jesus, fuck," Foster groaned. "Jesus, fuck, you're so beautiful. So sexy." He cupped my naked breasts, and shivers of need skated through me. I arched my back, my nipples tightening in the cool air. My breasts swelled as Foster's thumbs caught on the tight points.

Then he lifted my right breast as he bent his head, and his mouth was on me.

I reached for the side of the pool for purchase, struggling to contain my cry of pleasure.

"Foster, we can't ... ah ..." He sucked hard, shooting bolts of sensation between my legs. "Not here. Anyone might see us."

That seemed to be the splash of cold water he needed.

Foster lifted his head but pressed his body to mine.

He throbbed against me.

Then he kissed me again, hard and hungry as he squeezed and caressed my breasts like he couldn't help himself.

Finally, he released my mouth, the bristle of his unshaven cheeks scratching my skin as he whispered in my ear, "This is far from over."

He then pushed away, swimming at impressive speed across the pool.

My fingers trembled as I grabbed the strings of my bikini top and fumbled to cover up. Foster hauled himself out of the pool, his boxer briefs clinging to the muscles of his perfect ass and obvious erection. He shot me a look of heated promise over his shoulder, then bent down to scoop up his clothes.

"Holy. Crap," I murmured, touching my bee-stung lips.

So we were two completely different people, and we weren't ever going to be anything permanent ... but that didn't mean we couldn't indulge in a little after-hours fun.

Yeah, now that I'd had a taste of him ... this was definitely far from over.

CHAPTER SIX

FOSTER

It was serendipity. At least, that was the excuse Foster used as he pulled into the parking lot outside Ember's spa and store.

He stared up at the sign for the spa: House of Bonet.

And then to the sign above the attached store: Ember's Zen Den.

He smirked at her sense of humor, pulse racing.

Of all the places he could've been that afternoon, it had to be in town. Colt had set up a meeting with a guy looking to sell several properties he owned on the coastline. Unfortunately, Colt had a bad case of food poisoning after a sample day yesterday with their wedding caterer. Not only had he upchucked throughout the night, he and Jade now needed to find a new caterer.

And Foster had to cover his meetings.

The day after he almost screwed Ember Bonet in her swimming pool.

Definitely serendipity had kept him in town today.

The nanny would collect Georgie from school like always, so with time on his hands, he found himself heading toward Ember.

Despite knowing it was probably a terrible idea, he couldn't get the taste of her out of his mouth. If he didn't have her, he was pretty sure he'd never be able to concentrate fully on anything ever again.

Striding into Ember's store, he drew to a stop in disappointment to see a woman with long, black hair sitting by the counter. She eyed him suspiciously.

More than likely because he didn't look like their usual customer.

"May I help you?"

"Uh ... is Ember here?"

Instead of answering, she turned and yelled toward the doorway that presumably led to the storeroom. "Bonet, some hot dude is here to see you!"

He raised an eyebrow but didn't respond, only took a few steps toward the counter. It was a wonder Ember's employee couldn't hear his heart pounding.

"Is that really how you're going to address our customers?" He heard Ember say. "Raven, please—" She was suddenly there, staring at him open-mouthed.

"Hey." He took in her long dress, loving the way it hugged her breasts and waist before it flared out into a full skirt. The way she dressed was so different from the women he'd dated, but Foster liked it. Everything about Ember was enticingly feminine.

"Hey." Ember stepped toward him. "What are you doing here?"

"Had a meeting in town. Thought I'd stop by." He knew he couldn't hide the heat in his eyes.

He knew it in the way she sucked in a breath and addressed the so-called Raven in a breathy tone. "Honey, why don't you finish up early?"

"You sure?"

"Yeah, I'm sure."

"Sweet!" Raven hopped off the stool and grabbed a huge black purse. "For once, I can grocery shop without two teens chirping in my ear and adding fifty dollars' worth of crap we don't need, and can't afford, to my cart."

Ember gave her a strained smile. "Have fun."

"Sure, sure." Raven wiggled her fingers at Foster as she passed, but he could barely keep his eyes off Ember.

In fact, his attention was glued to her as her chest rose and fell with quick breaths while she followed in Raven's wake. Bemused, Foster turned to watch her sashay across the store and turn the lock on the door. She flipped the sign to Closed and then sashayed back.

"Come with me," she murmured as she passed him. Anticipation hung heavy in his groin.

Practically chasing after her like a panting teen, he followed her down two steps to the narrow corridor that led to the stockroom, the restroom, and her office. Ember's skirt disappeared into her office with her, and a haze of lust came over his mind.

As soon as he stepped into the room, he rushed her, pressing her against her desk, molding his body to hers. Foster's heart slammed against his ribs as their eyes locked, her soft body crushed to his, the fire between them blazing.

Her lips trembled, and the wild need took over.

Foster covered her mouth, swallowing her gasp of excitement. Her perfume, the heat of her beneath his hands, and the taste of her—that taste he'd gotten last night in the pool was an addictive elixir—it all overwhelmed Foster as he gripped the back of Ember's neck with one hand and slid the other down her stomach ... He smoothed it over her round hip and under her thigh.

She kissed him back harder, her arms circling his waist as she fell against the desk but clung to him, her fingers digging into his back as he tugged her thigh up so he could press deep between her legs. Her lips parted on a whimper of desire, and the sound aroused him beyond bearing.

His hand tightened around her nape and he groaned, desperate for more, for everything from her. They devoured each other like it was the last time they'd ever kiss. Foster lifted Ember's thigh and nudged her onto the desk, grinding his erection against her.

The feel of her hands sliding up his back and over his shoulders, her fingers sinking into his hair, only made him want more. He wanted her hands on his bare skin.

"Take off the dress." He broke the kiss to demand gruffly. Even as he uttered the words, he was shrugging out of his jacket.

Ember's eyes were smoky with passion as Foster stepped back to allow her room to undress. She gathered the full skirt in her hands, and he absently undid his tie as her long legs were revealed.

Then her soft stomach and her breasts as she lifted the dress over her head and dropped the fabric on the floor.

He swallowed hard, eyeing every magnificent detail of her. "Bra and panties too." He whipped off his shirt and started on his belt.

Watching her lick her lips as she stared at him was his undoing.

"Come on, gorgeous." He pushed down his suit pants and kicked them off. "I want to see every inch of you. I've wanted to see every inch of you since I saw you in that pink number at your sister's engagement party."

She flushed with pleasure at his confession and reached around to unclip her bra. Slowly, she let the straps fall, the cups catching on her taut nipples.

Finally, it released.

It had been dark last night in the pool.

In the warm light of her office, Foster could see Ember in all her glory.

"Fuck me, fuck me, fuck me," he muttered, almost stumbling out of his boxer briefs with excitement.

Her throaty laughter only made him harder, and his mouth went dry as she curled her fingers into her panties and pushed them down.

"Sit on the desk and spread your legs."

Ember bit her lip for a second, her eyes on his erection. "Are you always this bossy?"

"Just with you. You make me very, very impatient. And frustrated," he growled.

Chuckling, Ember sat on the edge of the desk and spread her thighs.

"I've died and gone to heaven, haven't I?" He fell to his knees before her, skimming his hands up her legs to push her open to his gaze.

"I think maybe I hav—ah!" Ember cried out as he licked into her hot depths.

Foster held back his grin of satisfaction and buried his head between her pearly gates.

EMBER

ALL RATIONAL THOUGHT left me the moment I saw Foster standing in my store with a look in his eyes I knew too well. He was here for one thing and one thing only.

And considering I wanted what he wanted just as badly, I'd lost my ever-loving mind.

Right then, I couldn't care.

My head fell back on a groan as he licked at me, his tongue flicking and tormenting my clit. "Foster, please."

I could feel it building already, the muscles in my thighs trembling and tightening.

And then two fingers pushed inside me.

Foster sucked and licked as his fingers played their part. My hips undulated off the desk, my fingers tightened in his hair, my senses on overload. Every time I felt the rasp of his unshaven cheeks against my sensitive skin, the tension inside me tightened further.

He sucked hard on my clit, and I exploded, my cries of pleasure so loud, I'd worry later if people in the spa might have heard.

Foster stood, wrapped my legs around his hips, and shoved his hands in my hair to hold me to him for his devastating kiss. I could taste myself on his tongue, and I moaned into his mouth.

Foster broke the kiss, his hot lips trailing down my neck, the bristle of his stubble scratching my skin. I arched my back, anticipating what he wanted, and thrust my breasts up for his exploration.

Quickly, the gloriously languid aftermath of my climax was fanned into a flame again. He cupped and stroked and kissed my breasts, learning every inch of them. And then he wrapped his mouth around my nipple and tugged, sucked, and licked it until it was so swollen, it became overly sensitive. I hissed, and understanding why, Foster moved on to my other nipple until my legs were climbing his hips, and I was writhing against his erection, desperate for him to take me.

"Come inside me, Foster."

He kissed me, one hand under my ass urging me up against his erection as he rubbed its hard heat between my legs, teasing me beyond bearing.

"Foster!" I broke the kiss, glaring into his dark, lust-filled eyes. "Now."

"You're on the pill, right?"

The question was almost pleading.

I nodded and looked down, fire in my belly at the sight of him, ready for me.

I licked my lips as my gaze traveled up his perfectly honed, muscular body. I'd never been with a man as beautiful as him before. Physical perfection was never enough to attract me. I always had to be attracted to some inner beauty.

And that was the truth.

Foster wasn't just beautiful to me because he was a handsome twenty-five-year-old.

He was beautiful to me because he was a wonderful father who was trying to do the best by his daughter, and when he wasn't being a thoughtless moron, there was a gentle kindness in him.

Fuck, I should stop this.

"Ember, I've never wanted a woman as much as I want you," Foster confessed against my mouth.

And just like that, I was lost again.

I kissed him, my tongue flicking at his lips. I took the silken heat of him in my hands and squeezed. Foster kissed me harder, gasping and panting as I stroked him with one hand and dug my fingers into his ass with the other, urging him to me.

I guided his tip to my entrance and smoothed my hand up his rigid stomach.

My eyes fluttered closed at the satisfying burn that turned to pure relief as he overwhelmed me with fullness.

"Ember, open your eyes," Foster demanded.

I opened my eyes and held his intense gaze.

"Keep looking at me." He thrust deeper, looking almost pained. "Jesus Christ, you're perfect," he whispered. "Keep looking at me. It's me fucking you, it's me that makes you feel this good."

I nodded, clinging to his shoulders as he tilted my hips farther to glide slowly in and out of me. I trembled against him as he took pleasure in taking his time.

"You're so perfect, so fucking perfect," he grunted against my lips, his speed increasing.

I moved against his thrusts, the blood rushing in my ears. "So are you."

"Ember." His grip tightened as he repeated my name like a prayer.

"Foster," I whimpered back as he thrust at just the right angle to brush my clit with his movements. My nails dug into his shoulders. "Oh, God, do that again."

Satisfaction made his expression harsh, and he drove into me harder.

My climax built, my neck arching, my cries echoing around the office.

"Come for me, Ember," Foster commanded. "I want to feel you come around me."

Just like that, the tension inside me peaked.

And peaked HARD.

I gasped as the first orgasm hit and was quickly followed by another bigger, more spectacular one that made me lose all sense of self. My cries filled the whole goddamn building. My fingers dug into his skin as I clenched around him, and my eyes rolled into the back of my head.

My pulse was loud in my ears as Foster thrust harder,

faster into me. A few seconds later, he buried his face in my neck and muffled his shout of release against my skin. His hips jerked against mine, and I felt him throb in pulse after pulse inside me, shuddering in my arms.

I held on to him as we tried to catch our breath. My skin was slick against his, my breasts crushed against his chest. I caressed his back, soothing him.

Eventually, he lifted his head and stared at me in awe.

And I knew, no matter how stupid we both understood it would be, that this wasn't the last time we'd find bliss in each other's arms.

CHAPTER SEVEN

EMBER

Foster's groan was loud.

I clamped a hand over his mouth as I undulated against him. "Shh."

His nostrils flared and his grip on my hips tightened. And in revenge, he began bucking his own magnificent hips beneath me.

"Oh, fuck," I huffed, releasing his mouth to brace both hands on his shoulders.

Suddenly, I was flipped on my back, my wrists captured above my head, and Foster took over.

Seconds later, he slammed his mouth down on mine as he felt my coming orgasm, and he swallowed my cry of release in his kiss. My cry was followed by his groan as he shuddered in climax.

We panted, tight, low sounds we attempted to keep barely audible, and Foster brushed his lips over mine again before withdrawing. This was the moment I usually slid out of his bed, cleaned up in his master bath, and tiptoed downstairs to return to my house. For the past month, we'd carried on our secret affair. On weekends, I'd spent more time with Georgie again. The two of us were as close as ever, and I was starting to worry that I wasn't the only one who would be hurt when this affair ended.

I had to end it.

Because I was falling in love with a man eleven years my junior who cared way too much about his parents' opinion.

"Don't go," Foster whispered, reaching for me as I moved to slide out of his huge bed.

While we tried to find moments to meet while Georgie was at school, between both our jobs, it was almost impossible. We'd instead fallen into a routine of me sneaking into the house once Georgie was asleep.

"I better," I whispered back. "We don't want to wake G."

"We won't." He rested his head on the pillow near mine and tugged on my hip in a silent plea for me to turn toward him.

I did. "You okay?"

Foster grinned. "What? You're surprised I want to spend time with you not having sex?"

"We spend time not having sex." In fact, our weekends with Georgie were the best. I'd never seen Foster so relaxed.

"I mean alone. Just you and me." He brushed my hair off my face, his expression tender and affectionate and so very bad for my heart. "Do you want kids? You're so good with G."

Shocked by the question, it took me a minute to answer. "I ... yeah, if it's in the cards for me, I'd love at least one."

"You'd make a great mom." He kissed my nose. "How are your sisters? I mean, I know how Jade is because Colt's told me."

I grimaced. "I feel for her. Jade is so not an elaborate,

spectacle kind of person, but this wedding planner they hired is going all out and constantly bombarding Jade with questions. She feels like the wedding has taken over her life."

"Colt feels the same. He told Jade to fire her and they'd have a small wedding instead."

"Which is sweet, and she appreciates it, but they've already put down deposits and ... well ... I think she thinks it's good for your business image. To have a big, lavish wedding."

"It is always good to advertise success when you can, as crass as that sounds." Foster frowned. "But not to the detriment of the well-being of someone we love."

I reached up to stroke his cheek, enjoying the feel of his stubble prickling my skin. "That is appreciated. Jade, however, is much tougher than she looks. School's out for the summer, so she has more time on her hands to deal with it. And it's not long now. Once it's done, it'll be done. Besides, she *is* looking forward to the honeymoon. A week in Japan, followed by a week at some luxury resort in Bali? Uh, yes, please. Lucky duck."

"Have you traveled much?"

"No." I lowered my gaze. "We traveled around the States with Mom and Dad when we were kids. But I've never had time to travel farther afield. Or the money."

"You own your own business."

"Yeah ... so I *could* afford to travel, but I like having a nest egg in case something happens. Mom and Dad left us the house. No mortgage. My dad inherited it and then we inherited it. And they left us some money, which helped take care of the costs of living in it. But it was a struggle for a while. We were on a tight budget and couldn't afford much besides the essentials. The girls decided not to go to school, and I still don't know if that was based on what they actually wanted or if they thought we couldn't afford it. I put myself through my massage therapy qualifications and took out a bunch of loans to make the business work, and I'm still paying those off. So ... traveling ... not so much for me."

Foster caressed my waist and hip in a soothing, comforting gesture. "You're amazing, you know that?"

I smirked. "If you say so."

"No, I'm being serious. You sacrificed so much for your family. I admire that."

"It didn't feel like a sacrifice."

"Which makes you all the more magnificent."

I grinned. "Magnificent. Ooh, I like that word."

But Foster didn't smile. He pressed closer to me, his expression intense. "I want to take you to Bali or wherever it is in the world you want to see."

Just like that, my humor fled. "Foster ..."

Realization flashed in his eyes and he lowered them, hiding from me. Yet he didn't let go. In fact, he banded his arm around my waist as if he didn't ever want to let go.

Incredibly sad all of a sudden, I leaned in and caressed his lips with mine. "I gotta go." I wiggled against his hold but instead of releasing me, he pushed me onto my back and kissed my breath away. "Foster," I panted.

"I want you again." His voice was gruff.

Heat flickered low and deep in my belly, and I melted into the bed, too eager to let him inside.

⚜

"THANK you for being so patient in there," Jade said as we walked along the hot city sidewalk. She knew I wasn't a fan of the place. The air was too thick with fumes, the smell of waste wafting up from the sewers now and then, and if I wore sandals on a warm day like today, my feet got covered in soot from the traffic.

Thus, I'd chosen to wear a light pair of boots with my dress, and my feet were too stuffy inside them.

Still, I wouldn't complain.

Jade rarely asked me to come into the city, and this was for the wedding. Anything to relieve her stress. Besides, it worked out. For the first time since our affair began, Foster was busy this Sunday. Georgie's new nanny, a college graduate named Anne-Marie, who was this sweet, shy young woman Georgie thankfully loved, was working overtime to watch G, since I was busy with Jade.

"Of course. Dress fittings are necessary for a wedding. And it was good of them to open on a Sunday."

"Yeah." Jade nodded. She shot me a look. "You're honestly happy with your dress?"

"Of course." My maid of honor gown was silver, as were the bridesmaids' dresses. Moon, Celeste, and Luna had joined us for the dress fitting, but Moon had hurried home as soon as she was done, and Celeste had gone back to Luna's to see the kids.

Jade and I wanted to grab something to eat together before heading home. With work, the wedding, and Colt, we hadn't seen a lot of each other lately.

"And your dress is to die for."

My sister beamed. "You think?"

"Colt is going to lose his—" I cut off abruptly.

"Ember?"

My pulse pounded in my throat as I halted in front of a restaurant.

Inside, clear as day, were Foster and his parents. A young, beautiful blond sat next to Foster, her hand on his shoulder as she leaned in to laugh with him about something.

"Em." Jade stood at my side.

His parents smiled at the young couple.

Were they a couple?

No.

Foster wouldn't—

The blond kissed his cheek, and he lowered his eyes almost shyly.

Foster?

"That's Heather Smyth," Jade said in my ear. "Colt told me Foster's parents have been trying to set them up for a while. I only know who she is because I met her at the office last week when I came into the city to have lunch with Colt. Heather works for a bank nearby. Colt told me she's gotten persistent. I guess Foster finally gave in."

He was seeing another woman behind my back?

"Ember?"

"He and I have been having sex for over a month." I looked at my sister, tears in my eyes. "And I stupidly fell for him. Like really, really fell for him, Jade. I'm such a fool."

Jade looked heartbroken for me. "Oh, God, Em."

Her sympathy only made me angry. "No one makes a fool of me." I glared back at the young couple. "I think we should stop by and say hi. It's only polite."

"Ember ..."

But I was already pushing open the door to the restaurant. I wouldn't make a scene. But I wanted him to know that I knew. A hostess stepped toward us but I shook my head at her distractedly, focused on the man I currently loathed.

As if he felt me, Foster turned his head in my direction.

His eyes rounded in surprise, and it was quickly replaced by a flash of something like panic. Then he was pretty much expressionless.

So good at masking his feelings. No wonder he'd duped me.

The blond and his parents turned to see what had caught his attention, and Madeline smiled at the sight of me and my sister. "Jade, Ember, how nice to see you."

"You too, Mrs. Darwin, Mr. Darwin ... Heather ..." Jade cut off at that, apparently unable to say it was nice to see Foster.

"We were just passing by and saw you in here ... thought we'd be neighborly." I forced myself to look at Foster.

I saw the slight shudder in his breathing that betrayed his discomfort.

"Yeah," Jade agreed, her fingers lacing with mine. "It was such weird timing, too, because I was just telling Ember about you and Heather, Foster."

Heather grinned, curling her arm around Foster. "It's nice to see you again, Jade. And nice to meet you, Ember."

Not her fault, not her fault, not her fault. "It's nice to meet you too."

"Well, we better get going." Jade tugged on my hand. She offered goodbyes to the Darwins and I followed her out, numb.

What a foolish woman I'd been.

"Are you okay?" My sister hadn't let go of my hand.

"I don't know." I looked at her. "I used to think Luna had bad taste in men ... but it's clear she and I share that particular trait."

"Were you exclusive?"

"No." I stopped, shaking my head in anger. "No ... but you tell someone you're sleeping with that you're sleeping with someone else too."

"You're right."

"Ember!"

I winced at his voice.

"Ember ..." He sounded out of breath, and I turned as Foster slowed from a run to a stop before us on the sidewalk. "This isn't—"

"Have you been fucking her while you were fucking me?" I cut him off, my voice harsh.

Foster flinched back. "Of course not."

"Then that's all I need to know." I turned to leave, and he grabbed my arm. I shook him off. "Don't touch me."

His expression darkened with frustration as he ran his hands through his hair. "You and I ... we ... and Heather is the daughter of a family friend ... and ..."

"And we were just screwing around," I whispered, hating him because I hadn't imagined his possessiveness or the way he acted like he wanted more than just sex.

He'd made me start to hope.

The cruelty of it was overwhelming.

"No." He tried to reach for me again, but I retreated. Anguish blazed in his eyes. "I care about you. I do. I just ..."

"You don't have to say it." Disgusted with him, I dragged my eyes down his body and back up again. "Your family's good opinion means too much to you, which means you think I'm not good enough—"

"No—"

"I know who I am. I know my worth. And I deserve better than you, better than someone who would try to make me feel horrible about myself because he can't stand up to his family. My mistake for getting involved with a *boy*."

He gaped at me, shocked, hurt, angry.

And it satisfied that spiteful part of me that wanted him to hurt as much as I did.

I whirled and stalked down the street, Jade's footsteps syncing with mine. By the time we reached the train station, we were both sweaty and out of breath.

Plus, I felt beyond nauseated. Every part of me ached.

"You were wonderful." Jade wrapped an arm around my shoulders as we waited on our train. "And you were right. He's just a boy who doesn't deserve you."

"What about G?" My lips trembled as tears stung my eyes. "I don't want to hurt her."

Jade rested her head against mine. "It's terrible and sad ... but a clean break for the two of you will be best."

"We live next door to each other."

My sister sighed. "I know you might not want to hear this ... but with me leaving ... perhaps it's time to sell the house."

Aghast, I pulled away from her. "What do you mean?"

"It's prime real estate. Even split five ways, your portion of the sale would buy you and Celeste a smaller place, maybe even somewhere closer to the beach."

"But ... it's been in the family for three generations."

"It's just a house. And maybe it's time to move on. Do you really want to watch Foster and Heather, or whoever he ends up with, start a new life with Georgie next door?"

CHAPTER EIGHT

FOSTER

Nothing felt right. He couldn't settle. He couldn't sleep. An anxious feeling stirred in his gut all the time. Guilt rode him hard. And dread. He didn't even want to analyze the dread.

Georgie missed Ember.

They hadn't seen her in two weeks.

She wasn't answering his calls, his texts.

She didn't swim at night anymore.

The few times he'd knocked on the door, Celeste answered, less than friendly, and told him Ember wasn't home.

Foster couldn't blame her. No, he hadn't slept with Heather. He hadn't even kissed Heather. But the strange double date with his parents was technically their second date because they'd had lunch alone in the city the week before. Something he hadn't told Ember.

The whole time, he'd tried to tell himself he wasn't doing anything wrong. The same at lunch with his parents.

And then Ember had walked into the restaurant.

The look in her eyes.

The betrayal.

Fuck.

He sucked in a deep breath and exhaled, the sound shaky to even his ears.

He missed her.

The sound of her laughter, the way her dark eyes danced with it. Her easy affection with G, like the two of them had been together their whole lives. The way G lit up for Ember in a way she used to only for him.

The way *he* lit up for Ember.

Her soft, breathy moans in his ears. Her hands caressing his back, gripping his ass. The dramatic slope of her narrow waist into curvy hips. Gazing into her eyes and feeling so fucking at peace, like he'd finally found something he'd been missing his whole life.

"If I hear you sigh like that one more time, I'll punch you."

Foster started, swinging his office chair around from the window to find Colt braced against the doorway.

His friend closed the door behind him and walked into the room. "It's like working with a zombie these days. You barely said two words to Jack Hunter in the meeting this morning."

"We made the deal, didn't we?" he grumbled like a petulant teenager.

Colt scowled as he sat down on his desk. "This has to stop."

"What?"

"Don't. Don't be an even bigger prick than you're already being."

SAMANTHA YOUNG

Indignant, he snapped, "I don't need this shit right now, Colt."

"Oh, I'm sorry, I forgot this was all about you." His friend looked at him with such disappointment in his eyes, Foster flinched. "Do you even give a shit how you made her feel, or do you only care about how you feel?"

Remorse sliced through him. "Of course I give a shit."

"Really? Because you're walking around here like you're the one who got fucked over when the truth of the matter is that you made a very special woman think that her feelings aren't more important than your parents' fucking snobbery."

"Colt—"

"Nah, listen." His friend pushed off the desk. "It's clear that you have real feelings for Ember. In fact, it's clear that you *think* you're in love with her."

"Think?" he snarled. How dare he—

"Yeah, *think*. You see, because *I* love Jade. I love Jade so much that the thought of hurting her, of putting my feelings before hers, makes me sick to my stomach. *You* don't love Ember. If you loved Ember, you would tell your father where to stick his opinions and his money."

Heart racing, Foster shook his head. "Family is important. Can't you understand why I don't want to disappoint my father?"

"No, actually, I can't. Here's your choice—on the one hand, Edward Darwin, who still makes fucking excuses for Georgie's selfish mom just because of her family's blue blood, a guy who bases his opinion of a person's worth off a family fucking name. That's who you want influencing Georgie's life? Or, on the other hand, Ember. Funny, gorgeous, kind. Is great with Georgie. And for some stupid reason loves you."

Hope was a knifelike pain in his chest. "She said that?"

Colt's expression was harsh as he gave a tight nod. "She *was* in love with you. But I guess she realized the age gap was

266

a problem after all. She said you had a lot of growing up to do, and she didn't have time to wait around."

He sighed. "I fucked up."

"She's putting the house up for sale."

Panicked, he barked, "What?"

His friend nodded, grim-faced. "That's how much you hurt her. So tell me ... can you live with that? Because if your answer is yes, you're not in love with her, man."

Foster's gut wrenched. "I love her. And I'm an asshole." He pushed out of his chair, his agitation visible. "You're right. You're so fucking right, part of me wants to punch *you*. I'm a father now. I can't keep making choices based on what's best for *my* father. It has to be for what's best for the people I love." Frantic with dread at the thought of losing Ember forever, he shook his head. "What if I can't win her back?"

Colt considered this, his demeanor toward Foster visibly softening. "Well ... here's some advice: With the Bonet sisters, actions speak louder than words. But actions accompanied by the *right* words is your best shot at getting her back."

CHAPTER NINE

EMBER

On the plus side, the rehearsal dinner was a smallish affair. Compared to the two hundred–strong guest list for the wedding, there were only seventy-five people at the rehearsal dinner.

I couldn't bear to think what this wedding cost Jade and Colt.

But I would ... because it kept my mind off someone else.

Three weeks had passed since I'd caught Foster at lunch with his other woman.

His calls and texts had stopped around ten days later.

However, for whatever reason, he'd started calling me again this past week. I had a bunch of texts from him pleading to meet—"We need to talk"—but I was half convinced he was just horny. Moreover, I didn't want my resolve to melt.

A guy who let me think I wasn't good enough was not the right man for me.

End of story.

I missed G terribly. And my guilt was overwhelming. Truth is, I wanted to see her, but my sisters held me back, telling me I'd only make it worse for the little girl in the long run.

I missed her giggles and her smile.

And I really hated the idea that I made her feel as abandoned as her mom had.

Tears choked in my throat and burned in my eyes, and I dropped my gaze to the table to hide my emotions.

As maid of honor, I was seated up front at a U-shaped banquet table.

Only a few seats down from me, at Colt's side, was Foster.

My skin hummed with awareness of him.

He hadn't brought a date.

I mean, neither had I ... but I'd worked myself up a lot about this rehearsal dinner because I was so sure Heather would accompany him.

Maybe she could only attend the actual wedding.

His parents were here. Colt had invited the Darwins out of respect.

I couldn't even look at them. I blamed them, too, for making it so Foster felt he had to please them with his choice of girlfriend.

Though, I wondered if any parent would be happy about their son dating a woman eleven years older than him? Forlorn, I reached for my champagne glass and emptied it in one chug.

I could feel Jade's eyes, but thankfully she couldn't question me because Colt was in the middle of his thank-you speech.

My attention moved over the tables before us, sliding

through the Darwins and past folks I recognized from the engagement party. Then on to the banquet table where my sisters sat with their partners. Moon, Linzi, and Jilly. Luna and her bored-looking husband Garret. And Celeste and the guy she'd been dating for the past month. He was a cute vet she'd met after accidentally running down a cat. Seriously, my sister's life was an ongoing rom-com novel.

They looked good together, and she seemed to really like this one.

Who knew, maybe I'd have to buy a one-bedroom house on the beach. Grow old on my own, no kids, no pool, just a cat that someone would run over one day and use as an anecdote at her wedding to the vet she met through my damn cat!

Shaking my head out of my morbid thoughts, I tried to zone back into the room.

Colt was thanking his beautiful fiancée. A sweet kiss on her lips.

We were to raise our champagne glasses—shit, mine was empty. *Hope no one notices.* I pasted on a strained smile.

After my soon-to-be brother-in-law settled back into his seat, the murmur of conversation started again, and Jade covered my hand nearest her. "Are you okay?"

I wanted to say I needed more champagne, but the last thing I should do was get drunk at my sister's rehearsal dinner in front of my ex.

Was he even my ex?

Did five weeks of mind-blowing sex really count as a relationship?

My heart throbbed in answer.

Opening my mouth to assure her, I was abruptly cut off by the chime of cutlery tapping against glass. Jade turned her head to the left and I followed suit, shrinking back in my seat as I realized Foster was standing to address the room.

Oh, gosh, were we supposed to prepare best man and

maid of honor speeches for the rehearsal dinner too? I thought, panicked.

"Uh, I'm not scheduled to talk tonight."

Oh, thank God.

"But Colt gave me permission to hijack the rehearsal dinner."

What?

A murmur of confusion shifted through the room.

"What is he talking about?" I whispered.

Jade shook her head, looking as confused as I felt.

And then Foster turned and looked directly at me.

His expression open, pleading, tender.

Holy. Crap.

"Months ago, at Colt and Jade's engagement party, I met a woman who knocked me on my ass. And I was so unprepared for it, so not in the place where I could handle it, that I was unforgivably rude to her."

Tears of shock glistened in my eyes, and I could hear my sister's indrawn breath.

"I never believed in fate." He shrugged, looking boyish and uncertain. "Not until you, Ember. Not until I bought the house next door to yours without knowing it. It's like the universe wanted us to be together."

"Foster," I whispered.

"And somehow, because you're a goddamn miracle and you're so kind"—his emotion made his eyes wet—"you not only forgave me for being an asshole ..." The room tittered, but I was barely paying attention to anything but him. "You took care of my daughter, and you helped us through a really horrible time."

He stepped out from his chair to approach mine, and I tilted my head to hold his gaze. "Ember Bonet, I know I don't deserve you. You are incredible, smart, kind, funny, loving, and passionate, and there is no doubt in my mind that someone who is your equal is out there waiting for you. But I'm a selfish bastard because the mere thought of letting him have you feels like my heart is being ripped from my chest.

"And that guy, whoever he is, might deserve you ... but I promise"—Foster lowered to his knee in front of me and reached for my hand—"I promise you that no man will love you harder than I do or work harder to prove it. Please forgive me for being a blind fool?"

I couldn't breathe.

Foster Darwin had just declared himself in front of all these people, including his parents.

"Let me make it up to you," he pushed, trepidation glittering in his eyes. "I will never give you cause to regret it. I love you."

"Okay."

His eyes widened. "Okay? Yes?"

I smiled, that damn ache in my chest easing. "Yes. But you have a lot of groveling to do, mister."

Foster grinned, standing up to pull me into his arms. He hugged me so tight. "Anything, anything." He kissed my temple, then my cheek, and then my lips.

A long, deep, hungry kiss that was only broken as the erupting cheers in the room finally registered with us.

Cheeks hot, I laughed, a little embarrassed by the public display as the room full of practical strangers celebrated our romance.

Well ... not the whole room.

They waited until all the guests had left hours later. We'd felt their eyes on us during the rest of the evening, but they never approached. I was tense. Foster kept whispering assurances in my ear. The man hadn't stopped touching me since I'd agreed to give him a second chance. He'd apologized to Jade for hijacking their celebrations, but my big sister was genuinely ecstatic for us.

"Here we go," Colt murmured.

Everyone had left except the four of us and the Darwins.

Colt took Jade's arm and strode toward the exit, nodding at the Darwins.

Foster's hand tightened in mine. "It'll be all right," he promised.

But I wasn't certain. There was a part of me that couldn't trust Foster completely yet. I knew he sensed that when his expression hardened with determination. "One day, you'll never doubt me," he vowed.

I squeezed his hand and took a deep breath as Madeline and Edward halted before us. Foster's mother looked uneasy, whereas Edward was clearly furious.

"What is the meaning of this?" Edward gestured between us.

"I think that's self-explanatory." Foster pulled me closer into his side. "I love Ember. We're starting a life together."

Oh, wow. Just hearing him say it again ...

"You can't be serious about this?" Edward sighed heavily, his focus on me. "I'm sure you're perfectly lovely. But tying my son down is incredibly selfish—"

"Dad—"

"No. She will hear this. You're, what, in your mid-thirties?"

"Thirty-six."

He huffed. "Eleven years older than Foster. How will that look when you're fifty and he's still not even forty yet?"

"I don't care. I love her."

"I'm talking to Ember." And he was. Prodding my insecurities. My own concerns. "You're not from the same community as Foster. You'll be pulling him and Georgie away from the life they're used to."

"Bullshit, Dad."

"Foster," Madeline admonished.

"No, I won't stand here and listen to you disparage the woman I love."

"And what about children?" Edward scoffed, ignoring his son. "Don't you want more children? A woman of thirty-six is past her prime."

That was it.

That was when I saw red.

"Past my prime?" I stepped away from Foster, bristling with rage. "I hate to shock you out of the nineteenth century, Mr. Darwin, but women are having babies in their thirties with a lot more ease than they were a hundred years ago. Children aren't out of the question. What is out of the question is your participation in our relationship. Your son is a man. A father. It's time you saw that."

Foster tugged me back into his side. "Ember's right. This is our decision. And I have no reservations about it. I love her. Georgie loves her. There is nothing you can say to change it."

"I'll cut you off."

The words sliced through the air, cold and harsh.

"Do it," Foster answered without hesitation. "I'm a successful man in my own right. I don't need your money. I don't need your blessing. It would be nice, but it's not a requirement." He looked at his mother. "I would think as my parents, you'd just be happy that I'm happy."

Madeline's expression softened, but Edward barked out a hard guffaw.

"We're not sticking around to listen to this ridiculous sentimental nonsense. When you come to your senses, you'll know where to find us." He turned and marched out of the room.

Foster's mom wavered, tears filling her eyes.

"Mom?"

She grimaced and then hurried to follow her husband.

Silence fell between us. I squeezed his hand, hating the forlorn look on his face. However, as soon as he turned to me, the melancholy melted away. "You okay?"

"Are we together?"

I nodded, torn between joy and concern.

Foster grinned. "Then I'm more than okay."

I hugged him, loving the feel of his strong arms so tight around me. "I think your mom will come around."

"Yeah, maybe." He turned, his lips brushing my ear. "I know I don't deserve it yet … but I can't wait for the day you tell me you love me too."

My pulse pounded in my ears as I eased away from him.

The smart, sensible part of me knew I should hold back.

But I'd never been the kind of woman who lied to herself or others. "I love you," I assured him. "I love you so much."

His answer was to kiss me with a fierce wildness that made me tremble from head to toe. "We need to find a bed. Now," he growled, guiding me toward the exit.

"Amen to that," I agreed, and then we were running and laughing like two teenagers, out of the building toward his car in the parking lot, desperate to finally really be together.

EPILOGUE

FOSTER

Fourteen months later

Because she was already a swimmer, the doc said it was okay for Ember to keep swimming during her pregnancy. Still, Foster sat on a lounger right next to the pool as G and Ember swam.

"They're fine," his mom reassured him from the adjacent lounger. "She's fine."

"I know." He nodded, not taking his eyes off them.

His mom laughed under her breath.

So he was being overprotective. He knew that. Wasn't going to stop him.

Foster's daughter and wife, and the little boy growing in her belly, were his entire world.

"I think I'll join them." Foster rose to stand.

"Nah, I'm going in." His dad lowered his glass of iced tea and stood in his swim shorts and T-shirt. "Need a reprieve from this heat."

Relaxing as his father climbed down the ladder into their pool, Foster watched as G played with her grandfather and Ember looked on, grinning as her stepdaughter splashed her grandpa.

"Cannonball, cannonball!" G demanded.

"Well, I'm going to get out of the way for that." Ember laughed, swimming toward the ladder.

"No, no," Edward called to her before he turned to G. "I can't throw you around the pool when your mom is in with us. Not safe for the baby."

"Okay." G pouted but let it go.

"No, really, I'm thirsty, anyway," Ember said and climbed out.

Foster's eyes zeroed in on her belly. She'd taken to wearing tankinis during her pregnancy, not because of the bump, but because she thought her breasts were obscene.

He wasn't complaining.

About anything.

Two months after they'd started dating again, he proposed, she said yes, and then a few weeks later, she moved into the house with him and G. Her sisters put their family house up for sale, and a new family moved in. The Bonets seemed surprisingly at peace with it.

As for him and Ember, they married in winter, a small ceremony, just family and a few friends, and much to Foster's relief, his parents attended.

For five months after the rehearsal dinner, they didn't speak. He missed his parents, but not enough to give up Ember. Thankfully, his mom convinced his father to stop being a stubborn ass. Edward missed his son and his granddaughter. And once he gave Ember a chance, Foster knew Edward came to respect and care for her too. So much so, he'd stopped making excuses for Carolyn. Carolyn, who no longer called to speak with Georgie. She'd halted her calls around three months after she left for Paris. The next thing Foster knew, he heard from her lawyers. She granted him sole custody.

She wasn't cut out to be a mom, she'd said.

G asked for her less and less every day until one day, she called Ember "Mom."

Ten minutes later, he'd found Ember crying in their bedroom. Part joy, part rage at Carolyn.

When Edward heard G call Ember "Mom" for the first time, he'd gone cold and quiet. Foster had worried he'd make an issue out of it.

However, on his next visit, he started referring to Ember as G's mom, too, proving that people can change for the better no matter what their age.

"Let me get you water," his mom said to Ember, standing from her lounger.

"I can get it."

"No, you sit here under this umbrella. You shouldn't catch too much sun."

Realizing she was right, Ember agreed and took his mom's place under the shaded lounger. Unable to resist, Foster got up and nudged her over so he could lie beside her on it. Then he rested his hand on her stomach.

"How's our little guy?"

"Kicking while I was swimming." She grinned. "I think he likes it."

Foster kissed her nose. Feeling how warm she was, he frowned. "I think you should stay out of the sun for the rest of the day."

Instead of stubbornly arguing with him like she usually

did, Ember snuggled into his chest. "Okay. This is nice, anyhow."

He nodded, holding her close, his hand on her belly, watching G squeal with delight as his father threw her into the air, the water splashing up over the sides as she dropped back into the pool. He knew his dad would tire quickly but would push through as long as Georgie wanted him to.

"I'm so happy," Ember whispered against his throat.

An ache flared across Foster's chest. He held her tighter. "That's all I ever want to hear."

A minute later, his mom returned with a tray of drinks, calling to her husband to watch his back.

It was a fairly ordinary domestic scene.

Yet to Foster, it was a beautiful goddamn miracle.

VILLAIN: A HERO NOVELLA

CHAPTER ONE

"Run with the twins with different fathers' story. See if we can get the mom in for next Monday," said my boss, Dick.

I caught Barbara rolling her eyes and hid my smirk. She was one of the hosts of the breakfast show *WCVB This Morning* and getting a little sick of our new boss. She wasn't the only one.

Dick cut her a dark look. "Problem, Barbara?"

"I was wondering when I get to interview someone about something important again." She shrugged.

Barbara had job security. She was much loved at WCVB and would be hard to replace. So she could push Dicky Dick a little further than the rest of us.

"You don't think twins that have different fathers is scientifically important?"

"I think it's scientifically rare. And there has been no mention of DNA tests, no doctors corroborating her story. This woman put the story up on social media and it got some attention. That's all. I call bullshit. Where's the evidence?"

"People don't want evidence. They want sex and scandal.

If she's lying, great. You get her on that couch and you grill her about why she's lying. If you can make her cry or storm off the set, even better." And apparently that was all he was going to say on the matter because he turned to me.

I hated this part of our early morning conference meetings: when Dick's lecherous eyes landed on me.

"Nadia, how is your weather report coming for next week? Anything there?"

My meteorology reports for this week sat in front of me. "The rain from this week will ease off into a heat wave. I'm guessing lots of people will be heading to the coast for a long weekend."

His black eyes ran over my chest and I wanted to shrivel inside myself. He grinned. "Fantastic. Let's get you to the beach next week in a bikini for Monday's weather report."

The thought made my stomach plummet. This was not what I signed up for. Russ, our last boss, the boss who hired me, was a brusque but professional man who would never have dreamt of putting me in a bikini on air. "Um ... I'm not comfortable with that."

Dick raised an eyebrow. "How so?"

Barbara huffed in annoyance for me. "She's not a Playboy Bunny, *Dick*."

"She's a weather *girl*. And her face, tits, and ass have shot our ratings through the roof. Can you imagine what they'd do if they saw her in a bikini?"

Anger bubbled under my skin. *She's a weather girl. And her face, tits, and ass have shot our ratings through the roof. Can you imagine what they'd do if they saw her in a bikini?* I memorized every word for my log file. "Actually, Dick, I'm a broadcast meteorologist, and I'm not reporting the weather in a bikini."

From the corner of my eye, I saw Barbara grin proudly.

It was difficult for me to stand up to Dick, which was infuriating because I'd never found it difficult to stand up to anyone. But I loved my job. I loved the challenge of getting on camera and having to think on my feet. I didn't have cue cards like the rest of my colleagues. It was just me, my report, a green screen, and coming up with a way to report the weather that was fun, witty, and fit with the theme of the breakfast show that day.

So I didn't want to lose my job after only six months, which was a possibility considering Dick had already fired our entertainment news girl and our chef and replaced them immediately with younger, more pliable employees.

If Dick was surprised by my mulishness he didn't show it. He opened his mouth to speak but was interrupted by Andrew, Barbara's co-presenter. "You can't force Nadia to wear a bikini, Dick, and harassing her about it violates a whole bunch of in-the-workplace legislation."

Dick's lips pressed together in irritation. He sighed. "Fine. But let's get you out on the beach. At least wear a summer dress or something a little enticing."

I shrugged, not agreeing or disagreeing. Which was better than getting up out of my chair and kicking him in the balls.

Relieved when he moved on to asking me what I had in mind for today's show, my tension slowly eased, especially when he eventually turned his attention to Angel, our entertainment news girl.

When the meeting was over, I stood, ready to head back to the makeup department. They'd already done my makeup but they had to put finishing touches on my hair before we went live.

People often asked me if the early mornings killed me but you got used to them after a while. Monday to Friday I got up at 3 a.m., got to work between four and four thirty, pulled together my meteorology reports, went into hair and makeup, joined the team for our conference meeting, finished hair and makeup, and prepared to go live. Our breakfast show started at six and finished at nine, and I appeared every half hour to do the weather. Afterwards I worked on my long-range meteorology reports so I had an idea of what was ahead, and then for the most part the rest of the day was mine. It meant early to bed, which played havoc with my social life but it was worth it.

"Nadia, see me in my office. Now," Dick said as the staff filtered out of the room. He followed them.

Barbara frowned at me. "Do you want me to come with you?"

I loved this woman. Grateful, I gave her a tense smile. "I think I better go it alone. I'll be okay."

"Are you still keeping that log?"

"I'm still keeping that log."

"Good." She squeezed my arm.

A horrible case of butterflies erupted in my belly as I strode to Dick's office. If he wanted to argue about the bikini, I had to push past my fear of being fired. Because there was no way in hell I was getting my ass out in a bikini on live television.

The tinkle of a text message on my phone brought my head down to where my phone lay on top of the folders in my arms.

The sender's name sent irritation through me. I flicked it open.

Please, darling, we need to talk. We both made mistakes. Let's put it behind us.

Darling. And to think I used to like it when he called me that. Now it made me want to smash my phone every time I saw the word. I wasn't his darling. I'd never been his darling. I deleted the text, like I'd done with all the others.

Dick had left his office door open for me. I rapped my knuckles against it and waited.

"Come in and shut the door behind you." Dick sat on the

edge of his desk, his ankles crossed in front of him, his arms crossed over his chest. As always, his dark eyes ran the length of my body, slowly, lasciviously, and in a way that one day might get him punched.

I reluctantly shut his door behind me and turned to face him, pressing my folder against my chest so I could at least conceal the part of my body that fascinated him so much.

What most people didn't know about me was that I was pretty insecure about my body. Growing up I was a chubby kid and had been bullied mercilessly until junior high. I'd stretched out, lost the puppy fat, and my waist shrank. The only part of me I'd never been insecure about were my legs. My mother had long, fantastic legs with perfectly toned calves, toned thighs, and a slim ankle. Great legs. And she'd given me those. But I still had big boobs, wide hips, a sizeable ass, and a curve to my belly that no amount of sit-ups could flatten. Everything about my body was exaggerated and I envied women who could slip on any dress and have it sit beautifully on their slender curves.

I wasn't a woman who could wear practically anything I wanted. Jeans made my ass look huge, as did most pants. Anything floaty made me look bigger than I was. Fitted fifties-style attire suited my figure best, so I dressed in a lot of pencil skirts and blouses.

It was a surprise to me that I became so popular on WCVB for my curves. Don't get me wrong—I'd had men in the past tell me how much they loved my curves, but I honestly thought they were lying in the way most men do when they tell a woman she's beautiful so they can fuck her.

But Boston liked my curves. I was "WCVB's Weather Pin-Up Girl." The attention was a little daunting at first, and truthfully I was at war with myself over it. Part of me got a huge confidence boost from it, and the other part of me was uneasy that they were focused on my appearance. Yet, I knew that was a huge part of the industry I was in, and I knew that before I got into it. Thankfully, as it turned out, just as many women liked me on the show as men did. They said I was funny and down-to-earth. Real.

That made me feel better.

Dick, however, never made me feel better.

He made me wish I could wear a burlap sack to work.

"Don't worry, it's not about the bikini." He waved the thought away.

Under normal circumstances I might have relaxed, but this was Dick.

So I didn't.

"I have a proposition for you."

I knew it.

This was the moment I'd been dreading.

Yeah, I was going to be sick.

"How would you feel about taking over Angel's job?"

Shock rippled over me, putting a pause on the nausea. "In entertainment?"

"Yes. She gets more airtime than you, which makes no sense considering you are why viewers are tuning in."

"Not all of them. They love Barbara and Andrew."

Dick rolled his eyes. "Right. Well, if it were up to me, you'd be getting Barbara's job but the powers that be upstairs like her so she stays. For now."

Bastard.

"But I want more of you on our show."

"I'm a meteorologist."

"Whether you like it or not, you're Boston's new 'it girl' and I want more of you on my show." His eyes bored into my folder, as if he stared long and hard enough, he'd see through it to my chest. "And I have a story that will get you there."

I didn't want Angel's job. I wanted to keep *my* job. "I'm not interested."

Dick's expression hardened. "I have a private investigator friend. Did you know that?"

It was never good when someone asked that question out of the blue like that, right?

My stomach flip-flopped.

"It always befits a boss to know his staff as well as he can. I know my staff very, very well." He stood up from the desk and I had to steel myself from pressing back against his door. "For instance, I know that you're not quite the sexy-but-nice girl next door you make yourself out to be. You're also not a natural redhead and your real name isn't Nadia Ray. And I know why."

Sudden understanding dawned.

The bastard thought he knew who I was because of my past. He thought I was *that* kind of woman. No wonder he was more abrasive with me than any of his other female staff.

Fuck.

"How do you know that?"

"It's easy enough to find out these things if you know where to look." He took a step toward me, smirking. "Somehow I don't think Boston's 'it girl' will fare too well when they discover she was a home-wrecker at the tender age of twenty-one."

I hated him.

I truly hated him.

"What do you want?"

"That's easy. I want to be the highest-rated breakfast show in Massachusetts. I've failed in the past, Nadia. Let's just say I didn't like the way I was treated while I was struggling to climb my way back up. Until now. With this job, I've been given a second chance. I can't fail again. And I think you're the key to my success. So, we're going to prove to the powers that be that you deserve the top spot. First, Angel's job ... then we'll work on getting you Barbara's."

"I don't want their jobs."

"It's not about what you want. Or haven't I made that clear?" He grinned as if he were telling a joke instead of blackmailing me. "And I have the seeds of what could be a brilliant story."

I thought about the log on my iPad. Since Dick started working here, I'd kept an exact account of every sexual comment he'd made to me. The plan had been if he pushed me too far, I would take it to the station executives. Unfortunately, I knew how these things went. Dick would be fired but eventually they'd find a way to get rid of me too, not wanting to be tainted by a sex scandal. And I was afraid there were few employers who would hire someone who'd accused a colleague of sexual harassment. I needed this job. This job was the first thing in a long time that made me feel good about myself.

"What's the story?"

"This one we'll need to be careful with, and it will test your research skills." Dick stepped toward me again and I braced myself. If he so much as touched me ... "I slept with an older woman this weekend while I was at a family wedding in Philly. She was drunk, we got to talking after sex, and she let slip something very interesting."

"What?" I snapped. I wanted out of his office. And I really, *really* didn't want to hear about his sex life.

"She let it slip that I wasn't the first younger man she'd been with. She developed a taste for living in Cougar Town after paying a hot young guy to fuck her. And do you know who that young guy was? Caine Carraway. CEO of Carraway Financial Holdings. She told me that while he was at Wharton, he prostituted himself to her and her wealthy friends. That's how he got the capital to invest."

Uneasiness crawled through me. If this was true ... Even I, a newbie to Boston, knew who Carraway was. He'd strode into Boston high society despite his lack of blue blood because he was immensely wealthy, intelligent, and ruthless. This story ... this story if true would be the biggest scandal to hit the city in a long time.

I didn't judge people. I couldn't care less if it were true and I wasn't in the business of destroying a person's reputation. I knew how that felt firsthand. "That sounds like nonsense and without proof, you're asking for trouble. Carraway is a powerful man, Dick."

"Exactly why we need evidence." He reached behind him and plucked a card off his desk. Handing it to me, he said, "My one-night-stand's card. She won't return my calls but she might talk to you. Try to get in touch with her. While you're at it, get digging. There's something here. Carraway is practically untouchable. Bringing him down would take this station to another stratosphere."

I stared at my boss in horror. He was truly a disgusting human being.

Reading my expression, Dick sobered. "I'm doing this for us both, Nadia. With sex appeal and charisma like yours, you deserve to be a star."

With a heart like yours, you deserve nothing. But I didn't say the words out loud. Instead I crushed the business card in my hand and turned to leave.

"Nadia."

I paused, not wanting to look at him again. I didn't think my stomach could take it.

"Remember what's on the line here."

I nodded, all my words choked down by rage, and then I got the hell out of there.

As soon as I returned to my workstation, I pulled my iPad out of my drawer and logged into my file. Quickly, I recounted everything that had happened in my boss's office and saved it. The iPad trembled in my shaking hands. What was I going to do?

Maybe ... maybe I could do a little digging. See what was there. Buy some time. Figure out how in the hell I could get Dick fired without losing my job at the same time.

CHAPTER TWO

S taring at my laptop screen, at the papers spread all over
the desk in my sitting room, a measure of relief washed
over me.

There was nothing here.

For the past two weeks, in my spare time, I'd been
researching Caine Carraway. I'd also used savings I couldn't
afford to use on a private investigator. I had him following
Dick everywhere in the hopes that he'd find something I
could use to blackmail my boss out of blackmailing me. It
made me sick to my stomach to even contemplate blackmailing someone but that's how desperate Dick made me
feel.

Since that moment in his office, I'd been walking around
with a constant knot in my stomach.

I pulled at my ponytail in frustration but not at the fact
that I'd found nothing on Carraway. That was the best news I
had so far.

The woman Dick had slept with, Imelda Worthington,
was refusing to take my calls. She'd hung up on me on our

first call, and now she was screening me. I'd left a number of messages but so far, nothing.

As for Carraway's history at Wharton, from what I'd discerned, he'd worked his way through business school as a waiter at a fancy restaurant on Society Hill. How he got the money to make his first investments seemed clear to me.

I pulled out a photograph of Henry Lexington from my research.

Henry was the son of Randall Lexington, the CEO of *Randall Lexington*, a domestic and offshore bank; he worked for his father, who happened to be Carraway's business partner. Henry was where Carraway got his money to invest, I was sure of it, because Henry and Caine were good friends and roommates at Wharton. As far as I could tell, they were still close.

I stared at their photos. God, the two of them were annoyingly good-looking. Where Caine was tall, darkly handsome, and brooding, Henry was tall with light brown hair, had a mischievous twinkle in his blue eyes, and overall polished, movie-star good looks. According to the society pages, he was a perpetual flirt, never seen with the same woman twice, and he was the ultimate catch. He and Caine were Boston's most eligible bachelors.

But they came from entirely different backgrounds.

Whereas Henry had all the luxury and opportunities in the world, Carraway had not.

He grew up in South Boston, son of a construction worker and a shop girl. His mother's body was found in a hotel room when he was a boy—a drug overdose. Three months later his dad walked into their cop neighbor's home, took the cop's gun, and blew his own brains out.

Carraway was put into the system.

A tragic early life.

It only made his successes more impressive.

I hated Dick. I hated that he would want to hurt someone who had strived so hard to put his past behind him.

There was no other scandal immediately to report. Carraway didn't seem to have a lot of connections in his life. If anyone knew anything remotely private about him, it would be Lexington. My eyes flicked back to the photo of the handsome blueblood. It was from yesterday's newspaper: a photograph of him at Richard and Cerise Anderson's anniversary ball at their home in Weston. On his arm was a very attractive, tall, enviously slender brunette. She was named as Alexa Hall, Carraway's PA. Henry had taken Carraway's PA to the ball?

Wait.

Hall?

Something about her name bothered me and I fumbled to find the file I had on Carraway's staff. As Carraway's PA, Alexa would surely know more about him than most but I'd eliminated her as a possibility because she had only recently started working for Carraway.

But her name ...

I pulled out her official employee file at Carraway Holdings. The file was confidential but my friend Joe had a friend who worked at Carraway Holdings and owed him a big favor. Joe and I met at college, we fell in love in a nonsexual way because he was attracted to men, and I rarely asked him for a favor so he cashed in this one for me. His friend got into the personnel files and made a copy for me. It had to be some big favor he owed Joe to risk his job like that, but Joe wouldn't tell me what. Joe was a whiz with a computer, though, so I hope it wasn't anything more illegal than copying some personnel files.

That's how I ended up with Alexa's file. And I knew why her name was bothering me.

Her file said Alexa Holland, not Hall.

Holland?

As in Holland Diamonds?

The Hollands were one of the oldest, bluest-blooded families in Boston.

Why would a Holland be working for Caine Carraway as his PA? And why would they lie about her name at the ball?

I Googled Edward Holland, the current patriarch of their mini empire.

There was no mention of a granddaughter called Alexa.

However, the story that caught my attention was his son's. Alistair Holland. Disinherited twenty years ago, Alistair Holland divorced his wife Patricia Estelle Holland, leaving behind her and their son, Matthew.

But where did he go?

I drew up his picture and then folded Henry out of the photo of him and Alexa and put Alexa next to Alistair. "Hmm." There was something in the chin and shape of their eyes ... but not enough to say they were related.

Flipping back to Alexa's file, I looked up her date and place of birth and called Joe to ask him for another favor. Ten minutes later, he called me back with results.

"Found her birth certificate. Her father isn't named on it. But her mother is Julie Brown."

"Thanks, Joe."

"I thought you didn't need anything else from me," he teased.

"I owe you another beer."

"Nah, this is fun playing detective. Arthur and I are considering doing a PI bit."

I snorted. Arthur was Joe's husband, and they liked to play out a different sex scenario every week. "Have fun with that."

"I'm thinking I'll be the PI and he'll be on the—"

"For future reference, I never need to know the details."

He laughed and hung up.

And I immediately searched for Julie and Alexa.

A few pages into the search, I found an article from eleven years ago, from a high school in Chester, Connecticut, a town about an hour from my own hometown of Beacon Falls.

Alexa and Julie had raised money together as part of a mother-daughter entrepreneurial challenge. All the money went to charity. They were photographed together at the high school and it was clear that Alexa looked more like her mother.

But that wasn't what made my heart rate speed up.

It was the profile of a man who appeared to be walking out of the shot.

I looked at Alistair Holland and then back to the newspaper article.

It was the same guy. Alistair.

Alistair Holland *was* Alexa's father.

He had to be.

But why didn't anyone know this?

Why was Alexa unacknowledged?

I turned my attention back to the mystery of Alexa Holland and started weeding through the stories of Alistair's disinheritance. At first I couldn't find anything about Julie or the reason why he'd been disinherited. The society pages speculated but no one really knew anything real. However, as the minutes gave way to hours and my eyes blurred, something pushed at the edges of my brain.

A date.

No.

I rifled through my folders and found the one I was looking for.

The articles on Caine's tragic childhood.

"The dates," I whispered to myself.

No. That was mere speculation too ... I had no evidence.

But everything somehow connected.

No. I shook my head. Surely someone else would have put this together if it did.

But then no one else knew about Alexa. About Julie.

My eyes flicked to the date on the short article in the newspaper about Caine's father's suicide. And then I looked at the old society pages announcing Alistair's disinheritance. They were only weeks apart.

All the information started whirling around in my head. Caine's mother worked in an upmarket shop in Beacon Hill. From the one photo I'd found of her, she was extremely beautiful. A beautiful shop girl in Beacon Hill would have tempted Alistair Holland, a known philanderer. Did they have an affair? From the stuff I had on Alistair, I knew he'd run into trouble in his youth with drink and drugs. Was there a connection to him and Caine's mother's death? Is that why Edward Holland disinherited him and he ran off to Connecticut to be with Julie Brown and his illegitimate daughter?

So why would Caine hire the daughter of the man who could've been involved in his mother's death?

"Your imagination is getting the better of you." I sank back in my seat, thinking perhaps I should have been a fiction writer instead of a meteorologist.

But the idea that there was something in the story made me antsy.

And I didn't want to stop until I'd proved or disproved my theory.

"Why?" I huffed to myself.

It wasn't like I had any intention of actually taking this story to Dick.

No ... but if there were truth in it, I could take it to Caine and tell him what Dick was up to. Seeing how easy it was for a nonresearcher to put the pieces together might light a fire in Caine to put a stop to Dick digging into his history. And consequently, hopefully, put a stop to Dick messing with me.

I stared at the photos of Alexa and Caine. Their mystery was intriguing but more than that, it could save my job.

My eyes flicked from Alexa to Henry Lexington. I'd bet everything I owned that handsome blueblood knew the truth.

I'd also bet everything I owned that he'd never tell.

His hand rested proprietarily on Alexa's slender hip. She looked like a lot of the women he dated, if not more striking than most. I wasn't exactly his type but it was possible, if I could find a way to meet him, the known womanizer might be swayed by my feminine wiles.

Or not, the insecure voice in my head said.

There had to be a way to find out the truth without turning to Lexington.

There just had to be.

ॐ

JOE WAS A BETTER researcher than I was and he'd managed to find me Caine Carraway's childhood apartment. My thinking was that perhaps someone who lived in the building at the time might still live there and be able to give me some answers.

It was a Saturday and I should've been spending the little free time I had relaxing or sleeping, but I had to follow up on my theory.

Dick had asked me into his office the day before, and it had lit a fire under *my* ass.

"Anything?" he asked as I'd closed the door behind me.

"Not a thing," I lied.

To my revulsion, he invaded my personal space, placing

his hands at either side of my head on the door as he leaned in. "I don't have to remind you what's on the line, do I?"

I'd wanted to lift my knee and slam it into his crotch but, as usual, I was wearing a tight pencil skirt, which restricted that kind of movement.

Instead I seethed. "You might want to take a step back."

He leaned in further until his breath whispered across my lips. His cologne was spicy, cloying, and might as well have been a pillow over my face for how suffocated it made me feel. "You might want to put a little more effort into this story, Nadia. One call to the right reporter and your career goes up in flames."

"Imelda Worthington won't take my calls."

"That's it?" he sneered. "That's all you've done?" His eyes washed over my face and then dropped to my chest. "So you really are just a piece of ass, huh."

One day I was going to snap. I could feel it. He was going to reduce me to physical violence. I hated him. "No, I've been looking. But if there's a story, Carraway has buried it deep. Which wouldn't surprise me considering who he is. He has money and resources we don't have. Plus, I have to be careful so I don't alert him that I'm looking into him."

Dick sighed. "Try Imelda again." He dropped one hand to my shoulder and ran it slowly down my arm, deliberately brushing the side of my breast with his fingers. "You have a week."

I shrugged his hand off and fumbled for the door handle. Yanking the door open with all my strength forced him to stumble back and I shot out of his office.

Not wanting to see anyone, I'd locked myself in the ladies' restroom and fought a battle with tears. There was no way in hell I'd let him get away with making me cry. I thought of his touch and the way it made my skin crawl, like a thousand tiny spiders had followed in the wake of his hand on my body.

This was the point I needed to tell the powers that be what he was doing.

Touching me was crossing the line.

But anger had started to course through me from the moment he'd put his hands on me, an anger so hot its flames burned all those creepy little spiders to ash.

No, he wouldn't get away with this, but I wasn't going to take it to the executives and eventually lose my job. I was going to prove my Caine and Alexa theory and use Caine as a weapon to destroy my lecherous, asshole boss.

So it was taking me down a dark path, making me like him in a way, yet right then, staring into the mirror at that angry, vulnerable woman, I didn't care.

All I cared about was showing Dick that *I* had power and he couldn't take it from me.

No one could.

Shaking off the memory of yesterday, I grabbed my purse and opened the door to my apartment with every intention of jumping in a cab to the address Joe had given me.

However, a man blocked my way.

He stood in my doorway, his fist raised as if to knock.

Shocked, I stared up at his familiar face.

Why the hell was Henry Lexington standing in my doorway?

His vibrant blue eyes met mine and for a moment, neither of us said a word. Silence stretched thinly between us, and I suddenly realized I was holding my breath.

Lexington quite abruptly broke the silence. "Miss Ray?"

"Yes, what—"

"We need to talk." He pushed past me and walked into my apartment without an invitation.

For a moment, I stood there with my mouth open, asking myself if that had just happened. Were people really that rude?

I stared after him, watching him disappear out of my hall and into my sitting room.

All my papers on Carraway were in there!

"Hey!" I called, shutting the door and hurrying after him. "What do you think you're doing?"

Lexington stood in the middle of my small sitting room, his back, thankfully, to my desk. His expression was sullen, cool, and calculating. This was not the charming, hedonistic millionaire I'd read about. "I could ask you the same thing, Miss Ray."

"Excuse me?" Cold sweat prickled under my arms. Did he know? How did he know? If he didn't know, why the hell else would he be here? Why was he here and not Carraway?

I waited anxiously for Lexington to stop boring through my face with his hard eyes. "I assume you know who I am."

"You're Henry Lexington."

"And you, Miss Ray," he turned and strode over to my desk, fingering my papers, "are going to let a certain story die."

My belly flipped unpleasantly.

Goddammit. "What?" I said.

Lexington raised an unimpressed eyebrow. "Imelda Worthington."

Fuck.

"That blank expression isn't fooling anyone, Miss Ray. I know she said a few unfortunate things to Richard Peters, your boss, and I know you've been calling her ever since."

Despite my guilt, despite knowing I was in the wrong here, this privileged asshole had burst into my apartment to intimidate me. Like hell! "You do, do you?"

His eyes narrowed. "Imelda informed me of what's been going on and asked me to kindly give you a message." He prowled toward me and I suddenly felt real fear. I didn't know this man and he was here to shut me up. How far would he go? I steeled myself, not wanting him to see my fear. If my expression gave me away, however, I didn't know; all I did know was that Henry Lexington stopped a good foot from me. It still wasn't enough. He stood at over six feet, his broad shoulders fitted into a perfectly tailored three-piece suit. He had big, masculine hands, one hidden in his pocket, the other resting on his flat stomach over a suit button. Henry Lexington had a swimmer's build— sleek but powerful—and I could only guess at the strength beneath his suit. I struggled not to feel overwhelmed by his large, magnetic presence, as much as I struggled not to feel fear.

"You'll leave her alone," he demanded.

Guessing there was no point in being coy considering he'd seen my desk, I asked, "Why are you here instead of Carraway?"

Lexington flashed me a wolfish grin that didn't reach his eyes. "Because I'm the nice one. Caine scares Imelda. He scares most people. Not you, though." He took another step toward me, seeming to be cataloguing every little nuance of my face. "And if you're not careful, that lack of fear could ruin you, Miss Ray."

If I'd been smarter, I would've told Lexington everything there and then. But his threats cut open the wounds Dick had caused. That others had caused. How I was sick of men trying to bully me. "I don't care how Carraway made his money in his youth, and anyway, there is no evidence to prove he did what Imelda told Dick he did."

It was a slight movement, so miniscule most wouldn't have noticed, but Lexington's shoulders lowered ever so, just enough to tell me he was relieved. Which meant there was probably truth in what Imelda had said.

Interesting.

"But that's not the story I found."

Lexington's jaw clenched and he cocked his head to the

side. There was something about being the sole focus of this man that made me nervous and insecure. I put it down to the fact that I was alone with him in my apartment and he'd politely threatened me.

"I've seen you in the morning doing the weather reports." He dropped his gaze for the first time, deliberately raking it over my body, before moving back up to my face. "You're hard to miss."

I kept my expression carefully blank, not liking his derisive tone. Not at all.

"How then," he took a step toward me, "does a weather girl end up chasing tabloid gossip?"

But he didn't give me a chance to explain, or to tell him what I'd already planned to tell Carraway. "Tabloid journalists are bottom feeders. Lowly scum on the evolutionary chain." His upper lip curled in distaste and I hated that it was directed at me. Defiance shuddered through me but I held it together. Who was he to judge me? He'd had money and power his whole life. He didn't know what it was like to be made to feel like a victim.

I flinched, goddamn him.

And he saw it. His brows drew together as he studied me and his tone softened ever so slightly. "Caine doesn't know you're digging, and he doesn't need to know. Stop."

He seemed to take my non-answer as agreement because he walked past me to leave.

What was I doing?

Just because this man was an asshole didn't mean Carraway wasn't still the answer to my problem with Dick.

I hurried after Lexington, and as he opened my door, I called out, "The story is about his mother's death and whether the Hollands are connected to it. Alistair Holland. Was he there when she died and did someone cover it up? Is

Carraway's PA Alexa related to the Hollands? And if so, why is she working for him?"

Henry whipped around and barreled me back into the wall before I could even blink, anger emanating from every part of his body as he trapped me. Infuriating heat and expensive cologne engulfed my senses. "How much do you want?" he seethed.

Shock and fear quickly turned to disgust and disappointment.

How stupid was I to think this guy could help me?

How stupid was I to think any man could help me?

I was right before.

I needed to fix this myself. Like always.

"You people think you can do whatever the hell you like, don't you," I said, my voice hollow in my ears, "Throw money at the problem and it'll go away."

"Don't pretend like I'm the bad guy here, Miss Ray. I'm not the cruel woman playing journalist, plucking guesses out of rubble and trying to put them together like a puzzle to wound strangers who don't deserve the consequences of your poisoned pen."

I wasn't trying to do that, you arrogant bastard!

I gave him a hard, mocking smile. "How poetic of you, Mr. Lexington."

"Don't think seduction will work here," he bit out, staring at my mouth, surprising me because seduction was the last thing on my mind. "Contrary to popular belief, I'm not swayed by every pretty face I see." He pushed off the wall and stepped back. "You will bury this story or I will bury your career."

Hurt kept me pinned to the wall. "And here I was led to believe you were the most charming man in Boston."

"Oh, I am. But some people aren't worth the energy."

And on that last well-placed parting shot, he marched out of my home, slamming the door behind him.

Feeling exhausted, I hurried to lock my door. Slumping against it, tears of anger pricked my eyes.

I hated Dick.

And I hated Lexington.

To spite him, I should give Dick the story. Clearly from Lexington's reaction there was truth in it.

But I wasn't a spiteful person and it wasn't Carraway's fault that his friend was a dipshit. And it certainly wasn't Alexa Holland's fault.

I'd still find a way to bury it, and not because Lexington had bullied me, but because it was the right thing to do.

CHAPTER THREE

I was in hell.
   More of a hell than usual.
Dining with Dick.

Which meant I'd barely eaten a thing and was getting lightheaded on wine.

It was a few days after Lexington had bullied me at my apartment and I was no closer to figuring out a way to get Dick off this story and off my back. Instead, Dick's boss, Jack, had asked Dick and I to wine and dine a possible investor in WCVB.

Mitchell Montgomery, the toilet paper king.

Yes, the guy made a lot of money in toilet paper.

It made sense, right? Everybody needed toilet paper.

And apparently the toilet paper king liked *This Morning* and he especially liked the weather reports. It was becoming clear on this little lunch why Mitchell Montgomery had earned the moniker, "The Asswipe."

Somehow I'd gotten through the meal but to my horror, Mitchell had insisted we join him in the cocktail bar for a midday Scotch.

"You know what I was thinking," Mitchell leered at me, "you should start wearing a bikini under a transparent rain-coat while you're reporting the news. That would be adorable."

Oh yes, adorable for sure.

"Great idea," Dick agreed.

Like that was a surprise.

I shot him a filthy look, the lack of food and three glasses of wine having lowered my survival instincts. "It's a little demeaning, don't you think?"

Dick kicked me under the table.

"Are you a feminist?" Mitchell scowled.

"Definitely."

"You don't look like a feminist."

What the hell did a feminist look like? Ugh.

"Nadia is joking, of course. All of your ideas—"

"Lexington!" Mitchell cut off my boss as he yelled over our shoulders.

My shoulders hunched up around my ears at the name he called out.

Seconds later a familiar deep, smooth voice said, "Mitchell, how are you?" And then he was there, standing over our table.

"Coming from a lunch meeting?" Mitchell asked.

"Yes, with Carraway. He's gone back to his office and I'm heading to mine." His eyes shot to me but he didn't give anything away before turning back to Mitchell.

"Join us for a little while."

To my horror, Lexington swiftly agreed and slid in beside Mitchell.

"Lexington, this is Dick and Nadia. This is Henry Lexing-ton. I'm sure you've heard of him. Lexington, Dick and Nadia are from WCVB." He reached over and squeezed my shoulder too hard. "You must have seen this gorgeous creature doing the weather."

My attempt at a smile failed, becoming more of a grimace.

"Of course." Lexington surprised me by throwing me a wide, flirtatious smile. "Nice to meet you, Nadia."

It was the first time he'd said my first name.

In that moment I had to wonder what meeting him would have been like if we didn't hate each other. To our companions, Lexington seemed charming as ever, but I saw the coolness in the back of his eyes when he looked at me.

"I'm thinking of investing in the station," Mitchell told him.

"Ah, I see."

"It would be a wise decision." Dick smiled at Lexington. "Food for thought."

Lexington chuckled. "Not my area of expertise. I'll leave the investing in media to Mitchell here."

"Well, I don't like to brag but I've got some ideas." Mitchell smirked. "I was telling them about one. Don't you think Nadia would look fantastic in a bikini and one of those transparent raincoat things while she reported the weather? That would certainly increase the ratings, right?" He nudged Lexington with his elbow and I suddenly felt like I couldn't breathe.

I was trapped in the middle of the good ol' boys club.

Something like irritation flickered in Lexington's expression. "And what does Miss Ray think of that idea?"

"Hates it."

Dick kicked me again and I winced.

Lexington studied me for a moment and then Dick, before he turned his attention back to Mitchell. He grinned suddenly and clapped the man on the shoulder. "It's a goddamn awful idea, Mitchell."

Surprise turned to more surprise when Mitchell laughed and agreed Lexington was probably right.

How did he do that? How did he criticize someone and get away with it?

They spoke for a little bit about our governor and local politics and then Mitchell turned back to me. "Now, now, we're being rude and neglecting my guest. We should talk about things more on her level."

Because politics weren't on my level?

"What would you suggest?" I attempted not to seethe.

Mitchell shrugged. "Shoes?"

He and Dick laughed but I noted Lexington didn't. He seemed embarrassed for me.

Or for my dinner companions?

"Oh, I know," Mitchell leaned toward me, "I have a question that's plagued me for a while now. Is ... is your ass real or is that surgery? Because if it's real ... Jesus H. Christ."

My stomach roiled as Dick laughed beside me and offered, "It's all real," like he knew from firsthand experience. Which he did not.

"Okay, gentlemen," Lexington patted Mitchell's shoulder again, "I think you've had too much to drink. I'll need to ask you to remember your manners."

"Oh, we're kidding. She knows that."

Inside I was screaming.

Two months ago my life was going somewhere. I was successful, respected, and popular.

Lately I felt like a play toy in a man's world, and I thought I'd left that feeling behind.

"Mitchell," Lexington warned.

The Asswipe sobered and held up his hands in surrender. "I apologize." He turned to me and took my hand in his to press his lips to my knuckles. "I apologize, dear lady."

I wanted to rip my own hand off and beat him over the head with it.

Instead I gave him a tight-lipped smile. "Excuse me, gentlemen." I used the term loosely. "I need to visit the restroom."

As I got up and walked away, I heard Mitchell say, "You've got to admit, though, that is quite the ass."

Alone in the ladies' restroom, I was shocked to discover how badly I was trembling.

No job in the world was worth this.

No.

Never.

Tears burned in my throat as I tried to catch my breath and make my decision.

I was quitting.

And tomorrow I was going above Lexington to tell Caine Carraway everything.

Decision made, I knew I couldn't crumble when I went back out there. I would excuse myself and then call Dick when I got home to tell him I quit.

Throwing open the door, I came to an abrupt halt at the sight of my boss glowering outside of it.

Dick gripped my right bicep and hauled me none too gently down the empty corridor out of sight where he practically threw me against the wall.

Fear and anger pulsed through me and I made to shove past him but he trapped me with the entire length of his body. His heat and hardness overwhelmed, his cologne suffocating me again. The feel of his hot breath on my forehead made my breathing tight and short. When you wanted a man's attention, the weight of his body could be comforting; when you didn't want a man's attention, the weight of his body could feel like a two hundred-pound prison.

Revulsion shuddered through me.

"What the fuck do you think you're playing at? When we get back out there, you're going to start acting like the little whore I know you are and get me this investment."

"You are so done," I hissed, enraged.

He bowed his head so his lips were almost touching mine and I struggled against him as he pinned my wrists to the wall at my sides. "There is only one way to get *your* way, Nadia. Appeasing me."

"Forget it," I tried to head-butt him but he jerked back in surprise. "That story on Carraway is never going to see the light of day. I was never going to let it."

Anger flooded his face red. "The only way that story will die, the only way you can get anything you want, is by doing what *I* want. I'm your boss, princess, and I make or break you." He rubbed against me. "We both know you've spread to get ahead before so let's stop playing the innocent virgin. It doesn't do it for me."

"I'd rather lose everything ... you piece of shit."

The scent of his cologne abruptly dissipated, my body released from the weight of his. I blinked as the blur in front of me focused into Henry Lexington pinning Dick to the opposite wall with an arm at his throat.

I thought I'd seen Henry mad before now.

But I was wrong.

His face was dark with fury as he bared his teeth at Dick. "Blackmail, Dicky boy? You are so fucked." He flicked a look back at me. "You okay?"

I glared at them both. "How long were you standing there?"

"I heard everything." He turned back to Dick. "And she's right. You are so done. Someone has been a very bad boss."

My stomach dropped.

He'd let Dick pin me to the wall that entire time?

He should have ripped the fucker off me as soon as he saw what he was doing, not stopped to eavesdrop!

Yes, by eavesdropping Henry gave me a witness to Dick's crimes against me, I knew that. I knew, somewhere in the back of my mind, that I should be relieved and grateful. The relief would come, but gratitude? No.

I couldn't get over the fact that Lexington had stood and watched Dick assault me and hadn't done anything to stop it until he knew I was innocent of crimes against his friend.

I was done. With both of these men.

So I left them to it, hoping they ripped each other apart until there was nothing left of them.

SUFFICE it to say I didn't sleep much that night. I vacillated between the horror of wondering how long it would've taken me or some kind stranger to save me from Dick's assault at the restaurant, and worrying about my future. When I closed my eyes, I could hear Dick calling me a whore, and I could feel his body on mine again. I'd shudder and my eyes would fly open in the dark. Keeping my eyes open was the only reminder that I was safe. But I wouldn't continue to be safe if I stayed in that job. Despite my anger toward Henry for waiting it out to hear what he wanted to hear before rescuing me, the relief *did* come. I finally had a witness to Dick's harassment. If shit hit the fan, I would hopefully have Henry's testimony. Until when, or if, that ever happened, I was walking away with my career untarnished.

So when I arrived at the station the next morning, looking like hell I might add, it was with every intention of quitting.

However, it soon became apparent that there would be no need for such drastic action on my part.

"Did you hear?" Barbara approached me as soon as I walked in.

"About?"

"Dick."

My heart thumped in my chest. "What about him?"

"He was fired. Apparently, he was arrested last night. Caught on camera slipping Rohypnol into a girl's drink at a private nightclub last month."

"What?" I breathed. "How?"

"Apparently the nightclub 'lost' the footage and then it miraculously turned up."

"Miraculously," I muttered.

Or not so miraculously.

My PI found nothing but apparently, Lexington's PI was better than mine.

"I'm running the show until they send us a new guy."

"Glad to hear it." I suddenly hugged her.

Barbara tensed in surprise and then hugged me back. "Sweetie, are you okay?"

The powerlessness I'd felt these last few weeks, the renewed shame and guilt, the exhaustion, and yes, the fear, coalesced inside me. My control was decimated. Tears filled my eyes and a sob slipped out before I could stop it.

"Nadia?" Barbara drew back, took one look at me, and hurried me into a conference room for privacy. "Did Dick do something to you?"

I couldn't tell her any of it because telling her would mean talking about Carraway and it wasn't my right to. I brushed away tears. "I just didn't like him."

"Sweetie, I've never seen you cry. There has to be more to it than that."

I shrugged, deciding to go with a half-truth. "He was getting more suggestive. And yesterday at lunch with Mitchell Montgomery ... they ..." More tears spilled as I remembered. "I felt like nothing. A piece of ass. Being there, letting them talk to me like that, it felt like I was giving them permission to do whatever they wanted to me. And that scared me. I was going to quit this morning."

"Oh, sweetie." Barbara hugged me again. "I won't let anything happen to you, okay? And next time," she pulled back to stare sternly into my eyes, "you tell me. There are a few bad apples still left in our line of work, and sometimes it's hard for a woman. But not if we stick together. Okay? Promise me."

I realized then that my tears were of relief. I sagged. "I'm glad he's gone."

"Me too. We can get back to normal now."

"Hopefully the next boss won't be an ass."

"We can only hope," she said dryly, and chucked my chin. "Now get into hair and makeup. I'm sorry to say it, sweetie, but you look like you haven't slept for a millennium while being dragged backward through a hedge."

"Funny, it feels like it too."

As I walked to hair and makeup, I realized I'd needed to cry to let it out of my system. I still felt exhausted but relief was slowly settling over me and my steps were lighter than they had been in weeks. Until my phone rang. When I saw the familiar number, a new sense of determination shot down my spine. For the first time since he'd started calling again, I answered. "I'm not playing hard to get. I don't want to hear from you. Ever. I'm changing my number."

I hung up and made a mental note to get a new number after work today.

My meteorology report was done and weather maps sent to the producers ready for the green screen when Lucy at reception called to say Henry Lexington was here to see me.

I glanced at the clock. It was 6 a.m. and I was due to go live in an hour. But I threw my shoulders back. It was better to get this over with now. I told Lucy to bring him to conference room one.

Where I was waiting so I could talk to him privately.

He stepped into the conference room and Lucy closed the door behind her as she left. Like always, Lexington's presence filled the room. I was trying to be cool and casual, leaning against the conference table with my ankles crossed in front of me. His eyes zeroed in on my face, and there was concern in them.

Too little too late.

"If you're here to check if I've dropped the story, you can rest assured I have. Of course, you did hear me tell Dick that last night, right?"

He nodded, taking a careful step toward me. "I came to see if you're all right."

I laughed and the sound was so harsh, it made him flinch. "Why do you care?"

"I deserve that. I admit I misjudged you and I apologize."

I slipped off the desk, standing tall and defiant as I crossed my arms over my chest. "Fine. You can leave."

Lexington suddenly looked exasperated. "I've tried to make amends."

"You got Dick fired." I nodded, having deduced that. "You must have quite the connections to have made that happen. Apparently the club in question doesn't like scandal."

"No, it doesn't, but rape isn't scandal. It's a crime."

Renewed anger rushed through me at the memory of Dick rubbing against me. "Funny, you didn't seem that bothered by it last night."

He looked like he'd been slapped. "Excuse me?"

"Last night," I bit out. "When Dick had me trapped against a wall ... you know ... *sexually harassing me*." Angry tears blurred my vision, which made me even angrier because he didn't deserve them. "You stood there and waited to hear what we were saying before you did anything."

Lexington stared at me a moment, seeming stunned.

"Fuck," he eventually breathed, remorse etched in his eyes as he moved toward me.

I cringed away, stumbling around the desk to put it between us.

He looked horrified by my reaction. "Nadia, please ... I didn't know what I was seeing when I walked into that hall. I thought it was a lover's quarrel. I didn't realize what was happening until I heard him blackmail you. I would never ...," his voice grew hoarse with sincerity, "stand by and let that happen to a woman. To anyone."

"Not even lowly scum on the evolutionary chain?"

"Jesus. I'm sorry. I didn't realize what was happening to you. Not with Dick's blackmail and not last night. I swear." He tentatively took a step toward me like I was an animal he might frighten away. "But I'm still sorry. I should have intervened right away and I regret not doing so."

My blood was so hot with resentment, it took me a moment to process his words, the sincerity behind them. Eventually, I calmed enough to make a decision.

I nodded, thinking maybe I believed him. However, I couldn't look at him anymore. His earnestness made me want to crumble, but I was still too angry. "I tried to tell you. When you were leaving my apartment. I was trying to tell you what I knew so you could help me stop Dick. But you jumped on me. *Pinned* me to the wall." My eyes flew to his so he'd fully understand the comparison I was drawing. "Bullied me." I jutted my chin out. "But I'm nobody's victim, Mr. Lexington. For future reference."

Not that I hoped to see him again. Ever.

"I screwed up."

Yeah, he did.

His piercing blue eyes flew to my face as if he'd heard my confirmation. "Nadia, I have no excuse, no good excuse. I'm very protective of my family. I thought you were trying to hurt a man I consider a brother."

And that was noble in a way.

However, it didn't soothe my outrage.

"Have dinner with me." He shocked the hell out of me. "Let me show you I'm not a bad guy."

"I don't need a guilt date."

"A what?"

"It doesn't matter. I'm not interested."

"If we'd met under different circumstances ... you'd want to have dinner with me." He offered me a boyish, coaxing smile that under different circumstances probably would have worked.

"You know I'm a little tired of men telling me who I am, what I'm worth, and what to do. I really don't need them telling me how I feel."

Lexington's expression sobered. "I know Dick treated you abominably, and I haven't done much better, but you are too young to sound that bitter."

His aim rang true and I winced from the hit.

He was right. I felt older than my years.

I was weary to the bone.

"Look, Mr. Lexington," I walked toward the door and opened it, "I really am glad you nailed Dick to the wall. Literally and figuratively. But I'd like to put all of this behind me. You're right ... I'm too young to be bitter. So I don't need reminders of this. And you're a reminder. I'll live quite happily knowing you and I will never cross paths again."

Striding toward the door, Lexington stopped so there was only inches between us. He wore that seductive, expensive cologne that tickled my senses. Those brilliant eyes stared deep into mine, searching them, and I wavered under their scrutiny.

"I don't want to never see you again," he confessed, sounding surprised.

I didn't know how to respond.

And apparently he didn't know what to follow up with because suddenly he walked away.

CHAPTER FOUR

"We're going to celebrate Dick getting fired. Come with us," Barbara had said after the show.

And I'd stupidly agreed.

It didn't seem stupid at the time, especially since we were celebrating at The Bristol Lounge, one of my favorite restaurants. It was part of the Four Seasons Hotel and directly across from Boston Public Gardens. The truth is I'd wanted a distraction from Henry's visit. It was ridiculous but I couldn't get his intense blue eyes out of my head. Or the remorse that had etched itself all over his face.

Maybe he really did feel bad for the way he'd treated me.

Yeah, maybe he did.

But did that change anything?

He'd still treated me poorly and who was to say he wouldn't again?

Just because people felt awful for doing something didn't mean they wouldn't repeat the crime.

The real problem was my attraction to him.

I could admit it.

I was attracted to the son of a bitch.

There was something deeply wrong with me that I could be attracted to a man I didn't even like.

Turned out that lunch with my colleagues was a terrible distraction idea. Because Henry was dining at The Bristol Lounge with none other than Caine Carraway.

"Maybe we should go somewhere else," I said as we stood in the lobby outside the restaurant. Henry hadn't spotted us yet.

Barbara frowned. "This is your favorite place. You love the Bristol Burger."

I *did* love the Bristol Burger.

And for the first time in weeks, I was hungry.

Dammit.

No man was chasing me away from my goddamn burger.

"You're right." I nodded, sounding more assured than I actually felt. "But I'll walk on your left side."

My friend eyed me in confusion as I huddled at her side, trying to hide behind her as the host led us up the few stairs onto the main floor of the restaurant and right past Henry and Carraway's table near the bar area, to a larger table at the back of the restaurant. As far as I could tell, he hadn't spotted me and there were now pillars between us that I could hide behind.

Relieved, I slid into my chair beside Barbara.

"Drinks?" the waiter asked.

We'd finished giving him our orders when the sight of Henry Lexington walking into view around one of those aforementioned pillars and toward our table made my pulse skitter.

He gave me a soft smile as if we hadn't been enemies up until twenty-four hours ago. "Miss Ray, what a pleasant surprise." That soft smile grew into a roguish grin. "Are you stalking me?"

I arched an eyebrow, wondering what the hell kind of game he was playing now. "A burger. I'm stalking a burger."

"The burgers *are* very good here."

"Mr. Lexington," Barbara said beside me, sounding delighted to see him, and awfully familiar. "What a pleasure to see you."

"You too, Barbara. And please, I've told you before—smart, beautiful women should call me Henry."

I didn't know what to do first: be surprised they knew each other or gag at his flirting with her.

"You know each other?"

"I know everyone worth knowing." He winked at Barbara and she tittered like a schoolgirl.

Dear God.

And then I was the focus of his attention. He leaned against Andrew's chair who was, as always, oblivious to anything but himself. "So this burger ... will it put you in a good mood?"

"Excuse me?"

Those blue eyes were too intense, much too intense. "A good enough mood to agree to have lunch with me tomorrow?"

I was going to kill him.

How dare he put me on the spot in front of my colleagues, in front of Barbara! What? Did he think I'd be civil to him because we had an audience? I scowled. "No."

"Are you seeing someone?" he persisted.

"No, she's not," Barbara interjected, giving me an "Are you crazy?" look. "And yes, she's free for lunch tomorrow. You can pick her up from the station at one."

"Fantastic." Henry gave her a grateful, gorgeous smile before turning it on me. "See you tomorrow."

He was gone before I could even get past the shock that had sealed my lips. Finally, they parted. "What was that?"

Barbara shrugged. "Me making sure you don't miss out."

"How dare you decide if not making a date with Henry Lexington is me missing out."

She raised an eyebrow at my snippiness. "He's Boston's most eligible bachelor, Nadia. For a reason." She gestured to where he'd been standing. "You can't tell me you don't find him attractive."

"I'd have to be blind," I gritted out begrudgingly. "But he and I don't exactly see eye to eye."

"Didn't seem that way to me. You could've cut the sexual tension with a knife." She shuddered, wearing a dreamy smile. "If a man looked at me the way Henry was looking at you, I'd slather myself all over him like butter on bread."

I chuckled because she was hard to stay mad at. "Barbara, the man is a known slut. He's not the settling-down type. When he looks at me, he's merely thinking about sex."

"Sweetie, so are most men and plenty of women," she patted my hand, "but is there anything wrong with sex?"

Only the fact that I hadn't had it in a while. "No."

"So why can't you go on a date with him expecting nothing but a free lunch and, if you're interested, the possibility of sex? I've heard he's very good."

"Well, he's had plenty of practice." I huffed. "I don't like him very much."

"Oh, sweetie, does everything have to be so serious? You don't have to like someone to have fantastic sex with them, believe me."

I stared at my friend, contemplating her advice.

She had a point.

I mean, it wasn't like trusting a man long enough to get into a serious relationship was in the cards for me at the moment. But I liked sex. My sex life didn't need to dry up because I didn't want to be in a relationship. And the last relationship I was in was over a year ago. Pete. He hadn't lasted long. Neither had Mike before him. Or Denny before that. I was kind of a serial monogamist because I wasn't very good at letting the men in my life really get to know me. Pete, Mike, and Denny had all dumped me for the same reason: I couldn't trust them long enough to be real with them.

But I missed sex.

Maybe I should start being more like Henry Lexington. A true bachelorette.

Maybe the man himself could teach me how, and by reducing him to no more than a one-time sexual partner, I could purge myself of the hurt that he'd added to when he'd treated me so poorly. Maybe I could dispel myself of some of the anger that had nestled, seemingly permanently, in a painful hollow in my chest.

ॐ

THERE WAS a big beautiful vase of flowers waiting on my desk when I returned after hair and makeup the next morning.

I admit to feeling a traitorous little thrill in my stomach when I saw the expensive calla lilies (how he knew those were my favorite, I did not know). Shaking my head in frustration that he could both piss me off and surprise me, I reached for the card.

Changing your number doesn't change how I feel. Darling, talk to me.

Fuck.

Of course Henry didn't know I loved calla lilies.

But *he* knew.

Worry pricked at me as I stared at the card. I'd told him too many times to count to leave me alone. I'd changed my number ... He wasn't going all stalker on me, was he?

Hating to rid my desk of the beautiful flowers, I flipped

the card and called the florist who was clearly up at the butt crack of dawn.

"Olivia's Garden, how can I help?"

"Ah, good morning, I received some flowers this morning."

"Miss Ray?"

"Yes," I said surprised.

"Yours were a very early delivery. Did you like them?"

"The flowers are beautiful. However, I really don't want contact with the man who bought them. Would it be possible for you to take them back and let him know that I sent them back?"

"I'm afraid flowers are nonrefundable."

"No, I don't care about him getting his money back. I care about sending a message."

"What flowers would you like to send him to do so?"

Was she for real? "No, I don't want to send flowers."

"We also send chocolates, gift hampers, and wine."

"Never mind." I hung up and slumped into my chair.

"Ooh, who sent the flowers?" Angel asked as she passed by.

"A misogynistic, egotistical, shallow, social climbing, cheating asshole."

She considered this. "He has good taste in flora."

Because she was funny, but mostly because I needed to, I laughed. Hard. And for a moment I felt better.

THE FLOWERS WERE another reminder of what happened when I trusted men. I wasn't saying there weren't men out there who could be trusted. Of course there were. I trusted Joe!

But that was different. When it came to men I was sexually interested in, I never seemed to be able to discern the trustworthy ones from the untrustworthy ones. Before Pete, Mike, and Denny, when I was still naïve enough to trust, I'd ended up choosing the latter, and paying for it emotionally.

It made me more determined to try things the way Barbara suggested, the way that Henry did things.

I didn't need to trust him to have sex with him, right?

I ignored the voice screaming in the back of my mind: *Wrong!*

It was Joe's voice. I'd called him the evening before to relay my thinking to him.

"No, no, no," Joe had cut me off. "Nadia, you are not the one-night-stand kind of girl."

"We don't know that," I'd argued.

"Yes, we categorically do. Don't do this, honey. You'll get hurt and you know I hate seeing you cry."

"Joe, I'm older and wiser now. Maybe this is the path my life is supposed to take."

"It's not. One day you'll meet a man you'll instinctively know you can trust. If you do this ... I think it's going to take you back to a bad place. You'll start hating yourself again and I can't watch you do that to yourself."

Uncertainty and unease, and maybe even a little bit of panic, settled over me at Joe's words. He was the only friend I had left from college, the only one who'd stood by my side, so he knew what he was talking about. Yet, I was tired of standing in one place. "Joe, I need to make a change."

He was silent for a while. "You're a grown woman, honey. You do what you have to do and you know I'll be here. But I am officially worried about this strategy."

"Barbara thinks it's a great idea."

"Barbara doesn't know what I know."

We'd ended the conversation soon after, and for a while I considered taking Joe's advice. But then I thought about my limitations as a girlfriend, and about Henry and how much I wanted to scratch that itch.

Then again, I might have been getting a little ahead of myself. Henry, when he wasn't being a villain, was naturally flirtatious and charming. That didn't mean he was attracted to me. This lunch could merely be an attempt to make amends and assuage his guilt over the way he'd treated me.

AT ONE O' clock on the dot, I found Henry waiting for me at reception. He drank me in from head to foot in a leisurely, decadent way, like he was savoring every minute of watching me walk toward him.

Okay.

So maybe he *was* attracted to me.

He held out his elbow and gave me an arrogant half smile that was much more attractive than I'd like. "Ready to go, Sunshine?"

For a moment I was caught off guard, not only by the nickname but by *him*. He was like a completely different person to the one who had burst into my home and threatened me against hurting his friend. This man was way more complicated than I think most people even realized.

I tried to shrug off the butterflies in my belly—they'd been there since lunch yesterday—and ignored his offered arm. "Sunshine?" I yanked open the reception door and held it for him.

Henry shook his head, laughing at my rejection, and wandered through the open doorway ahead of me.

"Well?" I said.

"Well what?"

But my query was lost in the feeling of being overwhelmed as the elevator doors closed me in the small space, *alone* with him.

My cheeks flushed. I could cook bacon on those things.

I shot Henry a look out of the corner of my eye seeing his continued amusement.

"What now?" I huffed.

"Nothing." He shrugged. "You're adorable when you're angry."

"If you knew anything about women, you would know that is the last thing you want to say to one who's angry."

"Actually, considering how adorable I find you when you're angry, it would make sense I'd want to keep you that way."

I rolled my eyes. "Very cute."

He nudged me playfully with his elbow. "We're just two cuties then, huh?"

The elevator doors opened and I strode out ahead of him. "*I'm* cute. You ... I'm thinking undiagnosed multiple personality disorder."

Henry's laughter rang out behind me and I had to suppress a smile at the compelling sound. He hurried to my side. "I'm growing on you."

"Like a wart."

He grinned and rushed to open the exit door. As I passed him, his blue eyes twinkled mischievously at me. "This is going to be fun."

I wasn't at all surprised to find Henry drove a silver Mercedes S-Class Cabriolet. He had the top down and as he opened the passenger door for me, I almost balked at sliding against the pristine ivory leather seat in case I marked it. Sinking into the luxurious car, I could only stare at the incredibly sexy interior.

Henry got in next to me and threw me the kind of excited grin a child might at Christmas. "Ready?"

"This is quite the car."

"The words say impressed; your tone does not." He observed as he pulled on his seatbelt. "Is it the top? Do you want it up so it doesn't mess your hair?"

"I don't care about that." I frowned, annoyed that he'd think I'd be *that* concerned with my appearance. "I care about how weird this is."

As we pulled into traffic, Henry slipped on a pair of aviator sunglasses. "What's weird about two adults having lunch together?"

"Because forty-eight hours ago, we were enemies."

"So melodramatic. We were merely mistaken about one another."

"*You* were mistaken about me. I think I have you pegged accurately."

"And that's why we're going to lunch because you don't." He shot me that sexy smirk. "You don't know the good stuff."

"Has anyone ever said no to you in your life?"

"Yes, frequently."

"Have you ever listened to them?"

Henry chuckled. "Rarely."

His laughter and the sight of him driving this beautiful car with lazy confidence, his strong hands lightly resting on the wheel, those ridiculously hot sunglasses—it all affected me. Greatly. A sensuous ripple fluttered in my lower belly.

Dear God, I *really* wanted him.

The realization caused my breath to escape from me in a shudder, drawing his attention. Quite abruptly, I made a decision. "I'm just going to put it out there in case you're planning to take me to a stupidly overpriced restaurant for lunch."

"*Okay.*" He drew out the word, sounding amused and wary at the same time.

"I don't particularly like you. In fact, you have become one of the villains in my story so far. I don't want to date you and I doubt very much that you are interested in dating me.

However, I also doubt that you feel so guilty about your treatment of me that you merely want to turn around my opinion of you. No, sir. I'm here because you're attracted to me. That's okay because apparently, I'm attracted to you too. You're hot and it's obnoxious but I can't deny it."

Henry's mouth twitched like he was trying to suppress a smile. "Okay."

"We're attracted to each other or you wouldn't have asked me out and I wouldn't have let myself be manipulated into saying yes. But let's not pretend this is something that it's not with chivalry and a date. You want to fuck me. And I'm amenable to the idea. So let's cut all the bullshit and just do it."

"Jesus." Henry almost ran into the back of a car that had stopped at the light, slamming hard on his brakes. He looked at me and even though I couldn't see his eyes, I knew his expression was incredulous. "You're amenable to the idea of me fucking you? Did I hear that right?"

I flushed. "I'm sure you're used to women with gentler manners but I'm a straight talker. I don't believe in flowering up a situation so as not to offend delicate sensibilities."

The traffic moved forward and Henry didn't speak.

In fact, he stayed silent for a while.

So long that I began to feel my cheeks burn with humiliation.

I'd read him wrong. He really did only want to make amends.

I wasn't his type.

Oh God.

This month had been really, really bad for me.

Finally, he pulled up outside a pizzeria on Tremont Street. Once he killed the engine he took off his sunglasses and turned toward me. His expression was surprisingly sober as he intently studied my face, as if he hoped to find answers there. "You're right," he said, his voice low, deep, "I want you. But I don't consider anticipation bullshit. We're going to have lunch. And you're going to agree to have lunch with me on Thursday. And then you're going to agree to be my date to the Delaney Charity Ball this Saturday. After which we'll go back to your apartment and I will happily fuck you into satisfied exhaustion."

For a moment, I couldn't speak because his last sentence turned me on, his words alone sparking delicious excitement deep in my belly.

What the hell would the rest of him do to me?

Of course, after a second or so of physical arousal, the rest of his words sunk in. "What?" I shook my head in confusion. "No. We don't need to have lunch or go to a *ball* together."

"No lunch dates, no date to the ball, no penis for you. And you don't want miss out on my penis. It's a good one."

God, I didn't want to laugh but he had the kind of irreverent charm that could melt the toughest critic. It was a gift. It was also a mask because I knew there was a dangerous character lurking behind it. Henry Lexington couldn't be trusted. The thought sobered me and Henry frowned. "What's the harm in a few dates, Sunshine?"

The harm was in him. I wasn't a naïve girl in a romance novel who thought she could seriously keep her emotions detached from a guy she was having sex with all the time.

Joe was right about me.

That's why it would be a one-time thing.

And even then, I was questioning my sanity over letting it happen that one time.

"This week, sex on Saturday after the ball, and then you and I are done."

Henry contemplated me a moment. And then he held out his hand. "Deal."

Tentatively, I slid my hand into his and had to fight

against a thrilled shiver as his thumb caressed my skin. "Deal," I managed.

He raised my hand to his mouth and gently pressed his lips to it. I stared at him, confused by the old-fashioned gesture as he let go. "Now, let's eat."

After hurrying around to open my door, Henry helped me out of the car; I was bemused when he held tight to my hand as he led me toward the restaurant.

We were having lunch at a pizza place?

I didn't know whether to be insulted or relieved.

As if he'd sensed my thoughts, he flashed me a grin. "I could've taken you to a fancy restaurant but I wanted to enjoy my lunch with you. And this here is the best damn pizza and ice cream place in Boston."

Relieved, I followed him inside. "You like pizza?"

His brows drew together. "Is there a person alive who doesn't?"

"Fair enough."

We were seated at a small table; I sat on the red leather banquette that stretched the entire length of the restaurant and Henry across from me in a black wrought-iron chair. I suddenly found I didn't know what to say or do now that we'd put our attraction out in the open.

Henry, however, never seemed to be uncomfortable with any situation. "So what made you want to be a meteorologist?"

"Um ..." I stared at him, confused. "Are we really going to do the 'getting to know you' thing?"

"What else are we going to do? Sit here and stare at each other? I could do that because the view is spectacular but I've always found a view gets even more beautiful when you know a little something about it."

"Do you always know the right thing to say?"

He smiled. "I asked a question first."

I sighed. "Fine. I grew up in Connecticut, a small town, and one day for career day in junior high, a broadcast meteorologist from the local station came to talk to us about her work. She was smart and glamorous and she was very kind to me." I gave him a wry, somewhat embarrassed smile as I admitted, "I was a chubby, awkward kid. Not very popular. Everyone else was clambering for her attention. But she picked me out and showed me how her job worked. I fell in love with it right there and then."

"One moment of kindness can change everything."

"Kindness costs nothing and yet it's worth everything."

His answering look was too soft, too tender.

And thankfully the waiter came to take our order at the right moment.

When he was gone, I changed the subject. "And you? Do you like working for your father's bank?"

"I do. I'm a managing director so I'm responsible for bringing in revenue. It means wining and dining clients, traveling a lot. It suits my personality."

"I'll bet it does." He was the perfect salesman—no smarm, just natural charm. "And did you become a managing director right out of college?"

"No. My father is grooming me to take over as COO shortly. He's been grooming me forever. I went into the bank after college as a junior analyst. Worked up to senior analyst, then to VP, then to director, and then to managing director. My father wanted me to understand how the business functions at every level. Well, not every level. He didn't start me in the mailroom."

"That's smart." I was impressed he'd worked his way up through the ranks, even if it wasn't from the mailroom. "And you genuinely like it? You wouldn't have wanted to do anything else with your life?"

Henry grinned at me. "I'm not a cliché, Nadia. I'm not a

poor little rich boy with a woe-me story of familial pressure and suppressed passions. I have a good family, a blessed life, and a job I like and can depend on."

I nodded, wishing it weren't rare to come across someone who was so content with their life.

"I thought you weren't interested in the whole getting-to-know-each-other thing?"

I rolled my eyes at his teasing. "I'm naturally a curious person. Don't get a big head about it."

"Curious, you say?" He raised an eyebrow, and I saw the sexual speculation in his gaze.

"One night, Henry. Not a lot of time to indulge my curiosity."

The blue in his eyes appeared to darken, to smolder. "It's time enough."

Arousal had deepened his voice and suddenly I was imagining all the things I'd like him to do. Lust shot through me, shocking the heck out of me. My breath stuttered and I even felt my nipples peak against my shirt.

Shit.

The pizza arrived, cutting through the tension-filled moment.

I stared down at the yummy-smelling plate, looking forward to tasting pizza that was famous for its charred crust.

"Nadia?"

Reluctantly, for I feared what looking at him would do to me, I lifted my eyes.

Henry stared at me like he wanted to devour me instead of the pizza. "The way you say my name gets me extremely hard, so you might not to want to say it in public too often."

As turned on as his cheeky words made me, they also gave me a little of my equilibrium back. "And you, Henry, might not want to divulge your weaknesses to me."

"Go ahead. Call me Henry. I'm perfectly comfortable

walking around aroused in public. I just thought it might embarrass you." He flashed me a mischievous grin before lifting a slice to his lips.

I tried not to laugh.

I did.

But damn, he made it difficult.

The sound of my laughter clearly delighted him, his answering smile big enough to light up Boston.

CHAPTER FIVE

"How much time do you have?" Henry said in lieu of "hello" as I met him at reception on Thursday. I was keeping up my end of the bargain and meeting him for lunch.

"Why?" I eyed him warily. Today he was dressed casually —instead of a suit, he wore a black, thin cashmere sweater with the sleeves pushed up his forearms, and slim-leg black trousers.

"Because I secured the afternoon off so I could spend it with you. Very difficult thing to do. You should feel honored."

"And what if I didn't have time to give you the entire afternoon?"

"Do you?"

"Maybe, but if I didn't ...?"

He grinned. "I'd convince you that what I have planned is better than whatever you have planned."

"What if what I have planned is sex with an exotic stranger?"

We stepped into the elevator and Henry pressed his hands to his chest dramatically. "Oh how she wounds me."

I laughed at his antics. "Okay. So what did you want

to do?"

"Well ..." he drew it out, waiting until we stepped out of the elevator, "if I recall, you told me on Tuesday that you hadn't toured Boston since coming to live here. Correct?"

"Correct."

Henry reached inside the back pocket of his trousers and produced two tickets. "Hop On, Hop Off, Red."

It was difficult for me to admit, but the man was continually surprising me. "A bus tour?"

"Not just any bus tour. You pay practically nothing for the whole day and you get off and on at whichever stops you want. It's genius."

I snorted. "I would've thought you'd want to tour in style. You seem the type."

"That's your problem." He tapped my nose playfully. "You see me all wrong."

"Hmm," I said, letting him know I wasn't convinced by his sincerity. "I'll need to change into something more comfortable."

"We can stop off at your apartment."

"If we're doing that, we might as well have sex and be done with this."

He wrinkled his nose, seeming to consider it, and then he shook his head. "Nah. I like my plan."

"You're seriously giving up the chance at sex for a bus tour?"

"Yes." He put his hand on my lower back and led me around to the passenger side of his car. That innocent touch made my blood heat.

Why wasn't it affecting him as much, dammit?

I glowered at him and he gave a bark of laughter as he got in the car. "I have had women pissed at me for fucking them and not calling them again. Never have I had a woman pissed at me for refusing to do just that."

"I'm smarter than most women."

Henry threw his head back in laughter. The gorgeous sound trickled away in the wind as we moved into traffic and I shook off the uneasy feeling that I was starting to like Henry Lexington.

And wasn't it a clusterfuck to like a man but not trust him.

⚘

"YOU HAD FUN, RIGHT?" Henry's eyes were filled with laughter.

We were currently sitting in Carrie Nation where I'd ordered the biggest burger along with the biggest cocktail. It wasn't the first time I'd been there. A date once brought me here and we sat in the intimate speakeasy section. Very nice atmosphere for a first date. If your date didn't spend the entire night talking to your breasts.

Thankfully, Henry was being a gentleman and he wasn't looking at my breasts, even though my shirt was soaked.

As was every inch of me.

I'd tried to dry as much of myself as I could under the hand dryer in the bathroom. I should've insisted on going home but Henry thought it was hilarious that we'd been doused in an unexpected rain shower after visiting the Old South Meeting House.

The cocktail bar and restaurant was a few minutes away. I hadn't known where we were going when Henry grabbed my hand and started running.

The waiter had laughed at us when we came through the doors.

Henry was fine. Wet shirt and hair and somehow he looked more lickable than normal.

I looked like a drowned cat.

"Super fun." He laughed at my deadpan tone. "Up until the rain, I mean."

Actually it had been fun. I thought Henry would get bored half an hour into it, but he seemed to enjoy the tourist thing as much as I did.

"You knew all the stuff we learned already, though, right?"

He shrugged. "It's good to get a refresher. Especially in such lovely company."

"You never stop."

"Nope." He eyed my burger. "Are you going to eat that?"

The truth was I never ordered a burger on a date. It was too hard to eat and look elegant at the same time. But in the moment it had sounded like a good idea. Now that my makeup was almost all off, my hair was limp and dripping, and my shirt was a wrinkled mess, I didn't think it was a good idea to add wolf-eating to the image I was creating.

My stomach grumbled.

Henry rolled his eyes. "I heard that. Eat." He lifted up his burger and bit into with no qualms.

Ah, screw it.

I bit off a chunk and closed my eyes in bliss.

"Good?"

I opened one eye and nodded.

Laughter danced in his eyes as it seemed to a lot when he was around me.

"I need to go to the gym," I said glumly after I swallowed. "I hate the gym."

"Then don't go."

"No, I need to. So I can eat like this."

"Thank God you eat." His eyes dropped to my breasts for a second and he shifted in his seat. Was it just me or were his cheeks a little flushed?

"Like what you see, huh?" I teased.

Henry's eyes smoldered so abruptly, my breath caught.

"Sunshine, you have no idea how much. I doubt there's a man alive who wouldn't like all that." He gestured to me.

I laughed. "You'd be surprised."

"Gay men."

"And straight men."

His outraged disbelief was extremely flattering. "Blind men."

"No." I shrugged. "Don't get me wrong. I get plenty of attention from men who have a thing for Christina Hendricks ... but it has been suggested to me in the past to cut out the burgers and pick up a salad."

"I hope you told the assholes to fuck off."

Annoyed at the flicker of tenderness I felt at his defense of me, I looked away, pretending to check out the people around us. "I may have even told one of them that if he wasn't into curves, he might prefer fucking himself. And that he should go do that. Immediately."

His chuckle caused a little flutter in my belly and I closed my eyes, trying to shut him out. My attraction toward him was too much for my liking.

"I like you, Nadia."

My gaze flew back to his in surprise. I struggled for a reply, scared to reciprocate, terrified that he was trying to suggest we nix the one-time-only deal. Eventually, I smiled and replied lightly, "I'm likable."

If he was disappointed by my reply, he didn't show it. Instead he stole a fry from my plate when he had plenty of his own.

"That was mean."

He grinned boyishly. "You don't like to share?"

"Not my fries when you've got your own. You've not got enough in life without having to steal my fries?"

For some reason he took my teasing question more seriously than I'd meant him to. "Do you think I'm just a rich asshole, Nadia?"

How to answer that?

The truth was I wasn't sure about anything when it came to Henry Lexington. Yes, he'd been an asshole to me so that would make him a rich asshole. But he was this other guy too. A funny, flirtatious, witty, thoughtful guy.

He could be the hero and the villain. Which one of those was the permanent resident and the other the visitor, I didn't know.

"I don't know who you are," I answered honestly. "And you don't know who I really am. But as agreed, we're not really sticking around to find out." To break the sudden heavy tension, I smiled flirtatiously. "But come Saturday night, you'll hopefully know something about me very few men know."

"Oh?"

I leaned over the table and his eyes fell to my lips. "The sound I make when I come."

His nostrils flared as our eyes locked and his voice was hoarse, "Have no doubt, Sunshine. I'll make you come so many times, I'll have the sound of it memorized."

My nipples hardened, my breasts swelled, and my skin flushed. Fingers tightening around the stem of my glass, I said, "Let's cut out the Delaney Ball and take what we want from this."

Henry reluctantly sat back. "Nice try."

"Come on, Henry, we both know what this is."

He raised his wine glass to his lips. "Do we?"

THE SPRAWLING STONE mansion was lit up in the dark by spotlights above the many windows, and going in and out of the huge double front door entrance were elegant couples in formal wear that veered from shimmering to starkly traditional.

After smoothing a hand down my dress, I noted how my fingers trembled and clenched my fist to stop the involuntary movement.

"You look beautiful," Henry said, caressing my waist as he led me inside with his arm around me. Since picking me up, he had showered me with compliments and then proceeded to stare at me heatedly the entire drive out to Weston.

There were a number of reasons I was so nervous walking into the Delaney Ball.

One, Henry had told me Caine and Alexa were going to be there and it was weird for me knowing I'd have to meet them and pretend I didn't know anything about them, let alone two of their darkest secrets.

Two, the people I'd be mingling with were Boston's elite. Although I'd met a few here and there, I'd never been to one of their events. I hated the idea of feeling like an outsider. Especially as I really was, considering Henry and I were extremely temporary.

Which brought me to the third reason I was nervous.

As soon as we'd gotten into the back of the Town Car, Henry had turned surprisingly serious.

"What's wrong? Regretting the dates? Wishing you'd gone straight for the home run?" I teased.

"You have no idea how wrong you are."

I squirmed under the intensity of his attention as he looked me straight in the eye. There was no sexual perusal of my body or cocky suggestiveness. "What do you want?" I huffed, feeling defensive for some reason.

"You," he replied immediately. "For more than one night."

My palms turned sweaty. "What?"

"I think it would be foolish not to explore what's between

us. No deadline, no fooling around, just you and me getting to know each other like normal couples get to know each other."

"You don't date," I argued, feeling my cheeks flush.

What was happening here?

Henry's expression turned tender. "For you, I want to."

"What? No. What?" I shifted uncomfortably, breaking his implacable hold on my gaze. "That's ... no. You and me? No." I looked back at him in outrage. "No."

He smirked. "Why not?"

"Because ..." I sputtered, trying to find the words. He had caught me so off guard. "It's us. No. No!"

"I reserve the right to change your mind. I have all night to do so."

I knew I was gaping at him like an unsophisticated middle grader, but I was in a state of shock. Henry Lexington didn't date. He played around. And suddenly, for me, he wanted to give dating a try? I wasn't buying it. Maybe he was under the illusion that there was something between us, but that didn't mean he wouldn't get bored in no time at all, and I'd be the one having to pick up the pieces of my pride as well as my heart.

Uh ... no thank you.

"I'll let you think about it." The bastard winked at me.

Butterflies had completely taken over my stomach as I tried to glide in my five-inch heels over the stone flooring in the Delaney's home. It was hard to describe the austere beauty of the ballroom we were led into. It wasn't as though I came across many homes that had an actual ballroom in it. The event was formally titled the Vanessa Van Hay Delaney Benefit for Alzheimer's. It was hosted by Michelle and Edgar Delaney, the children of Vanessa Delaney, a woman who'd been a pillar of Boston society for over fifty years before she was diagnosed with Alzheimer's. She passed away a few years after her diagnosis and ever since, every year, the Delaneys hosted their benefit to fund finding a cure. Only Boston's very elite were invited to come share their philanthropy, and that included my date and his good friend Caine Carraway.

I was merely the curvy treat of the week for Lexington but I'd done my best to make sure I wouldn't look out of place. Too much. Using my hard-earned savings, I'd bought a floor-length dress that hugged my upper body until it hit the top of my thighs and flowed out in layers of silk chiffon. It was the color of lapis lazuli, had wide straps over the shoulder, and a sweetheart neckline that screamed "This dress is all about the boobs!" With boobs like mine, it was very rare to find any piece of clothing that my boobs didn't immediately take command of. So it was easier to just go with it and let 'em shine.

Henry had only faltered once and that was when I opened the door to my apartment. I'd had to clear my throat loudly to get his attention off my assets. But from then on, he'd been a total gentleman, making direct eye contact only.

"Henry." A tall, lithe young woman laid a hand on my date's arm. As she pressed her boobs against his side, she smiled flirtatiously, a smile Henry easily returned. "You look wonderful as always." She trailed her fingers over his arm. I don't think my presence even registered on her radar. "We missed you at Fee's birthday bash last month."

"I was traveling. Work. Sorry I missed it."

Anger bubbled under my skin at the fact that Henry didn't force any distance between him and the woman. Anger I had to cool when his hand on my back tightened and he drew me closer. "Lana, this is my date, Nadia Ray."

Lana's eyes reluctantly swept from Henry's face to mine and she stepped back a little. "You look familiar."

Henry grinned proudly at me. "Nadia is WCVB's favorite broadcast meteorologist."

It was clear from the downturn of her mouth that Lana was less than impressed. "How diverting. I could never be a weather girl. Those early mornings have such a negative effect on the complexion."

I stiffened at the underhand insult but Henry laughed and patted Lana's arm, "Oh, be honest, Lana, you couldn't do the job because it would mean exerting yourself beyond the physicality of using Daddy's credit card."

I choked on my laughter as Henry guided me away from the socialite, her jaw almost to the ground. "I can't believe you said that."

Henry shrugged. "I hate cattiness."

"You slept with her, didn't you?" I covered my displeasure with a teasing smile.

"Once," he answered honestly. "It didn't mean anything."

To you it never does.

And there was the rub. I didn't believe Henry when he said he wanted more from me, more nights, more dates ... because he was saying that before we'd even had sex. I knew ... as soon as he'd had me, he'd walk out that door and I'd never see him again. There was absolutely no way I'd make myself any more vulnerable to the man than I already had.

"It means something to her. That's why she was rude to me."

Henry stopped from nodding at acquaintances as we passed through the mingling crowds to face me. "I don't want to talk about her. Or my past. I can't change it. But I can take charge of my future."

I shivered under the heated determination in his eyes, of the intent behind his words. "Champagne?" I squeaked out.

Laughing, he glanced around the room, perhaps searching for the alcohol, when his grin widened. "Caine's arrived with Alexa."

As Henry led me toward them, I tried to gain control of my nerves. I hated the fact that I had to lie to these people. Nearing the couple, I didn't know which one to look at first; they were so striking together. Caine was even more good-looking in real life than I could have imagined, but there was a cool hardness to his masculine gorgeousness. Alexa had a fresh-faced beauty with her high apple cheekbones, thick dark hair, and vivid blue-green eyes. She was tall with a slender figure encased in a stunning pale green and silver Jenny Packham dress. The dress's silhouette would have looked ridiculous on all of my exaggerated curves. Envy niggled at me. I'd never be able to pull off that kind of elegance.

"Alexa, looking more beautiful than ever," Henry said.

"Henry," she murmured, leaning into him with familiarity and affection as she kissed his cheek.

I stared at where he rested his hand on her waist a little too long and when I glanced over at Caine, I saw he was displeased by the embrace.

Jealousy pricked me for about a second until Henry caught Caine's scowl and rolled his eyes at him, taking a step back from Alexa. Something about Henry's amusement put me at ease. And then I saw the way Alexa turned to Carraway and stared up at his face, and I knew there was no reason to be jealous of her and Henry. I wondered if she knew her heart was in her eyes when she stared at her boss.

Interesting.

Henry nudged me forward. "Caine, Lexie, this is Nadia Ray. She's a local weather girl."

I tried not to read into the fact that he'd referred to my job title correctly with Lana earlier but called me a weather girl to his friends. I hoped it was just a slip and not an intentional attempt to rile me.

Recognition lit Alexa's eyes and unlike Lana, she did look

impressed. "It's nice to meet you," she said, and sounded like she meant it.

I grinned back tremulously, still unsure of how to act when I knew too much about her—more than I'm sure she'd be comfortable with me knowing.

Caine gave me a clipped nod that only made my nerves worse.

The man was intimidating without even trying.

"This place is insane, right?" Alexa said, bugging her eyes out as if to say, "What the hell do we do here?"

Relief at finding someone who felt like an outsider too made me laugh. "It's not what I'm used to."

"I hear you." She nodded, scanning the room. "But the mini crab rolls at these things are usually to die for."

"Nowhere near as good as the crab rolls we used to get at this little deli on campus at Wharton." Henry closed his eyes in exaggerated pleasure. "Oh, those were the days."

I chuckled because I equated good memories with good food too. Alexa smirked. "Crab rolls. That's what you remember most about business school?"

"I didn't say that." His eyes popped open as he grinned. "The women were also very memorable."

I refused to react because there was something about the way he deliberately didn't look at me when he said it that suggested it was for my benefit. Was he *trying* to make me jealous? Did he want a reaction? What kind of game was he playing with me now?

Despite the jealousy I did feel, jealousy that told me I should not be here or even contemplating letting this man anywhere near my bed, I pretended indifference to spite him.

"Oh, so it was the *crabs* you remember most?" Alexa cracked and I burst out laughing.

I had a feeling I was going to like this woman.

"I wasn't that bad." Henry snorted. "Okay ... I was almost

that bad."

"How did you put up with him? Or were you even worse than he was?" she asked Caine.

Caine didn't join in on her teasing. He was so cold and standoffish, I was suddenly glad I hadn't gone to him with what I'd found.

Alexa didn't seem bothered by his attitude at all. She huffed in exasperation. "Caine never talks about Wharton. It's like he's wiped it from existence."

Henry sobered as he and Caine shared a dark look; I shifted with unease. Oops. That's why Caine was looking so uncomfortable. The topic of business school. *Right*. Prostituting himself through school wasn't exactly something he wanted everyone to know about.

"We'll get you a crab roll in a minute," Caine suddenly said. "First we have to go over and say hello to the Delaneys." And without another word, he guided Alexa away from us.

She shot us an apologetic look over her shoulder.

"Well ... that was ... uncomfortable."

My date's demeanor changed so swiftly, he reminded me of the man I'd met weeks ago in my apartment. "She doesn't know and she'll never know. Understood?"

"I've already told you I have no intention of telling anyone."

"Good." He grabbed my hand and wrapped it around his arm. "Make sure it stays that way."

Bitterness reared its ugly head. "From the man who says he wants to date me."

"What does that mean?"

"It means there's no point in dating someone you don't trust."

"I trust you," he said. Taking in my disbelief, he wrapped his hand over mine, his expression softening. "Nadia, I trust you. That was ... that was a stupid thing to say to you. I ... I'm uncomfortable with the fact that Caine doesn't know that you know. I apologize."

And there he went, switching to the gentleman. You would think I'd relax but his ability to be these two different people unsettled me. Reluctantly, I muttered, "Accepted."

His eyes swept over my face, his features tightening. "Do you know how much I want you?"

"You've mentioned it once or twice." I turned away, not quite ready to return to that flirty place with him.

"I said I was sorry."

"I know." I eyed him now, trying to work this man out. I knew people were complicated—we all had good and bad in us. I couldn't work out how much of Henry was a good guy, and it bothered me more than it should considering I was only supposed to have sex with him once and be done with him.

"Then what's the problem?"

"No problem." I bit my lip as we studied each other. His unrelenting gaze made me sigh. "Okay ... You're so unbeliev-ably charming."

"That's a problem?"

"I bet nearly all the people in this room would be shocked to their core to learn that you have a side capable of pinning a man to wall, threatening violence, and getting him fired less than twenty-four hours later."

Understanding lightened his eyes. "And you'd be right." He shot me a wry smirk. He glanced around the room and turned back to me. "Caine and I get things done. But we choose a different path to the same destination. He comes off cold, he's intense, sometimes ruthless, and people fear him to the point where they don't want to piss him off—they want to be his ally. I, on the other hand, am all lightheartedness and effortless charm. People see a blueblood who got where he is because of his father. Most of them don't take me seriously."

He grinned and it was hard and wolfish. "They underestimate me to their own detriment."

His words caused me no small measure of uneasiness. They were in fact a reminder that Henry Lexington was a complicated man with more than one face. He could charm me effortlessly and then rip my heart out the next day. "Well, don't worry, Mr. Lexington. I for one won't underestimate you."

He immediately frowned and stepped into my personal space, crowding me. Henry searched my eyes, his expression unhappy. "You say that like you expect me to hurt you. I won't. I won't hurt you, Nadia."

I gave him a cool smile. "No, you won't."

Determination hardened his eyes. "This is happening between us and it's real."

I traced my finger down the lapel of his tuxedo and made a snake over his heart. "All that's going to happen between you and me is this ... you'll take me home, I'll invite you into my apartment, and then I'll invite you inside me. We'll have fun. You'll leave. And I won't see you again. Understood?"

Desire darkened his eyes as they fell to my lips. "I see we're doing this the hard way."

"I hope so."

He grinned at my innuendo. "Fuck, I like you."

"Henry, good to see you." We were suddenly interrupted by an older couple.

The smoldering in Henry's eyes disappeared as he turned to them and slipped easily into the charmer these people knew and loved.

⚜

FOR THE MOST part the people Henry introduced me to were friendly and inquisitive about my job, some of them knowing a lot more about meteorology broadcasting than I expected. But of course, we were surrounded by wealthy business people, smart people, and as much as some of them underestimated me, I'd probably underestimated and prejudged them too.

To my discomfort, I'd also underestimated Henry's flirtatious nature. Old, young, somewhere in between, if it was female, Henry went out of his way to make her feel like she was special. I don't think he even knew he did it—it was a natural part of who he was.

And as I watched him, I began to doubt every moment we'd spent together over the last week. Because the truth was, as much as I hated to admit it, Henry had made me feel special, interesting, intriguing, wanted. But he made every woman feel like that. It was a nice quality to have ... but not exactly one that gave me much faith in his so-called feelings for me.

We were talking to an elderly couple, Mr. and Mrs. Winston, when a petite beauty with masses of dark curls and huge dark eyes approached. She'd eyed me with distaste and then was overly fake friendly when Henry introduced us. She then insisted he come with her to sort out an argument with some person whose name escaped me. Despite what I thought was her obvious cattiness, Henry went, leaving me for the first time. I think he felt okay to do so because I was explaining my job to Mrs. Winston who seemed genuinely fascinated.

Five minutes later, he still hadn't returned and Mr. and Mrs. Winston had been distracted by an acquaintance.

I stood on the outskirts of the room, alone, confused, and wishing to God that I was home in my apartment watching a good movie.

"You look like you need this." Alexa approached on her own and offered me a glass of champagne.

Gratitude swept over me in such magnitude, I almost felt teary. I was miserable. I didn't know if I was miserable being at the party, or if I was miserable because of Henry, or how Henry made me feel. I didn't know. I was a mess.

I hid that mess behind a grateful smile. "Thank you. Henry was pulled away by some catty society girl and there really was no polite way for him to get out of it." I don't know why I said that. Maybe because I had hoped that's why he'd left me on my own. I almost flinched at how needy I was being. This so was not me.

"Henry's a catch around these parts." Alexa smiled sympathetically. "The women who have grown up in his circle think of him as theirs."

"I'm getting that." *They can have him!* I thought bravely, hoping that if I told myself I felt nothing for him, the feeling might actually take hold.

"Honestly, I think they bore him." She seemed to want to reassure me.

"Well, I'm from Beacon Falls, Connecticut, which is a slightly different crowd of people. Definitely not boring." Nope. Boring we were not. Or at least ... I wasn't boring. Not that my kind of boring was a good thing. I didn't want Henry to know how not boring I could be. The thought left a bitter taste in my mouth.

"I'm from Chester," Alexa exclaimed.

Unease pricked at me and I covered it with a chuckle. "No way. We grew up, like, what? An hour from one another?"

"It's a small world."

Yes, it was. Hopefully not too small for her to have heard anything about me. I shrugged off that concern, knowing even if she did know the story, it would have a different name attached to it.

Despite how I was feeling, Alexa was so easy to talk to that I found myself relaxing into her company. We talked about growing up in Connecticut, about college (not a lot because I didn't want to give anything away inadvertently), about Boston, and how I'd recently done the tourist thing. She told me about her favorite places around the city and I could see our tastes were similar. I enjoyed the fact that she didn't ask me about Henry, and because I already knew more about her and her boss than I wanted to, I didn't ask her about Caine.

We clicked, and in the back of my mind, I was already cursing Henry for introducing me to her, knowing that our friendship wouldn't last given he and I were ending this thing between us.

But maybe, somehow, I could still stay in contact with Alexa. She was the first person in Boston, other than Joe, who made me feel like myself.

"I'm sorry to interrupt, ladies." Henry appeared and gently tugged me toward him. I wanted to resist, considering how long he'd left me alone, but that conflicted with the fact that I was glad he had because it meant I got to spend time with Alexa. "My father is finally free from the bigwigs and I want to introduce you to him."

What the fuck?

His father?

Was here?

And he wanted to introduce me to him? No way. That was not in the plan!

"Your father?" I shot Alexa a pleading look even though I knew there was very little she could do. "Why are you introducing me to your father?" I hissed as he propelled me through the crowded ballroom.

"Because I want him to meet you."

I ignored his obvious amusement. "You're trying to torture me."

"Actually, I merely want you to meet my father. I like him

a lot and I like you a lot. It makes sense to introduce you."

"You're being pushy and obnoxious." My stomach twisted with nerves. "Really, Henry, I don't want to—"

"Father." Henry stopped in front of two men, and I was forced to shut up.

"Henry ..." The taller and older of the two men turned to us, his eyes flicking from his son to me. I'd seen Randall Lexington in the paper and already knew Henry got his good looks from his father. As trim as he must have been in youth, Lexington filled out his tuxedo as well as any man half his age. He had light gray eyes, not blue like Henry's, but they had the same smooth handsomeness. When he smiled at me, it was Henry's boyish, charming smile, and for some stupid reason, it made me relax a little.

"Nadia, this is my father Randall, and my colleague Iain Prendergast."

I stuck out my hand to his father, "Nice to meet you," and then to Iain.

"Nice to meet you, Nadia." Iain gave me a polite smile. "Henry, Mr. Lexington." He nodded at father and son and then left us to it.

"Miss Ray." Randall reached for my hand again, clasping it between both of his. His expression was warm and curious. "I've seen you on television. You light up the screen. I've never met a broadcast meteorologist before."

I was immediately charmed—he got my job title correct!

"Thank you. I love my job."

Randall let go of my hand and smirked at his son. "It only took you twenty-odd years to bring an interesting date to one of these things."

I laughed as Henry chuckled. "You've just insulted half the women in this room."

His dad shrugged. "Whoops."

Having not been what I expected at all, I found myself

relaxing even more. "Henry told me he had to work his way up in your company rather than going straight in at the top. I have to say I admire your decision to do that."

"Were you complaining again, son?"

"I'll never forgive you for the hardship."

I studied father and son as they teased each other, and liked what I saw.

"So, Miss Ray—"

"Please, call me Nadia."

"Nadia," his eyes searched my face, "a beautiful name for a beautiful woman."

"Hey now." Henry slid his arm around my waist and pulled me into his side. "Watch it. For all I know, my date has a thing for older men."

I tensed at the joke, immediately regretting it when Henry shot me a puzzled look. Forcing myself to relax, I smiled lamely.

"As I was saying," Randall smoothed over the moment, "Nadia, tell me, are you dying to get out of here as much as I am?"

There was no hiding my surprise at the question. Randall Lexington *was* Boston society. "What?"

Henry squeezed my waist. "My father hates these things. He only comes for the business opportunities and because my mother loves them."

"We could be doing better things with our time than standing around sipping champagne and gossiping," he said. I heard the tired derision in Randall's voice.

"This is a charity benefit."

"So let me write a check. Don't make me put on a damn penguin suit and stand in a ballroom having to converse with people, half of whom don't have an original thought between them."

I choked on a snort.

Seriously. I loved him.

Randall grinned at the noise. "I have a feeling Miss Ray shares my sentiments. Well, unlucky for you if you stick around with my son, you'll be subjected to more of this. It comes with the territory."

"I don't mind this stuff as much," Henry said.

"Now you don't. Give it twenty years. So ... do you like it?" Randall asked me directly.

I sighed. "It's really only my first society event."

"But?"

"I feel like a fish out of water," I answered honestly.

Henry's grip on me tightened. "Why?"

My answer seemed to have disturbed him.

"Uh, kids, maybe take that conversation elsewhere ..." Randall stared over my shoulder, "Your mother is headed this way."

Without even a goodbye, Henry took hold of my hand and dragged me in the opposite direction. "What is going on?"

He didn't answer me until we were on the other side of the ballroom with hundreds of couples between us and his father. Henry grabbed two glasses of champagne, handed one to me, and downed the other.

"Explain."

"You first." He crowded me against a window alcove, hiding me from the rest of the room. His hand rested on my hip possessively as he stared down into my face, looking as serious as he had in the Town Car earlier. "You feel like a fish out of water here?"

"Honestly, yes."

"Why?"

I cocked my head, studying him. Why did he care? "Why does it bother you if I do?"

"Because I have to attend these events. I hate to think of dragging you along to things you're not enjoying."

"There you go being all presumptuous again."

"I introduced you to my father, Nadia. I don't normally do that."

I scoffed. "So I should feel honored?"

"Don't do that." He leaned into me, pressing his body along mine. He stroked my chin and gripped it gently to tilt my head back. "Don't be cynical and distant. I don't like it. It's not you."

"You don't know who I am," I whispered, aroused by his proximity despite the mess of my emotions.

"No?" He bent down, his lips brushing mine. "Then tell me who you are."

I licked my lips deliberately so my tongue flicked against his mouth, and his eyes smoldered. "I'm the girl," I kissed him on the corner of his mouth, "wondering why a guy would introduce me to his father, but run like a bat out of hell from introducing me to his mother."

"His mother is wondering that also," a cool, feminine voice said behind him.

Henry froze. "Fuck," he muttered.

"I heard that."

For some reason, Henry looked pained as he pulled back from me. And apologetic. He gripped my hand in his and turned to face a petite woman who appeared younger than her years. A woman whose wealth meant life had been kind to her skin.

"Mother." Henry leaned down to press a kiss to her cheek without letting go of my hand.

Penelope Lexington had diamonds in her ears, around her throat, and around her wrist. In contrast to all the bling, her dress was black and simple. Henry had her lovely blue eyes.

She looked amazing for a woman who was mother to a

thirty-something-year-old.

Her full lips, however, were pinched with displeasure as she stared at me.

"Nadia, this is my mother, Penelope."

"Nice to meet you, Mrs. Lexington." I held out a hand to her, despite her chilly stare.

To my horror she stared at my hand like it was a bug. I dropped it, shocked at her rudeness.

"Mother, Jesus Christ," Henry snapped quietly.

"Don't you curse at me," Penelope huffed and then narrowed her eyes on me. "I can see what a marvelous influence the weather girl is already being on you."

I stiffened at her derision.

"Not. Here," Henry bit out.

"Not here?" She stepped closer to us and I glanced around the room. Mostly everyone was completely unaware of the tension happening among the three of us, but a group of young women to our right caught my eye. They were watching with glee.

"You're being rude."

"I'm being rude? You were supposed to attend the event with Portia Windsor. Instead you dumped her for a *weather girl*."

"Broadcast meteorologist." I threw my shoulders back, eyeing her in defiance.

Her upper lip curled. "Dress it up anyway you want, sweetheart, you're an overweight nobody whose breasts got her some attention. I know you. I know you better than you know yourself. And what I'm sure we can agree on is that you're not good enough for my son. I want you to leave."

"I can't believe you just said that." Henry stared at her in angry disbelief, two bright flags of red on the upper crests of his cheeks.

"I'm happy to leave." I stared through her for a moment,

hoping to make her flinch. However, she was cold as stone. As I moved to pass her, anger and fear that she was right mixed together. Maybe she was right. But how she'd treated me—humiliated me—was unforgiveable. I stopped by her side and stared down into her haughty expression. "I guess the saying is correct after all."

She raised a perfect eyebrow at me.

"Money really can't buy class."

Hot temper lit up her eyes but I walked away with my head held high.

I was halfway across the ballroom, which seemed to have tripled in size, when he fell into step beside me.

His hand rested on my lower back as he guided me out.

Neither of us said a word.

Not while we waited for the Town Car to arrive. And not while we sat in the Town Car.

Inside I was screaming. How she'd treated me reminded me of a time I'd like to forget. But I didn't feel like a victim.

I didn't feel angry at Penelope Lexington, who's attitude, unfortunately, was a product of the society she kept and being trapped in a time warp.

I was angry at myself because it was my own past actions that made me have such a low opinion of myself. A low enough opinion for me to believe Penelope Lexington was probably right. Joe was right. Being with Henry was taking me back to that bad place again.

Because who was I to have judged Henry all night? To stand there in my too-high heels and weigh whether he was a villain or a hero? If he was good enough for me?

I acted like my story deserved a hero.

But only a heroine deserves a hero.

And I wasn't a heroine. I couldn't be.

The truth was in someone else's story ...

I was a villain.

CHAPTER SIX

"What are you doing?"

Henry frowned at me as we stood on the sidewalk outside my apartment building. "Coming up with you."

The Town Car drove smoothly away. A trickle of fear, anxiety, and nerves mixed with the need to throw myself at Henry, to seek comfort in him with the added benefit of taking what Penelope Lexington didn't want me to have.

Yet my anxiety and self-derision were stronger in that moment, and after all the time I'd spent fighting to feel good about myself, self-directed anger started to brew. Because I should have listened to Joe.

And since I couldn't take it out on myself, I knew I'd take it out on Henry.

"Just go." I gestured toward the departing car. "Call him back." Turning on my heel, I climbed up the stairs to my door.

He climbed up the stairs right behind me.

My blood turned hot; agitation made me want to curl my toes inside my shoes, and the feelings stirring inside of me were so overwhelming, my hands shook as I tried to get the key in the door.

A small sigh sounded at my ear and suddenly his hands covered mine, pulling the keys out of my hold. I immediately stepped back, watching in mounting irritation as he let us into the building.

I tensed as he put his hand on my back, guiding me upstairs.

My throat felt hot, tight, swollen with words that I was trying to choke down. Hurtful words, hateful words. Words that would make him feel as badly as I was feeling.

"I told you to leave," I bit out, trying to stop him from coming into the apartment.

But looking up into his face, I could see I wasn't the only one struggling to hold on to a temper. Henry pushed inside, locking the door behind me, and I suddenly hated him for forcing me into this confrontation.

"I need to apologize," he said to my back as I hurried into my sitting room. My shoulders hunched to my neck at the words. I couldn't look at him.

What did he want me to say? That it was okay?

Because it wasn't.

No one, no matter what, should have to be subjected to what that woman said to me.

Henry's *mother*!

He was in Cloud Cuckoo Land if he thought this, whatever this was between us, could ever work out when his mother thought so little of me.

"Just go," I snapped, not looking at him.

"No," he said, his tone stern. "Not until you turn around and look at me."

I shot him a glare over my shoulder. "Satisfied? Now leave."

Instead of leaving, he studied my face, softening as if he understood what was going on behind my fury.

But he didn't understand.

"I cannot apologize enough for what my mother said to you. Frankly, right now I'm ashamed I share DNA with the woman. That was the reason I was avoiding her. She's ... bad with the women I date normally, even the ones she's set me up with. No one is good enough. Usually, it's merely irritating, but I didn't want to subject you to her. And if I had known how goddamn low she'd sink tonight, I never would've put you in that situation."

I heard his words, but I couldn't feel them. I couldn't feel the anger and worry in them that I'd later remember. In that moment, all I saw were the flowers peeking over the top of the trash can behind him. Flowers that had arrived at my apartment earlier that afternoon. Flowers that meant *he'd* found my home address. Flowers that taunted me, saying, "You can't be angry at Penelope Lexington when you know she'd feel smug with satisfaction if she ever discovered the truth." She'd feel vindicated in her opinion of me.

Worse would be how Henry would react if he knew the truth. How he'd never look at me the same way again. He'd never look at me in that way that was getting under my skin, becoming an addiction, despite all the defenses I'd tried to put up against him.

A chill shivered down my spine.

"Nadia, what can I do? What—"

"If you're not going to leave," I turned around to fully face him, "then we might as well get this over with."

Henry watched with narrowed eyes as I threw my purse on the couch and then removed my earrings. "What are you doing?"

Cold, toneless, I reminded him, "Our arrangement is almost over. A deal is a deal."

"A deal is a deal?" The muscle in his jaw twitched, his eyes flashing. "You're going to fuck me like some martyr?"

"Well, I'd prefer it if you leave but I don't welch on a deal."

"Nadia, don't hide from me." I could hear the barely contained fury beneath his words and in a twisted way, I reveled in it. I wanted his anger. I wanted to force him to walk away and walk away for good. "Talk to me."

I scoffed. "Why do you keep trying to make this more than it is? You wanted to slum it with the local weather girl. I wanted to get laid because it's been a while. You just happened to be there and I've heard you're good. That's all this ever was. And I'm not one of your uptight society princesses who needs to be assured you want more from me than a dirty fuck."

"Nadia ..."

I didn't heed the growl of warning in his voice. "Let me make it clearer," I hissed out, all my rage at myself redirected at him like I knew and feared would happen. "I don't do relationships with spoiled rich boys who run away from their mommas. I'll let a rich boy fuck me for the hell of it, but rest assured when I do let someone in long-term, it'll be a *man*."

Not even a second later, Henry crossed the distance between us, one hand tangling into my pinned-up hair, the other around my waist. He yanked me roughly against him before I could blink and slammed his mouth down over mine in a hard, punishing kiss.

And the war that was raging inside of me blazed outward as I pushed my hands against his chest, trying to get away, while my tongue danced with his with no thought to stopping. It wasn't a dream kiss, soft, sensual, seductive. It was harsh, wet, fast, breathless, just two mouths, two tongues, base need.

Arousal roared through me. I'd never been more aware of

my body in my entire life. My breasts were so swollen, so sensitive, it was a pleasure pain. My nipples hard, chafing against the lace of the bra I wore. The tingles between my legs were filled with such heat, the feeling almost burned, like flames and champagne fizz mixed together. Pain winced across my scalp, but knowing it was Henry's hand tangling tighter through my hair to pull me closer was erotic and thrilling. His other hand, his fingers, bruised my hip he clung to me so hard, forcing me against his body.

And causing the tingles to travel deep low in my belly, pleasure rippling, dampening my underwear with wet heat, was the feel of Henry's erection digging into my stomach. Suddenly I wasn't pushing him away anymore but curling my fingers into the lapels of his tuxedo jacket and rocking my hips into him.

Our harsh breathing filled my apartment as he broke the punishing kiss to glower at me in barely leashed enraged lust.

My heart raced, fearing he was going to walk away.

What a mass of confusion I was.

Quite abruptly, he pushed me backward and my dress got caught beneath my feet, tripping me. I stumbled against the wall and Henry was on me, pinning me there. His eyes never left mine and I could only stare up at him, panting, expecting, vulnerable and no longer caring because the calls of my body were louder than the calls of my fears.

Our eyes locked, our hot breaths whispering over one another's lips. My breasts heaved against his chest as he pressed into me. His hands smoothed lightly down my waist and goosebumps woke up along the curves of my chest as I swelled into him.

And then his hands stopped on the sides of my thighs, his fingers curling into the fabric of my dress. He pulled, bunching it, and cool air drifted over my legs, over my thighs, until it was gathered around my waist.

My breath stuttered as he pushed my legs apart with his feet and put his free hand on the inside of my left thigh. Not once did he break eye contact. I trembled, feeling like I was going to combust if he didn't do something soon. My body jerked as his fingers slipped beneath my underwear and slid easily inside me.

Henry's eyes darkened at finding me so wet, his features tightening ... and then it snapped whatever control he'd forced over himself in the last few minutes. He pulled back, my dress dropping to the floor again, and I trembled harder, staring into his eyes as he ripped off his tuxedo jacket. "Lift your dress," he demanded as he threw his jacket away.

I fumbled for the skirts, my knees shaking. He stepped back into me, his dress shoes hard and cold against my bare feet as he forced my legs even further apart. His hand gripped under my thigh, jerking my leg up around his hip, while the other unzipped his tuxedo pants.

I gasped at the heat of him throbbing between my legs and watched his blue eyes turn black just before he thrust into me. It burned a little, hurt. He was thick, bigger than I was anticipating. I'd never felt so full, overwhelmed.

But the discomfort melted, replaced with pleasure that tingled down my spine, through my legs, rippling in my belly as he slid out and then pumped back into me.

Our breaths puffed against each other's lips and I gripped his waist, urging him closer, harder. I wanted more. Everything. Now. I wanted to come. I didn't want seduction. I wanted him to shatter me. Immediately.

As if he felt my urgency or shared it, Henry picked up his pace. My head flew back against the wall, his bent, buried in my neck, breaking our eye contact.

And he fucked me.

There was no other word for it. It was hard, fast, angry.

It took barely any time for the tension inside of me to

spiral higher, higher toward the cliff edge. Then suddenly I was at the peak, and with one more hard drive into me, he pushed me over the top and I was flying and exploding at the same time.

A cry, almost a scream, tore out of me as my eyes rolled back inside my head. I'd never experienced anything like it—wave after wave of deep, hard pleasure rolling through me. And each strong ripple clenched around Henry's dick, the sensation goddamn glorious.

His long, guttural groan sounded in my ear and his grip on my thigh tightened to biting and painful as he came. His hips jerked against me as his wet heat released inside of me.

Our harsh breathing seemed to echo around the room as Henry slumped into me. He let go of my thigh and my muscles were too loose, too languid to hold it up. My leg dropped heavily to the floor, my skirts held up only by Henry's body against mine.

As my heart beat fast against my ribs, reality began to sink in, and he throbbed inside of me.

Inside of me.

A thought brought a shower of cold over me.

We hadn't used a condom. I was on the pill but that didn't mean we shouldn't have used a condom, especially considering how many women this man had slept with!

"Henry ..." I pushed against him.

He reluctantly lifted his head from my shoulder and stared at me, looking somewhat shell shocked.

"We didn't use a condom."

It took a minute for my words to sink in. "You're not on the pill?"

"I am," I hurried to assure him. "But we should have used protection."

The fact that we didn't shocked the hell out of me. I'd

never been so consumed with desire before that I'd forgotten about something as important as the condom.

Relief lit up his eyes. "I'm clean." He squeezed my waist. "I'm clean."

"You know for sure?"

"I get tested every three months. My last check was two days before we met. I haven't been with anyone since we met."

I let out a shaky breath, my own relief great. "I'm clean too."

His answer was to kiss me. Softly, sweetly. A complete contrast to the angry sex we'd had.

Guilt suffused me. "Henry."

"God," he groaned, grinding against me. "I love when you say my name."

My breath stuttered, surprise trembling through me as the pleasure started to wave through my lower belly again. Already. "I'm sorry for what I said."

His eyes locked to mine like he was trying to see down into the depths of my soul. "I take it that means you've stopped being pissed?"

"Have you?"

He grinned. "I just came harder than I've come in my life. What do you think?"

I laughed. "Men are so easy."

"Oh, I'm a man again, am I?" he teased.

"I said I was sorry." I stroked my fingers over his lips, feeling the sudden need to touch and taste him everywhere. "I promised you all night," I whispered, my voice hoarse with renewed lust. "Let me show you how sorry I am."

"I will." He kissed me, his tongue flicking lightly against mine before he pulled back. "But my turn first. I'm going to kiss and suck and lick every inch of you." His eyes dropped to my breasts and I gasped as he cupped them in his hands and squeezed none too gently. "Starting with these." He kissed the tops, dipping his tongue into my cleavage and making me clench around his cock that was growing harder inside of me. "You have no idea how many masturbatory fantasies I have had about your gorgeous tits."

I arched into his hands. "Henry," I pleaded.

"Fuck, you're going to be the death of me." Quite abruptly, he pulled out of me and wet came with him. He shoved a hand between my legs to feel his cum on me and I swear to God, I've never seen a man looked so turned on in my life as he rubbed his seed against my clit.

My fingers bit into his arms. "What are you doing?" I panted.

He didn't answer but locked eyes with me, watching me gasp and squirm as he plunged two thick fingers in and out of me while he rubbed my clit with his thumb.

Although my orgasm was slower in coming this time, it wasn't as harsh. It was sweeter, slower, more languorous.

"Do you have any idea how beautiful you are?" Henry kissed me softly as my skirts fell back to the floor.

Instead of answering, I kissed back, harder, wrapping my arms around his neck so I could feel every inch of him against me. This time our kiss was like a dream kiss—slow, sensual, arousing. I gave everything over to that kiss. I made it the best goddamn kiss I'd ever given. Because if tonight was all we had, I was going to make the most of it.

CHAPTER SEVEN

He woke me in the middle of the night, his mouth nuzzling mine. As soon as I started to return his kisses with fervor, I found myself pushed to my back as Henry settled his knees on either side of my waist.

There was tenderness mixed with the desire in his eyes and I was both thrilled and afraid. Hands braced on the mattress on either side of my head, he bent to graze his lips over mine. More nuzzling, soft, sweet kisses that gradually grew deeper. It felt like he was pouring his longing into me via his kisses and I wanted to cry because it was longing I returned. I was lonely. More than I'd realized. I'd been waiting for someone like Henry.

Tears burned beneath my lids because more than anything, I wanted to believe that these kisses were real. That his longing was as real as mine.

As if he sensed the change in my emotions, Henry's kisses grew rougher, more desperate, and I clung to his waist to meet him breathless kiss for breathless kiss. I gasped into his mouth as his erection stroked my belly. His lips drifted from mine to lace kisses across my chin, down my jaw, along my collarbone. He kissed his way down my chest, his mouth hot, searching, as though he was looking to discover all my secrets.

I held on, trailing my fingertips in light caresses across his muscled back, sliding my hands up into the silk of his hair, and curling them in tight when his hot mouth closed around my left nipple. He sucked it and my hips jerked against him in reaction. "Oh God." My thighs gripped him as I urged him closer, my back arching for more as he licked me and then sucked harder, all the while pinching my other nipple between his forefinger and thumb.

"Oh God," I moaned softly.

He lifted his head to watch my face as he moved against me, rubbing against my clit, building my need into craving. I groaned, tortured. "Henry," I begged.

His answer was to dip his head again, to lick my other nipple, and cup and squeeze my breasts in his hands. He lifted his gaze, releasing my nipple from his mouth. "You're so beautiful. I'm particularly enchanted by these." He squeezed my breasts a little harder. Arousal shot straight from where he was fondling me to between my legs and the coil of tension tightened in my lower belly.

I was panting hard, my fingers tugging his hair. "I want you inside me."

But Henry wasn't done making love to me. He created a trail of feathery, tormenting kisses down my stomach. I shivered at the touch of his tongue across my belly and melted into the mattress, my thighs falling open, guiding him to his southerly destination.

He kissed me there. Licked me. Sucked my clit between those clever lips until I was shivering and trembling, fingers curling into the sheets, flushed furnace hot, as he played me toward climax.

I lost my breath as the tension tightened inside me, my

hips stilling against his mouth momentarily as I reached my pressure point.

His tongue pressed down on my clit and that was it.

Over the edge I went as my orgasm seized me. I had no control over my body anymore as I pulsed and pulsed against his mouth.

Finally, cognizance returned as bliss faded to languid satisfaction. Henry moved back up my body and when I opened my eyes, I stared straight into his. He had his hands braced on either side of my head, his lower body pressed to mine.

Fear returned as he stared down at me with more hunger and want than any man I'd ever been with. He studied my face with his eyes and the gentle caress of his fingers, and something like panic squeezed my lungs. To escape it without escaping him, I pushed against his shoulder and shoved him onto his back. Anticipation flared in Henry's eyes as he lay back on the bed for me, his cock straining toward his belly. This was what I needed and wanted right now. And I wanted him to find as much euphoria as he'd given me.

I lowered my head and Henry muttered, "Fuck, yes," before I even touched him. When I wrapped my mouth around him, the muscles in his abs contracted and his hips flexed against me. His fingers threaded through my hair, "God, woman, you're a miracle."

I licked along the underside of his cock first, teasing him for only a few seconds before I began to suck, tasting the salty heat of him. At the same time as I moved my mouth, I pumped the root with my hand. His hisses and groans of need filled the room, and I got off on his noise of pleasure as if it were his touch. My nipples tightened into hard, achy peaks. I grew slick with heat between my legs and I found myself pumping my hips as I sucked him off.

I looked up at Henry's face from under my lashes, loving the sight of his tight, restrained expression and the glow of raw lust in his low-lidded gaze. The color was high on his cheeks and his chest rose and fell in shallow breaths as I vacillated between teasing licks of my tongue and hard pulls of my mouth. I slid my free hand up over the hot, damp skin of his lower abs, feeling them ripple under my fingertips.

I sucked him in deeper, and he squeezed his eyes shut, his teeth gritted together. "Nadia," he bit out, "fuck!"

That was my warning that he was coming and instead of jerking back, I sucked him through his climax, something I'd never done before, and he shuddered and shivered as he came down from the explosion.

When his cock softened, I pulled back to stare at him.

He stared back at me in awe.

But more ... there was so much more in his expression. Escaping it once more, I jumped off the bed and pulled on my robe.

"What are you doing?"

"Freshening up."

"Do it without the robe."

I stared back at him, unsure. It was different when two people were having sex—I lost my inhibitions as my desire for orgasm overtook every other feeling. But walking around my apartment naked in front of him, my ass jiggling and my boobs bouncing ...

Um ... *no*. Emphatically not. "I'd prefer not to."

Henry frowned. "You're beautiful. I don't want you to hide."

"I'm not perfect," I huffed. "I bet you're used to perfect. I don't have a flat belly and I have a jiggly ass ... there is fat on this body." I pointed to myself.

He grinned. "There are curves. And they're sexy as hell." He leaned up on an elbow and smoldered at me. "You're perfect to me."

Strangely, I sensed his sincerity.

What was I going to do with this guy?

Fine. I shrugged out of the robe and put my hands on my hips, trying to hide how self-conscious I felt standing naked before him. "Happy now?"

His darkened gaze swept down my body and back up again. "Sunshine, I won't be happy until I've screwed you six ways till Sunday."

I rolled my eyes, but some of my self-consciousness dissipated. "So romantic." Before he could respond, I walked out of the room and down the hall to the bathroom where I freshened up.

I returned a minute later and Henry stalked me with his stare, his eyes lowered to my breasts.

"Fuck," he groaned, reaching and placing me over him so I was straddling his hips. "I think I'm obsessed with your tits."

"I think you are too—ahh," I gasped as he cupped them and drew my oversensitive nipples into his mouth. I writhed as he played with me for what felt like forever until the blood surged back into his cock and it push against my belly.

My eyes dropped to his dick, excited and impressed.

Suddenly I was on my back, my surprised laughter swallowed up in his kiss.

Henry's lips were all over me again—my breasts, my stomach—and where his mouth went, his hands followed. He rested on his knees and I stared down at him, breathless with anticipation.

I cried out, feeling wrung out when his thumb pressed down on my clit. Even more so when he pushed two fingers inside me. "It's not enough," I begged.

"Jesus," he huffed, thrusting his fingers in and out of me. "You're drenched. You liked getting me off, Sunshine?"

"You might think about returning the favor," I bit out impatiently.

"God, I like you."

"Prove it."

"I will ... but I'm not going to fuck you, Nadia." He gently eased his fingers out of me and then coasted both hands up my body as he moved upward.

Confused, I watched him.

And then Henry, his eyes locked with mine, pressed my legs farther apart and slid inside me.

Easily.

Beautifully.

I sighed in utter sweet, shivering, erotic, slow, dizzying pleasure as he thrust in measured strokes. The swelling, overwhelming thickness of him inside me was a delicious kind of agony.

He was making love to me.

"Henry," I gasped, tears stinging my eyes before I could stop them.

"You are so sweet, kind, hilarious, exasperating, beautiful ..." he whispered and kissed me, never breaking his excruciatingly delicious tempo. He dragged almost all the way out of me in a slow, torturous stroke before pressing back in, in an equally tormenting slow thrust.

My eyes were locked on his face, mesmerized to see again the light of affection mixed with dark possession in his expression. He was such a complicated man.

And right then, I'd never felt anything more wonderful in my life than being with him like this. Every muscle in his body was locked, tensed, as he strained to be gentle, to be tender.

His eyes moved over me and his expression tightened even more as he got lost in watching my breasts bounce against his thrusts. His control slipped and I was surprised to find amusement in my pleasure.

He really was obsessed with my breasts.

"Nadia," he choked out as if in pain.

I caressed his back reassuringly. "Do it. Fuck me."

"This is more than this."

"Fucking can be more than just fucking," I managed before gasping against his harder, deeper thrust.

My words snapped what little control he was holding onto and suddenly his hips were pumping faster, pushing him deeper, giving me another orgasm that made my eyes roll back in my head. I was losing count.

His lips parted, his hips stalled, and he choked out my name on a harsh pant as he throbbed hard inside me.

My inner muscles pulsated around his straining cock and we shuddered together in climax.

Henry collapsed against me and I somehow managed to find the strength to wrap my arms around him.

As our breathing evened and he rolled off me, I was left stunned. Henry wrapped his arms around me and I cuddled against him as satisfied exhaustion stole us into sleep before I could fully formulate my panicked wonder at what had occurred between us.

***

I THINK it was the unfamiliar weight that woke me out of my sensual dreams. Heat was wrapped all around me, and there was a heaviness over my left thigh and across my waist. My face was pressed against something warm, smooth, and solid.

Slowly consciousness returned and with it the smell of cologne and the soft sound of someone else's breathing.

Last night came back to me in a rush of searing memories and emotions as I realized I was lying on my side, Henry curled around me. His leg was thrown over mine, his arm across my waist, and my head was buried in his chest. Unbelievably, his morning erection pressed against my belly. How on earth could that man still be turned on?

But then tingles awoke between my legs as I remembered what I'd been dreaming about. Even after the ferocious sex and stunning love-making, I'd been lost in an aroused fog, dreaming of Henry and sex.

For a moment, I lay there, enjoying the sensation of being in his arms. It was beautiful and unlike anything I'd ever felt before.

I felt safe in this man's arms.

Safe and even cherished.

It was possibly a million times more dangerous than my attraction to him.

His leg suddenly shifted and his arm tightened around my waist, attempting, it seemed, to pull me closer to him.

"I'm as close as you're going to get me," I mumbled against his naked chest.

It rumbled beneath my lips. "Not true," came his husky response. "My cock isn't inside you."

"Charming."

I felt him shake with laughter and involuntarily smiled in response.

He tangled a hand through my hair and gently tugged on it. I gave him what he wanted and tilted my head back to look into his eyes. Affection and heat mingled in his expression. "Good morning."

"Morning." Feeling stupidly shy all of a sudden, I blurted out the first thing that came to mind. "You don't snore."

He gave me a sleepy grin that was way too sexy for my comfort. "Well, you'd be the first to know."

"What does that mean?"

Henry shrugged. "You'd be the first nonrelated woman to know if I snored or not."

Understanding dawned and a mixture of triumph and uneasiness came over me. "Are you saying you've never slept with a woman before? How can that be? You've been monogamous with a woman for periods of time."

"Yes." He did me a favor by not asking how I knew that. "But I've never slept in their bed, nor they in mine." He reached up to curl strands of my hair behind my ear, and then he caressed my cheek with the back of his knuckles. I was breathless, watching him as he seemed to memorize every facet of my face. "Sleeping over usually sends the wrong message."

What?

Oh my God. "But ... you're happy to send this message ... to me?"

His answer was a long, sweet, drugging kiss that had my fingers curling into his biceps. When we finally came up for air, I felt a little lost.

"I can't imagine feeling like this with anyone else."

What? Was he saying what I thought he was saying? Or was this a phase for him, something new to try? "What does that mean? Exactly?"

"It means that waking up with you in my arms feels good." He brushed his mouth over mine. "And I want to repeat it."

"Henry ..."

"I love when you say my name." His kiss was harder, wanting, so I was surprised when he suddenly broke it with a miserable groan. "And I can't do anything about it because I have to go."

Surprise jolted through me. "You do?"

He kissed my nose as he lightly caressed my breast with his thumb, groaned in frustration, and then hopped out of bed. I wrapped the sheets around me, watching befuddled as he moved around the room, grabbing his clothes. As he pulled on his tuxedo jacket, reality came crashing back.

When he was so close, he had a bad habit of confusing me, bewitching me even. Now with a margin of distance between us, I remembered what *I* wanted and what I didn't want. And what I didn't want was to be that girl who was confused when a guy said he wanted you but then got out of bed right away to leave.

"Look," I sighed, "you don't have to do this."

Henry frowned. "Do what?"

"Pretend. I'm a big girl. And we had a deal. This was a one-time-only thing."

"Are you being serious?" he asked incredulously as he sat down to tie his dress shoes.

"Excuse me?"

"If I wanted out, I would have been gone as soon as we had sex last night. Were you not listening to anything I just said?" He gestured to the bed.

He didn't seem angry. More amused by me. "Henry ..."

I didn't know how to articulate what I was feeling, or if I even really wanted him to know what I was feeling, but he pulled out his cell and called someone before I could make up my mind. "Henry Lexington. A Town Car, please." He gave the person on the other end my address. "My apartment first. I need the driver to wait. I have an eleven o' clock flight ... Logan." He ended the call. "I have a flight."

"So I heard." Some of my uneasiness dwindled a little now that I knew he had a legitimate reason for leaving. "Business trip?"

"To the Caymans."

"Nice."

Henry didn't seem like he thought it was nice. Instead he sat down on the bed next to me and reached over to tug playfully on the sheet I had wrapped around me.

"Stop." I swatted away his hand.

He pouted playfully. "Please. I need a visual to get me through the next few days. From the Caymans I fly to

Panama, from Panama to Seattle. I won't be back until next Monday."

The news that he would be gone for over a week disturbed me. It was ridiculous! I would not be one of those women. "You have plenty of visuals from last night," I reminded him, "to get you through forever." I swatted his hand away again. "Henry, this was a one-time deal."

He got by my swatting, fisted a huge chunk of sheet in his hand, and used it to haul me up against him. His arms wrapped around me, trapping me. "I thought we came to an understanding a few hours ago ... when we came."

I would not laugh.

He saw my lips twitching and grinned. "Nadia, I like you. You like me. Let's not overcomplicate this. Let's see where it goes."

That was the problem. I did like him. And I liked that he liked me.

I wanted to see where this went, despite my reservations.

I think I wanted it more than anything. Which meant I had to hope he never found out the truth. With an exaggerated huff, I withdrew and lowered the sheet. His eyes immediately dropped and heated at the sight of my naked breasts. "Enough to see you through?" I quipped.

With a long, drawn-out groan, he dropped his face between them and mumbled, disgruntled, "It'll just have to be."

CHAPTER EIGHT

"Something is bothering you," Barbara said as she sat her pert butt on my desk and crossed her arms. She gave me an "I'm not moving until you tell me" look.

It was Wednesday.

And I hadn't heard a thing from Henry. At all.

I don't know what I'd been expecting but when he took my phone and programmed me into his before he left me Sunday morning, I assumed that meant I'd at least get a "I arrived safe and sound" text. Or something.

But nada. Zilch. Zippo. Nothing.

And I was back to feeling like an insecure high schooler.

I resented the hell out of him for it.

"Is it about Lexington?" Barbara asked.

Feeling vulnerable and stupid, I didn't want to explain. Barbara was so together about men. She was always the one in control. She surprised me by saying, "They have a way of fucking with our heads even when we think we've done everything to protect ourselves from it." She saw my surprise and nodded. "There was someone in my past I developed feelings for. Even when I meant not to."

"What happened?"

"He married someone else."

"Jesus."

She shrugged as if it didn't matter anymore. "It happens. So what's going on with Lexington?"

I found myself telling her all about our one-time-deal agreement, the charity ball, his mother, and in not great detail, our night together and the morning after. "Now he hasn't called and I'm feeling the way I promised myself I'd never feel. Insecure. Stupid. Vulnerable. He's ... God, Barb, he's such a flirt. And it's so natural to him, he wouldn't even know how to stop. So how do I know he's not in Panama with some beautiful Panamanian woman saying all the same things to her that he said to me?"

"You don't."

I winced at her bluntness.

"You don't, sweetie. I've known Henry Lexington longer than you and I can tell you that the man bores easily. You should not, I repeat *not*, be waiting around for him to call you." She stood, having no idea how much she'd trampled across my hopes. "Instead, I think you should do what you were doing. Have fun. Play the field." She grinned. "I'm setting you up on a date for tomorrow night."

"No." My stomach dropped at the thought.

"Yes, and not just any date. I'm setting you up with Micah."

"Who is Micah?" I asked warily since she'd said the name with sex in her voice.

"Micah is my young friend. He's gorgeous and he is never looking for anything but fun."

Understanding dawned. "You're setting me up on a sex date?"

"Yes. The only way to get over Henry is to have sex with

someone else who is fantastic in bed. And trust me ... No one will blow your mind the way Micah will blow your mind."

"Wait ... you're setting me up with your fuck buddy?" I hissed.

She shrugged. "I don't mind sharing."

"Barb—"

"Sex is a high." She grabbed my shoulders, giving me a little shake. "You had amazing sex with Henry and it has clouded your judgment. Having even better sex with someone else will put you back on the right course."

Joe's warning echoed in my head. He wouldn't think this was healthy. Or at all like something I'd do. "I don't know."

"I'm older and wiser. You're doing this."

৩৫৩

MICAH WAS a lawyer but I'm pretty sure he could have been a model instead.

I had never been on date with a man who was more beautiful than most of the women I'd met. For a while I could only stare at him, marveling at his chiseled jawline and his aqua eyes framed by the longest, thickest eyelashes I'd ever seen.

To be fair, Micah was doing his own share of staring.

It was Thursday and we were sitting in a hotel bar on Beacon Street. We'd tried conversation but it was stilted, and he didn't get my nervous jokes.

He studied me over the rim of his soda water and lime.

I studied him over the rim of my glass of wine.

"Barbara said you were luscious. She wasn't lying."

I flushed at the compliment. "She said you were gorgeous. She wasn't lying."

He nodded, taking the compliment as his due. Of course

he knew he was gorgeous. Still, the man never smiled. Or cracked a joke. Or teased.

Flashes of a boyish grin flitted before my eyes and I almost groaned at the intrusion. I did not want to be thinking about Henry right now.

"I've slept with all kinds of women, all different shapes and sizes," he continued, his eyes drifting over my body. "But not one as happily proportioned as you. You have outstanding curves in all the right places."

If Henry had said that to me, I'd pretend to want to smack him while truthfully enjoying the compliment. Because he would have said it in a teasing way, with a provocative grin, meant to flare my temper and turn me on.

Micah said it like he was a scientist analyzing data.

"Has anyone ever told you, you look like that actress out of *Mad Men*?"

"Yeah." I threw back a huge gulp of wine.

"Do you prefer rough sex or gentle?"

And I nearly choked on it. "Excuse me?"

His aqua eyes narrowed. "I like to know a woman's preference before sex. I want to make sure you get what you're looking for tonight. Barbara didn't specify."

An ickiness crawled over my skin. God! This felt like a business transaction. It wouldn't have surprised me if after we had sex, he'd turn around and say, "That'll be four hundred dollars, please."

"I can't do this." I slammed my wine glass down on the table, grabbed my purse, jumped off my stool, and hurried out with the image of his befuddled expression in my mind. As I stalked down Beacon Street, keeping my eye out for a cab with its light on, I fumbled for my cell phone.

Twenty seconds later I heard Joe's voice in my ear. "I think Barbara might have set me up with a prostitute," I said loudly enough to draw stares. I didn't care.

"What?"

"Micah. This lawyer who may as well have been a prostitute."

"Wait," my friend huffed. "Start at the beginning."

So I did. I told him everything that happened with Henry, how he made me feel, and Barbara's grand idea to get me over him. I wasn't surprised when Joe didn't say, "I told you so." He wasn't that person. Instead he said, "You're not cut out to be a player, Nadia. You know this."

"Clearly, you're right." I saw a cab and waved it down. "I'm not Barbara." That was the truth. As much as I'd tried, it was not who I was.

As I settled into the cab and gave the driver my address, I waited for Joe to give me some sage advice. "I don't know much," he said, "but I feel I have to remind you that Henry Lexington *is* a player."

Yes, he was. And now I was comparing every man to him ... which was such a stupid thing to do.

"What am I going to do?"

"You're going to go out on a date with someone who is looking for what you're looking for: a relationship."

"I'm not looking for a relationship," I argued.

"If you're not looking for just sex, then you're looking for a relationship, whether you want to admit it or not."

I thought about waking up in Henry's arms, how safe and wonderful I had felt.

Maybe that feeling wasn't about Henry. Maybe Joe was right. Maybe, finally, I was ready to get past my fears and try something real with someone again.

"Okay."

"I have a friend. James. He's a photographer and he's a little older than you."

"How much older?"

"About Henry's age. He divorced eighteen months ago and

has been on dating sites with no luck ... James deserves someone great. I'd be happy to set you two up. I know he has an early shoot in the city tomorrow, so why don't I set you up for lunch after the show?"

Something real. With someone who actually wanted something real.

The butterflies in my belly rioted at the idea.

"Go for it."

❧

JAMES WAS A GENTLEMAN.

When I walked into Anthem, this cool, casual upscale place at Faneuil Hall, I didn't have to ask the hostess to show me to the table because James stood up from a booth and waved me over.

My first (and shallow) thought was that he was shorter than Henry. And when I approached and he leaned in to shake my hand and kiss my cheek, my heart sank at the lack of butterflies. He was shorter than me when I was in heels. It sounded ridiculous to care about that stuff, and I knew when you met the right person, you didn't care about if he was short or tall, green or blue. But on first impression, it bothered me.

James was shorter than I was in heels, and he was slim and wiry, built like a cyclist. If we were to have sex, I'd feel super self-conscious. As "happily proportioned" as I was, I knew from experience that if the guy was not tall, well-built, or stocky, I tended to feel like a whale.

I didn't want to feel like a whale during sex.

I wanted to feel feminine and sexy and easily manhandled.

Flashes of Henry fucking me against the wall the other night hit so suddenly I stumbled, knocking over an empty glass on our table. "I'm so sorry," I gasped, my cheeks burning with mortification.

James gave me a kind smile, probably assuming I was nervous. "No worries."

We slid into opposite sides of the booth and I smiled back, trying to shove my thoughts of sex and Henry out of my head. "So, you're a photographer?"

We chatted a while in between ordering and waiting for our food to arrive, telling each other a little about our jobs. James was freelance and did a lot of work for a couple of newspapers.

"I've seen you on television." James suddenly looked a little shy. "You're as gorgeous and charismatic as you are on TV. I asked Joe about you a while ago, whether you were seeing anyone. But he said you weren't dating."

Suddenly I felt bad. Very bad. Because it would seem James had had a crush on me for some time and here I was already discounting sex with the guy because of his height and build.

Strike that.

If I was going to be honest with myself, I was discounting sex with the guy because of Henry Goddamn Lexington.

I desperately tried to shake him off. If I gave James a chance, something could develop between us and I wouldn't give a rat's ass that I weighed twice as much as he did. He obviously couldn't care less, if the way he kept running his eyes over me when he thought I wasn't looking was anything to go by.

"I was concentrating on my career for a while," I finally replied. "But I need to start prioritizing my personal life too."

"I get it." He nodded. "After my divorce I realized how little time I'd prioritized my personal life. It was why my ex left me. I knew then I had to make some changes."

"So ... you didn't want to get divorced?" I asked tentatively.

James shrugged. "I know it's for the best now. But at the time, I was pretty wrecked by it."

"Haven't you ever considered trying a reconciliation with your ex?"

He frowned at me and I flushed, realizing what a stupid thing it was to say on a date. "Well ... she started dating pretty quickly."

"So she's seeing someone."

"No. They broke up a few months ago."

"Maybe you should talk to her."

"Okay, wait." He held up a hand. "Are you counseling me to get back together with my ex on *our* first date?"

"It does sound like it," a deep, familiar voice said from behind me.

I tensed.

No. Way.

James looked beyond my shoulder and not wanting to but drawn to, I half turned in the booth to find Henry sitting in the one directly behind me.

Our faces were so close it took me a second to recognize the anger burning in the back of his blue eyes. It was still there even as he flashed me a cocky grin and stood. "Mind if I join you?" he said, and sat down beside me, forcing me along the booth.

This was not happening!

How was this happening?

He was supposed to be in Panama or Seattle or something!

"Henry Lexington," he held out his hand to James who shook it in bemusement. "A friend of Nadia's."

"Nice to meet you."

"You too. Although to be honest, I'm surprised to meet

you." I could feel him looking at me but I stared straight ahead at James. I was beyond tense, bracing myself for what Henry was about to say or do. "I was under the impression Nadia was off the market."

My jaw almost hit the table.

He did not just say that.

James looked between Henry and me. The smart man cottoned on extremely quickly. "Look, I don't want to get in the middle of something." He slid out of the booth and pulled out his wallet but Henry stopped him.

"Let me pay for your lunch. Compensation for a colossal waste of your time."

The anger slipped out in his words and James paused. He looked at me. "Nadia, are you okay with this guy?"

I gave him a weak smile, grateful that he'd asked. "I'm sorry, James. Henry and I have a little unfinished business. I didn't mean for you to get caught in the middle."

"As long as you're okay?"

I nodded and he pulled out money from his wallet and threw it on the table, despite Henry's offer. "It was nice to meet you anyway."

"You're a gentleman," I said as he walked away. And he was.

Why did I have to be attracted to the asshat beside me and not the one who was walking away?

I didn't even have to look at Henry to be overwhelmed by him. He was so much bigger than me in the booth, his heat and anger pulsing as he pressed his knee against mine.

"Look at me," he seethed.

Not wanting to be a coward, I finally did and winced at the awful look on his face. "Henry—"

"You can either play this out in public—and I can't promise it won't get loud—or you can get that sexy-as-fuck ass of yours out of this booth and into my car. Your choice."

"That's not much of a choice," I snapped.

"Nadia ..." he warned between gritted teeth.

With an exaggerated, exasperated sigh, I grabbed my purse and nudged him with my knee. He got out and despite his anger, he held out his hand, helping me up out of the booth. As soon as I was on my feet, his fingers curled tight around mine.

There was no hope of escape.

⚬⚮⚬

NOT A WORD WAS EXCHANGED between us as Henry drove through heavy traffic to Back Bay. The tension was so unbearably thick, I didn't realize until we pulled up to his building that I'd curled my fingernails deep into my thighs. My stomach was in knots, hating that he was angry at me, hating that I hated that he was angry at me. Why did it feel like I'd betrayed him?

I shouldn't care like this.

Ever the gentleman, he parked his car, got out, and walked around to the passenger side to open my door and help me out. Like at the restaurant, he held tight to my hand as he walked toward the apartment building on Columbus Avenue. Inside the grand marble entrance hall, Henry first nodded at a very tall security guard and then said hello to a well-dressed gentleman behind reception. "Mr. Lexington," the man nodded.

Henry led me into one of two elevators in the hall and I watched, somewhat taken aback, when he didn't hit the penthouse button.

He felt my stare, his eyes asking a belligerent "What?"

"You don't live in the penthouse?"

"Disappointed?" Acid dripped from the word and I hated it.

I wanted to kiss the attitude right out of him.

"Surprised."

"The penthouse is more Caine's taste. I don't need all that space."

As I discovered when Henry led me inside a modest but beautifully turned-out one-bedroom apartment with a view over Statler Park. "Nice space."

Right in the heart of Back Bay.

This place must be costing the man a fortune.

"I don't want to talk about my apartment."

On that note, I spun around to find him staring at me, wary, it seemed. I'd prefer a glower over wary.

"How did you know where to find me?" It occurred to me that there was a possibility I was already being stalked by one man. I didn't need another in my life.

"My mother." His anger leaked out in his words, despite his careful expression. "She found out I flew home early from my business trip, guessed why, and couldn't wait to inform me that you were seen on a date the other night. I went to the station today to find out what was going on and Barbara told me you were on another date."

"And she told you where to find me?" The traitor.

"I may have threatened bodily harm."

"Henry!"

"Christ, Nadia!" His control snapped as he came toward me. "What the fuck are you playing at?"

"Is your mother having me followed?" The idea filled me with horror. What if she did a little digging? Would she find out what I didn't want Henry to know?

"I don't want to talk about my mother and how fucking crazy she's acting. I want to talk about you and how fucking crazy you're acting."

"Stop cursing at me!"

His hands came up and he clenched them into fists, as

though he were trying to stop himself from wrapping them around my neck. "Nadia, stop avoiding the question."

"Your mother hates me. That's a huge problem."

"Nadia ... I won't. Say. It. Again."

"Don't threaten me!" I pushed against his chest, and he didn't budge. "You're the one in the wrong here! Pushing me around! Interrupting dates!"

He gripped my biceps, yanking me into him. "We had an understanding when I left. I'm not the one in the wrong here, Nadia. Why the fuck!" He stopped, took a breath, and his voice lowered, calmed, "Why can't you trust me?"

At the hurt, the vulnerability I heard behind those words, I sagged against him. "Henry, I don't do trust very well. And you didn't call or text so ..."

His hands tightened around me as he searched my face. "So what? I was on a business trip. I told you that. I was under the impression you understood and that when I got back, I'd call."

I nodded, feeling foolish. Not for going out on other dates but for wishing he would have *wanted* to call or text me despite being on a business trip. I tried to pull away but he held me tighter. I looked anywhere but at him and he ducked his head to look into my eyes.

"I wanted to call," he said, his words low, gentle. "But I thought you needed some space after what happened. If I knew you would go out with the first guy your friends could set you up with, I would have called."

"Henry ..." I tried to withdraw again but his hands slipped down my back, forcing my body against his. I flushed at the feel of his arousal digging into my stomach.

His voice was hoarse. "Do you think I'd put up with this much drama from anyone else?"

I glared at him. "*You* cause the drama."

He grinned at my flare of temper. "Really?"

"This is too much." I pushed ineffectually against his chest, looking up into his too-handsome face. God, I loved his face.

"Why do you keep fighting me?" he whispered against my lips. "Can't you see how much I care about you?"

I sucked in a breath at the words, my heart racing at the sincerity behind them. "Henry."

If anything he grew harder against me. "You have no idea what my name on your lips does to me."

"I think I do," I whispered back.

But he didn't smile. Instead his expression turned pleading. "Why?"

I knew what he was asking. What he'd been asking all along since he'd crashed my date. And I knew if I didn't tell him, he'd walk away. Despite all my insecurities, being in his arms now seemed to obliterate them all.

My fingers curled around the lapels of his wool blazer. He had shown me his vulnerability. He'd dropped his veneer of charm to give me something real.

I believed he deserved *real* in return.

"My dad is a cheat," I said, my eyes dropping to Henry's strong throat. "My mom knows and she ... stays with him. And it's not like he's in love with two women and can't pick. He just screws anything that has a vagina. I didn't know until high school and parents knew and suddenly kids knew and then I knew. I even caught him once." I swallowed back the remembered misery of that time. "My mom suffered through the humiliation and she made me suffer through it with her by staying with him."

"Sunshine," he whispered, caressing my back. "I'm sorry."

I finally made eye contact with him and found myself falling into his concern and tenderness. He cared.

He really did care.

I pressed closer, wanting to bury myself inside his arms

forever. "I wish it hadn't affected me, but it did. And having a boss like Dick, and being treated like a sex object by men like Montgomery Mitchell, it only made it harder for me to trust men. And the way you treated me ..."

His fingers bit into my waist, almost bruising. "If I could take—"

"No." I cut him off. "I'm not dredging that up to make you feel bad ... I'm trying to explain why I haven't exactly made this easy for you. Because ... it isn't easy for me, Henry." I curled my hands around his neck. "I care about you too. I *want* to trust you."

Wrapping his arms around me, he bent his forehead to mine, his breath caressing my lips. "Then try."

I nodded. "I will. I promise."

CHAPTER NINE

"Now let's take a look at the weather forecast. Nadia, what is in store for us?"

I took my cue from Barbara, spotting the camera with the red light and throwing the audience a beaming smile. "Well, Barbara, you and the rest of Boston will be relieved to know that the sun is sticking around this week, right through Saturday. We're looking at clear skies for game day at Fenway. Even better, while temperatures soar today and tomorrow to ninety-five, the Red Sox can rest easy that they won't be melting on the field on Saturday, as the temperature falls to a milder eighty degrees over the weekend."

"That's good to know. I don't want my makeup running off while I'm in the stands." Barbara threw the camera a flirtatious smile. "You never know who you might meet at a game."

"Games are sacred, Barbara," Andrew said and gave her a droll look. "They're not a live version of Tinder."

"Why, Andrew, I'm surprised you even know what Tinder is. Relics don't usually take to new technology."

I tried not to laugh, even though I wasn't on camera, because my mic was still live.

Andrew gave the camera a weary look and I saw the crew laughing. And then he turned to me and I was back on camera. "Will you be at the game, Nadia?"

"Of course," I lied. The city of Boston didn't want to know I wasn't a hardcore Red Sox fan. I wasn't a baseball fan at all. Henry was but he thankfully wasn't into forcing someone to a game just to keep him company. Plus, Caine had a box at EMC Level and Henry always went to games with him. That meant I got to enjoy my first weekend on my own in a while. I couldn't wait. I had a pile of movies and a bottle of wine waiting for me.

We finished up our program for the day and when I got back to my desk, flowers waited for me. Peonies. A few weeks after Henry and I started dating and were photographed together in the society pages, the text messages stopped and so did the calla lilies. *He* finally got the message.

But he'd ruined calla lilies for me. When Henry asked me what my favorite flowers were, I told him peonies.

Henry sent them every week.

❧

"Did you get my flowers?" Henry caressed his thumb over the top of my knuckles.

We were seated at the Bristol Lounge for lunch as was our weekly tradition. It had become apparent in the last few months that Henry was incredibly affectionate. No matter where we were, there was hardly a moment he wasn't touching me. I didn't even think he was aware of it half the time. For instance, we'd sat at the table, me adjacent to him, and I'd fiddled with a fork, my mind on work. Henry had automatically reached for my hand and hadn't let go of it while we waited for our food.

I smiled at him. I had no idea where he got peonies, considering they were out of season in this state, but every week, without fail, peonies turned up at the station.

"You know I love them." And I did. "Where are you getting them?"

He grinned. "I'll never tell."

I rolled my eyes. "Infuriating man."

Henry tugged on my hand. "You love it."

Any attempt to remain expressionless were obliterated under his deliberately heated stare. No matter how many times I tried to not react, I failed. I laughed and shook my head at him.

Our meal arrived and I attempted to let go of the uneasy butterflies in my stomach so I could enjoy it. This was my treat. Every week, a burger at the Bristol Lounge.

I was digging in and made the mistake of looking up from my burger as I chewed.

Henry was staring, a small smile curling his lips.

Swallowing, I put my burger down and wiped my mouth with a napkin. "What?"

"Nothing." He dug into his *filet*.

"It was something." I huffed. "You don't stare at a woman when she's eating a burger, Lexington. It's rude."

He chuckled. "I'll keep that in mind."

"Come on. Seriously. What were you staring at?"

Henry leaned toward me and said quietly, "I like watching you. Whether you're eating a burger or coming around my cock, I like watching you."

Did I mention he had a tendency to say filthy things to me in public? I threw my napkin at him and he laughed, ducking to avoid it.

"Well, you wanted to know."

The truth was I loved our banter. I loved how playful he was and I was never bored when we were together. In fact, I looked forward to seeing him like an addict looked forward to their next fix. It was dangerous, I knew it, but I couldn't stop myself. And I really believed Henry felt the same way. No one could look at someone with the deep intensity he looked at me with and not feel the same way, right? My past lovers had told me that they cared but now I knew, after feeling the sincerity in Henry's words, those prior words were merely letters put together on the tongue.

"Henry."

The voice abruptly yanked me from my sweet musings.

It was a voice I did not want to hear.

"Mother." Henry pushed back his chair and stood. I finally drew my gaze upward to watch him round the table to kiss his mother's cheek. She stood before us looking ill at ease. Behind her was another well-put-together woman around her age and a young, beautiful brunette, likely in her early twenties.

To say things had been strained between Henry and his mother was to put it mildly. It had gotten to the point where he'd stopped visiting his parents' home, and I could only surmise it was due to her opinion of me. I truly didn't know what I'd done to upset this woman so much, but it was clear she detested me, and even more so now that her hatred had damaged her relationship with her son.

It was horrible to be the cause of their discord, and I'd tried talking to Henry about it but he didn't want to discuss it.

"How are you?" he asked.

Her expression said, "You'd know if you called more" but she kept those words to herself. "Well, thank you. You remember Edina Hamilton?"

Henry nodded and held out his hand to the older woman. "Nice to see you again."

"You too, Henry." Her eyes ran over him appraisingly and there was something in them that made me stiffen. I realized what that something was when she practically yanked the young brunette into Henry's personal space. "You remember my lovely daughter June. She graduated from Yale this summer."

His smile was lazy and flirtatious as he shook June's hand. "Congratulations."

"Thank you." She beamed up at him. "I still can't believe I graduated."

"June was pre-law," her mother preened. "She'll be attending Harvard Law in the fall."

"Impressive. Smart *and* beautiful." Henry winked.

I hated him.

His mother shot me a smug look while he wasn't paying attention and I squirmed in my seat.

Yes ... the last few months with Henry had been blissful. With one exception.

His inability to not flirt.

I'd tried to not let it bother me.

But it bothered the heck out of me.

"Well, our table is waiting," Mrs. Lexington said. "Before we go, Henry, I was thinking you could introduce June to Caine as she hopes to go into corporate law. It's best to make all the connections she can now, am I right?"

"Definitely," Henry said affably.

"Oh, wait." June dug into her purse and produced a card. "My number."

He took it. "Have a lovely lunch, ladies."

As they walked away, Henry returned to the table and I wondered how much of a scene I'd make if I stuck my fork in his hand. I tried to tell myself that his flirting didn't mean anything, but I guess I wasn't thick-skinned enough to be able to put it to one side.

I didn't want him telling other women they were smart and beautiful.

I didn't *see* other men anymore. I only saw him. And it hurt to think my feelings were more involved than his.

My appetite gone, I shoved the burger around my plate.

"Are you okay?" He frowned at me after a few minutes.

I nodded, afraid to speak in case I screamed at him.

He sighed. "I know it was rude of me not to introduce you but I was going to before my mother said they had to get to their table."

My answering smile was tight.

"Is it because of my mother? Because I told you not to worry about that."

In that moment, I wanted to claim a headache and leave him there but that would mean doing so in front of his mother, and I didn't want her to think she'd won. Instead I said, "No, it's not that. I just have a bit of a headache."

"We can leave."

"No. Finish lunch."

Afterward we strolled out of the restaurant with Henry's hand on my back, and he nodded at his mother and her companions as we left.

"Why don't I drop you off at my apartment? You can get some sleep, get rid of that headache, and I'll take care of you when I get back from the office." He kissed my hand as we sat in his car outside the hotel restaurant.

His words were sweet but I was still pissed way the hell off. I shrugged my hand out of his. "You know I really just want my own bed."

Henry searched my face and I did my best to keep my expression neutral. With a heavy sigh, he drove out of the hotel driveway and joined the traffic, heading toward Lower Roxbury.

Outside my apartment I gave him a quick peck on the cheek and jumped out of his car before he could question why I was acting so strangely.

Once inside I leaned against my door, trying to catch my breath. It felt like I'd sprinted home. I was jealous and hurt over Henry's flirting but did I have any right to be? Surely he didn't mean anything by it. But me? I was keeping the truth from him.

I was all wrong for this man.

He needed a woman who accepted him for who he was.

He needed a woman who could be totally open with him.

Ten minutes later, my phone beeped. It was a text from Henry.

Are we okay?

I wanted to tell him no. We weren't. And we probably weren't going to be.

Then I thought how wonderful it felt when we lay in each other's arms at night and talked until we fell asleep.

So I replied:

Of course. I'm just tired. We'll talk soon. xx

ONE OF THE best things about dating Henry was the fact that he'd introduced me to Alexa. It would be an understatement to say that she and Caine had been through the ringer over the summer. If I told you what had happened to her, to them, you'd think I was making the whole thing up.

Alexa—or Lexie, as I called her—was fully recovered from the disaster, thank God. Even better, she and Caine were a real couple now. It turned out Caine was head over heels in love with her. I didn't think it was possible for Carraway to love anyone more than business, but after witnessing him with Lexie these last few months, I knew it to be true. He stared at my friend like there was no one else in the world like her.

And he never flirted with other women.

Ever.

He didn't even look at other women!

Suffice it to say, I was envious.

Things had been strained between Henry and me since our lunch. I'd put off seeing him before the weekend, and I had my quiet Saturday at home while he was at the game. I couldn't shake him on Sunday without causing drama, and honestly, as much as he'd pissed me off, I missed him.

And that's why I found myself having dinner with Henry, Caine, and Lexie at Caine's penthouse. It wasn't the first time I'd been in the amazing space but it was my first dinner there. The penthouse was on Arlington Street, a two-minute walk from Henry's apartment. There were floor-to-ceiling windows everywhere, giving him awesome views of the city. The apartment was open-plan living and on a raised platform was a stylish eight-seat dining set so we could enjoy that view while we ate.

Conversation was going well—we were bantering back and forth—when Henry ruined it.

"I bumped into Edina Hamilton and her daughter June the other day," he said to Caine. "June is starting Harvard Law in the fall. She's going into corporate law and I promised I'd introduce you."

"Why?" Caine frowned.

Yes, why, Henry?

"She wants to start making the right connections now. You know how these things work."

"And does she seem like the kind of thick-skinned, hard-nosed lawyer I'd have at my firm?"

Lexie snorted and shot me a smirk.

I didn't pay much attention to her amusement. I wanted to hear Henry's reply.

He shrugged. "It was a two-second meeting. She graduated from Yale and got into Harvard Law. Clearly she's smart."

"And beautiful." The words were out of my mouth before I even knew what was happening.

Everyone looked at me because I'd not only said the words, they were so filled with resentment, even I flinched.

"What?" Henry said.

Well, it was out there now. "That's what you said to her. You told her she was smart and beautiful and then you winked at her." Out of the corner of my eye, I saw Lexie and Caine shift uncomfortably. *Shit.* "Never mind."

"Oh no." Henry sat back, dropping his fork. He crossed his arms and grinned at me as if he was actually enjoying my bout of jealousy. "Please, go on."

Hurt scored across my chest like whiplash. He thought this was funny? He thought this was a moment for our playful banter where we pretended to be irritated with each other? My expression smoothed to politeness. I didn't want to cause a scene in front of our friends.

I turned to Lexie who was staring at me in concern. "Did you say Mrs. Flanagan gave you the recipe for this?" I indicated to the paella. Mrs. Flanagan was Caine's neighbor and a good friend to both him and Lexie. She was all I could think of in the moment to talk about.

"Yes," Lexie answered slowly. "Would you like it?"

"That would be great."

I could feel Henry staring at me but I refused to look at him. Instead I gave Lexie a somewhat tremulous smile. "Have you managed to talk that banoffee pie recipe out of her yet?"

"No," Lexie said, thankfully going along with me. "I beg

and I beg. If Caine asked, she'd probably give it to him but he won't." She threw him a teasing look. "He does it to torture me."

"No. I keep telling you Effie guards her pie recipes with her life. You'll get them in her will. You just have to be at peace with that."

When Caine was relaxed, making jokes, I could definitely see why Lexie fell for him. The man had a quick, dry sense of humor, and he stared at my friend like she was a miracle.

I understood that too.

I had a woman crush on Lexie. She was funny, smart, determined, loyal, and truly kind. She was everything I hoped I could eventually become.

A little while later, I excused myself to the bathroom, mostly to get away from the tension Henry and I were causing at the table. The lower-level bathroom was getting a facelift so I climbed the spiral staircase that led upstairs. I was walking down the hall when I heard my name murmured below. Like a big kid, I tiptoed back down the hall to eavesdrop.

"It was nothing," I heard Henry say.

"It's not nothing, Henry. You called a woman smart and beautiful in front of Nadia. And winked at her," Lexie huffed.

"So?"

"Are you kidding me? I thought when you started dating Nadia that you'd stop flirting with other women."

"I don't flirt."

"You flirt all the time."

"If I do, it doesn't mean anything. Nadia knows that."

"No." Lexie sounded despairing. "God, Henry, do you not know anything about women?"

"Carraway, help me out here."

"Sorry," Caine's voice rumbled up to me, "I can't. If Lexie flirted with other men, it would piss me off."

See! Thank you, Caine!

There was silence and I was about to head back to the bathroom when Lexie said, "It wouldn't bother you if Nadia flirted with other men?"

More silence, and I found myself leaning further toward the staircase, desperate to hear his answer.

To my disappointment, he didn't respond. With an inward sigh, I found the bathroom, washed up quickly, and wandered as casually as possible downstairs.

Henry stood from the table. "There you are. Time to go."

Taken aback, I could only nod and quickly thank Lexie and Caine for having us before Henry grabbed my hand and led me out. Just as we walked into the hall, I looked over my shoulder and caught Lexie grinning mischievously at me.

Confusion wrinkled my brow.

Inside the elevator, his grip on my hand tightened. I dared to look at him. He was staring straight ahead, the muscle in his jaw twitching.

"Months ago when I crashed your date with that photographer, I was jealous as hell," he bit out. "And I made that clear."

My heart started to race. "Yes?"

Finally, he looked at me, his expression unsure. "You've been pissed all week because of June Hamilton and you didn't tell me. How many times have I pissed you off and you haven't told me?"

"Not pissed," I said, my words so low I was almost whispering. "Hurt."

Remorse and something else flicked across his gaze. "That's a million times worse. Why didn't you say anything?"

"Because you're a flirt." I wrenched my hand away. "That's who you are. I can't change who you are, Henry. And I can't change the fact that I'm the kind of woman who wants the guy she's with to pretend that he doesn't see how beautiful other women are. I don't *see* other men when I'm with you. They don't exist. Not like that. All I ever see is you. And yes ... it hurts that you don't feel the same way."

He cut me a disbelieving look.

Yet he didn't speak.

He didn't speak at all. However, when the elevator doors opened, he grabbed my hand and marched me down the street to his apartment. I didn't know what was going to happen next. Uneasiness made me tighten my hold on his hand and he squeezed back. In reassurance?

I didn't know.

The doubt was obliterated as soon as I stepped inside his apartment.

He slammed the door shut behind us and pinned me against the wall, towering over me, covering me, staring down into my eyes with a fierceness that made me breathless.

"What I say to other women ... it's merely years of culti-vated charm. A veneer. A mask. And I've been doing it so long, it naturally happens." He cupped my face in his hand and leaned down so our noses were touching. There was nowhere for me to look but deep into those vivid blue eyes. "But I can promise you that you are all I truly see. You're all I think about. All the time. And I've been trying my damnedest to give you space when you get distant with me like you did this week ... but I'm not winning either way here so I might as well just say what's been building inside me for months." His thumb slid over my lips as he drank in my every feature. "Nadia, I am so in love with you. Every moment we're not together, I miss you. I miss you like I haven't seen you in years. The thought that I've been hurting you these past few months kills me. I'll be more aware of the flirting thing. I won't do it. I promise you. But you have to promise me that from now on, you're going to talk to me. You're going to tell me when I've made you happy and when I've pissed you off ... and if, and I hope I don't, hurt you."

Nadia, I am so in love with you.

Never before had I felt such a mix of agony and euphoria. His words meant everything to me ... yet they also terrified me.

The fear won and it closed my throat and any response I might have had.

That was when Henry Lexington proved to me he was someone very special.

He brushed his lips gently over mine and whispered, "I can wait, Sunshine. You take all the time you need."

CHAPTER TEN

"I can't believe you talked me into this." Anxiety surged through me.

"We have to face her together. It might as well be now."

Face Henry's mother. Together. At a Sunday luncheon. A garden gala. Whatever that was. "Why is there always an event every weekend in your circle?"

He shrugged. "Charities, political campaigns, celebra—"

"People with too much time on their hands."

He chuckled. "Please don't say that in front of my mother."

"She doesn't like me, Henry. Nothing I say or do will change that."

"Well, she needs to come around because you're not going anywhere. And that's why you're here. So she can see that."

I nodded, leaning into him a little more. "I know. I'm sorry. I'm just nervous."

"Lexie is here somewhere," he offered, knowing her presence would soothe me.

As we made our way around the lawn, people stopped to greet Henry, some I'd met at previous events, others who I hadn't and were intrigued to meet the woman Henry had given up bachelor life for. I'd asked Lexie what I should wear to a garden gala and we'd gone shopping together. I was pleased to see my friend had steered me correctly. The women were dressed in a similar style—classy summer dresses with cardigans or blazers since the weather was turning cool.

I was wearing a blue dress in a stretchy material that hugged my body. The hemline sat an inch or so above my knee showing plenty of leg, but the neckline was slashed in a straight line below my neck and it had cap sleeves. It was sexy, demure.

Lexie had also given me little plastic heel cups for my stilettos so I didn't sink into the lawn.

"Henry, Nadia." Randall Lexington suddenly appeared, looking dapper in a blue cashmere sweater and tan trousers. He shook his son's hand and then leaned over to kiss my cheek.

I relaxed a little, knowing at least one of Henry's parents liked me. According to Henry, his father was trying to get Penelope to come around to us. Apparently he wasn't having much luck.

"You look beautiful," Randall said as he pulled back. "And I'm pleased no one's run you off."

We all knew who "no one" was.

Henry's arm tightened around my waist. "I'd only chase her if she ran."

I rolled my eyes and Randall gave a bark of laughter. "Who are you and what have you done with my son?"

"That is what I'd like to know." Penelope sidled up to our group.

She had a habit of doing that. Appearing out of nowhere like magic.

Like a wicked queen in a fairy tale.

"Penny," Randall warned under his breath.

She gave him a weary look but moved into his side. He automatically embraced her and she leaned deeper into him. Their public affection was surprising.

I'd noted that a lot of couples in Henry's set were so proper and aloof with one another in public. It took me aback to see Penelope Lexington, someone who came off as so cold, be an exception to the rule.

"Mother," Henry said as he dutifully let go of me to lean over and kiss her cheek.

Her expression softened a little but then tightened when he immediately returned to slide his arm around my waist.

"You're still here." Her gaze landed on me.

"Mother." It was Henry's turn to warn her.

But as intimidating as she was, I didn't want Henry to think I needed protection from her. "Mrs. Lexington, it's nice to see you."

"Liar."

"Penny," Randall groaned.

"I'm not going to pretend I'm happy Henry is dating this woman, and that's final."

"You pretend you like people all the time, Penny. You can't stand half the people at this party and yet you'll smile and compliment them, lying through your teeth."

I shifted uncomfortably but decided to be just as direct as Henry's mother. "Henry and I are together. I won't be chased off no matter how rude you are to me. So, you can either pretend to accept this *fact*, or you can embarrass us all. That, however, is only going to lead to people gossiping about us, about you. Worse, *pitying* you. Poor Penelope Lexington having to put up with that woman dating her son." Henry's hand on my back tensed. "Or you could smile and pretend that you're happy with Henry's choice, and that you're so far above them, only your opinion matters."

Henry's parents were silent for a moment but Randall wore a small, impressed smile.

Penelope eyed me like she'd never seen me before. And then she nodded. "You're right."

"Thank God," Randall muttered.

Heeding my advice, Penelope pasted on a welcoming smile and gritted out between her teeth. "You're very manipulative."

"Mother," Henry snapped.

"Smile, darling." She grinned, looking around. "I might dislike your weather girl but at least she understands how things work around here."

I looked up at Henry, disheartened, but relieved that there would be no public humiliation. He stared down at me, eyes apologetic. He had nothing to be sorry about and I kissed him to say so.

And also to annoy his mother.

***

A VILE TASTE filled my mouth and I tried not to show it, I really did, but my God.

"Here." Caine noted my expression, grabbed my arm, and turned me so my back was to the crowd and facing the woodlands that bordered the house. "Spit it out there."

"Blech." I did, wiping my mouth and turning quickly around as if nothing had happened.

Henry was shaking with strained amusement while Caine smirked.

Lexie gave me a sympathetic smile. "I tried to warn you."

She did.

She did try to warn me that the square pastry with the orange stuff on it was the worst canape she'd ever tasted in her life.

"You didn't warn me it tasted like fusty balls."

Henry spat out the soda water he'd just sipped and Caine and Lexie jumped back to avoid it.

"What exactly do fusty balls taste like?" Caine said so seriously, it made me grin.

"Try one and you'll find out."

After wiping his chin with a napkin, Henry said, "Tell me, how on earth you know that the canape tastes like fusty balls?"

"Are we really having this conversation?" Lexie glanced around to see if anyone was paying attention to us.

"Because I've tasted fusty balls." I shrugged, like it was obvious.

"Oh dear God." Lexie looked up at the sky as if she were really calling to Him.

"Not mine," Henry said indignantly.

"No, handsome, your balls are fine."

"Only fine?"

"Now I feel a little sick." Caine gestured to his stomach, looking pained.

"They're better than fine," I hurried to reassure my boyfriend. "Best balls ever."

Lexie and Caine locked horrified gazes. "This isn't happening."

"So who had the fusty balls?"

"It is happening. Somehow it's happening," Caine said.

Henry and I both ignored him. "A guy I dated. It didn't last past the fusty balls."

"I'd think not." Henry nodded. "I'm sorry that happened to you."

"I'm sorry this entire conversation happened to us," Lexie said to Caine.

Henry winked at me and I hid my mischievous smile as I

sipped my champagne to rid myself of the fusty balls taste in my mouth.

I WASN'T surprised Caine and Lexie found a way to ditch us not too long later but it was worth it. Even more so because Henry was doing something for me.

He wasn't flirting with any other women.

Of course he was always polite and friendly, but there was a noticeable difference in his demeanor. Some noticed, some seemed to think it was sweet, giving us this "aww" look; others glowered at me like I was the devil incarnate.

For some reason, even though this was what I wanted, I was also left uneasy.

"Can we go inside for a minute? Find somewhere quiet?"

Henry's brow furrowed in concern but he nodded and immediately led me away from the crowd and into the house. We wandered through the halls until Henry stopped outside double doors. "This is Jeff's office."

"Who's Jeff?"

"Lydia's husband."

"Who's Lydia?"

He chuckled. "You don't even know whose garden gala we're at?"

"Nope."

Once inside, he closed the door and I was surprised by how small the space was. In any normal house, it would be a big office but in this one, it wasn't. It was cozy and masculine compared to the airy feminine style of the rest of the house. Lots of dark wood, dark fabrics, and lots of books.

Henry stopped near Jeff's desk, watching me as I skirted the room, taking it all in. "So what did you need quiet for?"

Right.

That.

I grew still and reluctantly faced him. He was going to think I was unbalanced. "I'm worried that you're not flirting with anyone."

His eyebrows almost hit his hairline. "Excuse me?"

"Not that I want you to," I hurried to say. "But I'm worried that you're changing yourself for me."

Thankfully, he looked more amused than angry. "Of course I'm changing for you. But you're changing for me too."

Surprised, I blurted out, "No, I'm not."

"Yes, you are." Affection and desire mixed in his eyes. "You didn't want this. You didn't trust this. But you let down your guard to give me this." He gestured between us. I held my breath as he continued, "I can make the effort to not send signals to other women than I'm interested in them when I am absolutely not. I can make the effort so that you know I only want you. And I can do that because you made an even bigger effort to give a man, with not the greatest track record for monogamy, a chance."

Love for this man moved through me and I wanted to proclaim it . Yet I couldn't. Maybe I had let down some of defenses.

But not all of them.

Henry patted the large desk. "Now come here."

I raised an eyebrow. "You want me to sit on a stranger's desk? Whatever do you have in mind, Mr. Lexington?"

"I just want to talk to you."

"Liar." I grinned but I strutted across the room, swaying my hips for his benefit, and sat on the desk. My dress tightened and shifted higher up my thighs. Henry's eyes narrowed with wicked intent as he spread my legs and insinuated himself between them. I instinctively wrapped my legs around his hips and we locked gazes as his hands drifted under the fabric of my dress on either side of my thighs. He slid them upwards, taking the dress with them until it was bunched around my waist. "We really shouldn't do this."

"Once more with feeling. Naughty girl. The only one I see." His voice deepened with emotion. "Only ever you, Nadia."

A rush of possessiveness coursed through me and I clasped him by the back of the neck to slam his mouth down over mine. He grunted in approval, the sound vibrating through me, as he returned my demanding kiss.

I wanted to mark him. I wanted to ruin him for any other woman. If ever in the past he'd snuck off to have sex at one of these goddamn events, I wanted this encounter to be the one he'd remember above all others.

Henry broke the kiss, pulling back only to grab the hem of my dress in his hands and yank it upward. I lifted my arms, helping him out. It went flying behind him seconds before he unsnapped my bra.

My heavy breasts swelled under his perusal, my nipples turning to hard pebbles. He cupped my breasts and I arched my back on a sigh as he kneaded them, his touch shooting liquid heat straight through my belly and down between my legs. "I miss these whenever I can't see them," he grumbled adorably, making me shake with laughter.

"You're definitely obsessed."

He nodded, completely serious. "I am."

Chuckling, I covered his hands with mine. "I'm naked on some blueblood's desk, Henry. We don't have time for you to cherish these today."

"Promise me something and I'll speed things up."

Normally I would've laughed but there was something so solemn in his voice and his eyes that I nodded mutely.

"Promise me that these are mine." He squeezed my aching breasts. "Because I love them and I think it would kill

413

me if ever there came a time when some other man got to be with them like this."

I stilled.

Because we both knew he wasn't actually talking about my breasts.

I still hadn't told Henry I loved him.

Not because I didn't feel it but because I was terrified of losing him, and admitting that I loved him out loud would only make things ten times worse when he did eventually go.

This ... however ... this I could give him. "Yes, they're yours."

His eyes smoldered and his reply was to pull gently on my hair, arching my neck and back further and lifting my breasts closer to his mouth. He bent his head, his hungry eyes locked with mine. I shivered, thrilled to see the mirrored possessiveness in his gaze before he closed his hot mouth around my right nipple.

I whimpered at the molten pleasure that rippled through my lower belly and I clutched to the nape of his neck with one hand while the other caressed his upper back, wishing he wasn't wearing a damn blazer over his shirt. Too many layers! He sucked hard, causing a sharp streak of pleasured pain, and then he licked the swollen nipple before moving on to the other.

"Henry, come inside me," I whispered.

He looked up at me and smirked. "Mouth first."

I groaned, growing more wet at the mere thought, but I was also still perfectly aware that we were in an office at someone's else house surrounded by guests. "We could get caught."

"I know. Just imagine people walking in while I'm on my knees licking your pussy." His words were scratchy with arousal. "They'd condemn us but at night, they'd draw up the image of you naked, writhing on a desk with my head between your legs, and they'd get off on it, Sunshine. How could they not? You're the sexiest thing they'd ever see in their entire lives."

His words turned me on so much, I was shocked. The thought of being caught was suddenly incredibly exciting. Perhaps when my head cleared from lust I'd be mortified but right then, it all so very tantalizing.

My belly squeezed deep down low and I knew I was more than ready for him. As his fingers curled around my underwear, my breath came in harsh pants. I stopped touching him to brace my hands on the desk at either side of my hips so I could lift my ass. Henry peeled my damp underwear down my legs, staring up at me with this devilish look I'd come to know and love.

"You're soaked." He bit his bottom lip, studying me for a moment. "I guess we'll be finding more public places to fuck in the future."

"Henry ... stop teasing me," I huffed. "Or we really will get caught."

In answer, he lowered himself to his knees and his hands pressed my thighs apart.

I watched, lost in my daze of utter need, as he licked me.

"Fuck," I hissed, my hips writhing against him. "Henry ... Henry ..." Every time I said his name, his licks over my clit grew more enthusiastic. Then he circled it with his tongue, pressed down it, and repeated, teasing me toward orgasm. It was just out of reach. "Oh God!" My head fell back, my eyes rolled, and then he slid his fingers inside me.

I tensed.

He sucked on my clit. Hard.

I shattered, my climax pulsing through me and I bit my lips to muffle my scream of release.

Still shuddering through the remnants of my orgasm, I was barely aware of Henry standing and unzipping his trousers. Within seconds he was gripping my thighs, pulling me to the edge of the desk. My palms were flat to the piece of furniture, my arms braced a little behind me. It was a good thing too. I was steady and prepared when Henry thrust into me. Hard.

I cried out, closing my eyes to savor the rough but pleasurable assault on my senses.

"Look at me," he demanded, his voice guttural.

My eyes opened on command and there were all my feelings reflected back at me.

Pure primal possessiveness.

My lips parted as he continued to pump into me, another orgasm building as he fucked me, reminding me of our first time together.

"Nadia," he panted, his hot eyes never once leaving mine.

"Yes," I answered breathlessly.

"You're mine."

"Yes."

"I'm yours."

"Yes."

His grip on my legs became almost biting as his thrusts came faster. "You need to come," he panted harder, a bead of sweat glistening on his forehead from the strain of holding back his own climax.

"I am," I said breathlessly, jerking my hips in rhythm to his thrusts.

And then I tensed before the next thick drag of his cock inside me shoved me over the edge. His lips crashed down on mine to swallow my cry of release and seconds later, he stiffened and we were kissing to muffle his long, deep groan. His hips jerked against me while he came.

The sound of laughter outside the door brought our heads up and reality cooled the heat of passion.

"Shit." Henry pulled out of me, tucking himself back in before he turned frantically to find my dress and underwear.

"I thought you wanted us to get caught?" I said, hopping off the desk as he handed me my things.

He glowered at me. "Not in actuality. No one gets to see you naked but me."

"Caveman," I muttered as I tugged on my underwear.

"You have no idea." He started pulling my dress on over my head before I was ready and my arms got caught.

"Jesus," I laughed. "Henry."

"Fuck." He pulled and tugged until my dress was back on. Only then did he slump with relief.

I stared at him, dying to laugh even more. "What was that?"

Looking disconcerted, he snapped, "Apparently, the thought of someone catching us having sex is merely okay as fantasy."

"Well, the dress is only part of the problem." I squeezed my legs together. "I need to find a bathroom pronto. To clean up."

His eyes darkened with desire and the muscle in his jaw clenched.

"What now?"

"I want you all the time," he grumbled, putting his hand on my back to lead me out of the office. "My cock is going to fucking break off."

"You?" I huffed. "What about my poor, abused vagina?"

"You weren't complaining earlier," he pulled open the door, "when my tongue was on it."

A throat cleared and we both froze.

Alexa suddenly stepped into view and she looked like she was struggling not to laugh. "I was just on my way to the restroom."

"You're alone." Henry looked around us.

"Now I am. Thankfully."

"I'll join you." I grabbed Alexa's arm. "I need to use the restroom."

"Oh, I bet you do," she muttered.

We strode off together down the hall and I glanced back at Henry.

Love.

There was nothing but love in his eyes.

But something else too.

Longing.

And you could only long for something you didn't think you really had.

You have me, Henry, I wanted to reassure him.

But will you still want me when you know me? Really know me.

Instead of reassuring him, I faced forward and walked away.

CHAPTER ELEVEN

Henry had been gone on a business trip for four days and although we'd talked, I missed him. I missed him so much that I thought for sure when I saw him, those three words he was waiting on me to say would burst out of me.

He was returning on a Sunday, my day off work, so I had plenty of time to ravish the heck out of him when we reunited. I was supposed to be going to his apartment but that morning, there was a knock on my door. When I looked through the peephole, Henry was on the other side.

I threw open the door and jumped him.

To his credit, he caught me and didn't even groan at the weight of me hitting him. Instead he wrapped one arm around my waist and the other under my ass and walked into the apartment like I weighed nothing.

He laughed while I peppered his lips and face with kisses. "If this." Kiss. "Is how." Kiss. "You're going." Kiss. "To greet me." Kiss. "Every time I come back." Kiss. "From business." Kiss. "I might do it more often."

My head snapped back. "Don't you dare. Ahhh!" I

squealed as he pushed us over the edge of the couch and fell on top of me, catching his weight at the last minute.

"Fuck, I've missed you." He kissed me long and hard until I was panting for breath when he finally let me up for air.

I hugged him hard, every part of me giddy and happy to have him home. "I missed you so much." God, I loved his face. I loved his nose. His eyes. His smile. I loved, loved his smile.

We cuddled and petted and kissed each other, talking quietly about his business trip and about my week at work until his words grew slower, sleepier.

Lying side by side on my couch, I'd curled my leg around his hip to stop him falling off the narrow space. As he stroked my collarbone, I took note of the dark circles under his heavy-lidded eyes.

"Handsome, you're so tired," I whispered.

He smiled wearily. "I am."

"You should have gone straight to your bed."

"I wanted to see you first."

I kissed him softly, grateful for him more than I could say. The truth was that these last weeks with Henry had been the first time in a very long time that I hadn't felt lonely. Not even a little. "Let me take care of you," I said, caressing his unshaven cheek. "If you could have anything right now, what would it be? Nonsexual," I hurried to add.

He smirked, his eyes glazing with exhaustion. "Sunshine, I couldn't even if I wanted to."

"Then what do you want?"

"I've been craving banana bread from Flour," he mumbled, snuggling into me.

I grinned against his ear. Banana bread was not what I'd been expecting but the bakery was only a twenty-minute walk from my apartment in Lower Roxbury. "I'll go get you some."

"You don't have to."

I kissed behind his ear. "I want to."

"Okay. That'd be nice."

How could this man be so sexy and yet so adorable? I gave him a quick kiss on the lips and climbed over him to get off the couch. He was so out of it, he rolled into the space I'd left. As always, I was overwhelmed by the sheer affection I felt for him. To stop myself from bursting into tears like the emotional watering pot I'd become lately, I dragged the throw off the back of the couch and covered him. Then I removed his shoes and placed them on the floor by the couch.

Less than five minutes later, I was walking out of my apartment on a mission to get Henry's banana bread.

Cool fall wind whipped my hair behind me and I shrugged the collar of my coat up around my neck. We were having a particularly cold October this year, something my viewers were not happy to hear. They were tweeting me during the show, some pleading with me to give them good news, others cursing me like it was my fault our fall weather was off to a crappy start.

To be honest, I didn't mind the cold. I hated the wind and the rain but I liked the dry, crisp, cold mornings. Especially if the sun was out like it was today.

At Flour, I was lucky to get the last of the banana bread and I threw in some cinnamon crème brioche for myself, even though I wouldn't have time to go to the gym today to work them off. Grabbing coffees to go, I could only describe my mood as blissfully content. I was having one of those days where every negative thought was banished under the naïve belief that things could really stay in a suspended state of "fucking great."

I think I could have gotten through the entire day on that feeling.

But someone else had other plans.

Daydreaming about future Sundays with Henry, I was jolted into reality when I turned the corner off Washington and walked into a solidly built male.

The coffee I was carrying was knocked out of my hands, hitting the ground and splashing over both our shoes and calves. "Shit, I'm sorry," I gasped, as we both instinctively jumped back.

And then I looked up into his face to apologize again. Fear froze the words in my throat.

Quentin James was frowning down at his shoes and trousers.

He looked up, irritation mixed with something akin to smugness. "Not exactly how I was planning for us to meet."

"What are you doing here?"

The loud buzz of traffic blared behind me, drawing his annoyed gaze. "Let's walk."

"Let's not." I stepped back. "Move out of my way."

"Is that any way to greet an old lover?" He smirked.

Staring into his dark eyes, I wondered how I could have been so naïve as to once think he had the eyes of a poet. Dear God, I was such an idiot. Once upon a time, I'd thought he was the most beautiful man I'd ever seen with his perfect thick hair waved back from his face and full mouth like a sullen male model's. His irresponsible lifestyle seemed to have caught up with him, however, because there were deep lines in his face that hadn't been there before, and his hair was almost completely gray.

He used to have a year-round smooth tan; now he was pale, and his cheekbones looked hollow, like he'd lost quite a bit of weight.

"I thought when you stopped calling and sending me flowers that you'd finally gotten the message than I'm not interested in talking with you ever, let alone reconciling."

"Oh, we're past that," he narrowed his eyes on me, "since you started spreading for someone higher up the food chain."

Rage coursed through me. "It was never about that for me, you son of a bitch."

He tsked. "I wouldn't piss me off, darling. I hold all your dreams of marrying a Lexington in my hands."

As quickly as I'd flushed with anger, I was suddenly chilled to the bone. "What do you want?"

Quentin scowled. "I'm in a bit of financial bother. Some gambling debts."

I waited, a knot tightening in my stomach.

"I saw how well you were doing for yourself and thought maybe you might have the money to help me, but you aren't the doe-eyed girl I remember. So I found the money elsewhere."

Revulsion that I'd slept with this man, a man who had chased me down after years only to get money out of me, rolled through my stomach. "What the hell are you doing here now?"

"I'm in trouble again. And apparently, you're practically engaged to one of the wealthiest men on the East Coast."

A ringing sounded in my ears. Astonishment. Disbelief. What the fuck? "Seriously?"

"Let's not make a scene."

God, he was such a smarmy, sleazy asshole! How could it be possible that his grimy hands had touched me?

"I *hate* you."

"I couldn't give a damn." He sighed impatiently. "I'm just going to lay it out for you. I need fifty thousand dollars. You're going to return to that crappy little apartment of yours and tell the man who is currently inside of it that you're in trouble and need the money. If you don't, I will tell him who you really are and what you're really capable of."

He'd been watching me. Us. Nausea surged and only my anger kept it at bay. "I didn't do anything."

Hatred burned out of his eyes. "We both know that's not true. You ruined lives. Why should you get to ride off into a fairy tale while the rest of us are destroyed?"

Furious tears stung my nose and eyes. "You're disgusting."

"I'm resourceful. There's a difference." He stepped to the side, gesturing for me to pass. "You've got forty-eight hours until I knock on your door."

Shooting him one last murderous glare, I hurried past, needing to put as much distance between us as possible. I spent the rest of the walk back to my apartment alternating between looking over my shoulder and screaming inside my own head.

I didn't know what to do.

What the hell did I do?

Once inside, I found Henry still asleep. Leaving him there, I put our baked goods in the kitchen and then quietly shut the door to my bedroom to change out of my coffee-covered jeans. My hands shook the entire time.

I made my way into the living room again and sat down in the armchair across from Henry, cuddling my knees to my chest.

There was no question now as I looked at him about what I'd do. In reality, there had never been a question.

I would not be blackmailed and I wouldn't resort to extorting money from the man I loved.

Instead, finally, I was going to face what I'd known I would have to face all along.

The truth about who I once had been.

She wasn't someone I was proud of but she also wasn't me anymore. And I had to hope that Henry would see that. That he would forgive me for hurting an innocent person as badly as I had.

I don't know how long I sat there, watching him sleep, waiting with knots in my stomach for him to wake up and thrust us into cold reality.

Finally, I heard his breathing change, he made a little groan, and he slowly turned on the couch. His sleepy eyes snagged on me sitting in the corner and he rubbed his forehead. "What time is it?"

I glanced at the clock on the radio. "One thirty."

He groaned again and sat up, running his hands through his hair. "I didn't mean to fall asleep," he finished on a yawn.

When I didn't respond, Henry looked over at me, studied me, and quickly grew alert. "What's going on?"

My lips trembled. Every part of me was shaking. "Something," my voice croaked and I cleared it, "something happened while you were sleeping."

Henry threw off the throw and swung his feet to the floor. "What?"

I didn't answer.

"Nadia, you're chalk white. What happened?"

"I went to Flour and I got your banana bread. It's in the kitchen. I got some cinnamon crème brioche too for me," I recounted inanely. "And coffee. But it got spilled because ... I bumped into someone. Someone I knew once."

His brows creased in confusion. "Who?"

"His name is Quentin James. Professor Quentin James." I released my knees and sat forward, expelling a shuddering breath. "Henry ... I'm in trouble, I think. This man ..." I looked at my feet. "He's ... I need to start at the beginning."

"Nadia, look at me."

"I can't." Tears escaped beneath my lids. "I'm ashamed and I can't look at you and watch your expression when I tell you what I have to tell you. I ... went to college in Florida. One of my favorite professors was Quentin James and in my senior year, we grew close." I remembered the day we'd met in his office to discuss some connections he had in Florida in broadcasting. He'd been off, acting distracted, and at first I'd put it down to the fact that he'd separated from his wife not long ago, something he'd told me a few months before. When I asked him what was wrong, he said he knew it was wrong, but he had feelings for me.

"I'd been so excited, so naïve. We started an affair. He told me that he and his wife had been separated and that he was falling in love with me. And like an idiot, I believed him."

"Nadia, look at me."

I shook my head. "It went on for months and then one night we were fooling around in his office when someone let themselves in. His *wife* let herself in." I closed my eyes remembering the way she crumbled in pain upon finding us together. Her anguish. Her hurt. And worse ... "His *pregnant* wife."

"Nadia—"

"I should have apologized, I should have felt remorse, but all I felt was betrayed and desperate. Later he told me that they had been separated but she found out she was pregnant so they were trying to make it work. He seemed so broken. He told me he loved me but that we had to stop because he had a responsibility to her. I didn't want to hear it." I forced myself to meet Henry's gaze but I couldn't see anything in his expression; all I could see were images from the past. "I was twenty-one and I thought I was in love. There's no excuse for what I did next. I told you my dad wasn't a good guy, Henry." I wiped at my tears. "That he cheated on my mom constantly and I was pretty much invisible to him. My mom was so wrapped up in trying to keep her marriage together that I barely made a blip on her radar. I'd been a chubby, awkward kid and boys didn't pay attention to me in high school either, and when they did, I soon found out they only wanted one thing.

"Quentin had been different. He made me feel special and needed. And I thought I was so mature back then. I thought that it would only hurt everyone in the long run if he stayed with his wife for the sake of the baby. So I went to talk to her alone.

"It blew up into an argument almost right away. I can still hear her screaming at me to get out of her house." I flinched. "But before that, she told me that they had never been separated and that I was the third student she'd caught him with in the last two years." I choked on a sob. "She looked at me like I was this evil whore and I was so ashamed and so betrayed and so sorry. She kept screaming at me to leave and I didn't, I just kept trying to apologize, to tell her I didn't know that he was still with her. Finally, she threatened to call the police and that got through to me. I left. But a few days later ..." I stared in horror at Henry. "The baby went into distress. She lost it," I choked out.

Henry's eyes closed tight, his lips pinched together at my revelation.

I looked away. "Everyone in my class found out. Other professors. Quentin turned it all on me. Blamed me for his wife leaving, for her losing their kid. Said it was my fault, that I'd agitated the situation. He lost his job and everyone hated me. Those last few months were the worst of my life. I went home to escape but I didn't know that the cousin of one of my classmates lived in our town. It was a chance in a million. But they all found out and my mom could barely look at me, let alone allow me to explain. She thinks I'm just like my father.

"I couldn't get a job anywhere, and it felt as if everyone in goddamn Connecticut knew the story. And the more people make you feel like the bad guy, Henry, the more you believe it, you know. There has to be some truth in it. When I looked in the mirror, I hated my reflection. So I wanted to escape that person. I changed my name, dyed my hair, and moved to New York. I worked for an online meteorology broadcaster where my old boss at WCVB spotted me and offered me a job. I moved to Boston."

Silence engulfed my small apartment as I waited for the man I loved to either forgive me or condemn me.

When he didn't say anything, I stared straight into his expressionless eyes and whispered, "I'm sorry for being a hypocrite in the beginning. For making you feel like you didn't deserve a chance with me when the truth was the opposite."

His mask dissolved into anger. "Don't. That's not true. I'm ... I'm sitting here, trying to work out how I tell you that ... I know Nadia is your middle name and that your real name is Sarah Nadia Raymond."

What?

"What? How?"

Henry blanched. "My mother. After she found out I was bringing you to the Delaney charity ball, she had a private investigator look into you and she found out everything about Quentin and you. Except she made it out like you knew you were getting involved with a married man. My father once told me that when he and my mother were engaged he had a drunken indiscretion with a friend of hers. They separated for a while before he convinced her to take him back. He's been loyal to her ever since, but cheating is a sore point for my mother."

"Which explains why she hates me so much."

"She doesn't know you," he said. "She told me about Quentin thinking it would change how I felt about you, but it didn't. Because I knew there had to be more to the story." He got up and crossed the room. I stared at him in stunned disbelief, veering between joy and confusion as he lowered himself to his haunches in front of me.

Henry took my hands in his and I was beyond relieved to see there was nothing but love in his eyes. "We all make mistakes and you were only a kid. For all I know, I've slept with someone's wife or girlfriend because they lied to me about it. People lie, Nadia, and they can betray us, but we learn from it ... and I know you. I know you learned from it. You have turned this into something much scarier in your head than it is. You didn't murder anyone."

"But their baby," I whispered.

"Nadia," pain brightened his eyes, "Quentin James was a serial cheater who got off on screwing innocent students, and you were merely one of the many times he hurt his wife. You simply happened to be there when the stress of his betrayal became too much for her. And he's the asshole who put all the blame on you when everything that went wrong in his life was down to his own damn selfish disregard for those around him."

"You really believe that?"

"I told you I loved you after I found out," he reminded me.

"Why didn't you tell me you knew?"

"Because I wanted you to trust me enough to tell me yourself ... and God, Sunshine, you kept me waiting. I thought I'd be waiting forever."

"I love you," I blurted out, sliding my hands up his arms to his shoulders and leaning into him. "I love you so much."

Suddenly I was in his arms and he was kissing me, pouring every ounce of his love for me into our connection. When we finally broke apart, breathless, Henry stared at me in wonder as he brushed my hair from my face.

Then quite abruptly, he scowled. "You said you met the bastard outside."

And that's when I laid out the rest of it. Quentin's stalkerish behavior a few months ago and now this—his blackmail.

Henry grew very still, very quiet, and it concerned me more than an outburst ever could.

"I'm going to kill him."

He sounded so sincere, I gasped. "No, you are not."

"Yes, I am."

"No, you're not."

"I'm going to eviscerate him."

"That's the same as killing him, Henry, except more descriptive."

He shot me a look before he got to his feet and began pacing my small living room. "I thought this man was supposed to be smart," he spat. "Does he have any idea who he's dealing with? I can end him without killing him."

Yes, but Quentin was relying on the woman who felt so ashamed by her actions that she'd changed her name and appearance to escape her past. He was relying on her to have the same kind of self-preservation as he had. However, I wasn't Quentin. Unlike him, I would never betray the person I loved most in the world.

"He was counting on me to keep this from you. To want to keep this from you more than anything. Also, he probably knows this could ruin my career. It wouldn't be the first time someone has held it over my head."

Henry stopped mid-pace. "What does that mean?"

"It's what Dick was blackmailing me with."

"Fuck," he hissed. And then he was across the room pulling me into his arms, hugging me so tight, his grip was almost bruising.

"What's this for?"

"Because it's a fucking miracle you even gave me a chance considering how many bastards you've had to deal with."

I sunk into his embrace and he relaxed a little. His familiar scent, a mix of cologne and something that was all Henry, was just as comforting as his hard, strong arms. I'd never wanted to rely on anyone. The thought scared me. But I was coming to realize relying on Henry was no longer a choice. I needed him. I craved his love and support. Even more so now that I knew he loved me despite all my mistakes.

"What are we going to do?" I whispered.

Henry was quiet a moment as he rubbed soothing circles over my back. "Right now I'm taking you to bed and you're going to tell me over and over that you love me while I'm inside you. And afterward we'll eat banana bread and brioche in bed and forget anything else exists. Tomorrow, I'll deal with Quentin." He felt me tense and kissed my hair. "I won't kill him but when I'm done with him, he'll wish I had. All you need to know is that he is out of your life for good and nothing will come between you and your career, or more importantly, between you and me."

I lifted my head to stare up into his beautiful face. "You're the best person I know." I reached for his lips and pressed the softest, sweetest kiss to them. "So I think you'll understand why I can't let you take care of this."

"What?" His eyes narrowed.

Determination blazed out of me. "I have to deal with Quentin. I'm honest enough and I think strong enough to admit that I need you. I do. But I'm also still trying to be a better person, and to do that, I must shut Quentin down myself. And I can do that knowing that I have your support. He has to know I'm not that naïve, starved of affection, help-less girl anymore. I'm a successful career woman," I grinned saucily, "with friends in high places."

"Fine," he bit out. "You can be the one to talk to him, but I'll be nearby watching. No arguments. And if your way doesn't work, then we do it my way."

"Done."

Henry suddenly grinned. "We're good at this."

"We are good at this." I grabbed his shirt and pulled him backward toward the bedroom. "But I hope not too good. I quite like arguing with you. I especially like the kissing-making-up part."

Quite abruptly, Henry swung me up into his arms and smirked. "Sunshine, kissing isn't the making-up part." He threw me and I gasped in surprise, bouncing on my bed. I stared up in anticipation as Henry practically ripped off his shirt, dropped it, and crawled onto the bed up my body. His eyes smoldered. "*This* is the making-up part."

"But we haven't argued," I teased.

"It doesn't matter," Henry said, his voice hoarse as he reached down and unzipped his pants slowly. A fizzle of pleasure tingled between my legs. "I'm going to fuck you like we have." His fingers curled under the waistband of my yoga pants and underwear and he tugged.

"And then we'll make love?" I asked breathlessly as he divested me of my clothes.

"Someone once told me fucking can be more than just fucking. Fucking, sucking, licking, pawing, grabbing, groping ..." He caressed my inner thighs, heading to the ultimate destination in this scenario. "With you, it's always making love."

I laughed softly, shaking my head in amusement. "You're such a smooth talker."

He gave me a killer-watt smile, his eyes so filled with happiness, I shook with my own giddiness. "It's also the truth."

"I know," I reached up to cup his face in my hand, "I believe you."

EPILOGUE

Fourteen months later ...

"Well, we're coming to the end of today's show," Andrew said to the camera, "but we had to make time to say a proper goodbye to Barbara."

On our cue, Angel and I walked on camera, Angel carrying a mammoth bouquet of flowers while I held a basket of wrapped gifts from us and the crew. Barbara gave me a kiss on the cheek, accepting the presents. She even accepted a kiss on the cheek from Andrew.

"I am going to miss you all so much. Thank you. And Nadia, good luck with this one," she cracked, gesturing to Andrew.

My stomach did a little flip as we all laughed while Andrew rolled his eyes. On Monday I was taking Barbara's spot as co-anchor on the breakfast show. It wasn't something I thought I ever wanted, but when Barbara told us all she'd accepted a job as a breakfast show anchor in LA and our new boss Kelly offered me her spot ... I found myself excited by the prospect.

It wasn't something I'd wanted when I'd first started here, and definitely not when Dick was trying to blackmail me into it, but I found I needed a new challenge.

That didn't mean I wasn't nervous as hell.

We wrapped up the show with Barbara thanking our viewers, surprising us all when she got choked up as she said she'd miss Boston. But like me, she needed a new challenge and, she joked, a new pool of men.

Afterward we all went out for our last lunch together and I grew tearful when it was finally time to say goodbye. Barbara and I may have been different kinds of women but we'd still connected.

Heading toward Henry's apartment, *our* apartment now, via the Public Gardens, I'd stopped to sit on a bench despite the cold. After calling Joe to check if we were still on for dinner the next day, I sat there a while, enjoying the peace. The sun was out, low today, cutting through the bitter January we were experiencing. I spent a lot of time in the gardens now that I lived so close. There was something tranquil about them no matter what time of year it was.

"It's freezing out here."

I was startled out of my thoughts about my new job, wide-eyed as Henry sat down beside me. He was bundled up in a wool coat and the scarf I'd bought him for Christmas. He slid his arm around me and pulled me into his side; I soaked up his warmth and his scent.

"What are you doing here?"

He stared down into my face lovingly. "Cut out of work early because I thought you might be here either crying about Barbara or worrying about the new job."

"I cried first. Now I'm worrying." I grinned at how well he knew me.

"You're going to do great, you know that. This city loves you."

The last was said with a grumble that made me laugh. Henry vacillated often between being proud of me and smug that I was his woman, and territorial and annoyed that my local fame partly meant I got hit on often.

"So you came to meet me? That was sweet of you."

His arm tightened around me. "I actually came to ask you something."

"Oh?"

Something in his voice, something nervous and wary, unsettled me. For the past fourteen months Henry and I had been nothing but honest with each other every step of the way. After my standing up to Quentin did little to make him back off, Henry told me up front he was going to take a turn. He didn't go behind my back about it, even though he knew his interfering would piss me off. We argued about it, but Henry said it was clear Quentin was a misogynist and didn't see me as a threat. Also it became clear Quentin was going to continue to be a major pain in our ass, so I had to let Henry try. I didn't know what was said or done between them; all I knew was that Caine had Henry's back, and Quentin never bothered us again.

A few months later when Alexa and Caine got married in a tiny, private ceremony only we and a handful of people were invited to, Henry asked me to move in with him. That meant we had lots more opportunity to argue and make up, and we did because we were kind of brutally honest with one another.

We trusted each other enough to be that honest with one another.

So it was no wonder that Henry's caginess lately had bothered me. I'd walk in on him on the phone to someone and he'd abruptly stop talking and end the call. Or he'd be on his laptop when I got home and he'd shut it and push it away, avoiding me when I asked what he was up to.

He'd been a little distant, preoccupied, and when I asked him what was bothering him, he said nothing. We both knew that was a lie but rather than fight about it like normal, his behavior bothered me so much, I wanted to pretend everything was okay by not pestering him.

It appeared, finally, that Henry might be ready to talk about what was going on.

"What's happened?"

He gave me a shaky, apologetic smile. "I know I've been preoccupied lately, and I'm sorry if I've worried you."

"Henry ..."

"You know," he laughed but the sound was also shaky, "I thought when I decided to do this, it would be easy because it's you and me. I know how we feel about each other ... but I guess in every decision we make, there's that tiny percentage of doubt in the back of our minds. And in this case that doubt, that fear, is paralyzing because if this doesn't go my way, it could ruin everything. It could ruin what I've come to consider as *everything*. You," his grip on me tightened, "you are everything to me."

No ... no way ... "Henry...?" I tried to keep the hope out of my voice.

He licked his lips nervously, something I had never seen him do, and I found it adorable. He'd roll his eyes if he knew I thought of him as even remotely adorable. "I thought about where and how and when ... and everything I thought seemed too grandiose and cheesy and so sentimental, it lost true sentimentality. I thought about our first date at a pizza place," he grinned, "and our second getting drowned in the rain on the Hop-on, Hop-off tour. I knew from the moment I met you that you were the one woman I wanted to be real with, to be me with, and I knew for some reason I can't explain that I could be. I didn't have to hire a Town Car and take you to the opera or a concerto, wear a tux, and buy you diamonds. Nothing had to be a game, a show of money and charm. It could be real. It could be simple. And as it turned out, be fucking extraordinary in its simplicity."

His eyes brightened now and tears spilled down my cheeks as the months, the ups and downs, the reality of being in love with him flashed by me. Because he was right. Our lives together felt extraordinary. I felt so goddamn lucky to have him.

Henry slid off the bench, getting down on one knee in front of me, and my heart threatened to explode out of my chest. I watched, happiness I didn't even know I was capable of feeling building inside of me as he reached into his overcoat and pulled out a blue velvet ring box. He watched me, not once looking away, as he opened the box and revealed an engagement ring. The most beautiful engagement ring I'd ever seen.

It looked vintage. Tiny diamonds lined delicate scrollwork in the metal that swirled to a peak atop the band where a single bright diamond winked nestled in its grasp.

"It was my grandmother's," Henry said. "My mother thought it might suit and when I saw it, I knew it was perfect."

His mother? "Penelope?"

"She's coming around, Sunshine." He grinned. "And she's pissed that I'm not doing this at a garden party, or in Paris, or on a gondola in fucking Venice ... but I felt like this had to be a moment only for us. Somewhere real. No grand gestures, no flash mobs, no fireworks. We don't have ordinary lives, you and I. People photograph us and put us on front pages, and they like to think they know who we are. Grand gestures and fireworks are part of our lives; they're not extraordinary to us. But when we get home and we close the door behind us and it's just you and me ... that's our extraordinary, right?"

I nodded, hardly able to make out his face I was crying so much.

"I was born into a life of privilege ... but I never knew true wealth until I met you, Nadia Ray. Will you make me the richest man on earth by doing me the honor of marrying me?"

"Yes!" I sobbed, throwing myself at him, his laughter vibrating against my lips as I kissed him. I must have looked ridiculous crying and laughing as I peppered his face with kisses but I didn't care.

Eventually, Henry had to gently push me away so he could slip the ring on my finger.

"It's perfect. It's so perfect." I clasped his face in my hands and kissed him with a little more restraint.

We were smiling so hard, I thought our faces might crack. Henry's arms wrapped tight around me and I noticed his eyes shift over my shoulder. He gave me a rueful smile. "We're being photographed."

I snorted. "I guess I won't get the chance to tell Lexie first after all."

He chuckled and helped me to my feet. Our coats were soaked but I didn't care. "She already knows."

"What?" We turned to walk toward the path and I discovered Henry was right. People passing must have seen him down on one knee and stopped to be nosy.

They clapped and shouted congratulations to us as we passed.

"Lexie and Caine already know," Henry continued once we'd gotten through the small crowd and headed toward home. "I asked Lexie for her opinion on the ring."

"I thought you said you knew it was perfect," I teased as I held up my hand to stare at the stunning piece of jewelry.

"Like I said before, I felt this weird niggle of doubt about everything."

"There was no need." I squeezed him close.

"Really? Because it apparently didn't even cross your mind that my secretiveness was because I was going to propose." He arched a brow at me. "What did you think I was hiding?"

I knew what he suspected I thought. "I didn't think you were cheating." I shoved him, annoyed. "Are we really going to argue seconds after getting engaged?"

"Not if you tell me what you thought I was hiding."

"I didn't know. I thought maybe something was really wrong at work and you didn't want to worry me."

"Oh." He relaxed but I still glowered at him.

"Trust goes both ways, you know."

"No." He shook his head. "We're not arguing. We don't need to argue to get me hard," he promised, and not quietly. "You saying 'yes' gave me a surprisingly substantial erection."

I threw my head back in laughter as he grinned happily down at me. "God, I like you," I repeated words he'd said to me many times.

"Good." Henry drew me to a stop outside the gardens to kiss me. "Because you're stuck with me."

We kissed on the sidewalk until some grumpy person who clearly wasn't getting laid knocked into us and told us to get a room. Breaking apart, we laughed quietly against each other's lips.

And then it hit me that those lips were my lips forever.

That he was mine forever.

"By the way," I whispered, "seriously epic proposal."

"Yeah?" His expression softened.

"You started us off as we mean to go on ... not needing all the bullshit people tell us we need. Because if one day something happens and we lose all the material stuff that makes us privileged, I know we'll be okay. As long as we've got this," I tugged on the lapels of his coat, pressing his body against mine, "we'll make it through the good and the bad."

He nodded and then I saw a twinkle of mischief enter his eyes. "You know, my mother is going to want the biggest, most expensive society wedding you can think of."

I shrugged. "Then we'll give it to her. The only thing that matters is that you and I get married, right?"

"She'll drive you nuts."

"Henry ... do I get you at the end of it?"

"Yes." He smiled. "You get me now, during, and after."

I shook my head at the innuendo in his voice but said, "Then let her drive me crazy. All I care about is you."

Henry's hands curled around mine and he leaned his forehead against mine.

We closed our eyes, the sounds of the city disappearing around us, as we just breathed.

Together.

ALWAYS.

ONE DAY: A VALENTINE
NOVELLA

CHAPTER ONE

The Cairngorms, Scotland

One day.

"One bloody day," I muttered in irritation as I shoved into my walking boots. I fumbled with the torch on my phone and grabbed my last roll of toilet paper. "Bloody hell." I'd need to get more when the rest of civilization eventually woke up.

Typical, I thought, as I jumped out of the camper van I'd borrowed from my brother. Shivering in the freezing-cold February morning, I swung my torch toward the woods and contemplated hurrying back into the van for my coat.

But the pressure on my bladder insisted I move. Quickly!

Uttering obscenities under my breath, I moved toward the woods, cursing this cursed fucking day to hell.

Valentine's Day!

Not once on this camping trip had I needed to pee this early in the morning. But on Valentine's Day, on a pitch-black, Baltic Valentine's Day at five o'clock in the morning, of course, I was so desperate for a pee there was no way I could wait until the public toilet opened.

To make matters worse, I was parked on a lay-by next to Loch Alvie. I was surrounded by hamlets. The nearest frickin' town was Aviemore, which, to be fair, was only ten minutes away, but ten minutes was a long time when your bladder was screaming at you. Plus … again … no public toilet was open at this time!

"The woods are probably cleaner," I huffed, thinking of some of the dodgy public loos I'd used in the past week.

"Ah!" I slipped on mud in the woods. My heart, already beating hard, pounded faster. "I'm going to die," I whispered, my eyes round as I tried to see by the light of my phone. This was how horror stories started. I could see the headlines now: LONE WOMAN FOUND MURDERED IN WOODS BY LOCH ALVIE.

Locals suspect mythic woodland beast!

"Oh, shut up, Hazel," I murmured and stopped, feeling far enough away from the road to not be seen by any early traffic. "You're more likely to be mauled by a red squirrel, unable to defend yourself because they're a bloody endangered species." And they could be vicious little buggers.

As I unzipped my walking trousers and pushed them and my underwear around my ankles, I cursed bloody Valentine's Day all over again. Squatting, peeing in the woods in the blistering cold, I sighed. It was as though this day had it in for me—for the past ten years. What the hell had I done to piss off Cupid?

Physical relief moved through me as the pain in my bladder eased, and just as I was about to let out a grateful sigh, my whole body froze at the sound of cracking bracken. I looked up and to my shock saw a light dancing nearby.

Suddenly I was blinded by said light.

A frozen scream stuck in my throat.

I *was* going to die!

Someone else was in the woods, watching me pee, and I was going to die!

Don't just sit there, you moron!

My body unlocked and I jerked my arm to hold up my phone. The torch on it did little to help me see in the dark. What I did see was the shadow of a great, big, hulking figure.

That scream escaped, and I tried to yank up my trousers and underwear at the same time as I ran. Except I couldn't remember which direction I'd find the road!

"Wait!" I heard a man's deep voice. "I'm not going—"

But whatever he said was muffled by hard dirt slamming into my body as I fell. The blood whooshed in my ears as my heart hammered against my ribs. The crack of woodland told me he was following me. I scrambled to my feet, desperately trying to get my trousers on. I'd succeeded with the underwear, but the fucking trousers had fucking fallen again and fucking tripped me up.

"Come on!" I whisper-screamed, tears burning my eyes. Then I was out of the trees and—"Ahhh!" I scrambled to a stop, slipping on the large pebbles on the loch shore. I whipped around as that bright light bounced out after me.

I was *not* going to die here.

I rushed the mammoth man with all my strength and collided with his solid body. My hope was he'd go down and I'd get past him. But he grunted as we both tripped over the loose rocks and fell headfirst toward the woods. My skull thudded against earth, the breath knocked out of me.

"Fuck," I heard the voice say. "Shit. Are you okay?"

I stilled at the concern in the stranger's voice, and instead of taking the opportunity to run like hell, I wheezed, "Are you American?"

He shifted beside me, and I realized we were tangled up

in each other. He gently extricated his heavy legs from mine and placed his light between us. A ghoulish face looked at me. I imagined my own face was just as ghoulish in the torchlight.

His eyes, however, were not the eyes of a madman. They seemed to hold genuine concern.

"Yes, I'm American. Liam Brody." He held out his hand, but I just stared at it, still not convinced I wasn't in danger. "You can call me Brody."

I continued to study his hand, wondering if I moved now, might I get away?

"I'm not a homicidal maniac," he said, amusement in his words, "I promise. I left my tent because I needed to pee, and after I did, I saw your light in the woods and then I saw you … well … and then you were screaming and running. I realized I'd scared the shit out of you, and probably in hindsight shouldn't have given chase. I only wanted to reassure you I wasn't a murderer. So … sorry about that."

If I hadn't been shaking from adrenaline (and blaming him for it), I might have grinned at his explanation. "Where's your tent?"

He swung the torch to my left, and it lit up the shallow, rocky bank of the loch. In the distance, I could see the outline of a tent.

"I think that might be illegal," I said. "And bloody idiotic in this weather." I looked back at him. "You must be freezing."

"I'm not the one wearing only a sweater."

True enough, I could see and feel the puffy jacket he was wearing. "I've got two T-shirts on underneath my jumper."

Liam ignored that. "Where's your tent?"

"Camper van," I said, moving to stand. "Parked on the lay-by."

He got up, too, towering over me by a good nine or ten inches. I was small at five five, so it was easy for a really big guy to look like a giant next to me. Feeling intimidated, I retreated.

"Can you find your way back?"

"Sure, I—oh, balls in hell!" I bit out.

"What is it?"

"I dropped my phone."

"I have a good sense of direction, if you want me to take you the way we came?"

I contemplated him for a moment. "You promise you're not a homicidal maniac?"

"I promise. Although for future reference, a homicidal maniac would probably promise that, too, right before he killed you."

I stared at him in horror.

"But I'm not one."

"You really know how to reassure a stranger lost in the woods with only you and your torch to rely on."

He gave a huff of laughter and strode past me into the dark cover of the trees. "You can hold on to my jacket if you want. Or I could take your hand."

"I'll manage," I insisted, thinking a little distance wouldn't be a bad thing, in case I did need to run for my life. "Fucking Valentine's Day," I muttered.

"What was that?"

"Nothing."

The only sounds around us were the creaking woods, the early-morning whisper of bugs and birds, and in the distance, a vehicle driving by.

"Kind of bold of you," Liam suddenly said.

"Huh?" I'd been intent on watching my footing in the dim light his torch left behind as he moved in front of me.

"Peeing in the woods by yourself."

"It was that or pee myself."

"You could have peed on the lay-by."

Was I really discussing public urination with a strange man? I snorted at the thought. "People use that lay-by. I wasn't going to pee on it. Plus, anyone passing would have seen my bare arse."

"And you'd deny them that pleasure?" I heard the laughter in his words and couldn't help but grin in response.

"How do you know it would be a pleasure? I might have an arse like a moon crater."

Liam chuckled. "I know for a fact that's not true."

Mortification flooded me as I realized he'd probably caught sight of my bare arse fleeing him! "Fucking Valentine's Day."

"Do you keep muttering 'fucking Valentine's Day'?"

"Yes. Because it is. Fucking Valentine's Day."

"That it is," he said, sounding grim.

Could it be? Had I actually found another human being who understood that VD was not a day for celebration but a cursed, commercial piece of bullshit lorded over by a tiny, cherub-shaped tyrant?

I grunted in acknowledgment.

"Any sign of my phone?" I said, hoping we'd find the damn thing. It cost a small fortune.

"We're getting closer to where you were peeing."

I flushed at his casual mention of it. "You know, you could stop talking about the fact that you've seen me in such a vulnerable position."

"We all need to pee," Liam said matter-of-factly. "It's not like I caught you taking a sh—"

"Tra-la-lah!" I cried to shut him up.

He laughed and stopped to look back at me. "I can't believe you actually tra-la-lah-ed. No one tra-la-lahs."

"I do ... when I'm trying to stop rude Americans from discussing my bodily functions."

"We all need to sh—"

"Tra-la-la-la-lah, la-la-la-lah!"

His shoulders shook in front of me. "You do realize you're tra-la-lahing to 'Deck the Halls'?"

I played the Christmas song quickly in my head. Damn. I *had* just tra-la-lah'ed to it. "Stop talking about ... certain things, and I'll stop tra-la-l—"

"Got it!" he announced triumphantly. He bent over, and when he straightened and turned around, he had his torch aimed at my phone. "Looks okay."

"Oh, thank heavens." I grabbed it. "Thank you. Any chance my loo roll is there?" I gestured beyond him.

He swung back around, bent down again, and retrieved the toilet paper.

"Thank God." I took it.

"You need help getting back to your van?" His words were tinged with laughter.

I hated to admit it, but it was either wander lost by myself for a while or take a chance that the American wasn't a serial killer. "Yeah. Please."

"No problem."

I followed him again, using my phone to light my way.

"You know, you should invest in an actual flashlight," Liam said. "The one on your phone won't get you very far."

"It got me far enough to pee," I said, forgetting momentarily that I'd insisted we not talk about bodily functions.

We broke out of the woods, stopping at the bottom of the slope that led up to the lay-by. Liam climbed it and then turned around to hold out his hand to help me up.

I grasped it, and a shiver ran through me at the feel of his calloused skin. His hand was huge compared to mine, and he pulled me up like I weighed no more than a feather. Putting the shiver down to the fact that it was freezing outside, I ignored the sharp heat of awareness.

His torch swung over my brother's camper van.

It was about eight years old and not the prettiest thing. Still, it was comfortable inside. Along with plenty of sleeping space, it had a sink to wash in, as well as a burner to make tea and to heat up soup and beans.

I thought about Liam in his little tent in the cold. If I were wise, I'd get in my van and leave. However, I seemed plagued by a sense of gratitude toward the American, and an even weirder feeling of not wanting to say goodbye just yet.

Which was ridiculous because I'd spent the last week avoiding men and loving every minute of it.

"Wait there," I said, striding past him. I climbed into the back of the van and opened the drawer under the burner. Grabbing the penknife inside, I clambered back out with the knife switched open.

"Do you want a cup of tea?" I said casually.

His torch swung from me to the knife. "How do I know you're not a homicidal maniac planning on killing me for my handsome pelt?"

A smile prodded the corners of my mouth at his teasing. "I keep this for protection. You get a cup of hot tea, or you can wander back into the woods to your cold, wee tent. What's it going to be?"

"I'll have the tea, thanks," he said, striding toward me.

The light from my van spilled over his face.

Holy fuck.

He had a chiseled, stubbled jawline, and short, closely cropped, dark-blond hair, and he was ... well, he was hot.

Really hot.

He wasn't joking about his handsome pelt.

I gave him a weak smile and gestured for him to climb in, suddenly rethinking this idea. I wasn't exactly immune to a pretty face, and I had sworn off men for the time being.

"I hope you realize how much of a chance I'm taking," he

said, somehow gracefully managing to get his large body inside my van. "You could do anything to me in here."

I grinned at his teasing, charmed already (and inwardly cursing myself for it!), and got in after him. After pulling the doors shut to block out the cold, I placed the penknife on the unit by the burner and hurriedly slipped on my jacket. As I did, my eyes clashed with Liam's, and in the van's bright, overhead light, I noted that his eyes were gorgeous. Light green and expressive.

He was unfairly good-looking.

I set about boiling the kettle over the burner, self-conscious because I could feel him watching my every movement.

He reached out to touch my arm, and I jumped.

"Your hand. You've got a cut," he explained.

I turned it over and saw he was right. It must've happened during one of my falls. "It's not too bad."

"You should clean it. Use some of the hot water from the kettle and a cloth. Have you got a first aid kit?" he asked, looking around the van.

"Behind my rucksack." I pointed to the large bag I'd placed behind the driver's seat and watched as Liam crawled over to it. His jacket shrugged up his body and his walking trousers tightened over his arse.

That is a very, very good arse.

"Got it," he said, and I dragged my gaze away before he caught me ogling him.

Damn it.

"Fucking Valentine's Day," I muttered, rummaging through a plastic carrier bag I kept tea towels in. I found one and carefully poured hot water on it.

"Here."

I looked up at Liam.

"I'll do it."

Deciding to trust the apparent sincerity in his beautiful eyes, I crawled over and held out the cloth. He gently took it and my hand and cleaned my cut.

I stared determinedly at what he was doing rather than at his face. "Thanks," I murmured.

"You're welcome." His voice was deep and far sexier than any man's voice had a right to be.

A flip in my lower belly caused tingles to rush between my legs, and at the same time, my nipples tightened against my bra.

It's the cold! I assured myself, even though I knew it wasn't.

Of course, I'd meet the most attractive man ever on Valentine's Day. It was official: Cupid hated me.

It seemed to take forever for him to clean my cut, apply antiseptic, and then seal with a plaster. Or a Band-Aid, as he called it.

"You're all good." He stroked his thumb over the top of my hand, and my eyes flew to his.

His gaze roamed my face in this interested, appreciative way I knew too well.

I yanked my hand from him. "Tea?" I said, hurriedly crawling away.

I thought I heard him chuckle behind me before he said, "Tea would be great."

"I have milk in a chill box," I said, pulling it out and opening the ice-filled rectangle. Nestled within was the fresh milk I'd bought the day before, along with cans of Diet Coke.

"Milk would be great."

"Sugar?" I threw over my shoulder.

That made him grin. "No, thanks."

I made us both tea (mine with milk and two sugars), and handed him his mug. Our fingers brushed as I did so, and that rush of awareness flooded me again.

Jesus Christ.

Liam took a sip as he looked casually around the place I'd been living in for a week. "So ... you know my name," he said, his gaze swinging back to me, "but I don't know yours."

Deciding there was no harm in giving him my name, I said, "Hazel."

"Hazel. It suits you."

"It would have suited me even better if I had hazel eyes." My mum had hazel eyes. I'd seen the photos. And all my siblings had hazel eyes. Instead, I got my dad's eyes. Big, dark eyes, so dark brown they glittered like jet in a certain light.

"No." He shook his head, but didn't elaborate.

"So ..." I searched for something to ask him. "Are you just visiting Scotland?"

Liam stared into his mug, hands wrapped tight around its heat. "No, I live here."

"In a tent?"

"No. I'm doing a camping thing right now."

"Me too. Except in a camper van. I don't think I could sleep in a tent in this weather."

"It's not too bad. I'm from Gunnison, Colorado, so I know cold. This isn't it." He grinned.

He had a good smile. No, a great smile. His teeth were white, not perfectly straight, his grin a little crooked. It was boyish *and* sexy.

Fuck.

I ignored the sudden heat in my skin. "How cold does it get there?"

"Minus seven."

That didn't seem so bad.

He must've read the thought on my face because he said, "In Fahrenheit, not Celsius."

I winced. "Bloody hell. Note to self: Avoid Gunnison, Colorado."

Liam laughed. "At least in the winter."

"So, why Scotland?" I asked, intrigued to know more about him. Far more intrigued than I'd like to be.

"I studied here. My postgrad. University of Aberdeen. Liked it so much, I stayed."

I smiled. It was inherently Scottish to be pleased when a foreigner said they liked our country. We were such proud creatures, we Scots, easily flattered when an outsider understood the beauty of our land, a beauty I'd spent the last week getting to know better, developing a deeper bond with the Highlands.

It had all been going so well ... until now.

No work, no men, nothing but the stunning lochs, valleys, and mountains, and my own thoughts.

Until Liam Brody.

To my utter annoyance, I wasn't upset about meeting him (now that the initial shock of our unusual meeting had worn off), which was exactly why I needed to get away from the American as quickly as possible.

"How long have you lived here, then?" *Yes, because more questions will get rid of him.*

He blew air out of his lips as he thought about it. "About ... ten years."

"That makes you ...?"

He smiled at my nosy question. "Thirty-two."

"What did you study? At uni?"

"Forestry."

I raised an eyebrow. It wasn't every day I met someone who'd studied forestry. "And what does one do with a postgrad degree in forestry?"

"Become a forest engineer."

I had an image of him in an open plaid flannel shirt, his rippled torso gleaming with sweat while he swung an ax. I squashed the delicious lumberjack fantasy, but my voice was hoarse when I asked, "What does ... what is that? What does that involve?"

Almost as if he knew what I was imagining, his eyes gleamed with amusement. "Log removal from timber-harvesting areas."

The sexy image fluttered across my eyes again. "Physically? By yourself?"

Liam grinned. "No, it's a little more complicated than that."

Knowing he'd been in Scotland so long made me more aware of his accent, and I noted that he ended some of his words with a Scottish burr. Hot.

"How?" I was actually interested to know.

"I survey the timber-harvesting area. That means drawing maps of the land's topographical features using a computer program, then planning and directing construction of roads and rail networks needed to transport logs from the harvest area to a safe storage and loading spot. I ensure the safe, efficient removal of the logs by planning and overseeing construction of campsites, loading docks, bridges, equipment shelters, and water systems. And I select the methods and equipment we'll use for handling the logs."

There wasn't anything about his explanation that wasn't interesting or appealing, and I couldn't explain why.

Okay, maybe it was the lumberjack fantasy.

"Forest engineer." I nodded. "Good job."

He laughed. "Glad you think so. What do you do, Hazel?"

As good as my name sounded on his lips, it wasn't good enough to dig a real answer out of me. I did not want to tell this big, handsome forest engineer that my job sucked. "I'm a journalist," I evaded.

"What kind of journalist?"

"The kind of journalist who takes a break from her life by borrowing her brother's camper van."

The kind of journalist who didn't want to talk about it.

I threw back the rest of my tea.

Liam seemed to get what I wasn't saying and followed my lead. He handed me the empty mug, something resembling disappointment in his expression. "I guess I better get out of your hair, then."

Feeling rude and guilty since he'd politely answered my inquiries, I took his mug without meeting his gaze. "Yeah, I should get moving."

"Okay." He slid toward the back of the van and I opened the doors for him, watching as he climbed out.

He looked back at me as he turned on his torch. "It was nice meeting you, Hazel."

I wished he'd stop saying my name like that.

Ignoring the sudden urge to ask him not to go, I gave him a tremulous smile. "Thanks for not murdering me, Liam."

His eyes flashed at my words in a way that gave me the tingles again. With one last crooked smile, Liam Brody disappeared into the dark woods by Loch Alvie, leaving me with a strange ache in my chest.

He was gone for good.

"It's for the best," I whispered, closing the van doors. "Fucking Valentine's Day."

CHAPTER TWO

A while later, I had a quick, cold wash over my sink, brushed my teeth, put on a little makeup, changed into clean clothes, and climbed into the driver's seat.

According to my brother Johnny, who'd done this Highland trip a few times in his camper van, there was a great place for breakfast near Newtonmore. It was a middle-of-nowhere diner where lorry drivers stopped to eat.

Apparently, the breakfast was *good*.

Following Johnny's directions, I made my way there in what was turning out to be a beautiful, sunny, but crisp, cold morning. It had been raining the past few days, but of course, the sun would come out on Valentine's Day.

I thought of Liam in his tent by himself, wondering what his breakfast plans were. I also wondered about his method of travel. There wasn't another car in the lay-by ... was the idiot walking everywhere?

Well, that was a sure way to get killed.

But that wasn't any of my business. I frowned.

Maybe I should turn back and get him.

Or maybe not!

I ignored my concern for a complete stranger, found the diner, and parked beside an articulated lorry.

Inside wasn't the most attractive place I'd seen. Everything was a grimy beige, the floors scuffed with rubber marks, and the leather on the booth benches had seen better days. But it was clean—and it was busy.

I took a seat at the first empty table I could find.

"I'll be with you in a minute," a waitress said as she took down an order from the guys at the table in front of me.

I nodded and stared at the menu, even though I already knew I wanted a big, fat, Scottish breakfast.

My belly rumbled in anticipation.

"Coffee, tea?" The waitress appeared at my side.

"Tea, please. And orange juice, if you have it."

"Aye, sure. Ready to order?"

"The full Scottish breakfast."

Her gaze raked over me. I was not only short but also small-boned, slender. "It's a big portion, mind."

I may be small, but I could pack it away when I wanted to. I grinned. "Perfect.

"Eggs?"

"Scrambled."

She strode away with my order just as the diner door opened.

A small, bearded man walked in, and I was about to drop my gaze when it snagged on his companion.

Liam Brody.

No. Fucking. Way.

As though he sensed me, his head swung in my direction, eyes widening in recognition.

So ... it would seem the universe was determined to put this American in my path.

Johnny, a bit of a hippy who believed in the spiritual world, fate, destiny, and all that, would say this was kismet.

With his voice in my head, I thought, *Oh, what the hell*. I smiled at Liam and waved.

He accepted my invitation, clapped the small, bearded man on the shoulder in what appeared to be thanks, and weaved over to me.

Liam grinned as he slid his big body into the small booth. His jacket was open, and peeking out of it was a red flannel shirt like the one I'd fantasized about earlier.

I tried not to flush like an idiot. "Hello, stranger."

"This is just weird," he said, still grinning.

"How did you get here?"

"I was walking down the B9152 when that trucker"—he gestured behind him—"Pete, stopped and told me I was going to get myself killed."

"He's not wrong." I frowned. "Why are you walking?"

He grimaced. "My car died just before Aviemore. I put it into a garage, but it was going to take too long to fix. I decided to walk."

"I can't believe you ended up here." I surveyed the diner, avoiding his penetrating stare.

"Apparently, the universe wants us to spend some time together."

My eyes jerked back to his, surprised he'd said what I'd just been thinking. I gave a huff of laughter. "Apparently."

"What can I get you?" The waitress was back.

"Uh ..." Liam glanced over the menu and asked me, "What are you having?"

"Full Scottish breakfast."

"I'll have the same." He handed the menu to her. "Scrambled eggs. And a coffee, please."

She took it from him without a word and walked away.

"It's certainly a friendly diner," I cracked.

"Yeah, but Pete said the breakfast is delicious."

"My brother said the same thing. That's how I knew where to find this place."

"The same brother who owns the camper van?" Liam asked cautiously, like he was afraid any personal questions might send me fleeing.

Oh, what the hell, I thought again. "The very same. I'm running from life for a while. I was inspired by Valentine's Day."

Appearing as though he was trying not to laugh, Liam said, "Is that so?"

"The day is cursed. For me, anyway."

"Sounds like an interesting story."

I settled back in the leather booth and stared at his too-handsome face. "You want to hear my story?"

He mirrored my actions, relaxing in his seat. "Definitely."

"Okay … first off, I have had grand plans of being a feature writer for a newspaper like *The Herald* or *The Guardian* since I was thirteen. But my brother talked me out of journalism and I ended up training to be a psychotherapist. I started working for the NHS but it wasn't for me, so I went back to school and studied journalism. First job I landed was an advice column because of my background. Now I'm twenty-seven and still writing an advice column in a women's magazine I would rather eat than read."

Liam covered his mirth with a cough.

"It's okay, you can laugh." I smirked. "It's pretty pathetic."

"You just … you have an amusing way of putting things."

"And that's why my editor won't promote me out of the advice column. It's not being the advice columnist that's really the issue. I'm quite an opinionated person, and I quite like offering advice. But I get some great letters, from people with real, troubling problems, and my editor won't let me respond to those. All we publish are saucy affair problems, and 'my boyfriend or my cat' ultimatums... It's frustrating to say the least."

"So you hate your job and presumably loathe yourself for sacrificing your happiness for money."

"Wow." I narrowed my eyes. "You're good at that summation crap, aren't you?"

He grinned.

"Yes. I make good money writing my pithy, often sarcastic, bordering on insulting column that our readers love. I've sold my soul for a mortgage and a MINI Cooper. That's one of the reasons I'm taking a break."

"The other reason?"

"Fucking Valentine's Day."

Liam chuckled. "Explain."

Our breakfast arrived before I could, and as we were both apparently ravenous, we were quiet a moment while we dug in.

Finally, Liam swallowed a bite of haggis and scrambled eggs and said, "You were saying?"

"The dreaded VD." I scowled just thinking about it. "Ten years ago, I was dating a musician who was two years older than me. He dumped me on Valentine's Day for another girl. He said *she* actually appreciated his music." I made a face at the memory. "Three years later, my boyfriend of a year sat me down on Valentine's Day and told me he was gay."

Liam choked on his breakfast, and I slid my glass of juice across the table. He took it gratefully.

"I'm fine now," I assured him as he looked at me with watery-eyed shock. "It was quite a surprise then, and I did wonder why me for a while."

Dropping his eyes to my chest, Liam said, "Yeah, you'd think he'd go for a more boyish type of girl."

I was fairly well-endowed, despite my slender frame. My sister, Heather, who was built like me but with no chest, often told me enviously that God had clearly loved me more than her when He saw fit to gift me with my figure. Heather was beautiful and had nothing to complain about. However, I always secretly thought that God probably might love me more but only because Heather learned to be a bitch by the age of seven, and over the years became proficient in it. She was now a *raving* bitch.

I laughed at Liam's brazen ogling, putting thoughts of Heather out of my head. "Right? So ... yes, surprised. But I got over it. And then a year later, I was dating this wannabe bad boy, a bit like the first boyfriend. He was shagging a friend of mine." I fluffed the truth a little, not wanting to open *that* can of worms. "I found out on Valentine's Day.

"Two years after that, still not over my attraction to the idiot bad boy, I got dumped by my second musician when he decided to go with his band to the US. Having finally realized I was getting nowhere with bad boys, I started dating good guys. Unfortunately, the first bored me to tears, so I ended it. Finally, three months ago, I started dating a scientist. He was nice enough, quite good in bed, so I thought it might work out."

"I'm guessing it didn't," Liam mused.

"Nope. He told me he loved me a few weeks ago. I didn't say it back because I didn't feel it yet. He knew about the other Valentine's Day disaster dumpings, so he kindly told me last week that he was breaking up with me now to save me from the humiliation of a fifth VD dumping. I decided then it was a good time to take a break from my life. Gather some perspective and get to know my country better while doing it."

Liam stopped eating to stare at me. "You do realize that VD also means venereal disease?"

"I do. I think it's quite fitting for Valentine's Day. But just to be clear, I wasn't dumped because I had VD."

461

Laughter in his voice, he said, "Thank you for sharing that."

"Do you have VD?"

He choked again, banging his fist against his upper chest. His words were hoarse. "That might be the weirdest, most intrusive question anyone has ever asked me."

I shrugged, grinning. "I'm kind of a strange person."

His eyes gleamed with humor and if I wasn't mistaken, a little bit of sex. "Strange can be good."

I didn't understand what he meant exactly, but there was definitely flirtatiousness in his voice. "Did you just say something dirty to me?"

He threw his head back in laughter but didn't answer.

I narrowed my eyes at him before diving back into to my food. To be honest, I was excited he might be flirting, but I was also wary. After all, it was fucking Valentine's Day. And Liam Brody was too charming for his own good.

"Are *you* a bad boy?" I asked.

His expression sobered, and a glimmer of pain flashed in his eyes before he lowered them. "Not even in the slightest."

Hmm. There was a story there. But before I could ask, he said, "So, have you found what you're looking for on this break of yours?"

"Not yet," I said, disheartened. I'd hoped that by some stroke of luck or magic, I'd stumble across life's answers. However, I'd come to the conclusion that life wasn't really like that. There was stumbling involved, but it was *through* life.

"Where are you going next?"

"Fort William, but I thought I'd stop at Laggan first."

His study of me was intense. I almost squirmed in my seat.

"What?" I said.

He shrugged. "Well ... I'm making my way to Fort

William. To climb Ben Nevis, to be exact. But I could stop in Laggan."

"You're looking for a free ride," I teased.

"I could get that from Pete."

"The bearded truck driver you just met?"

Liam grinned. "We have a bond, Pete and me."

Chuckling, I shook my head. "I'm not sure I should offer a free ride to such a charmer. It can only end badly."

"You think I'm charming?"

I sighed as if I found his charm insufferable. "Only in the worst way."

"There's a bad way to be charming?"

"On fucking Valentine's Day, yes."

"What if I promise you that I hate Valentine's Day, and that I'd like to spend the day with a woman who shares my revulsion?"

Smiling and curious, I cocked my head in curiosity. "Why do you hate it?"

"Because ..." He hesitated, as if unsure whether to share with me. "A woman upended my life a few weeks before Valentine's Day. I've disliked the day ever since."

"Kismet," I murmured, feeling a thrum of energy heat my blood at his confession.

"What?"

"Nothing." I shook my head, trying to control the pounding of my heart. "Just something my brother would say."

He threw his napkin on his empty plate. "So? Do you want to spend today with me pretending it's just another day?"

"What the hell." I shrugged, throwing my napkin on my plate too. He grinned, pleased. "Just remember—I have my penknife on me at all times."

He slid out of the booth, pulling his wallet from his back

pocket. "You know, you don't need that knife to force seduction on me." He winked.

And before I could respond to his flirtatious remark, he strode away to pay for his breakfast. I had just reached the counter to pay for mine when he turned and took hold of my hand. "Put your money away."

"You paid for my breakfast?"

"Of course," he said gruffly.

"Uh ... thank you."

"You're welcome."

He led me to the other side of the diner where the bearded lorry driver Pete sat with another man. "Hey, Pete, I need to grab my stuff."

Pete looked from Liam to me and grinned. "So I see. Got another ride, did you?"

Ignoring the insinuation in his tone, I waited as he handed his keys to Liam. "Bring them right back."

Still holding my hand, Liam strolled outside toward a smaller truck parked at the opposite end of the car park. "Do people always automatically trust you?" I asked, referring to the fact that Pete had given his keys quite happily over to the American, and I'd let him into my van this morning.

He threw a cocky smile over his shoulder. "I just have one of those faces."

"Tell me about it."

"What?"

"Nothing."

When he let go of my hand to jump up into the lorry for his large rucksack, I tried not to feel bereft at the loss of his touch. I should have been annoyed that he was holding my hand. It was completely forward of him to do so!

But I wasn't annoyed.

Damn.

"Where are you parked?" he asked as he locked up Pete's lorry.

"Behind that big artic." I pointed.

"Okay, I'll meet you there." He threw me another quick, crooked smile that made my belly flutter and hurried back inside the diner.

"You're in trouble," I muttered as I walked to my van. "Big trouble. Biggest." I slammed into the vehicle, half excited, half annoyed at this whole kismet thing and at Johnny for always talking about crap like fate.

Thanks to him, there was a possibility I might lose my knickers tonight.

The back of the van opened, and I craned my neck to see Liam's huge rucksack getting thrown in. And then he was getting into the passenger side.

He stared at me, smiling with those gorgeous eyes.

Yup.

There is a definite possibility I will lose my knickers tonight.

CHAPTER THREE

Boating was a bad idea. I knew it from the moment we got in the damn boat.

It turned out Laggan was a tiny village with very few buildings interspersed throughout the gorgeous surroundings. There were stores—a quaint, beautiful old building with a white-painted sign that declared LAGGAN STORES. There was also a country hotel up the hill, and a few homes here and there. But mostly there were green, rolling mountains as far as the eye could see, dipping down into the beautiful valley that homed the River Spey.

Liam had suggested we rent a canoe and take in the scenery from a new vantage point.

I tried to tell him I was useless with a paddle.

"You keep veering toward the bank," he said, grinning at my uselessness.

I huffed, "Well, dear God, man, you're stronger than I am. Surely you can stop me."

He laughed. "I don't think an army could stop you if you put your mind to something."

"I'm not exactly putting my mind to paddling us in the

wrong direction." I looked down at the paddle in my hand. "How is it possible to get this wrong?" I dragged it out of the water.

"Here, I'll show you." The boat wavered as Liam leaned toward me.

"Don't do that!" I cried.

"Nothing is going to happen."

He moved again, and the boat wobbled even more. My instinctive reaction was to try to stabilize it with my own body, and I moved to center myself.

However, I completely forgot I had a large paddle in my hand, and as I moved, it came up out of the water.

"Hazel, shit—"

My heart rammed against my chest as I realized the paddle was coming for Liam's head. I was about to drop it, but his reflexes were faster. He ducked to avoid it, over-throwing his balance, and then—

SPLASH!

Horror moved through me. I had no idea how deep the river was, how good of a swimmer Liam was, and it occurred to me I might have to jump in to save him!

"Liam!"

I moved to do just that when the water rippled and splashed again as Liam soared up out of it and onto his feet. He stood, the water at waist level, and wiped the river off his face.

I eyed his dripping clothes in guilt. "It's shallow water here, then?"

His eyes danced with humor.

"Sorry."

"My own fault. I should have listened to you."

I smiled sheepishly and pointed to myself. "Bad at boating."

My heart lurched as he grabbed the sides of the canoe,

and for one second, I thought he was going to topple me into the water in revenge. Instead, he gently dragged the boat to the riverbank and helped me onto land.

"You need to get out of those wet clothes."

"Ah," he said, smirking, "this was your master plan, was it?"

I made a face. "I assure you, I don't need to resort to almost drowning a man to get him naked."

"I bet you don't," he murmured sexily.

Trying not to flush, and failing, I gestured to the boat. "What do we do with this?"

He spun around, looking up through the trees. "I'll get my stuff from the van while you tell the boat rental guys where to pick up the boat. And then we find someplace where I can take a shower."

"No. You come with me to the boat hire guys. If they see the state you're in, they might not be mad that they have to go find their damn canoe."

That's exactly what we did.

And I was right.

The guys were too busy lecturing me about not going out in a boat when I wasn't confident in one, thereby putting my companion in danger, to care about having to rescue their canoe.

I took the admonishment, all the while wanting to kill Liam who was trying his hardest not to laugh.

"Amused, are we?" I grumbled as we climbed the hill to where my camper van was parked.

"Just a little."

I rolled my eyes and shook my head. "Fucking Valentine's Day."

"You know, you curse a lot."

I did swear a lot. Will, the scientist who dumped me last week, said it was the one thing about me he didn't find attractive. Unfortunately, it was a hard habit to break. I'd grown up with three big brothers and an aggressive older sister. There was a lot of swearing in our household. You swore that much, you became attached to the words. Take *fuck*, for instance. It could be put in front of almost any other word and still make sense. There was beauty in that!

"I'm not criticizing you," he said softly at my silence.

"Oh?"

"It was just an observation."

"Three big brothers," I explained. "It's a bad habit."

"I don't mind it," he assured me. "You make *fuck* sound cute."

Laughing, I shook my head. "I'm sure."

"It's true." He threw me a grin before he opened the van doors and rifled through his rucksack for dry clothes.

While he did that, I grabbed a coat hanger from one of my carrier bags, shoved my sleeping bag and duvet aside, and pulled down a hook attached to the ceiling. "Give me your jacket."

"It'll drip all over the place," he said, realizing what I meant to do.

"We'll wring it out a bit."

After he shrugged out of the jacket, we each took an end and did just that. When we'd squeezed as much of the water out as we could without ruining the damn thing, I hung it up in the van.

He gave me a grateful smile.

"Now what?"

"We passed a guest house," he said, pointing in the direction we'd trekked back from the canoe. "When we were on the water, I saw it."

"And what are you planning on doing?"

"Charming my way into the owner's shower."

Laughing, I followed, carrying his dry clothes for him so

they wouldn't get wet from the clothes he was currently wearing. I had no doubt he could charm his way into a convent.

The guest house, as it turned out, was a moderately sized home with the most stunning views over the River Spey. I had my doubts that the owner would let a strange man use their shower, and my doubts were founded when an elderly woman opened the door and stared at Liam like he'd just come out of the swamp. She was perhaps in her seventies, wearing walking trousers and a thick, cable-knit jumper. Her white hair was thick and full and twisted in place by a large barrette. Her skin was weatherworn, and she had a no-nonsense air about her.

As he explained what had happened, her eyes shot to me and she tsked. "Never go out on a boat if you can't even handle a paddle."

I winced. "Yeah, I get that now."

"I'd be grateful if you'd let me use your shower," Liam said. "I'll pay."

The elderly woman studied him carefully. "I'm not in the habit of letting nonpaying guests use my facilities. What if this is a scam to steal from me?" Her eyes swung to me suspiciously, and my lips parted in indignation.

Why was I the more likely culprit?

"I promise." He tried to smile but his teeth chittered together. "We're n-not thieves."

"Och, look at you." She heaved a heavy sigh, taking in his dripping clothing. She stepped aside. "Come in before you catch a chill."

"Thank you. You're so kind." He gave her that boyish smile and to my surprise, she preened under it.

"That one is certainly a charmer," she observed as she let me inside her home.

"I'm aware," I replied dryly. "I'm Hazel, by the way."

"Belinda. Everyone around here calls me Belle."

"Liam," he said as we paused in the entryway. "I'd offer you my hand, Belle, but it's covered in river grime."

Belle chuckled, shaking her head. "Falling in the Spey on a February morning. Were you trying to kill him?" she teased.

"Yes, were you trying to kill me?" Liam cocked his head, his eyes bright with mirth and flirt.

I smirked. "Not today."

The old woman laughed and then gestured toward a room on the right. "Have a seat in there, Hazel, while I show your boyfriend to a shower."

I opened my mouth to correct her, but Liam spoke first. "You have a beautiful home, Belle," he said as she led him upstairs.

Rolling my eyes, I wandered into the sitting room and took a seat on a pink velvet chair. "Could charm his way into a convent," I muttered.

Not too long later, Belle reappeared in the sitting room. "That's him all settled. Would you like a cup of tea while you wait?"

"Oh, I don't want to put you out."

"Not at all. I only have a few guests staying at this time of year, and they're all out and about wandering. It's quite nice to have the company."

"If you're sure."

She gave me a nod and then paused, looking thoughtful. "Towels. I haven't gotten around to changing them over for the evening. He has no towels." Before I could say anything, she was gone, the stairs creaking as she climbed them.

It only seemed like a few minutes later when she reappeared in the sitting room, this time wearing an amused smile.

"Is everything all right?"

The stairs creaked and footsteps sounded down the hall

toward us before she could speak. Suddenly, Liam was in the doorway.

I was momentarily frozen at the sight of him in jeans, one boot, a sock, and well ... nothing else.

He was ripped.

Like ... seriously ... his abs!

My fantasy of him had nothing on reality.

He shoved on his other boot and then strode in with his laces undone. Before I could speak, he bent close and handed me his wet clothes. "We need to go now," he said under his breath. "Ogle me later."

Confused, I tore my eyes from his torso to his face.

He looked supremely uncomfortable, and if I wasn't mistaken, there was a flush on the crest of his cheeks. I stood up as he shrugged into his jumper, and my eyes flew to Belle in question.

She looked like she was on the verge of laughter. "Some tea, then?"

"Oh, thank you, but no," Liam said without meeting her gaze. "We're in a rush. But thank you again."

In answer to my frown, his eyes widened. He was trying to send me a message, but I had no clue what that message was.

"We need to go." He took his wet clothes back from me. "Don't we, sweetheart?"

I raised an eyebrow at the endearment but went with it. "Yes." I turned to Belle. "My accidentally dunking him in the river threw us off our schedule for the day."

Belle's lips twitched. "Oh well, then. I'll see you out."

"Thank you again," I hurried to say since Liam refused to look at her anymore.

"You're welcome." She held open the door for us, and Liam quickly stepped outside. She grinned at him and then gave me a wink. "And lucky you."

I had no time to ask what she meant because Liam was

practically running. Chasing after him, I finally caught up once we were out of sight of the guest house.

"What on earth happened?" I asked, trying to match his long strides.

He threw me a look over his shoulder, and I realized it was one of pure mortification.

Suspicion dawned, and laughter trembled in my voice. "She didn't ..."

"Walk in on me while I was naked in the shower?" he said, clearly horrified.

"What?" *Do not laugh, do not laugh!*

"I was in the damn shower, and she walked in with a bunch of clean towels. While I was naked. In the shower."

"She was just being helpful," I said, losing my battle with amusement.

Hearing the laughter in my words, he cut me a dirty look. "She stared at my ..." He gestured to his dick.

"Was she coming on to you?"

"No." He shook his head, the color still high on his cheeks. "She was very matter-of-fact, actually." He stopped and scowled. "She congratulated me on my penis."

As much as I tried to stop the laughter from taking over, it was too much. I threw my head back and burst into stomach-cramping hilarity at the image of big Liam Brody standing in a shower while Belle congratulated him on his dick.

Now I understood her words at the door: "And lucky you."

"Ha!" I laughed harder.

By the time I regained my control, Liam was wearing a reluctant grin, staring at me with warmth in his eyes that made *me* flush.

"I can't believe that happened to you," I said, a little out of breath. We walked again. "Actually, I can. Fuc—"

"—king Valentine's Day," he finished, smiling widely now.

And then something occurred to me, my eyes zeroing in on his crotch before I could stop myself. "Just how big are you?" I blurted.

He had no blush on his cheeks for *me*. Instead, he cut me a hot look that sent tingles all over. "Wouldn't you like to know."

Actually, I would. That's why I asked.

I shrugged, nonchalant. "I'm not interested in a penis that probably hundreds of women have seen."

"Not hundreds," he said, eyeing me thoughtfully.

I wasn't sure I believed that. "Really?"

"Really," he said, sounding quite serious. "I guess I'm one of those old-fashioned types who has to actually like a woman before I'll sleep with her. The sex is better."

Liking that answer more than I should, I tried to shift my wayward thoughts, imagining Belle congratulating him. What a character! Part of me wished we'd had the chance to stay and get to know her better.

Just like that, I was off again, laughing more at Liam's mortification than anything else. This time his deep laughter joined in.

CHAPTER FOUR

"This is more like it," I mused, relaxing as the distant sun warmed my face.

We'd grabbed sandwiches and snacks from the store at Laggan and then we found a lay-by on the A86 at Loch Laggan in Ardverikie. We took our small picnic down to the beach by the loch where I'd spread a couple of towels for us to sit on.

There was no one else around, and the loch glistened in the winter sun.

It's hard to explain what a Highland view does to me. How just sitting by the water of a placid loch, surrounded by the rugged beauty of the Cairngorms, instilled a peace I couldn't find anywhere else. I'd discovered this peace in the last few days and found I was becoming addicted to it.

"There's nothing like it, is there?" Liam said.

I glanced at him. "Like what?"

"The peace you find in places like this."

I stared at him, slightly awed. "I was just thinking that same thing."

He studied me as I studied him, and my chest constricted

with the kind of emotion I wasn't prepared to feel toward a man I'd met less than twenty-four hours ago.

"Tell me about your family. Those three older brothers of yours," he said, biting into his sandwich.

Unnervingly, I found I wanted to tell him anything he wanted to know. "I have three big brothers and an older sister. My mum died after she gave birth to me."

"I'm sorry," he said quietly.

I gave him a sad smirk. "Hence all the swearing. My brothers pretty much raised me because Dad kind of gave up all responsibility after Mum died. My oldest brother, Grant, is more like my dad. He's a lawyer." I smiled fondly. "He's kind of got a stick up his bum. I tease him all the time. Drives him nuts."

Liam grinned at me. "I bet he adores you."

I shrugged because I knew Grant loved me, but Scottish men weren't very comfortable expressing those kinds of emotions. Or at least my brothers weren't. Except for Johnny.

"Then there's Douglas. He was a professional football player. Never has to work again. Invested his money, made the right choices, is forever lecturing me about my lack of direction and passion. I know it's because he worries, but one of these days, I'm going to knee that man in the goolies just to shut him up."

He winced. "For his sake, don't."

"And then there's Johnny. A total hippie. Believes in auras and spirituality and destiny and all that rubbish. Invested money into a software program when he was twenty, and now lives off the rather bounteous fruits of that nonlabor, traveling all over the world, taking beautiful photographs he sells to magazines."

"Your siblings are successful."

"A bit." The lead weight in my stomach returned. I felt like an utter failure in comparison.

"And your sister?"

The lead weight grew heavier. "Heather is ruthless, ambitious, and beautiful. She had an affair with her best friend's husband who also happens to be the CFO of a telecommunications company. He left his wife for Heather, married her, and when she refused to get pregnant for fear of ruining her figure, he agreed to adopt children and hire a nanny."

Liam was quiet a moment. "You don't get along with her?"

"That friend I told you about ..." I glanced up at him, squinting against the sun. "The one who shagged my boyfriend ..."

Sympathy darkened his eyes. "Not a friend. Heather?"

I nodded and looked back out over the loch, searching for that peace. "She was always horrible to me growing up. Tearing me down about how I looked, about my accomplishments at school. Starting fights with me. I mean, hair pulling, nail scratching, vicious fights." I shuddered remembering them. "She made me tough, I'll give her that." And then I uttered something I'd never said out loud to anyone before. "She hates me because she thinks I killed our mum."

"Jesus," he said, his voice hoarse. "Surely not?"

"She told me. When I asked her why she slept with him, with my boyfriend, she told me it was revenge."

"That's fucked up."

I laughed humorlessly. "Tell me about it."

"No, I mean ... she has *issues*."

This time I laughed for real. "Yeah, she does. The boys and I aren't close with her at all anymore. She blames me for that too." Hearing the dullness in my words, I shook my head, embarrassed. "I'm sorry. I got all serious and depressing on you there."

He nudged me with his shoulder. "You can get all serious and depressing on me anytime."

I smiled gratefully and nudged him back. "What about you? Your family?"

"Back in Colorado," he said. "I try to visit every couple of years. They can't really afford to come here."

"Do you miss them?"

"Yeah. But we video call. I catch up with them often."

"Brothers? Sisters?"

"Both. My parents wanted a big family, and they have it." He grinned out at the water. "I have a big sister—Melanie— she has four kids. Then there's me. No kids." He shot me a grin. "Yet. Next are the twins, Kyle and Leeanne. They have two kids each. And then my baby sister, Beth. No kids. She's in college."

"Wow. That *is* a big family."

"Yeah. We have our dramas like everyone else, but it's a good family to be a part of."

"They must miss you horribly."

"For all you know, I could be a terrible brother and they're glad to see the back of me," he teased.

"No way." It wasn't possible.

"No?" He gave me a sexy, inquiring smile.

There was that flip in my lower belly again. Feeling brave, I gave him a cheeky smile in return. "You're too likable."

He narrowed his eyes, his expression playful. "Oh, I get it. You're attracted to me."

Cocky bugger. "So. *You're* attracted to *me*."

Liam's gaze dipped to my mouth. "You are not wrong."

My breath stuttered, wondering if he would kiss me. The blood whooshed in my ears, blood that grew hotter as I waited for him to make a move.

I was yanked from the moment when he abruptly looked away, staring back out at the water. "I can't make up my mind if it's those beautiful eyes or those sexy-as-fuck dimples. It might be the dimples."

"Huh?" I said, confused, dazed, wondering why we weren't kissing.

"Your dimples. They slay me."

Amused at the thought of my dimples slaying anyone, I pointed to the one that creased my right cheek as I grinned. "These little things?"

Amusement danced in his eyes. "They have power over me. I imagine they have power over many men."

I laughed, delighted by the thought. "If only I'd used the power for good instead of evil."

Chuckling, Liam reached for a bottle of water, but he made no move on me at all after that.

Instead, openly admitting our mutual attraction only intensified the awareness between us. Sexual tension was strung taut like a live wire. And every time our hands or arms brushed, tingles shot to all my girly parts.

"If you have such a wonderful family, why are you here instead of over there?" I asked, breaking the silence.

He narrowed his eyes in thought. "When I came here for college, it was for an adventure. I'd always planned to go home and be a forest engineer there. But something happened when I got here." He looked at me. "I fell in love."

For some reason, the thought of him in love with some other girl made my heart twist in my chest. "Oh?"

"With this country. I fell in love with this country."

Inexplicable relief moved through me. "It's a seductive place."

"It is that." He sighed. "I'm more at home here than I am back in Colorado. The country, the people, the humor. It fit better. But I love my family too. It was difficult. I was split in two."

"So how did you come to the decision to stay?"

"I went home for a while, and I missed being here. My

family told me to go back to Scotland. They knew I wasn't happy."

"They sound like a good bunch," I said, and I found myself wanting to meet them.

I realized I wanted to know everything about Liam Brody.

The connection I felt toward him was crazy, but I couldn't deny it.

"They definitely are that."

"And do you love your job?"

"I do." He nodded, serious. "I don't want to do anything else."

"Why the camping trip?"

I thought I saw him tense at the question, my curiosity piqued.

"I just ... I needed to get away. Some alone time. Sometimes we all need that, right?" he said pointedly.

"And here I am intruding on it," I teased.

"I'm intruding on yours too."

"You're taking my mind off things."

"Like Valentine's Day?"

"Well, you were until you mentioned it." I shoved him playfully. "Nah. My job. I was talking about taking my mind off my job. I don't know what the hell I'm going to do about it."

"Quit."

Startled by the blunt response, I said, "Are you insane?"

"No." He looked deep into my eyes in a way that made my breath stutter again. "You're smart. You're funny. You can do whatever you want. Don't wake up ten years from now, Hazel, and regret your life because you were afraid to lose your house or your MINI Cooper."

"And what do you suggest I do?"

"What do you want to do?"

"Write about real people, real issues, maybe try to help

them."

"Then do it."

I guffawed. "It's that easy, is it?"

"Yes," he insisted. "Fight your editor harder. Or find another magazine that likes your ideas. Do something. Anything. Annoy people, piss them off, but get in their face and make them sit up and pay attention to you. That's how we do it in America. You all are too polite here."

His words percolated.

"Better yet," I whispered, an idea forming, "my brother ... he has tons of contacts in social media ... I could write an advice blog." I stared at Liam, dumbfounded that I'd never thought of this before. "I could write a blog, and Johnny might be able to help me spread the word online about it. If it got big enough, I could make money from ads ..."

"That sounds like a great idea."

"But I'd need money to support me in the meantime." I sighed. "I have some in savings to keep me going for a bit ..."

"Give up the car. Give up the mortgage. Are they really that important at the end of the day? You've been living happily in a camper van for a week. Surely a small, inexpensive rental flat with an internet connection is a step up?"

It was crazy. A totally bampot idea.

But it excited me. And I hadn't been excited about anything in a really long time.

I grinned. "I'm glad I met you, Liam Brody."

"I'm glad I met you, Hazel." He grinned back, and then he said, "Even if you keep on calling me Liam when I told you to call me Brody."

"I like Liam." It suited him better than Brody.

We stared out at the loch again as we fell into comfortable silence.

And then, just as my eyes drifted closed against the sun, I heard him say softly, "And *I* like you."

CHAPTER FIVE

The sun was setting as I pulled into the car park outside the pub and inn that Liam directed me to in Fort William.

"I'm taking a room here tonight if they have one," Liam said. "I need a good sleep if I'm going to climb Ben Nevis tomorrow."

"It seems nice," I said, unhooking my seat belt as I looked up at the white stone building.

"It is. I stayed here a few years ago when I climbed Ben Nevis for the second time."

"I've never climbed it. It would probably be the end of me if I tried," I said. "Not really the athletic type."

He nodded, as if distracted, and just as I was about to get out of the van, he said, "Can I say something without it pissing you off?"

The question made me apprehensive. We'd enjoyed a great day together. The best, in fact. I didn't want to get pissed off and ruin it. "Try me," I finally said.

"I don't mean to go all macho caveman on you, but could

you not sleep in your camper van tonight? Or any night from now on?"

"Huh," I uttered, confused.

Liam glanced back at my sleeping arrangements, scowling. I also noted the muscle in his jaw flexing with annoyance.

"Are you trying to scare my sleeping bag with a scowl?" I teased.

He didn't laugh. "It's dangerous. I can't believe your brothers let you take off in this thing. Sleeping in a camper van in a lay-by in the middle of nowhere? Are you trying to get yourself hurt, or worse?"

Oh.

He was concerned about me.

My belly fluttered. "I have my penknife."

"A lot of good that would do if someone bigger and stronger broke in to attack you."

Now I was scowling. "Are you trying to scare me?"

"Yes. Out of this van."

"I'm very careful, you know. Almost bordering on paranoid."

"Yeah, I can see that, what with you letting a strange man into your van and then spending the entire day with him, alone."

"You found me out," I said dryly. "I'm a thrill seeker." Shaking my head at his nonsense, I pushed open my door.

"Hazel …"

When I looked back at him, I stilled at his somber expression. "If you sleep in this van, I'm going to worry about you."

My chest tightened with that strange, swelling emotion I'd experienced earlier. After a moment or two, I finally managed to find my voice. "I'll get a room at the inn too."

He gave me a small, relieved smile. "Thank you."

It turned out they had space available, and we dumped

our stuff in our separate rooms. I needed a shower, so I told Liam I'd meet him downstairs for dinner.

A hot shower, after a few days of none, could make you feel completely human again.

As I dried my hair, I contemplated my clothes. I didn't have anything nice to wear, so I had to make do with a fitted turtleneck and my black skinny jeans. I also applied a wee bit more makeup than I'd been wearing lately. My reflection didn't scream seductress, but I looked a damn sight better than I had when we arrived.

Liam seemed to think so, too, his eyes raking over me slowly and deliberately as he stood from the table he'd gotten us in the busy barroom. "You look great," he said, surprising me by pressing a kiss to my cheek. "Fuck, you smell great too."

I shot him a saucy smile as we took our seats near the crackling fireplace. "You're not shy with compliments, are you?"

"I say what I think," he said. "Never seen the point in not."

"I'm not complaining," I assured him.

Soon our meal arrived, along with ale, and we talked about everything and nothing. I told him what magazine I worked for and that my column title was "Dear Hazel." I regaled him with tales of the older women who wrote to me about wanting to bonk their personal trainers, and my sarcastic but hopefully helpful advice.

He told me about his friends at the forestry commission and how wild their Christmas staff parties could get. We laughed as we enjoyed the warmth of the pub and the delicious food while loud Celtic music filtered through from the other side of the inn.

"There's a ceilidh on tonight," the waitress said, setting

our dessert on the table. "It's always a good night here when a ceilidh band is playing."

My eyes lit up at the thought. "I haven't been to a ceilidh in years."

"Yeah, me either," Liam said and then moaned over a forkful of cheesecake.

"Good?" I teased.

He nodded, clearly too in love with dessert to form words. I watched him devour his slice as I slowly ate mine, but I wasn't really focused on dessert. Flushed with food and ale (I was a lightweight), I couldn't stop myself from blurting out, "This has been the best day ever."

The words made him still, his expression soft. "Yeah, it has."

I beamed at his agreement, and his study of me became intense. "What?" I whispered.

"I just met you. Less than twenty-four hours ago." He dropped his fork on his plate and rubbed his hand over his short hair. "I shouldn't feel like this."

"It's insane, I know." I leaned forward, relieved I wasn't the only one feeling this crazy connection. "But not impossible."

"No?" He reached over and fiddled with my silver bracelet.

"Have you ever seen this old 90s show called *Dharma & Greg?*"

Liam shook his head.

"They meet and fall for each other in a day. In fact, they get married the day they meet. Not that I'm ... that we're ... pfft," I stammered, embarrassed. "That came out all wrong."

He chuckled, trailing his fingertips from my bracelet down over my hand. "Do you want to dance?"

My gaze flew to his. "At the ceilidh?"

"Yeah."

I nodded, excited by the idea of any kind of physical activity with him. "Let me just use the ladies' room first."

Once I stepped inside the tiny, empty restroom, I stared at myself in the mirror. My dark eyes glittered, my cheeks were flushed, and I swear my boobs had swelled to attention. Everything about me said, "Liam, take me now."

Because I wanted him too.

I'd never, not once, had sex on the first date ... but this was different. This was ... "Kismet," I whispered. "Fucking Johnny. Fucking Valentine's Day." I laughed softly and then went about my business.

I was drying my freshly washed hands when my gaze snagged on the unit attached to the wall next to the air dryer.

A condom dispenser.

Without overanalyzing it, I grabbed my purse and bought a packet, tucking the condoms into my shoulder bag.

Belly fluttering intensely, I tried to appear calm and nonchalant when I returned to Liam. It was hard, though, as I suddenly imagined his face between my thighs, that sexy stubble of his scraping my skin ...

"Let's dance." I grabbed his hand, needing the distraction.

The room brimmed with people—some sat at tables crowded around the edges, drinking and clapping along to the music. The ceilidh band was set up on a small stage at the far end, and in the middle, people danced.

At present, they were doing the Highland Barn Dance, one that took me straight back to school and our Christmas dances.

"Come on!" I cried over the music, pulling Liam into the crowd.

We were immediately welcomed, and Liam caught on quickly to the steps, making me laugh as he did an exaggerated hop before skipping sideways into the center of the room, while I skipped toward the edge with the rest of the women.

By dance three, we were sweaty and pink-cheeked. It was a night of heat and laughter, capping off a perfect day.

But as the music started up for the Gay Gordons dance, Liam took my left hand in his, pressed my back to his chest, and clutched my right hand at my shoulder.

My laughter faded.

Feeling him pressed against me, a dance that had always been light and playful turned seductive. In fact, after the polka—jarring movement completely out of sync with how we were feeling—Liam nudged me out of the circle of the dancers and led me into the quieter, empty hallway.

My hands rested on his chest, his heart thumping wildly beneath my fingertips. He nudged my shoulder bag aside to grip my hips.

We stared into each other's eyes for a long moment, everything around us fading.

"Let's go upstairs," I said, feeling like I might burst out of my skin if I didn't get him inside me soon.

The feeling only worsened when his erection prodded my stomach. He closed his eyes, as though in pain, and when he opened them, they blazed. "I don't have anything," he said, voice hoarse. "Protection, I mean."

Excited laughter trembled on my lips as I pressed deeper into him. "I do. There was a condom dispenser in the ladies' restroom."

He smirked. "Well, that was awfully presumptuous of you."

Grinning, I slid my hand down his hard stomach and between our bodies to cup his growing erection. "Awfully," I whispered. "But you did say you like me, and you also said you only fuck women you like."

He hissed under his breath. "Hazel." His grip on my hips turned bruising as he ground into me. "I was wrong earlier."

"About?"

"When I said you were cute when you use the word 'fuck.' Not cute." He shook his head, suddenly edging us backward. "Hot. Fucking hot." And then suddenly, he let go only to bend down and scoop me up.

I squealed, wrapping my arms around his neck to hold on as he powered up the main staircase to his room.

As soon as the door slammed behind us, he gently eased me to my feet, removed my shoulder bag, and yanked me back against him. Liam's lips crashed down on mine as I stood on tiptoes; my hands fisted the back of his sweat-soaked T-shirt. Two seconds later, he gripped my bottom in his hands and lifted me for easier access. I obliged and wrapped my legs around his waist, our kiss hard, hungry, and wet, a possessive kiss that got me in all my tingly places.

I loved the way Liam held me—one arm hooked under my bum, his other hand threaded through my hair to hold my lips to his. No escape.

He was in control, and he pulled back first. We panted against one another's mouths, trying to catch our breaths.

This feeling ... these feelings between us ... it was nuts! But it was also amazing.

I looked into his green eyes and swore I was falling.

And then I literally was because he threw me onto his bed, caveman style. He followed me down, kissing me, his hand in my hair. His tongue stroking mine, the taste of him, his scent ... I had never been more turned on in my life.

I broke the kiss, my skin on fire. "Clothes off," I murmured against his mouth, trying to push him up.

He took the hint, pulling back to straddle me as he whipped off his T-shirt.

I reached out, dazed, to run my hands over his abs. "How

do you gem mm mmm ..." My question was muffled as Liam yanked my turtleneck, and thus my arms, over my head, throwing my top behind him.

My hair clouded wildly around my head, but Liam wasn't paying attention to my mad hair. He was already reaching for my bra.

Cool air tightened my nipples as he pulled the material away and threw it behind him. His eyes glazed over as he stared at me, probably feeling what the same thing I did when I looked at his fine abs.

"Do you even realize how sexy you are?" he asked hoarsely as he cupped my breasts in his large, hot hands.

I moaned as his touch sent sparks of arousal down my belly and between my legs.

"Hazel," he groaned, leaning over to press soft kisses down my chest and over my breasts. When he wrapped his mouth around my right nipple, I gripped his head in my hands and held on as desire rippled through me. My hips undulated against him, impatient to get to the main act.

As if he'd read my thoughts, Liam's fingers went to the button on my jeans. He pulled away from my now-swollen nipple to yank the jeans down my legs. He slid off the bed to do so, and then immediately got to work on removing his own jeans and underwear.

He stood naked before me, and my mouth went dry. He was tawny and sculpted, with deep cuts in his obliques that told me he was used to *a lot* of physical activity.

"Condoms?" he said, his voice guttural.

"Purse." I gestured to the floor where he'd dumped it as soon as we got in the room.

I almost whimpered with bliss as he turned around. His arse. Oh my God, his arse was quite possibly the finest thing I'd ever seen.

"Get back over here," I said, panting. "Now."

Smirking arrogantly in a way that only increased my lust, Liam crawled back onto the bed and lowered himself over me. I dropped my gaze to his cock. He was so hard, the thing was almost touching his belly.

My eyes flew to his face, and we stared at each other a moment, both of us breathing rapidly.

"I don't think I've ever been so wet in my whole life," I said, apparently unable to control my filter around this man.

My words seemed to snap whatever control Liam had because suddenly he was tearing at the condom wrapper with his teeth and rolling it onto his impressive hard-on, all in three swift seconds.

And then he was kissing me again, his stubble scratching me in a way that made the hair on my arms stand up.

Everything about this man was knicker-melting sexy.

My fingers tightened in his hair, and Liam's fingertips glided down the curve of my waist, across my belly, and between my legs. I moaned into his mouth as he pushed two fingers inside me, the moan turning to whimpers as he pumped them in and out. He left my mouth, his lips trailing down my chin, my throat, my chest, before they tickled across my left breast and closed around my nipple. I threw my head back on a deep groan as the pull of his mouth shot more streaks of heat to my sex.

I clasped his head to my chest as he sucked and licked my nipples. All the while, my hips flexed against the thrust of his fingers between my legs. It wasn't enough. I needed more.

But Liam seemed intent on making me come, and soon my nails were curling into his broad shoulders, his name escaping in panted gasps from my lips as the tension inside me increased. It tightened and tightened until I froze, breathless.

And then the tension exploded.

"Liam!" I cried out, his name ending abruptly in a

whimper as my climax rolled through me, my inner muscles squeezing around his fingers as I jerked against them.

I didn't even have time to catch my breath as he slipped his fingers out, braced his hands at either side of my head, and pushed inside me.

I spread my legs wider for him, holding on to his waist as he nudged deeper. Swollen from my orgasm, it was a tight fit, and Liam gritted his teeth as he sank into me.

"Oh God!" I cried, overwhelmingly full.

I clutched on to him, watching how his eyes flared.

"So tight," he groaned, moving his hips gently and groaning again. "Jesus, Hazel, you feel fucking glorious."

Wow.

No man had ever said anything so wonderful to me during sex. I flexed my hips against his, urging him to move. And move he did. My fingers dug into the supple muscles of his back as he pumped into me in deep, hard drives that threatened to blow me apart.

We gasped each other's names as the pleasure escalated with each thrust.

"Harder, Liam," I begged, my fingers digging into his skin. "Oh God, harder."

"Fuck," he grunted, his powerful drives slamming into me until the headboard banged against the wall. I didn't even care if anyone heard us. All I cared about was the pleasure burn of his cock dragging in and out of me, setting my nerves on fire.

It came. My body stilled for a fraction of a second, and then, "Yes!" I screamed as the most exhilarating orgasm moved through me.

My inner muscles rippled hard around Liam's cock, tugging intensely on him, so intensely he swelled even thicker inside me before he shouted my name. His hips shuddered against mine in quick, deep jerks as he came.

He collapsed over me, his mouth against my neck as he panted.

"Fuck me," he groaned, pressing a kiss to my sweat-dampened skin. "Fuck me." He rolled off, giving me room to breathe, but he lay close and curled his hand around my breast as we panted.

"That was ..." I searched for the right word.

"Mind-fucking-blowing," he offered.

"Yeah, that."

My limbs were useless. It was if they'd melted into the mattress.

After a minute or so of silence, Liam got up and disappeared into the bathroom. When he returned, the condom had been disposed of. I watched him stride across the room, confident in his nakedness, and if I wasn't mistaken, he was sporting a semi.

"I'm impressed." I nodded toward it.

"I want you again." He shrugged like it was a given. And then he collapsed next to me on his back. "First, I'm going to taste you."

I sat up and looked at him, already pulsing at the thought. "Taste me?"

"Taste you." His eyes smoldered. "Climb aboard, beautiful."

So I did, holding on to the headboard as I straddled his face. When his tongue thrust into me, I was lost all over again.

My climax this time was slower, sweeter, but no less wonderful, and when I was done, Liam flipped me over onto my stomach. He guided me up onto my hands and knees, and then his heat disappeared.

Glancing over my shoulder, I watched as he grabbed another condom from the packet in my purse. He stilled at the sight of me, his eyes darkening, his features hardening with lust and determination.

"You are the sexiest fucking thing I've ever seen in my life," he said, his swelling erection proving he meant it as he hurried back to me.

My head fell between my shoulders, my hair brushing the bed, and my belly fluttered with anticipation at the crinkling of the condom wrapper.

"Ah!" My back bowed as he slid slowly inside me, torturously slowly. "Liam," I begged. "Oh God."

But he was determined to take his time, smoothing his hands over the globes of my arse as he glided in and out of me in gentle thrusts. Those magic hands coasted up my ribs, and he wrapped his arms around me.

He pulled me up off my hands, until I was sitting on him, my head resting against his shoulder.

"You are so beautiful," he said hoarsely, cupping my breasts in his hands and giving them a delicious squeeze that made me cry out. "And you feel amazing. So amazing."

I curled my arm around his neck and closed my eyes as I bounced up and down on his cock in slow, deep drives.

This *was sex*, I thought, euphoric. Finally, this was good—no, great sex—no, AMAZING bloody MAGNIFICENT sex.

CHAPTER SIX

The first thing that seeped into my consciousness was the hard heat of a body pressed against the whole length of me. Legs tangled with mine. Slightly hairy legs that tickled my skin.

I grinned, still not quite awake, as the memories of last night played behind my eyes.

Warm lips kissed my shoulder. "Good morning," Liam whispered in my ear.

Turning my head toward his, I pried my sleepy eyes open and stared into his blurry, handsome face. "Morning." He smelled of soap, and his hair was damp. He must have showered already.

"We need to check out really soon."

"What time is it?" I mumbled. I was exhausted.

"Ten fifty in the morning."

I groaned. "We only fell asleep a few hours ago." We'd had lots of sex. Lots and lots of fantastic sex.

He smiled, but it was the first smile he'd given me that didn't reach his eyes. "I'm aware."

Feeling cold and tense, and very much awake all of a

sudden, I froze, watching him climb out of bed. As he pulled on his underwear and jeans, I asked, "Are you okay?"

Having never slept with a man on the first date before, I had to wonder, with dread in my gut, if this had been a one-night stand and only I hadn't known it.

Liam stopped to look me directly in the eyes as he buttoned his fly. "We need to talk."

The dread spread through my whole body, and I quickly shuffled out of bed, ignoring the ache between my legs and the twinge in my muscles. Uncaring of my nudity, I picked up all my articles of clothing from the floor. I could feel Liam's eyes on me, but unlike last night, it didn't make me want to throw him on the bed and have my wicked way with him.

Once I was dressed, I snatched up my purse.

Liam frowned. "Where are you going?"

"Well, this is the brush-off, isn't it?"

He scowled, looking pissed. "No, it's fucking not."

I crossed my arms over my chest, astounded that this man could make me feel more vulnerable than any of the men I'd dated for much, much longer than a day.

Waiting as he shrugged on a T-shirt and his flannel, I tried to imagine what on earth we needed to talk about. If he wasn't giving me the brush-off, and he wore protection, then I couldn't think what could be responsible for the serious crease between his eyebrows.

He gestured to the bed as he stepped toward me. "Sit?"

I did so, and Liam sat close beside me, our legs touching.

His continued silence drove me nuts. "Are you planning on saying anything anytime soon?"

Heaving a sigh, his nod was somewhat reluctant. "Do you remember I mentioned a woman who upended my life before Valentine's Day?"

The dread intensified. "*Yes,*" I drawled slowly.

"Well ..." He rubbed a hand over his short hair nervously. "It was kind of *this* Valentine's Day."

"Explain," I bit out, feeling my blood burn with anger as I guessed at his meaning.

"I'm engaged." He cut me a soulful, searing, apologetic look, as if that could somehow soothe the emotional punch he'd just thrown into my chest. "I mean, I *was* engaged."

"Are or was?" I snapped. "Two different things."

Liam flinched. "Was. I mean ... her name is Fiona. We met three years ago. I thought we were happy ... until a few weeks ago, she told me she'd fucked her colleague. Multiple times. On different occasions."

I couldn't even bring myself to feel sympathetic because I was reeling from this bombshell news he could have imparted any time in the last twenty-nine hours!

"She still wants to marry me, but I ... I told her I needed space. That's why I'm on this camping trip."

Hurt, a deep, wrenching hurt, cut across my heart. "So am I revenge?"

"God, no." He gripped my hand, but I snatched it away from him and took my whole body with it, crossing the room to put much-needed distance between us.

I stared at the door, wondering how it was possible to hurt this much over him.

"Hazel, I never expected to meet you."

"What does that even mean?" I whispered.

"That we have a connection."

I whirled around, glaring at him. "You had sex with me multiple times last night. Never once did *Fiona*, your fucking *fiancée*, cross your mind?"

"No." He stood, his expression hard. "Not once. I was caught up in you last night. And you can't tell me you weren't just as lost in me."

"But I don't have a fiancé."

He scrubbed a hand down his face and groaned. "This is so messed up."

"You could have told me about her at any point yesterday. It's not like we didn't talk. In fact ... I've told you things I haven't told anyone."

"I know. I just ... I wanted to keep you for a while. I thought if I told you, you'd take off."

"I would have," I agreed. "Because I don't know you, Liam. Not really. Who is to say that you're not just a player?"

"I'm not." He strode over to me and gripped my biceps, pulling me into him. "You know I'm not. I've never done anything like this before. I wasn't planning anything. It—"

"—just happened," I finished, the words bitter.

"Don't." He pressed his forehead to mine, and I hated him for the way I wanted to sway into his hold. "It doesn't make sense ... but you *know* me. And I know you."

It didn't make sense. Up until two minutes ago, I'd been thinking the same thing. But this was reality, not some fucking fairy-tale, insta-love story.

"Are you going back to her?"

Liam pulled away and nodded slowly, every nod cutting me deeper. "To talk things out. You and I ... This is crazy, right? We've known each other a day. I've known her three years. It would be unfair not to ... I mean ... what I mean is ... fuck." His gaze darted to the alarm clock on the bedside table. "We need to check out. Grab your stuff from your room and meet me downstairs. We'll go somewhere and talk this out."

Go somewhere and talk? About what? About how he was going back to his fiancée? There was no need to talk about that, other than to have him say sweet things to me so he didn't feel like a shit when he left.

I nodded numbly, not wanting to argue.

Falling for a guy after a day.

What a moron.

Once I was outside his room, I moved fast. At super-speed. All I needed to grab was my still-packed rucksack, and I nearly tripped down the stairs as I fled with it on my back. My room was charged to my card, so I didn't waste time on that. Liam could check me out. It was the least the bastard could do!

Adrenaline flooded me. I was shaking as I hurried out to my camper van and threw my rucksack inside. With one quick glance back at the inn, the tears started to fall. Fury and hurt surged through me. I wanted to scream.

I jumped into the driver's seat and probably left rubber marks, I reversed so hard and spun so fast out of there.

I glanced through my tears in the rearview mirror and saw Liam run into the car park, shouting after me. He dropped his rucksack and kicked the hell out of it. Just as I was about to disappear from sight, he fell to his haunches, his head in his hands.

And then I was gone.

"Fucking Valentine's Day," I sobbed.

CHAPTER SEVEN

My life had changed in epic ways since meeting Liam Brody.

Sometimes I couldn't even believe it.

To begin with, I'd never been as lonely as I was when I drove back to Glasgow and returned to my family and friends. How could I tell them that by some absurd twist of fate, I'd met a man, fallen in love, and had my heart broken, all in one day?

It sounded ridiculous even to me.

But my chest ached constantly. I cried at romantic comedies, and not happy, joyful, mushy crying. No, I cried hateful, envious, bitter tears and then threw stuff at the television.

Nothing excited me. A pall had settled over my days.

Friends commented on it. Johnny took one look at me and said my aura had splotches of black in it, whatever that meant. Even the answers in my column had become so pessimistic and depressing that my editor warned me to "buck up your ideas, or find yourself out on your arse."

That was actually the moment that saved me.

I did need to buck up. Liam Brody was not going to do

this to me. No man was! I had a life to get on with.

The first thing I did was talk to Johnny. My brother was the most enthusiastic man on the planet. How he'd ended up with his fiancée, Marie, a woman who apparently didn't know her cheek muscles could move into what we humans called a smile, I had no idea. Anyhow, his enthusiasm for my career change was exactly what I needed.

While Grant was extremely concerned when I quit my job and put my small, two-bedroom house on the market, Douglas was impressed with my take-charge attitude. With mixed reviews from my big brothers, I had to shut their opinions out for once and just go with my gut.

Johnny had gotten a friend to create my website, "Ask Hazel," for free, and I got a deal on all the maintenance charges. He was also using his contacts to spread the word about it, and I'd already gotten a lot of shares on my opening article, enough to receive my first lot of emails from people asking for advice.

They were strong starter emails. One was about a woman who was a recovering alcoholic; she'd married a recovering alcoholic. Recently, his son from his first marriage had died in a car crash, and her husband had started drinking again. She loved him, but she couldn't seem to get through to him and was afraid of losing herself in the process. It was a tough one to reply to, but that's what I needed. The challenge of really helping someone who desperately needed help.

My advice to the first two letters got a ton of comments and loads of shares on social media. People thought I was insightful and kind, but also funny. I wasn't going to lie—it was a bit of an ego boost. Even better than all that was the response emails I received from the original writers, telling me that my advice helped and it meant a lot to them. It made me feel good about myself, and about what I was doing, for the first time ... in, well, ever.

More emails came in from people looking for guidance, and I was optimistic.

I'd sold my car, and my house was on the market. I was hoping to sell soon. I planned on moving back to Hamilton, where I grew up. There were a few one-bedroom flats in the area I could afford while I tried to get my online career off the ground.

"I can't believe I've let you do this to me twice now," I groaned to my friend Shona. As part of my plan to keep so unbelievably busy I wouldn't think about a certain American, I'd decided to let my super-fit friend, Shona, take me out for morning runs.

Within five minutes, my chest was on fire and my legs felt like they were strapped with weights. I hated every minute of it.

She handed me bottled water as we walked around the corner onto my street. "You just need to build up your stamina."

I shot her a look. "Why is it necessary to be able to run a long distance?"

"What if you got followed home one night and needed to outrun your would-be attacker? Or *The Walking Dead* became a reality?"

"If *The Walking Dead* becomes a reality, I'm throwing you at the zombie fuckers to distract them long enough for me to get away without my lungs exploding."

Shona smirked. "I love how you love me."

I pulled my key out of the little pouch I had tied around my waist and let us into my house, stooping to pick up the mail as Shona passed me.

"Have you any fruit?"

"Some bananas, maybe," I grumbled, shuffling through the letters. To my surprise, this week's copy of the magazine I'd worked for was in the bundle.

"Speaking of bananas," Shona said as I wandered into the kitchen. "There is this delicious new intern in my office who I think you'd love."

"Intern?" I said distractedly, throwing down the mail and pulling the elastic band off the magazine. An envelope with just my first name written on it fluttered out from between the pages.

"Yup. He's a wee bit younger than you, but I swear his arse is worth the disparity in maturity levels. Plus, rumor has it"—she held up a banana and grinned—"he's well-endowed."

"Not interested," I muttered, pulling a note from the envelope.

"It's been months. Much too long for any woman to go without a good seeing to."

"I have a vibrator."

"It's not the same."

"Shona, shut up for a minute."

"Very nice," she grumbled.

I shot her a look and she frowned, coming toward me. "What is it?"

I held up the note. Scrawled in feminine writing were the words:

I THOUGHT you might be interested to read this week's advice column.

YOUR SUCCESSOR,
Dear Lola

"WHAT THE HELL?" Shona murmured, reading it over my shoulder.

I shrugged casually, though I was anything but casual. In fact, I felt as if I'd been hit with a shot of adrenaline, like my whole body was anticipating something, even though I didn't know what that something might be.

Hands shaking, I flipped open the magazine to the column.

Once upon a time on this page, there'd been a cartoon of a girl who looked a bit like me with the words *Dear Hazel* scrawled next to it. It had been replaced with a photograph of a pretty, stylish redhead and the words *Dear Lola* above it.

Every week, the most interesting letter was featured in the middle of the column in a colored box in a larger font than the rest.

My heart started pounding as soon as I scanned it. Shona read it aloud behind me:

Dear Lola,

This letter is actually intended for your predecessor, Dear Hazel. As I have no other way of contacting her, and your annoying boss wouldn't give me her personal details or even just pass along a message (helpful guy, that one), I thought this might be my only way to reach her.

So, Hazel, I have to hope you still read this column out of curiosity, or rely on the kindness of your successor to send you a copy. If you're reading this, I need you to know that I'm sorry. What I should have said to you that morning was that even though, rationally, I knew falling for you in a day didn't make sense, it did happen. I did fall for you. I had no intention of walking away from that. I just wanted to talk about where we'd go from here. After all, I had unfinished business I needed to resolve first before I could imagine a fresh start with you. But I wanted that. With you.

And I should have made that crystal clear.

I swear, I've never felt worse than that moment in the parking lot, watching you drive away, not knowing anything about you but your name. Not even a surname. Just Hazel.

Do you know how many Hazels live in Scotland? A lot. A depressing number of Hazels. Watching you go, feeling desperate and powerless, it made me realize that I don't give a damn if this is crazy. I don't. I even watched Dharma & Greg. *It was funny. I liked it. I got it.*

Do you get it? Did you fall as hard as I did?

If you did, I want you to meet me at the pub where we spent the night together. Meet me there May 16 at 3 p.m.

I miss you every day.

Liam

SHONA TURNED TO ME, her eyes tracking the tears running down my face. "Who the hell is Liam? What did I miss?"

Instead of answering, I threw my arms around her, and she caught me. I cried into her shoulder as she shushed me gently. Finally, when I managed to calm myself, she let go. I swiped at my wet cheeks with a trembling hand. "Fucking Valentine's Day." I laughed through a sob.

She frowned in concern. "What?"

"I met a man on Valentine's Day. I fell in love."

"In a day?" she asked, incredulous.

I nodded. "In a day."

For a moment, my friend stared at me like I was a loon, and then she sighed. "Are you sure you both weren't just really, really drunk?"

Knowing she'd never understand without the whole story, I started from the beginning—from the moment he caught me with my underwear down in the woods to my speeding away from him without giving him a bloody chance to explain.

By the end of my tale, she gazed at me in amazement.

"That is the most fantastically, romantic fucking thing I've ever heard in my life."

"Yeah."

"You're going to go, right?" She snatched up the magazine and waved it at me. "You have to!"

I snorted at her sudden turnabout. "Yes, I'm going."

She squealed and bounced up and down like a kid. "Oh my God, oh my God! What date did he say again?"

"The 16th"—I hurried over to my phone—"which is …"

"Today! Fucking today!" Shona cried.

I whirled around, realizing she was right. "Fuck."

"Okay, what time is it?" She glanced at the oven's digital clock. "Okay. It's eleven o'clock. Plenty of time."

"The pub is in Fort William—as in over three hours away! I'll need to borrow your car. And I need to shower. I can't turn up all sweaty and icky. Ahh!" I rushed by her, thundering upstairs.

"You'll make it!" she yelled after me. "You have to bloody make it! I'm invested in this now! If you don't make it, I'll kick your arse!"

Since she had a black belt in tae kwon do, I had no doubt Shona could do just that.

I'd never showered faster in my life.

❧

THE WHOLE WAY UP to Fort William, I had to coach myself to stop speeding. Now and then, my foot would take on a life of its own and I'd check the speedometer on Shona's Golf and see I was ten miles above the limit.

My brain whirred the entire time.

I kept lecturing myself about how mad this all was, and then my heart would tell my head to fuck off as it remembered the way Liam made me feel. One day. Just one day. But he had made me feel more interesting, more at peace, and safer than anyone ever had.

And the sex.

"Oh, the sex," I moaned, remembering. I had gotten through many vibrator-induced orgasms replaying the details of that night over the past few months.

And his letter!

My God, how romantic was that?

But Lola ... I had a mind to kill her! I could understand my editor refusing to pass on a message because he was a crusty old git who was pissed off at me for leaving the magazine. But Lola! She could've just sent me Liam's letter rather than waiting until publication day. The day I was supposed to bloody well meet him! For all she knew, we met in a pub in Istan-fucking-bul!

"Advice columnists," I huffed. "All about the drama."

Gravel kicked up under the tires of Shona's car as I whizzed into the pub's car park at five minutes to three. Not wanting to appear that I'd dashed up to Fort William like a maniac, I got out with a casualness I did not feel. In fact, I very much felt like a little girl at Disney World, like one who'd spotted her favorite Disney princess but whose mother wouldn't let go of her hand, so rather than running and throwing herself at the princess, she had to walk at the agonizing, sedate pace her mother had set.

My legs were a little wobbly as I walked in my low-heeled boots across the car park and into the cozy pub. I gave the bartender a tremulous smile as I entered the barroom and then swept the space for Liam.

He wasn't there.

My heart fell.

What the ...?

The grandfather clock in the corner read ten minutes to three.

Okay.

Shona's car clock was fast. I was early.

"Can I get you anything?" the bartender called to me.

"Soda water and lime, please," I said, needing to be completely sober for this moment.

"Grab a seat. I'll bring it over."

I nodded my thanks and took my shaking legs to a table by a window that faced the car park. I wanted to see Liam arrive so I could ready myself.

That thought made me snort.

How could I possibly prepare for this?

I smiled my thanks at the bartender as he set my drink on the table and left.

Not only was I excited about the prospect of seeing Liam again, but I was also terrified. What if that one day we'd spent together had become so mythical that it didn't live up to the actual reality of being with him?

And if we did decide to be together, how were we going to work it all out? He lived outside Aberdeen. I lived in Glasgow.

You could live anywhere.

I tried to ignore that insistent thought. It would be insane to move to Aberdeenshire to be with a man I'd known a day.

But you want to.

I did.

Oh hell, I was so screwed.

"I hoped you'd come."

I froze, every little hair on my arm rising at the sound of his voice behind me. Turning to look, I stared up at Liam Brody as he walked around the table and took the seat opposite me. Those gorgeous green eyes of his never left my face.

My God, he was even more handsome than I remembered.

"Christ, you're beautiful," he said softly. "I forgot just how beautiful."

I smiled as stupid, girly tears pricked my eyes.

"There they are." He grinned back. "Those dimples."

"These?" I pointed to them, teasing.

He nodded and let out a long, shaky exhale. "I was worried. Really worried. I thought you might not see the letter."

"I did. This morning. I may have broken the speed limit a couple times getting here."

He laughed, and that warm ache, that ache only he could make me feel, suffused my chest. For what seemed like minutes but was perhaps only seconds, we just sat there staring and drinking each other in.

"There were moments over the last few months that I wondered if you were real."

I nodded. "I've had those moments."

"I've missed you."

"I've missed you too." My smile faltered a little. "But ... Fiona?"

Liam sighed. "I went home and broke it off with her for good. That was my intention all along. Even before we met. I couldn't be with someone who'd betrayed me. And I realized that if I could meet a woman and fall harder for her than I ever had for anyone in just one day, then what I had with Fiona wasn't real, anyway."

"I fell for you too." I reached across the table and covered his hand with mine, delighting in the feel of him. "I'm sorry I didn't let you explain. I just ... I didn't want you to see how much it would hurt when you told me you were sorry but you were going home to your fiancée."

"I figured as much." He clasped my hand tightly.

Laughter bubbled past my lips as excitement and fear mingled inside me. "We're crazy. Everyone is going to think we're crazy."

He leaned over the table. "Fuck everyone else. And anyway ..." He suddenly stood, tugging gently on my hand so I had no choice but to stand too. He pulled me into his body, and I had to tilt my head to meet his gaze. I'd forgotten how bloody tall he was.

Brushing my hair back from my face, Liam cupped my cheek in his palm and leaned down to murmur against my lips, "What a great story to tell our grandkids."

I laughed at his outrageous romanticism, secretly loving it, and relaxed as I gave into this madness. "What? That their grandfather caught their grandmother with her knickers down in the woods?"

My body shook against his as he laughed. "Great fucking story. For the rest of my years, I will not forget the sight of your cute little ass running away from me in those woods."

I snuggled closer, wrapping my arms around him. "So what now?"

"One day at a time. Together." He kissed me softly, but I sensed the bite of his hunger in his grip on my waist, hunger he was holding back because we were in public.

"Let's get a room," I whispered.

His eyes darkened. "I already did."

I smirked. "Well, that was awfully presumptuous of you."

He patted my arse. "Awfully."

Without any fight at all, I let him lead me out of the barroom and upstairs.

"And just think," he murmured, his hands roaming over my body as if he couldn't help himself. "Our anniversary will be on Fucking Valentine's Day. Suddenly your name for it has taken on a whole new meaning."

I shivered in anticipation at the sexy promise in his eyes. "In that case, let's make every day Fucking Valentine's Day."

Liam slammed the door behind us and guided me toward the bed. "I'm planning on it."

AFTERWORD

I would never advise any woman, caught by a strange man with her knickers around her ankles in the woods, to invite said strange man back to her camper van. Or follow him around for the day.

Unless, of course, he's Liam Brody.

The author of the bestselling sensation On Dublin Street
returns to Scotland in a brandnew series readers have called
'absolutely breathtaking!'

HERE WITH ME
(The Adair Family Series #1)
*Settled in the tranquil remoteness of the Scottish Highlands, Ardnoch
Estate caters to the rich and famous. It is as unattainable and as
mysterious as its owner—ex-Hollywood leading man Lachlan Adair
—and it's poised on the edge of a dark scandal.*

After narrowly escaping death, police officer Robyn
Penhaligon leaves behind her life in Boston in search of some
answers. Starting with Mac Galbraith, the Scottish father
who abandoned her to pursue his career in private security.
To re-connect with Mac, Robyn will finally meet a man she's
long resented. Lachlan Adair. Hostility instantly brews
between Robyn and Lachlan. She thinks the head of the
Adair family is high-handed and self-important. And finding
closure with Mac is proving more difficult than she ever
imagined. Robyn would sooner leave Ardnoch, but when she
discovers Mac is embroiled in a threat against the Adairs and
the exclusive members of the estate, she finds she's not yet
ready to give up on her father.

Determined to ensure Mac's safety, Robyn investigates the
disturbing crimes at Ardnoch, forcing her and Lachlan to
spend time together. Soon it becomes clear a searing
attraction exists beneath their animosity, and temptation
leads them down a perilous path.
While they discover they are connected by something far
more addictive than passion, Lachlan cannot let go of his grip

on a painful past: a past that will destroy his future … if the insidious presence of an enemy lurking in the shadows of Ardnoch doesn't do the job first.

READ ON FOR THE PROLOGUE & CHAPTER ONE

PROLOGUE

ROBYN
One year ago

Boston, Massachusetts

The rain lashed our patrol car as we sipped our coffees, waiting for a crackle on the radio.

I was enjoying the peaceful lull created by the sounds of raindrops on metal when a pop of color in the overwhelming gray beyond my window caught my attention.

On the sidewalk, a woman in a navy coat, one hand holding a black umbrella, the other a leash, was halted by the dog on the end of it. From here, it looked like a Lab. The dog wore a bright red raincoat. And he'd sat his ass down on the sidewalk as if to say, "I'm done with this shit. Make it stop."

I laughed under my breath as the woman gesticulated wildly, as if to reply, "What the hell do you want me to do about it?"

Her arms thrown wide, head bent toward the dog staring back up at her, became a snapshot in my head. I wished I had my camera. I'd use a wide aperture and my 150mm lens to blur out the gray, movement-filled background and focus on the woman and her stubborn dog.

"Jaz thinks you should dump Mark." My partner, Autry Davis, yanked me out of the mental photography processing in my head.

Smirking at the comment, I ignored the uneasiness that accompanied it. "Oh, *Jaz* thinks that?"

Jasmine "Jaz" Davis was pretty outspoken, but Autry had made it clear he didn't like my boyfriend Mark from the moment he'd met him.

"Sure does." Autry stared out the window at the passing traffic. We were parked on Maverick Square in East Boston, near a bakery we both liked. They did good coffees. And Boston creams. Not that we were trying to live up to the cop cliché. We allowed ourselves a Boston cream once a week. It was our treat. "She thinks he thinks what he does is more important than what you do and that he never prioritizes you."

That did sound like something Jaz would say.

Mark was a prosecutor and very good at his job. His success was appealing because I found hardworking guys sexy. But lately he'd been pushing me to make a change. He thought I should work my way up, apply to become a sergeant detective and then move up to lieutenant.

He didn't understand I didn't want that because he was the most driven son of a bitch I'd ever met. Like I said, that was hot until he tried to make me into someone I wasn't.

"Well, you can tell Jaz I'm breaking up with him."

Autry tried not to look too happy about that and failed. "Yeah?"

"Yeah. He's too much like hard work."

"Not that I want to talk you out of dumping the guy, but you do realize relationships *are* hard work. Right?"

I snorted. "Says the man with the wife and kids he adores."

"Doesn't mean it isn't hard work."

"I know that. But you've got to *want* to work hard at it, and I don't want to with Mark. Last weekend, he blew up at me for buying a fish-eye lens for my camera. Told me an expensive 'hobby' was a waste of my mediocre income, and he wasn't about to *indulge* me in a pastime." My skin flushed hot with anger at the reminder. I'd emotionally and verbally shut him out ever since.

"He said what?" Autry frowned. "Yeah, you need to dump his ass, pronto. Shit, can you imagine Jaz if I tried to condescend to her like that? He's lucky he's dealing with you and not my woman. He wouldn't have come out of it alive. And I'm not telling her what you just told me, 'cause he still might not. Damn, Penhaligon. Life is too short for that bullshit."

"The sex is pretty good, though." I said it mostly to be funny. No sex was worth being with a guy who made me feel small and unimportant.

Autry cut me a warning look. "Don't want to hear it."

I laughed under my breath and sipped my coffee.

Straight out of the academy at twenty-one, I was introduced to Autry Davis, my beat partner. A tall, good-looking man seven years my senior with a quick sense of humor and a warmth that could melt even the coldest soul. I'd developed a crush on the man. A crush that soon faded into friendship and trust. Especially when I met his wife Jaz and their two young daughters, Asia and Jada. In the last six years, the Davises had welcomed me into their family. Autry now was like an older brother. Like any brother, he didn't want to hear about his little sister's sex life.

And like any little sister, I deliberately ignored his pleas to stop torturing him with the details.

"I mean, there's room for improvement, but he's definitely better at it than Axel." Axel was the guy before Mark. A musician. Self-involved. Selfish in bed. And out of it. When I was sick with a bad head cold, he didn't opt to check in on me or offer to buy me groceries so I could stay in bed. Nope. He disappeared and said he wouldn't be back until I was well again. Jaz and Autry took care of me. Axel didn't come back when I was well again because I told him not to. Mark wasn't that giving in bed either, to be fair, but at least with him, I reached climax.

"I can't hear you." Autry scowled out the window. "I am no longer in the car. I am someplace where the world is good and right and the Celtics are winning the season."

"So the land of make-believe, then?"

"Don't you come at the Celtics."

I chuckled, opening my mouth to continue teasing him when the radio crackled.

"Domestic disturbance. Lexington Street, apartment 302B. Neighbor called it in."

Autry reached for the radio. "Gold 1-67. Three minutes out."

"Roger that."

I'd already started the engine and was swinging the car into traffic.

"What do you think it is this time?" I asked.

"Affair."

"You always guess that."

"Because I'm nearly always right."

"Last time you were wrong."

"What was last time?"

"Oh, Davis, you're getting old," I teased. "Girlfriend found out boyfriend had gambled all her savings. She beat the shit out of him."

"Oh yeah. That was a nasty one. That man will never be able to have children after what she did to him."

Unfortunately, probably true. I winced at the memory.

Only a few minutes later, we pulled up to the apartment building on the corner of Lexington. It had the same architecture as all the buildings in this part of Boston—narrow with wooden shingle siding. This one was painted white years ago and was in dire need of a repaint. It had two entrances, one for the downstairs apartment and the other for the upstairs. A woman in bright yellow pajamas, her hair covered with a matching bandana, stood outside the first-floor apartment door. She approached us as we got out of the car.

"They've been yelling up there for the last thirty minutes, and then I heard things crashing and she started screaming and crying." The neighbor looked shaken. "He's shiesty as fuck, that one. Think he's into drugs. Thought I better call it in."

I gave her a reassuring smile and was about to speak when a terrified shriek sounded from above. Autry hurried to the door. Turning back to the neighbor, I ordered, "Please return to your apartment, ma'am."

As I watched her do this, Autry banged on the door to the upstairs apartment. "Boston PD, open up!"

An angry male voice could be heard yelling obscenities upstairs. I caught "fucking bitch" in among the rambling, followed by loud sobbing broken by intermittent, garbled screaming.

Autry looked at me, face grim, and my hand went to my holster.

I nodded.

He turned the handle on the front door and it opened.

As we moved into the cramped hall, to the stairs leading steeply up to the next floor, I followed Autry and took out my gun. The occupants of the apartment no doubt couldn't hear us over their argument. As we climbed the stairs, it became apparent, from what I could make out, that this altercation was about drugs. He seemed to think she was skimming money off the top while selling his product. Not an average domestic disturbance call after all.

I steeled myself.

The stairs led to a hallway with two doorways opposite each other. We peeked in one and saw it was the bedroom; it appeared empty. Then we moved just beyond the door into the other, which took us into a small kitchen/living space. The place was trashed. Coffee table on its side, TV smashed, photographs falling out of broken frames and glass littered in their midst. A stool at the mini breakfast bar lay on its side.

A young woman huddled on the sofa, face streaked with mascara, fear in her liquid eyes as she stared up at a tall, skinny guy who held a handgun in her face.

We raised our guns.

"Boston PD. Lower your weapon," Autry demanded.

The man looked at us without doing as warned. He scowled. "What the fuck are you fuckin' bastards doing here? This ain't your business. Did that nosy cunt downstairs call the cops?"

His pupils were dilated, his speech slurred.

The guy was high.

This situation just got better and better.

I repeated, "Sir, lower your weapon."

"Or what?"

"If you do not lower your weapon, it will be construed as a threat and I will shoot you," Autry warned.

"I didn't understand half that shit." The gun wavered dangerously in his hand.

"Davis," I murmured and turned my head ever so slightly to look up at my partner—

Movement flashed in my peripheral. Adrenaline shot through me as another guy came charging into the room, handgun raised and pointed at Autry's back, finger on the trigger.

There was no time for anything but to move in front of my partner.

To shield him.

With threats front and back, I had no choice but to fire at the threat from behind. Two gunshots sounded, louder than a clap of thunder above the building. The sound ricocheted through my head at almost the same time that the sharp, burning sensation ripped through my chest.

Another bang. Another burn. And another.

I slumped into Autry as more gunfire sounded above my head.

There was noise. Groaning. Screaming.

Autry's voice calmly telling me I would be okay.

"Three people with gunshot wounds. We got an officer down. She's been shot multiple times. I need ambulances to 302B Lexington Street."

The pain in my chest seemed to spread through my whole body as I felt pressure on my wounds. "Shit, Robyn, shit," Autry murmured in my ear. "Why, why?"

I understood what he asked.

I wanted to answer, but I couldn't make my lips move, and there was something wrong with my vision. Black shadows crept around the edges, growing thicker and faster.

"Stay with me, Robbie. Stay with me."

I wanted to.

I did.

I wanted to reach out and grip tight to him and not let go.

But my body and mind felt disconnected, my mind pulling me farther and farther away ...

CHAPTER ONE

ROBYN

PRESENT DAY

Ardnoch, Sutherland,
Scotland

For once, I wasn't thinking about my camera or the scenery or the perfect shot. Amazing, really, when I was in one of the most beautiful places I'd ever been in my life.

Yet, it was difficult to see it right now when I was minutes away from meeting my father.

A man I hadn't seen since I was fourteen years old.

People called the nervous flutters in their stomach butterflies. Butterflies didn't cut it. Surely butterflies were when you were excited-nervous? What was happening in my gut right now made me feel physically ill. Even my knees shook.

And I hated that my birth father, Mac Galbraith, had that power over me.

I got out of my rental and forced my shoulders back, taking a deep breath as I strode down the gravel driveway toward the enormous security gates built into brick pillars. Those pillars flowed into a tall wall. On the other side of the gate, the drive continued, fading into the darkness of the woodland that shadowed its edges.

As I grew closer, I searched for a call button or cameras. Nothing. Stopping at the gate, I gave them a shake, but they were made of solid iron and immovable. Eyes narrowing, I searched beyond into the trees, trying to listen past the chirping of birds and the rustle of leaves in the wind.

A slight whirring to my left drew my attention, and I caught the light glancing off the movement of a lens. Ducking my head to look closer, I saw the security camera camou-flaged in a tree.

I saluted the camera with two fingers off my forehead to let whoever was behind it know I'd seen them.

Now all I could do was wait.

Just what my nerves needed.

I turned, leaned against the gate, and crossed my arms and legs in a deliberate pose that said, "I'm not going anywhere until someone comes out here."

Not even a few minutes later, I heard an engine and the kick of gravel. Pushing off the gate, I turned and watched the black Range Rover with its tinted windows approach from the other side.

My nerves rose to the fore with a vengeance.

Why oh why did my father have to be head of security at one of the most prestigious members-only clubs in the world?

Oh right.

Because of Lachlan Adair.

Jealousy and resentment that I hated I felt burned in the back of my throat. Ignoring the sensation, I crossed my arms over my chest and tried to look nonchalant as the Range

Rover stopped. The driver door opened, and a man wearing black pants, a black shirt, and a leather jacket approached the gate.

I noted the little wire in his ear.

He was security.

But he was not my father.

"Madam, this is private property," the guy said in a Scottish brogue much like Mac's.

"I know." I stared him down through the gate bars. "I'm here to see my father."

"I'm afraid only members and staff are allowed entrance onto the estate. I'll have to ask you to return to your vehicle and leave."

Like I could give a rat's ass that Ardnoch Castle and Estate was home to actors and movie and TV industry types who paid a fortune in annual fees just to say they were a member. "My name is Robyn Penhaligon. My father is Mac Galbraith. Could you let him know I'm here?"

The security guard was good—he didn't betray his reaction to this news. "Do you have identification?"

Knowing they'd ask for it, I'd stuck my driver's license in the ass pocket of my jeans. I whipped it out and handed it over.

"One second, please." The guy returned to the vehicle and opened the driver's door. He got in without closing it, and I heard him murmuring.

While his conversation with whoever went on, I returned to my car to get the sweater I'd thrown in the back seat. I'd been too hot with nerves when I'd left the hotel, but the chilled spring air now made me shiver.

A few minutes later, the guy returned to the gate. "Ms. Penhaligon, I must ask you to hand over any recording devices you have on your person, including any smartphones."

"Excuse me?"

"Nonmembers are not allowed onto the estate with recording devices. This ensures the privacy of our guests."

"Right." At least that meant Daddy Dearest didn't intend to turn me away.

Shit.

A little part of me almost wished he had.

I grabbed my phone out of my car, glad I'd had the sense to leave my camera in my room. I trusted no one with my baby.

"Is that everything?"

"Yup."

"Please return to your vehicle. The gates will open momentarily, and you will follow me onto the estate."

I nodded and got back into my rented SUV. A four-by-four had seemed like the right choice for spending time in the Highlands, and this one was affordable. Deciding to fly to Scotland without booking a return ticket gave my savings account serious palpitations. I had to be careful with my money while I was here.

As soon as the security guy couldn't see my face anymore, I let out a shaky exhale and waited for the gates to open. While I did this, the guy turned the Range Rover around and drove up the gravel drive to give the gates room. They swung inward seconds later, and I drove forward.

The driveway led through woodlands for what felt like forever before the trees disappeared to reveal grass for miles around a mammoth building in the distance. Flags were situated throughout the rolling plains of the estate—a golf course. Tiny distant figures could be seen playing.

Eyes back on Ardnoch Castle, I sucked in another breath.

I'd never felt more out of place.

It was a feeling I was used to when it came to Mac.

I never felt a part of his world.

He'd never let me.

The castle was a rambling, castellated mansion, six stories tall and about two hundred years old. I knew from my research that while it was the club's main building, there were several buildings throughout the twelve-thousand acre estate, including permanent residences members paid exorbitant amounts to own. According to Google, the estate sat on the coast of Ardnoch and was home to pine forests (which I could attest to), rolling plains (again, saw that), heather moors (really wanted to see those), and golden beaches (really, really wanted to see those). While I wasn't sure how this visit with my father would go, I kind of hoped it went well enough for a tour of the estate.

Even if I did feel like a fish out of water.

As I followed the Range Rover up to the castle, I mused over the security here in general. While there was a great big gate and walls at the main entrance, how did they ensure members privacy when there were twelve thousand acres to manage?

Something to ask Dear Old Dad if we ever got past the awkward, "Why didn't you love me enough to stay in my life, leaving me with rampant abandonment issues that have impacted me to almost fatal levels?"

There went my stomach again, roiling like a ship caught in a storm.

"Jesus Christ," I whispered as I pushed open the driver's door. The castle was like Downton Abbey on steroids. There were turrets, and a flag of the St. Andrew's Cross flew from one of the parapets. Columns supported a mini-crenellated roof over an elaborate portico that housed double iron doors.

As I got out, the wind blew my ponytail in my face and battered through my sweater. It was much windier here without the protection of the trees. And it had an icy nip that surprised me, considering it was almost April. The smell of saltwater hung in the air despite the fact the castle sat two miles inland.

I loved the air here. Crisp and fresh. It filled me with energy.

Neck craned, I stared up at the flag and heard the creak of the iron doors opening. A man wearing a traditional butler's uniform, including white gloves, stepped out as if to greet me.

But then he was halted by the appearance of another man.

Drawing a breath, I stepped out from behind the driver's door and closed it, forcing myself to look at the very tall, broad-shouldered figure heading my way.

A mixture of overwhelming emotions flooded me as I recognized the man. He wore a tailored gray suit that didn't quite civilize him. His thick, salt-and-pepper hair needed a trim and curled at his nape. His cheeks were unshaven.

He appeared to be in his late thirties but I knew him to be forty-four years old.

Expression neutral, he strode toward me with determination. As he drew closer, I realized how much I looked like my father. His hair was darker. But I had his face shape and his eyes.

Those were definitely my eyes. The same light brown around the pupil, striations of gray and green bleeding into the brown from the edges of the iris.

Mom always said at least my father had given me something good.

Mac Galbraith stared at me stonily. That bland countenance disappeared as he swallowed hard. "Robyn?"

"Mac." I held out my hand to shake his.

He stared at it for a second as if not quite sure what to do.

Manners compelled him to shake it finally. He squeezed my hand before seeming reluctant to release me. The action caused a complex response I hadn't expected. Tears threatened, and I glanced away, as if casual, unaffected. Staring at the castle, I said, blasé, "This is some place you have here."

"It's not mine," he replied. "It's Lachlan's. The Adairs."

Yeah, like I didn't already know that. There was that awful resentment again. I forced myself to look at my father. "I guess you're wondering why I'm here."

"Aye. Not that it isn't a nice surprise."

Was it?

I narrowed my gaze, trying to discern the truth in his statement. "It's not something I can just blurt out on the driveway of a castle with a man I barely know hovering at my back." I referred to Security Guy who was still with us.

"Sorry about that. Protocol."

I nodded. I knew all about protocol.

"You'd know all about that," Mac said, as if plucking the words from my head. "Last I heard, you were a police officer."

He looked pleased about this. As if it connected us. I hated that it did. After all, he'd been a cop once too. But so was my stepfather, Seth Penhaligon. "Family business, I guess," I replied. "Wanted to be like my old man, Seth." When I was 16, I'd decided to change my name legally from Galbraith to Penhaligon. After two years of no contact with Mac, I'd wanted to sever our connection as well as have the same name as the family who were in my life daily.

While Mac was very good at hiding his reaction, there was a flicker of something in his eyes that suggested I'd hit a sore spot.

Hmm.

"I'm not a cop anymore."

"Oh?"

"Like I said, I don't want to chat on a driveway. I know this place doesn't cater to riffraff, so can you get away?"

Mac frowned. "My daughter isn't riffraff. Come inside. We'll talk and then I'll give you a tour."

I thumbed over my shoulder. "Is this guy going to babysit us the whole time?"

Mac glanced at his colleague. "Jock, why don't you take the vehicle back to the mews and return to your duties."

"Yes, sir."

"Shall we?" Mac said to me, gesturing to the castle entrance.

"Isn't there a servants' entrance that would be more suited to my position?"

"There's a delivery entrance, but we're usually prepared for *those* packages." He shot me a sardonic look and walked toward the castle.

"What about my car?"

"It's fine there. We'll move it later if we need to."

I studied the back of Mac's head as he strode in front of me. My father had to be around six feet four and was physically fit. He made an intimidating figure. At forty-four, he had the physique of a man half his age. He looked great. Ruggedly handsome. Successful. He didn't look old enough to be my father. But for a kid who got his older girlfriend pregnant when he was only sixteen, he'd done okay for himself.

But I guessed a person could when they went out into the world to succeed by sacrificing their relationship with their child.

So lost in my thoughts, it took a second for my surroundings to hit me.

Holy shit.

I stopped just inside the door and gaped.

Yeah, I definitely felt like a fish out of water.

"Wakefield, this is my daughter Robyn." Mac stopped next to the guy in uniform. "Robyn, this is Wakefield, the butler at Ardnoch."

A butler. Of course. "Nice to meet you."

The butler bowed his head, expression stoic. "Welcome to Ardnoch Estate, miss."

I nodded vaguely, my attention returning to the space beyond us as we stepped inside.

"Impressive, aye?" Mac said, grinning at my expression.

It was mammoth.

Polished parquet flooring underfoot made it appear even more so. The décor was traditional and screamed Scottish opulence. The grandest staircase I'd ever seen descended before me, fitted with a red-and-gray tartan wool runner. It led to a landing where three floor-to-ceiling stained glass windows spilled light down it. Then it branched off at either side, twin staircases leading to the floor above, which I could partially see from the galleried balconies at either end of the reception hall. A fire burned in the huge hearth on the wall adjacent to the entrance and opposite the staircase. The smell of burning wood accentuated the coziness the interior designer had managed to pull off despite the dark, wood-paneled walls and ceiling. Tiffany lamps scattered throughout on end tables gave the space a warm glow.

Opposite the fire sat two matching suede-and-fabric buttoned sofas with a coffee table in between. More light spilled into the hall from large openings that led to other rooms on this floor. I could hear the rise and fall of conversation in the distance beyond.

In one of those doorways appeared a man as tall as my father. He paused at the sight of us and then made his way across the humongous reception hall.

As he drew closer, I recognized him.

Millions of people across the world knew this guy's face.

Wearing a fitted, black cashmere sweater that caressed his muscular physique and black dress pants, the man wore casual chic beautifully. He had the body and swagger that fashion magazines loved in their Hollywood actors.

And that's what he'd once been.

An A-list Hollywood actor.

Lachlan Adair.

Normal women would swoon at his dark blond handsomeness, his lovely blue eyes and brooding mouth, the short, almost dark brown beard. While obviously good-looking, there was a rough edge to his masculine beauty that made his face substantially more appealing. And he was well known for the wicked twinkle in his eyes. From what I could tell, he hadn't been a bad actor either, although typecast in mostly action movies.

I didn't swoon as he approached.

I was nervous, but not because his charisma and fame intimidated me.

Beneath my calm facade, I held a deep reserve of resentment toward this guy. It wasn't his fault. Not really. But this was the man my father abandoned me in favor of.

When Lachlan Adair broke out in Hollywood at twenty-one with a huge action blockbuster, he hired my father as part of his private security. Perhaps it was that they were both Scots that drew them together. I wouldn't know. I only knew they became close. So close, Mac went everywhere Lachlan did, even if that meant missing out on my teen years. My birthdays. Graduation. And then they moved back to Scotland when Lachlan retired to turn a family-owned estate into this exclusive, members-only resort.

Mac was head of security and lived in the village.

"I heard you had a visitor," Lachlan said. His attention moved beyond us and he addressed the butler. "Wakefield, there seems to be a problem with a guest in the Duchess's Suite. Would you mind assisting?"

The butler strode past us. "Right away, sir." He disappeared up the grand staircase, moving with efficient speed without looking like he was in a hurry.

Adair focused his stony gaze on me even as he addressed my father. "Mac, it seems an introduction is in order."

"Lachlan, this is my daughter, Robyn. Robyn, this is Lachlan Adair."

Neither of us reached for the other's hand. Awkward tension fell between us.

I didn't know what his problem with me was.

I wasn't the one who'd stolen *his* father.

"I know who he is," I said, unimpressed.

Lachlan's eyes narrowed ever so slightly. "I've heard a lot about you. It seems strange to have been in Mac's life for almost twenty years and never have met his daughter."

"Yeah, that tends to happen when a father abandons his kid to follow an *actor* around the world." I didn't dare look at my father. Despite my complicated feelings, I hadn't come here to attack him. There was a small part of me that understood why Mac hadn't been around.

"Excuse me?" Adair's tone had a dangerous quietness to it.

I ignored him and turned to my father. "Can we have some privacy?"

"Of course," Adair answered. "Forgive me for intruding." He gave Mac a look of concern. "Just wanted to make sure everything was okay here?"

Mac nodded, his expression guarded. "If you would prefer us to go off the estate, we can."

"Don't be daft." Adair took a step back. "Give Ms. *Penhaligon* a tour."

Did he just emphasize my surname?

For a moment, Mac pressed his lips together in a tight line and seemed to give Adair a warning glance. The lord of the castle lifted his hands in a gesture of surrender and without looking at me, turned on his heel and walked away.

Overall, he'd been as rude to me as I was to him.

But I had an excuse for my rudeness, even if it was unfair to blame him for my father's actions.

What had I ever done to Lachlan Adair?

SHOP NOW

ACKNOWLEDGMENTS

Novellas are often more challenging than full-length novels. To condense the craft to a shorter time on the page and still ask readers to fall in love with the characters. However, when I wrote these novellas, I wrote them as short, fun, escapist reads for my newsletter subscribers during the difficult year of the pandemic. For once, I didn't write with the pressure of obtaining impossible novel length goals in a quarter of the words. I just wrote for fun. And to my surprise and gratitude, these characters resonated with my readers. It seemed only right then to collate these stories together and release them just in time for the holidays. I hope you've enjoyed the romantic escapism of it all!

For the most part, writing is a solitary endeavor, but publishing most certainly is not. I have to thank my wonderful editor Jennifer Sommersby Young for always, *always* being there to help make me a better writer and storyteller.

Thank you to Julie Deaton for proofreading the collection. I appreciate you so much!

And thank you to my bestie and PA extraordinaire

Ashleen Walker for handling all the little things and supporting me through everything. I appreciate you so much. Love you lots!

The life of a writer doesn't stop with the book. Our job expands beyond the written word to marketing, advertising, graphic design, social media management, and more. Help from those in the know goes a long way. A huge thank-you to Nina Grinstead at Valentine PR for your encouragement, support, insight and advice. You're a star!

Thank you to every single blogger, Instagrammer, and book lover who has helped spread the word about my books. You all are appreciated so much! On that note, a massive thank-you to the fantastic readers in my private Facebook group, Sam's Clan McBookish. You're truly special and the loveliest readers a girl could ask for. Your continued and ceaseless support is awe-inspiring and I'm so grateful for you all.

A massive thank-you to Regina Wamba for a beautiful photograph that I just had to have on the cover of this collection. And to the awesome Hang Le for transforming that photograph into stunning cover design. As always, you amaze me!

Thank you to my agent Lauren Abramo for making it possible for readers all over the world to find my words. You're phenomenal, and I'm so lucky to have you!

A huge thank-you to my family and friends for always supporting and encouraging me, and for listening to me talk, sometimes in circles, about the worlds I live in.

Finally, to you, thank you for reading. It means the everything to me.

ABOUT THE AUTHOR

Samantha Young is a *New York Times*, *USA Today* and *Wall Street Journal* bestselling author from Stirlingshire, Scotland. She's been nominated for the Goodreads Choice Award for Best Author and Best Romance for her international bestseller *On Dublin Street*. *On Dublin Street* is Samantha's first adult contemporary romance series and has sold in 31 countries.